"I don't wa
trying to ge
clarified.

But no clarification was needed. That wasn't the grip of a woman planning to seduce a man to get him to back off. Or even to soften him up. Her touch was tentative, but the tentativeness didn't make it to her eyes.

She inched even closer. "And this has nothing to do with you being a bad boy."

"Good thing. Because I lost my bad-boy status years ago." Yeah, it was a poor attempt to lighten things up, but since she looked ready to shatter into a thousand little pieces, he thought she could use the levity.

It worked.

The corner of her mouth lifted just a fraction. "I don't think it's a status you can lose. It comes with the looks and the attitude."

He was in trouble here. Yeah, she might not be trying to seduce him, but she was doing it anyway.

Maybe she was right. Once bad, always bad. That was the only explanation Slade could come up with as to why he lowered his head and brushed his mouth over hers.

RENEGADE
GUARDIAN

BY
DELORES FOSSEN

First published in Great Britain 2013
by Mills & Boon, an imprint of Harlequin (UK) Limited,
Eton House, 18-24 Paradise Road, Richmond, Surrey TW9 1SR

© Delores Fossen 2013

ISBN: 978 0 263 90381 2

46-1113

Harlequin (UK) policy is to use papers that are natural, renewable and
recyclable products and made from wood grown in sustainable forests. The
logging and manufacturing processes conform to the legal environmental
regulations of the country of origin.

Printed and bound in Spain
by Blackprint CPI, Barcelona

Imagine a family tree that includes Texas cowboys, Choctaw and Cherokee Indians, a Louisiana pirate and a Scottish rebel who battled side by side with William Wallace. With ancestors like that, it's easy to understand why *USA TODAY* bestselling author and former air force captain **Delores Fossen** feels as if she were genetically predisposed to writing romances. Along the way to fulfilling her DNA destiny, Delores married an air force top gun who just happens to be of Viking descent. With all those romantic bases covered, she doesn't have to look too far for inspiration.

Chapter One

Maya Ellison spotted the man the moment she stepped out of the grocery store.

He would have been darn hard to miss, especially since he was leaning against her car. Except he wasn't just leaning. It was more as if he was lounging while he took in the scenery. Arms folded over his chest. Jeans-clad legs, outstretched and crossed at the ankles.

Waiting.

Maya had no idea who he was. Or what he wanted. But he appeared to be waiting for her.

She walked closer, her steps slow and cautious while she kept her attention nailed to him. Even with the lounging pose, she could tell he was well over six feet tall. Solid build. Dark brown hair that fell slightly long against his neck. Even though he was wearing a black Stetson, the cool October breeze had rifled through what she could see of his hair and had left it rumpled.

He reminded her of an Old West outlaw. And that was the reason she tightened her grip on the infant carrier that held her son, Evan.

The man lifted his head, snagging her gaze, but he said nothing as he pushed himself away from her car. The simple gesture nearly caused her to turn and run back into the store, but Maya reminded herself she was on Main

Street, in broad daylight, no less. Plus, this was Spring Hill, a sleepy Texas town that was as close to crime-free as a town could get.

Bad things don't happen in Spring Hill.

It was the reason she'd moved here. A safe haven to raise her child. She hoped she hadn't been wrong about that.

"May I help you?" Maya asked, and silently cursed the polite tone. She added a glare for his leaning on her car.

"I'm Slade Becker," he said, not answering her question. He reached into the pocket of his black jacket and pulled something out. Before Maya could react to the possibility that it might be a gun, he produced a wallet and held it up for her to see.

Not a wallet.

A badge.

She eased a few steps closer so she could get a better look at him and that star shield. It wasn't a cop's badge, but now that she had a better look at him, his steel-blue eyes seemed as if they did indeed belong to a cop. He didn't just look at her. He studied her from the top of her head to her sensible leather walking shoes. Then that gaze went to the carrier.

To Evan.

Because of the way she was holding the carrier and the single plastic bag of groceries, the man could likely only see the top of Evan's head, which was covered by a blue knit cap. Still, even that seemed intrusive, so she turned, hoping that would shift his gaze off Evan and back to her.

It didn't.

Maya decided to do something about that. She gave the carrier another adjustment so that it was as far behind her as she could position it. The shift caused her arm to ache, and she wouldn't be able to stand there long. Not that she intended to do that anyway.

"You're a U.S. marshal," she said, making sure she sounded impatient, which she was. Even though it was a beautiful autumn day, she suddenly wanted nothing more than to get home.

And away from this lawman with the haunting blue eyes.

There was something downright unsettling about him, and it didn't have anything to do with the car-leaning or memorable eye color. Maybe it was his looks. Edgy, along with being drop-dead gorgeous. He was the kind of man she usually avoided but found herself attracted to anyway.

Maya choked back a huff. No way, no how would she feel anything but wariness when it came to this man. She wasn't at a point in her life where she was looking for a relationship, especially one with a man like this.

"Yeah, I'm a marshal," Slade confirmed, and the wind had another go at his hair. "You didn't know I was coming." It wasn't a question, nor did he wait for her to answer. "I was on my way out to your house, but I spotted your car in the parking lot and stopped."

"But why?"

He opened his mouth, maybe to explain why she would have known he was coming or why he was indeed there, but her phone rang. The sweet lullaby ringtone didn't mesh with the syrupy tension in the air.

Even though she was on an extended leave of absence from her job as a victims' rights advocate, Maya couldn't risk not checking the caller-ID screen to see if this was someone from the office. She set down the carrier and grocery bag and snatched the phone from the diaper bag she had looped over her shoulder. She then picked up Evan again as quickly as she could, making sure she didn't let the stranger get a good look at her baby.

"Saul Warner," she mumbled, reading what had appeared on the screen of her phone. It wasn't a name she recognized.

"That'll be my boss," Slade provided, his rusty growl of a voice slicing through the lullaby notes. He leaned against her car again to resume his waiting.

Yet another piece to this puzzle. Why would his boss want to speak to her? "Maya Ellison," she answered.

"Marshal Warner," the man greeted. "I'm sorry I'm just now getting around to calling you, but I got tied up with something. It's possible that Slade Becker is already there in Spring Hill."

"He's with me in the parking lot of Hawthorne's Grocery Store on Main Street." Maya met his gaze again. Frowned. "But why is he here?"

Marshal Warner made a slight sound in his throat, as if the answer were obvious. "Because you need someone there with you, and when the FBI put out the request, Slade volunteered."

Okay. "Uh, why would I need a marshal, and why would the FBI request anything that had to do with me?"

No obvious throat sound that time, and Slade's left eyebrow slid up. It was a question. But Maya didn't know what exactly he was asking.

"You've heard about the kidnappings, of course," Warner continued.

Kidnappings? That kicked up her heart rate. She had seen something in the headlines of a newspaper in the grocery store, but she hadn't read the article.

"I haven't heard much news in the past several days. I just adopted a five-week-old baby, and—" Maya stopped herself from gushing about the joys and challenges of being a new mom and remembered she was talking to a federal marshal.

"Who are you?" Maya asked flat out. "Not your name. I got that. But why are you calling me?"

"The FBI asked us to help and Slade volunteered his services. Actually, he insisted on personally taking this case. Like the rest of us, he doesn't want another baby to go missing."

Her chest was suddenly so tight that Maya was afraid she wouldn't be able to speak, or breathe. "Why would you think anyone would want to take my baby? His birth mother willingly gave him up for adoption. And everything's in order with the paperwork. I should know because I'm an attorney."

The marshal paused. "You really haven't heard?"

"Heard what?" Maya snapped, though her sharp tone was more from fear than temper.

Another pause, longer than the other. "Marshal Becker will fill you in." And with that, Warner hung up.

She would have huffed if her breath hadn't been stalled in her lungs. "Your boss said you'd tell me what's going on," Maya relayed, hitting the end-call button.

He looked around. Another lawman's glance. "We should sit inside your car while I explain. Best not to spend any more time out in the open."

The hairs on the back of her neck started to tingle. But Maya didn't budge and she didn't fall back on a polite response grilled into her with her Southern upbringing. "I'm not getting in a car with you. In fact, I think it's time to call the sheriff."

Slade shrugged. "I'm sure Sheriff Monroe already knows what's going on, but he might not have figured it all out yet. The FBI phoned him a little while ago and faxed him my photo, my file and a copy of the police reports on the kidnappings."

"Figured out what?" Her voice was so loud that it woke

up Evan, and he stirred in the carrier. Maya wanted to throw her hands in the air but that would have meant putting down Evan again. She wasn't letting go of her baby.

Slade made another glance around. His attention landed and stayed on the car and truck that were stopped at the traffic light just up the block from where they stood. "Two baby boys have been kidnapped in the past couple of days. Both were from the San Antonio area."

Maya swallowed hard. "I'm very sorry for the families." They had to be suffering. She would be completely distraught if she were to lose Evan. Even though she'd only had him a week, she couldn't imagine what her life would be like without him.

"Yeah" was all Slade said.

The one-word response was laced with a ton of emotion, but it was short-lived. His shoulders went back. His chin came up. And anything that he'd been feeling was once again concealed behind that lawman's facade.

"Neither of the babies has been recovered," he continued a moment later. "*Yet.* Now we have to stop any others from being taken."

There it was again. A threat. Not from him, of course. Despite her earlier thoughts of his dangerous and dark air, he probably wasn't a kidnapper. *Probably.* Unless he wasn't really a marshal and this was some kind of ruse to get her to go with him.

Yes, she really did have to speak to the sheriff.

"I have to get home," she insisted. And run by the sheriff's office so she could have a look at this man's file and those police reports.

Maya walked right up to Slade, looked him in the eye and waited for him to back away. He did. Finally. She shoved her phone back into her shoulder bag and used the keypad on the door to unlock the car.

"You're sure you want to go home? Alone?" he added.

Maya huffed and threw open the back door so she could set the carrier in the specially designed car-seat holder. It made strapping in Evan a cinch, which she needed right now because her hands were shaking. Also, thankfully, her son had gone back to sleep. With luck she'd be home before he started to demand his two o'clock bottle. She had some formula with her, but she preferred to feed Evan at home.

Away from Slade Becker.

"I have a security system," Maya let Slade know. "And a gun."

That last part was a lie, plain and simple, but she made a mental note to consider buying one. She tossed the grocery sack on the floor of the backseat and started to close the door so she could then get inside and leave.

"The other families had security systems," Slade informed her.

That did it. Maya had had more than enough. With her hand still on the back door, she whirled around to face the doom-and-gloom marshal. "Look, those kidnappings have obviously concerned you, but I don't live in San Antonio any longer."

"No, but your son was born there." His words were slow and deliberate, as if he was emphasizing each one.

"So? Lots of babies have been born in San Antonio," she pointed out.

He nodded. "About twenty-five thousand each year. Your son was born September 16, a light day for deliveries because on that day only sixty-two babies were born. Twenty-eight were girls, thirty-four were boys. Of those thirty-four boys, twelve weren't Caucasian. So that brings the final figure of possible victims to twenty-two, and two of them are already missing."

"Victims," Maya repeated. The blood rushed to her

head. "What are you saying—that someone might want to kidnap my baby?"

"Yeah." He let that hang in the air for several seconds. "Both of the kidnapped babies were Caucasian males born on the same day as your son."

Oh, God.

She heard her own sharp intake of breath but tried to tamp down her reaction. This didn't make any sense. "Why would anyone want to kidnap Evan? Or either of those children who share his birthday?"

Slade took his time shaking his head. "We hoped you'd be able to tell us."

"I have no idea why!"

Again her voice was too loud, and it caused Evan to stir. He whimpered, and his mouth pursed as if he was about to cry. Maya caught onto the car seat and jiggled it gently, rocking him.

"But if you're right, if your numbers really add up, there are twenty babies." She made sure her voice stayed calmer. Hard to do. "*Twenty.* So why would you think someone would come after my child? Why not offer your services to the other nineteen?"

Slade studied a dark green SUV that was slowly making its way past the parking lot. Not a newer-model vehicle but a big sturdy gas-guzzler.

"Because of the sixty-two babies born that day, only four were placed up for adoption," he said. "One girl. Three boys."

Her heart went to her knees. She didn't want Slade to confirm anything else, but she couldn't stop him. Maya could only stand there and try to brace herself for the worst.

The worst came.

"The adopted boys are the ones who've been kidnapped," Slade said, his words echoing through the thick pulse that was now pounding in her ears. "And your son, Evan, is the final one on the list."

Chapter Two

Because Maya looked ready to fall face-first onto the concrete, Slade took her arm and forced her to sit in the driver's seat of her car. He had no intention of letting her drive off, but he doubted she was capable of doing that right now anyway. Not with her hands shaking and her breath gusting.

"Evan is the final one on the list," she repeated, though her voice didn't have a whole lot of sound.

For that matter, she didn't have much color, either. The natural blush had drained from her cheeks, leaving her bone-white.

She groaned and pressed her fingers to her trembling lips. A helpless, panicked sound shivered deep within her chest. "Oh, God. This can't be happening."

Slade didn't want to comfort her.

Okay, he did.

He was a sucker for a damsel in distress, always had been. He blamed that on his upbringing at the hellhole, also known as the Rocky Creek Children's Facility. There was forever a boatload of people who needed some kind of protection, and he'd always been good with his fists that way. But he didn't want to soothe Maya's fears. He wanted her to realize just how serious this situation was.

He wanted her to need him.

But he'd settle for her just accepting that she should

have his services, because he wasn't going anywhere. This was his case.

In more ways than one.

"Move over a bit," he instructed.

Maya looked up at him and blinked. Her eyes were brown. Not just any ordinary brown. More like a really good single-malt scotch. They were a nice contrast to all that flame-red hair that dangled and coiled around her face.

"Why do you want me to move?" She glanced around the parking lot, her gaze landing on each car before she scanned the trickle of traffic on Main Street.

"That's why. I'd rather not be standing out in a wide-open parking lot if the kidnapper decides today is the day he comes after that little boy in the backseat."

She nodded. But she darn sure didn't move. Her gaze came back to his, and she sat there staring at him. "Why should I trust you?"

Good question, but Slade couldn't tell her the real answer. He certainly couldn't tell her the real reason he'd insisted on this assignment.

"Because you have to," he settled for saying. "Because I can stop the worst from happening. I've tracked down kidnappers like this before, and I can do it again."

Slade put his hand on her arm and gave her a nudge so she'd get moving, but she still didn't slide over.

Part of him admired her defiance. Lack of trust and skepticism were a big help to staying alive in a dangerous situation. But another part of him hated that she was making this so damn hard. They didn't need to be here where it would be next to impossible for him to protect her and the baby.

"You didn't read about the kidnappings," he said, trying a different angle. One that would be hard to hear, but maybe it would be persuasive. "You didn't know this mon-

ster nearly killed one of the adoptive parents who was trying to prevent the baby from being taken."

The fear was instant. It flashed through her eyes, widening them, but she shook her head. The wind and the motion
sent her hair swishing against the shoulders of the cream-
colored top she was wearing.

Without saying anything, she thrust her hand into the
bag still looped on her shoulder. For a moment Slade
thought she might pull out the gun she said she owned.
If she even had one, she didn't have a permit to carry it.

But no gun.

Maya grabbed her phone and frantically scrolled through
the numbers. She jabbed the call button.

"Sheriff Monroe," she said. It wasn't a bluff, either.
Slade could hear the man's voice on the other end of the
line. "I'm in Hawthorne's parking lot, and I've been approached by someone from the marshals—"

Slade waited to see what the sheriff had said that'd
caused her to stop, but while he waited, he glanced at the
carrier seat. He couldn't see the baby, because he was facing the rear of the vehicle, so Slade leaned a little to the side.

The newborn was wearing a cap that covered his head,
and he was snuggled deep into thick blue blankets that hid
his body and chin. His eyes were closed. Sound asleep. And
his mouth was pursed as if sucking on a nonexistent bottle.

"I see," Maya said.

Her comment would have drawn Slade's attention back
to her eventually, but her touch drew it a whole lot faster.
Except it was a little more than just a touch. Maya caught
onto the sleeve of his jacket and gave it a sharp yank. Her
eyes were narrowed now—and he could see the question
in all those shades of brown.

What was he doing looking at her baby?

Slade put a quick stop to the looking. Best to keep focused only on convincing Maya to accept his help. Because she had no idea yet just how much she needed it.

"Yes." She continued with her phone conversation. "He's about six-two. Brown hair. Dark blue eyes." She paused. "Right. No visible scars, but I don't see a tattoo."

"Six-three," Slade corrected under his breath. "And yeah, there's a tattoo, but unless you're planning to strip-search me, it's not visible."

That earned him a top-notch glare.

A moment later Maya pulled in a long breath. "So Slade Becker really is a marshal," she commented to the sheriff. "You're positive? Because his hair seems too long for him to be a lawman."

"I just came off a month-long assignment chasing down fugitives and didn't have time for a haircut," Slade provided, though he wasn't sure she heard him. Maya jammed her finger in her left ear as if she intended to shut out anything he said.

She paused again while she continued to throw glares at him. "All right. No. I don't think it's necessary for you to come here, but you're right about it being a good idea for one of your deputies to drive out to my place and have a look around. Thank you, Sheriff."

The moment she ended the call, Maya studied him, specifically his eyes. "The sheriff confirmed your identity. He knew you were coming to town. He'd already left a message on my answering machine at home and has someone headed to my house now to make sure no one is there."

"Good," Slade mumbled. But he wouldn't trust the locals on this. If and when he got to Maya's house, he'd go through it again himself.

"The sheriff said I could wait here until he's made sure everything is safe at my house," she added. She stared at him a moment longer, huffed and then moved across to the passenger's seat so he could get in behind the wheel.

"Thanks." But Slade was pretty sure his tone didn't sound sincere, especially since he was merely thanking her for learning the truth. Still, he couldn't blame her for wanting to confirm his identity. In addition to that one, maybe she'd be willing to take other precautions.

Lots of them.

"What now?" Maya asked.

"We go to your place so I can have a look at your security system." Slade watched her glare turn to a frown. He did some frowning of his own. He wanted to offer her an alternative like a safe house, but he couldn't press this too hard, too fast. He darn sure couldn't have Maya demanding that he be removed from this assignment. "Or we wait here for the sheriff to call."

She looked ready to jump on that second choice, but then Maya glanced over the seat at the baby. She reached out and touched Evan's hand. Then his forehead. Probably checking to make sure he wasn't too cool or too warm.

Maya opened her door, and with the driver's side still open, the breeze flowed through the car. The breeze also caught her scent and it drifted Slade's way. Something feminine and musky.

It wasn't the kind of scent that came from a bottle.

"We wait for the sheriff's call," she said. "And before I take you back to my house or anywhere else, I want you to fill me in on this kidnapper. You said the cops don't know why the babies are being taken, but you must have an idea."

"Several of them." None of them would make her breathe easier. "There's the obvious—maybe this person is a baby snatcher. A woman who either is unable to have a child of her own or has recently lost one."

Of course, that didn't explain why she'd take two babies, both of them adopted.

"You have any suspects?" she asked.

"Just a person of interest who's missing, but the FBI, Marshals and the police are going through records and searching for any eyewitnesses."

Slade caught a flash of green out of the corner of his eye and looked in the direction of the traffic light again.

Hell.

There was the green SUV again. It'd just come this way several minutes earlier.

"Is something wrong?" Maya asked.

He glanced at her and confirmed she had followed his gaze to the SUV. "You recognize that vehicle?"

"No. But it's fall break for some of the schools. It could be someone visiting from out of town." She sounded hopeful. And concerned.

Slade took out the small notepad and pen from his jacket pocket and jotted down the license number. Maya was probably right. It could be nothing, but with the other kidnappings, he had to assume it could be something.

"Is that how the other babies were taken?" Maya's attention stayed on the green SUV. "Someone grabbed them from a public place and drove away with them?"

Slade nodded. "The second one went down that way. The adoptive mother was coming out of her pediatrician's office in downtown San Antonio. It was late. She had the last appointment of the day, and as she was getting into her car, someone bashed her on the back of her head. When she came to, her baby was gone, and there were no witnesses to the crime."

The traffic light changed, and the green SUV started to inch forward. The windows had a heavy tint, but he could just make out the silhouette of the driver. A man, judging from the size. There didn't appear to be anyone else in the vehicle.

"And the other kidnapping?" There was a lot of breath in her voice, and Maya was watching the SUV as if it were a jungle cat stalking them.

Slade almost hoped it was indeed the threat that his body was preparing to take on.

A showdown.

Right here, right now.

Part of him wanted nothing more than to stop this dirt-bag and put an end to the danger. But he also didn't want a shoot-out with the baby in the backseat.

He put Maya's question on hold for a moment, took out his phone and called the dispatcher at the marshals' office in Maverick Springs. All five of his foster brothers worked there. All five would do whatever he needed. But Slade didn't want his brothers to know about this yet. In case it turned out to be nothing.

The agency dispatcher answered right away, and Slade read off the numbers of the license plate.

"Call me when you know who owns the vehicle," Slade instructed. He put his phone back in his pocket and slid his hand over his gun, which was in a waist holster concealed beneath his jacket.

"The SUV isn't stopping," Maya said practically in a whisper.

No, it wasn't. The driver crawled past the grocery store and headed east on Main. Slade shifted a little in the seat so he could spot the SUV if it doubled back.

Maya's soft gasp, however, had his attention going right to her. "You really think you'll have to use a gun here?" She tipped her head toward his holster.

He thought about answering yes in the hopes of drilling home that it wasn't a good idea for them to be sitting in a parking lot, but she already looked scared enough. "I want to be ready," he said. "Just in case."

"Oh, God." She shook her head and repeated it. "This is for real, isn't it?"

Slade settled for a "Yeah."

Yeah, it was for real, and yeah, all of this was starting to hit her like a sack of bricks.

She pulled off her shoulder bag, dropped it on the floor and folded her arms around her. Her motions were borderline frantic, no doubt matching the intensity of the emotion going on inside her.

"A baby snatcher wants my child," she mumbled.

"Well, that's one possibility." He paused and gathered his thoughts so he could try to word this the right way. "The babies could have been taken to cover up something illegal about the adoptions themselves."

Maya was shaking her head before he even finished. "There was nothing illegal about Evan's adoption. I used a reputable agency and started the paperwork nearly three years ago—"

"You did that after the doctors told you that you'd never be able to carry a child of your own," Slade supplied. But he regretted that little revelation when Maya turned those accusing brown eyes on him again. "I checked into your background. Into all the adoptive parents' backgrounds," he amended. "I was looking for a connection."

"And did you find one?" she snapped.

"No. You're the only single parent of the three. The only one who's an attorney."

Maya huffed. "But there has to be something. Maybe a connection with the parents. Their jobs. Their ages. *Something.*"

Yeah. There was. And that was something she wasn't

going to like much. Of course, he hadn't done or said anything so far that would make this a fun experience.

"The parents of the first child own a successful business. Several of them, in fact. The second couple are both teachers. You're thirty-two, and their ages ranged from twenty-six to forty-three. But I don't think any of that information is relevant. I've gone through the files, and the only thing that connects all of you is the fact you adopted baby boys who were born on the same day."

She stayed quiet a moment and stared at the dashboard. "Maybe that *is* the only connection. Maybe the kidnapper is looking for a specific child."

Slade couldn't dismiss that, but there was a problem with that theory. "Neither of the stolen babies was returned."

Still, that didn't mean they wouldn't be or that this particular predator was indeed searching for one child. Maybe a child he'd already found. Maybe not. And maybe returning the babies was just too risky.

Judging from the way she dragged in her breath, Maya had just figured that out.

His phone rang. Not the lullaby tune like the one on Maya's phone. His was the standard annoying ringtone, and after seeing the call was from the dispatcher, Slade knew he had to answer.

"You ran the plates?" he asked.

"I did," Todd Freeman, the dispatcher, confirmed. "The owner's Randall Martin from San Antonio. He owns a bowling alley and has a record for assault eight years ago but nothing recent."

"Ask someone to run a deeper check on him. I want to know if this guy has family or business in Spring Hill. Then check and see if he has a girlfriend or a wife who recently lost a child. It might have even been a miscarriage or fertility problems. I also need to know if he has any connection whatsoever to Maya Ellison or the other two families of the missing babies."

Todd confirmed he would get someone right on that, and Slade ended the call.

"You have a lead?" Maya asked.

He lifted his shoulder. "Just checking all angles."

There was a sound from the backseat. First it was a whimper. But within seconds it changed to a full-fledged cry.

The baby was awake.

"He's hungry," Maya announced. She dug down into the shoulder bag and produced a bottle filled with formula. "I need to feed him."

Slade volleyed glances between their surroundings and Maya while she leaned over the seat. She unhooked the safety belts that held the baby in the carrier and car seat, and she scooped him into her arms.

"Hi, sweetheart," she murmured, kissing the baby's cheek. She returned to a sitting position and cradled Evan in the crook of her arm. He latched on to the bottle the second it touched his mouth.

Despite the horrible news Maya had just learned about Evan possibly being in danger, she smiled at the baby and continued to mutter things to him.

But Slade didn't hear what she said.

That's because his heartbeat suddenly got the best of him, and he couldn't hear over the sudden roar in his ears. He could only sit there, watching. Staring.

And wondering.

Maya pulled off the little blue cap and Slade's heart pounded even harder. He saw Evan's dark hair. He saw the baby's eyes.

Blue.

All babies had blue eyes, didn't they?

He couldn't let his mind run wild. He darn sure couldn't jump to conclusions.

But that was exactly what he was doing.

Maybe all babies had blue eyes, and plenty had dark hair. However, Slade thought that maybe he could see himself in that tiny face. His features. His blood.

His baby.

God, was this his son?

Chapter Three

Maya was glad she was holding Evan. Just having him in her arms steadied her and reminded her that she couldn't fall apart. She had to face this danger head-on because she didn't have a choice. She had to do everything within her power to keep her baby safe.

She glanced up from Evan to see the sheriff's white cruiser pull into the parking space next to her car. The tall, lanky lawman stepped out and he tucked a manila folder beneath his arm. Hopefully, he hadn't come there to tell her there was a problem with the security at her house.

And then Maya caught Slade's gaze.

He wasn't looking at Sheriff Monroe. Or even at her. He had his attention fastened to Evan. As he'd done in the parking lot, he examined Evan's face, with his forehead bunched up as if he was trying to figure something out.

"Maya," the sheriff said, approaching her car. He stooped down so he could see inside and looked past Maya and at Slade. "Marshal Becker. I'm Sheriff Wilbert Monroe."

Slade nodded, acknowledging the introduction, but he was still staring at Evan. And that wasn't alarm he was showing. Too bad Maya couldn't figure out exactly what was behind the marshal's intense expression.

"I checked your house," the sheriff said to her. "No sign

of anything out of the ordinary, but none of your neighbors was home. Would have been nice if they'd been able to tell me if there'd been any unusual vehicles in the area."

Maya nodded and gave Evan's bottle an adjustment. "But there might have been a suspicious vehicle near here." She leaned closer to grab Slade's attention so he'd quit looking at Evan.

He did, and for a moment he seemed as if he'd been pulled out of a daydream.

"Marshal Becker's having someone look into it," she explained. "But after we have answers about that, I'd prefer someone else guard Evan and me."

The silence was instant, and Maya glanced at both of them. The sheriff looked a little surprised, but it was Slade's reaction that she noticed most. Was that anger she saw in his eyes? Whatever it was, it was powerful stuff.

"I see," the sheriff finally said. "I'll make some calls—"

"You don't have time to hire anyone else," Slade interrupted. He turned his attention to Maya. "This kidnapper isn't going to wait for you to put security in place. He'll probably hit today."

Today? God, so soon?

Maya had to tamp down her nerves so she could speak. She also had to loosen her grip on Evan's bottle. The hard plastic felt ready to snap. "I'm sure the sheriff will assign a deputy for protection until I can get a bodyguard out here."

"A deputy." Slade repeated it like profanity, and he turned toward her so they were facing head-on. "Look, I know you have a problem with me. My hair's too long. I don't look like a marshal. Heck, I think you're even scared of me. But I don't want any of that to stop you from getting the best protection for that baby." He rammed his thumb against his chest. "And I'm the best."

"He's right," Sheriff Monroe agreed, apparently taking

up his cause. "My deputies have been trained, but according to his file, Marshal Becker has more experience than all of them put together."

Maya didn't doubt that, but she doubted she'd be comfortable with this man. But she immediately rethought that. One of the main reasons for her discomfort was this tug she felt deep within her belly. Slade was attractive, and she was attracted to him. But she was also smart enough to know he was hands-off.

Plus, there was the way Slade had looked at Evan. That was unsettling, too. It was almost as if this case was personal to him. And maybe it was. Maybe he, too, had lost a child.

Still…

Maya shook her head, but she didn't get to repeat that she wanted another bodyguard, because Slade spoke before she could.

"I'll protect Evan with my life," Slade insisted. "I won't fail at this."

Maya stared at him. And despite all her other concerns, she knew what he was saying was the truth. He would protect her son at all costs.

Later she wanted to know why.

But for now she'd settle for answers that would help her make a decision about whether to keep him as a temporary bodyguard.

"What makes you think the kidnapper will strike today?" Maya asked Slade.

"The first kidnapping happened day before yesterday. The second, twenty-four hours later. At five p.m. another twenty-four hours will have passed."

Maya checked her watch. That was only about three hours from now. Not nearly enough time to find a bodyguard and get him out to her house. Heck, it might not even be enough time for the sheriff to assign her a deputy and have him in place, since that would no doubt involve juggling some schedules.

"The police and FBI don't have anyone in custody," Sheriff Monroe continued. "They're narrowing down suspects, but it could take precious time for them to get close to making an arrest. What we need is for the marshal here to capture this person so the danger will be over and the kidnapper can tell us where the other babies are."

Of course. The families of the missing children would be well past the point of waiting on pins and needles. They'd be in panic mode.

"But Slade has no idea who might come after us," Maya pointed out. "This could turn dangerous, and I don't want Evan used as bait."

"He's already bait." Slade's mumbled words seemed to echo through the car.

Worse, Maya couldn't deny that it was true. The kidnapper might already have Evan in his line of sight.

"According to the info the marshals sent over, they're looking into several possibilities as suspects," the sheriff continued, drawing Maya's attention back to him. "There's a woman, Andrea Culberson. She's a nanny who might have kidnapped her employer's baby. He was the first child taken who shares Evan's birthday."

"Andrea Culberson," Maya repeated. The name meant nothing to her. "They're sure she took the baby?"

"Not sure at all. She's missing, and someone burned the Colliers' estate to the ground. If she's not the kidnapper, then it's possible the real kidnapper did something to make her go on the run. Or maybe just did something to *her*." The sheriff extracted a three-by-five photo from the file and held it out for Maya. "That's Ms. Culberson. Have you seen her before?"

Maya studied the photo of the woman with spiky blond hair. She was young, mid-twenties at most. "No. I don't think so."

"The police don't know where she or the baby is," Slade provided. "She disappeared, and since then her former employers have discovered that she had some problems."

"What kind of problems?" Maya asked, afraid of the answer.

"Depression, for starters. Andrea Culberson had a miscarriage exactly a year prior to the first kidnapping. It's possible she's taking the children to make up for the one she lost."

Extreme measures, but they might not seem so extreme to someone who was desperate for a child. Maya understood that desperation. To a point anyway. She'd wanted a child with all her heart, but she wouldn't have resorted to kidnapping.

Maya studied the photo, committing the woman's image to memory. She prayed she didn't come face-to-face with Andrea Culberson anytime soon.

"Plus, there's another possible suspect," Slade continued. "The person who's behind the wheel of the green SUV that circled the parking lot."

"Yeah, I got a call from the marshals about that SUV on the drive over," the sheriff added. "We're trying to get a photo of the owner, Randall Martin."

A photo would help. Well, maybe. It would at least alert her if she saw someone who looked like Andrea Culberson or Randall Martin. But there was the frightening possibility that it was neither of them.

Evan stopped sucking the bottle, and when Maya looked down at him, she realized he'd fallen asleep. Not good. He would spit up if she didn't burp him, so she eased the bottle from his mouth and placed him against her chest so she could pat his back. The motions weren't routine yet, but she was far more comfortable with her mothering duties than with what she had to do next.

She had to make a decision about accepting, or declining, the marshal's help.

The sheriff checked his watch. "I need to head back to the office and bring everyone up to speed on what we've learned." He glanced at Slade, then Maya. "I hope you'll allow Marshal Becker to go with you to your house, at least until we can make other arrangements."

Maybe. The verdict was still out on that. Maya couldn't dismiss the way Slade had looked at her baby. "I'll think about it."

The sheriff gave a frustrated sigh, aimed another glance at Slade that smacked of *Convince her* and walked back toward his car.

Slade shifted in the seat so he was facing her again. "What part didn't you understand when I said it was dangerous for us to sit here in the parking lot?"

"Oh, I understood all the parts. I'm just not sure I can trust you."

She didn't know who was more surprised. Maya, for actually speaking her mind, or Slade, for being on the receiving end of it. Something went through his eyes. Hurt feelings, perhaps? Or maybe it was something deeper than that.

"Did you lose your own child or something?" Normally that was a question she wouldn't ask, either, but this was far from a normal situation. She needed to understand Slade's response to Evan.

Slade didn't look at her. He started surveillance of the parking lot and traffic light again. "Yeah."

So that explained the long look he'd given Evan. Well, maybe. "There's more," Maya insisted.

She waited for him to deny it or to tell her that it was none of her business, but he sat there silently for several moments before he spoke.

"I had a relationship with a woman that ended, well, pretty bad."

There was no good way to respond, so Maya just waited for him to continue.

"Months after things were over between us, I found out she was pregnant with my child." Slade paused, and even though he didn't move even a muscle, she could feel the storm brewing just beneath the surface. "She disappeared before I could find her or the baby."

Maya automatically pulled Evan closer and kissed his cheek. "I'm sorry."

Well, that explained why he'd volunteered for this case. Now, the question was—did she intend to let him help her?

Maya glanced at Evan. Then at Slade. And she knew she had to do everything to protect the precious baby in her arms. Everything, including accepting temporary help from this man.

"All right," Maya said.

That was apparently all the confirmation Slade needed, because he put out his hand. "I'll drive, but I need your keys."

Maya first leaned over the seat and strapped Evan back into his carrier, and then she retrieved the keys from her bag on the floor. She reached out to hand them to Slade, but movement caught her eye.

It caught Slade's, too.

His head whipped toward the back of the parking lot. Maya followed his gaze and saw the green SUV. The same one that she'd noticed at the traffic light earlier. But it was no longer at the light.

There was a squeal of the tires, and the green SUV came right toward them.

Chapter Four

"Get down!" Slade shouted to Maya.

He drew his gun and pushed her lower onto the seat. It wasn't a second too soon, because the green SUV slammed into their front bumper, jolting not just Maya's vehicle but the two of them. Evan, too.

The baby immediately started to cry.

Slade had tried to brace himself for something like this, but bracing obviously hadn't done a darn thing to stop it. Here they were right in the middle of what had to be a kidnapping attempt.

Or maybe even something worse.

After all, the kidnapper had already tried to kill one of the adoptive parents, so it wouldn't be much of a stretch to guess that he would attempt murder again.

The green SUV shot past them, the back end clipping Maya's car, but the vehicle didn't speed away as Slade hoped it'd do. With the tires squealing, the driver did a doughnut in the parking lot. He didn't bolt forward, but Slade heard the driver rev up the engine. The revving wasn't nearly as much of a concern as was the SUV's position.

It'd blocked the exit.

"I need the keys," Slade insisted. And despite her hands shaking like crazy, Maya somehow managed to give them to him.

Slade started the engine, kept his gun ready, but that was all he could do. There was no way out unless Slade tried to bash the vehicle from the front of the exit. Not a wise choice since the SUV was bigger than Maya's car.

His other option was to stay put and hope the sheriff would arrive in time to scare this guy off, because Slade wasn't sure he could drive over the foot-high concrete barrier that divided the parking lot from the sidewalk. He'd wreck for sure, maybe even collide with other cars traveling on the street.

And even if they weren't hurt in all of that, it'd make them sitting ducks.

Besides, he needed to be able to aim in case this guy started shooting. With the other customers in the parking lot and the wall of glass at the front of the grocery store, Slade didn't want this bozo firing shots.

The fear crawled down Slade's spine. He'd hoped to have had the baby in a safe place before confronting this kidnapper, but it was too late for that.

The kidnapper was here.

And the stakes were sky-high.

Even if that baby in the backseat wasn't his, Slade couldn't let the newborn be taken. God knows what this SOB had done with the two children he'd already kidnapped.

Maya didn't stay down. Despite the fact that Slade was practically on top of her, she fought to get away.

"Evan," she repeated.

Slade knew that her every instinct was probably screaming for her to get in the backseat with the baby. His certainly were, and while it was a risk for her to move, it was an even bigger risk for him to have to struggle with her when he should be getting them away from the danger.

But the danger came at them again.

The driver jammed his foot on the accelerator just as Maya crawled over the seat. Slade didn't bother to check and make sure she was using her own body to protect Evan. She would be.

"Hold on," he warned her, and Slade threw the car into gear.

He didn't completely manage to avoid a collision with the other vehicle, but he stopped them from taking a direct hit. Still, he heard Maya's sharp gasp of surprise, and he felt her slam against the back of his seat. Thank God the baby was strapped in and semiprotected. But Slade wasn't sure how much longer Maya's car could hold up with this battering.

The green SUV backed up, and just like before, it came at them again. Slade jerked the steering wheel to the right, but there wasn't enough space for him to get them away from the impact. He grazed a van with what was left of the front bumper, and the driver plowed right into the passenger's side of Maya's car, crushing it in so far that the door ended up near the gearshift. So did the sheet of safety glass that was knocked from the window.

"Stay as low as you can," Slade shouted out to Maya. "And if you can, call 911." Though someone had no doubt already done that. Still, the sheriff needed to know what he'd be up against when he came rushing to the scene. "Tell them the person in the SUV is attacking us."

Evan's screams were louder now, but Slade tried to tune out the sounds and focus on what he had to do.

And what he had to do was stop this idiot.

Yeah, it was a risk, but anything was at this point. With the glass gone from the window, Slade had a direct shot at the SUV.

He took it.

The bullet he fired was deafening, even over Evan's

cries and the roar of the engines, and it tore through the front windshield. The safety glass cracked and webbed, but it didn't give way, and that meant Slade didn't even get a glimpse of the driver.

The guy was no doubt armed.

And that's why Slade threw the car into Reverse and got out of the line of fire. He figured the kidnapper wanted the baby alive and that he wouldn't shoot. Still, Slade wanted to put as much distance as he could between them and the SUV. Backward he flew across the parking lot and tried to dodge as many cars as he could.

"Someone's trying to kidnap my baby," he heard Maya relay to whoever had answered her 911 call. She gave the info about the SUV and the location and then begged the person to hurry.

She sounded many steps beyond frantic, on the verge of all-out panicking. No surprise there. This was probably the first time in her entire white-picket-fence life that she'd been attacked. But Slade hoped she could hold it together. The last thing he needed was her to be hysterical.

Slade finally heard a welcome sound. Sirens. Thank God the sheriff was on the way. Better yet, the kidnapper must have heard it, too, because the driver turned the SUV. Not toward Maya's car...but in the opposite direction.

He was trying to escape.

Hell.

That definitely wasn't good. Slade wanted to stop him. Wanted to drag him from the SUV and beat some answers out of him. There were two missing babies, and this same moron had just tried to take another.

"Wait here," Slade ordered Maya.

He reached to open the door, but reaching was the only thing he managed to do before he caught the movement from the corner of his eye.

Not the SUV.

But there was someone seated in a black two-door sedan parked in the corner of the lot. He'd noticed the vehicle, of course, when he'd first arrived at the grocery store and spotted Maya's car.

But he darn sure hadn't seen anyone inside.

Well, he saw that someone now—the shadowy figure behind the steering wheel—and an uneasy feeling snaked through Slade. He'd been a marshal for nearly ten years, and that was more than enough time for him to sense something was wrong.

Slade kept one eye on the SUV as it sped out of the parking lot, but he turned his weapon toward the sedan.

Mercy.

Was this some kind of trap?

If so, he'd nearly fallen for it because he had been within a split second of running after the SUV. If he'd done that, it was possible that he would have left Maya and the baby completely vulnerable to an attack.

Slade stayed put. Not easy to do. His body was in the fight mode, but he also felt something else. That overpowering instinct to protect this child. He'd never considered himself father material. And maybe he wasn't. But that didn't seem to matter to whatever was firing the emotions inside him. If necessary, he would die to protect the baby.

Slade glanced at the green SUV as it disappeared out of sight. The sirens got closer, and thankfully the cruiser didn't pull into the parking lot. The driver went in pursuit of the SUV. Good. Maybe the locals would manage to collar the guy—alive—so that Slade could question him.

But that left the person in the black car.

Maybe it was just a case of wrong place, wrong time, but Slade wasn't taking any chances.

"What's going on?" Maya asked. She would have no

doubt lifted her head to look over the seat if Slade hadn't pushed her back down.

"There might be a second kidnapper."

Her breath rattled in her throat. "What do you need me to do?" The question rushed out with a rise of breath.

"You're doing it. Just stay down." Maya had already plastered herself over the baby again, and thankfully Evan's cries were now just soft whimpers.

Even though the windshield of the black car was heavily tinted, Slade detected some movement inside. The driver started the engine but didn't move. He just sat there as if daring Slade to come and get him. Slade figured if he did that, he'd be instantly gunned down.

The moments crawled by, and though it seemed to take an eternity, Slade figured it was less than a minute before he heard a second siren. Backup. This cruiser, too, might go in pursuit of the SUV, but if it turned into the parking lot, that would free up Slade to check out his theory about the second kidnapper.

Except the kidnapper obviously had a different plan.

The black car inched forward, and Slade cursed. Because he thought the guy was about to bash into them again. Slade took aim at the driver but held back pulling the trigger just in case this turned out to be nothing.

But it sure didn't feeling like *nothing*.

The driver didn't come toward them but instead turned toward the exit. He didn't screech out as the SUV had done. He simply drove away as if he'd finished whatever routine business he had.

"You recognize that car?" Slade asked, and he made a mental note of the license plate.

Maya lifted her head just a fraction and looked over the seat and Slade's shoulder. "No. But if he's the kidnapper, he's getting away."

Slade was well aware of that. "Call 911 again and give the dispatcher a description of the vehicle. I want this guy followed." Slade rattled off the license plate that he hoped wasn't fake.

Maya made the second call, but this time she didn't stay down when she finished. She watched the black car drive out of the parking lot. Again, not hurried. The driver was doing nothing that would draw attention to himself, but the fact that he'd been there during the kidnapping attempt drew all of Slade's attention.

Two vehicles, two drivers. And it could be just the tip of the iceberg. Maybe the kidnapper wasn't working alone, and if so, it only proved just how determined this guy was.

But why?

If someone was kidnapping babies for emotional reasons, then an attack like this didn't make sense. The person in the SUV had been determined. Desperate, even.

And that brought it all back to Slade.

"What's wrong?" Maya asked. "You're breathing funny."

Slade hadn't noticed any change in his breathing, but he immediately tried to fix it. He didn't want to have to give Maya an explanation that the kidnappings could be connected to him.

But they could be.

Yeah, it had crossed his mind, but it was something he'd tried hard to dismiss. Well, he couldn't dismiss it now. There were some criminals he'd arrested who would no doubt like to give him a dose of revenge. What better way to do it than to kidnap his child and use the baby to get back at him?

Slade mumbled more profanity. He needed answers. About Deidre. About her death. About everything. Because if this was indeed connected to him, he had to stop it.

And learn if one of these three baby boys was his.

In fact, the kidnapper might already have his child. That only made his stomach knot even more, but Slade couldn't dismiss the punch of emotion he'd gotten when he looked at Evan's face. He wasn't the sort of man to believe in woo-woo junk, but he couldn't deny that he'd felt…something.

Something he pushed aside when the police cruiser came flying into the parking lot.

Maya lifted her head again. "It's Sheriff Monroe." And she might have bolted from her vehicle if Slade hadn't caught onto her and held her in place.

Her eyes widened, and she shook her head as if considering the impossible. "You think someone else is out there?" But she didn't wait for his answer. Her gaze fired all around the parking lot.

"We don't know how many people this kidnapper could have hired to help him," he settled for saying.

Slade kept hold of her until Sheriff Monroe and a deputy exited the cruiser. Both lawmen had their weapons drawn, and like Maya, they were looking for any sign of danger.

Unfortunately, the danger had driven away.

Slade stepped from the car but motioned for Maya to stay put. "Please tell me you have someone in pursuit of the SUV and the black car," he said to the sheriff.

Monroe nodded. "I've called for backup and road-blocks."

Slade hoped that would be enough. If they got lucky, the missing babies might even be in one of the vehicles. Though it was an unsettling thought to consider the babies—any babies—going through that kind of danger.

"Did you get a good look at either driver?" Monroe asked.

"No." And Slade knew that would be the first of many questions he'd have to answer the same way. On the surface the attack might have looked sloppy and unplanned, but Slade figured the opposite was true.

The deputy stayed diligent, looking around, and Sheriff Monroe hurried past Slade and made his way over to Maya. "Are you okay? Were either of you hurt?"

Maya shook her head, but she was far from okay. Slade could see the terror and the wildfire adrenaline on her face and in her eyes.

Slade went closer, too, and was relieved when he saw that the baby had not only stopped fussing but had fallen asleep. He wasn't sure how that was possible, but he was grateful for it.

"My truck's over there." Slade tipped his head to the side of the grocery store where he'd parked. "I can drive you to the sheriff's office, and we can wait there until we figure out the next step."

"Not home," she mumbled.

And it wasn't a question. Yeah, the impact of the danger was really starting to settle in now, but she still managed to give him a look that Slade had no trouble recognizing.

She didn't trust him.

Too bad. He hadn't exaggerated when he'd told her that he was her best shot at keeping the baby safe.

Slade took her by the arm and helped her stand. Good thing he didn't let go, because Maya wobbled and landed with a smack against him. Despite the hell they'd just been through, Slade felt another jolt. Not from the danger this time but from the realization that Maya was a damn attractive woman.

And she was in his arms.

She quickly remedied that. "Sorry." She pushed herself away from him but not before Slade caught another look in her eyes. Not distrust.

Oh, man.

He had to be wrong, but it seemed as if there was that little spark. Well, he had too much on his mind and plate to be dealing with that, and he told his body, and hers, to knock it off.

Maya reached for the baby, wobbled again and Slade stepped around her to unstrap the carrier so he could lift it and the car seat. He didn't have anything resembling a car seat in his truck, and the baby had already been put in enough danger.

Clearly, Maya didn't like him handling her baby even while Evan was in a carrier, but even she couldn't argue that she wasn't steady enough on her feet to make the short trek across the parking lot.

Slade kept his gun ready in his right hand, shifted the carrier to his left and gave Maya a nudge to get her moving. However, they only made it a few steps before the sheriff's phone rang.

"Sheriff Monroe," he answered, and Slade saw the immediate change in the lawman's body language.

That stopped Slade in his tracks. Maya, too. Hell, Slade hoped this wasn't bad news, because they'd already had enough of that today. Him and Maya and waited and fortunately didn't have to wait long.

"We got him," the sheriff announced the second he ended the call.

Maya made a sound of sheer relief. But not Slade. He just waited for the sheriff to continue.

"Well, we got one of them anyway," Monroe explained. "My deputy just cuffed the driver of the black car and he's taking him to the sheriff's office now."

"Is he talking?" Slade immediately asked.

The sheriff shook his head.

Slade got Maya moving again. "I'll do something about that."

One way or another, Slade would get answers. And not just about the kidnappings but about the baby's paternity. The moment he had Maya and the baby inside his truck, he took out his phone and started a text to send to one of his brothers.

"Please tell me nothing else is wrong." Maya leaned over as if trying to see what he'd typed.

But Slade fired off the text before she could see it. At least he thought he had.

Maya looked up at him with suddenly accusing eyes. "Why…?" That was all she managed to say for several seconds. "Why did you ask for a DNA kit?"

Chapter Five

Maya groaned when she checked the clock on the office wall again and wished the minutes would stop crawling by and speed up. It'd been nearly an hour since Slade and she had arrived at the sheriff's office. Almost immediately he'd disappeared into the interrogation room with the sheriff and their kidnapping suspect.

The man from the black car.

No one had filled her in on what the man's role had been in the kidnapping. Or if there'd even been a role. Basically, she'd just been left in the room with the promise from Slade that he'd get answers. Well, that wait for answers was testing her already frazzled nerves.

She was thankful that her son wasn't in on that frazzled part. She'd given him the rest of his bottle not long after they'd arrived, and the full tummy did the trick because Evan was sound asleep.

Unlike Maya.

She was too exhausted to pace across the sheriff's private office, but she couldn't stop her mind from racing. The attack in the parking lot was partly to blame for that. *Mostly to blame.*

But some of that mind racing was because of the cowboy-lawman in jeans and a Stetson who'd rescued Evan and her. She should be thanking him a hundred times over, but it wasn't a boatload of thanks that was in that whirl-wind inside her head.

It was the uneasy feeling she had about him.

Since she wasn't about to lie to herself, she admitted part of that uneasiness had to do with his looks. Alarmingly handsome. With a dark and dangerous edge. It wasn't even the *edge* that troubled her. In fact, that only made parts of her body notice him even more. But she couldn't shake the feeling that Slade was as uneasy about her as she was about him.

But why?

And did it have something to do with the DNA test he'd requested in the text? Slade hadn't answered her question when she'd asked him about it. There hadn't been time. They'd been in a rush to get to the sheriff's office and he had said something to her about needing to keep watch. Which he had certainly done. She had, too. But she'd soon demand the answer.

The office door opened, and despite her fatigue, Maya jumped to her feet. Just like that her body went on alert, preparing her for another fight. But it wasn't a kidnapper who came through the door.

It was Slade.

He paused in the doorway, looking first at her before his attention landed on Evan. She'd put the carrier on the sheriff's desk because the chair next to her hadn't been wide enough to hold it.

"Did he confess?" Maya asked.

"To some things." And with that somewhat cryptic statement, Slade closed the door and walked closer. His attention was still on the baby, and he sank into the chair next to her.

"His name is Morgan Gambill, and yeah, he has a police record for various drug offenses. He claims someone paid him to go to the parking lot and sit there. He says he didn't know anything about the green SUV, the attack or the kidnappings."

A frustrated sigh left her mouth. "You believe him?"

He shot her a "What do you think?" look. "I never believe anyone with a record that long, especially a drug user who looks like he'd sell his soul for his next fix."

Maya couldn't help it. She shuddered. This was exactly the kind of person she'd tried to distance herself from. "Who hired him?"

Slade shook his head. "Gambill claims he doesn't know, that it was all done via email and a wire transfer. We'll confiscate his computer and go through the account."

But he didn't sound very hopeful that they'd find anything. And they likely wouldn't. She couldn't imagine the kidnapper making a mistake that would be so easy to trace.

"Gambill wasn't armed when the deputy caught up with him," Slade continued. "But he could have tossed a weapon out the car window. Sheriff Monroe has someone out searching the sides of the road now. How is he?"

Since Slade didn't pause before that last question, it took her a moment to realize he was asking about the baby. "He's fine," Maya practically snapped. "Sorry," she added in a mumble.

Slade's gaze came to hers. Even though she hadn't thought it possible, those blue eyes were even more unsettling when aimed at her rather than the baby.

"How are *you?*" he asked.

Maya considered a lie but figured he'd see right through it. "Scared to death and even more afraid of trusting you."

Slade stayed quiet a moment, that steely gaze still drilling into her, and he nodded. "For the record, I don't trust you much, either. I figure first chance you get, you'll try to ditch me and that'll only put you and that boy in harm's way again."

His instincts were spot-on. She had already considered ditching him.

"I can't do much to change your opinion of me," he went on, his voice a husky drawl with a touch of gravel in it. "Can't deny this attraction between us, either. That won't help," Slade concluded.

Again she considered a lie. Again dismissed it. "Last time I acted on an attraction, I got burned—badly."

"Yeah." For one word, it encompassed a lot.

Sweet heaven. Did he know that she'd been attacked and left for dead four years ago?

No doubt.

Slade was a lawman, after all, and he'd known about her desire to have a child. But it only added another level of uneasiness that he knew about the attack. Had likely seen photos, too. Those nightmarish images flashed through her mind. Always there. *Always.* And she had the physical scars to prove it.

"I learned a lot from that attack," she mumbled.

"Bet you did. It's the hard lessons we remember most."

That was the voice of experience, and she made a mental note to do an internet check on Slade. She was betting he had some secrets.

Dark ones.

"I need you not to run," Slade tossed out there. "This investigation will be dangerous enough without you making it worse."

Maya pulled back her shoulders, about to assure him that she wasn't going to make things more dangerous. But she had to rethink that. What if Slade was her best bet at keeping Evan safe? The marshal certainly seemed determined to do just that. And in that particular area, they were on the same page.

"Let's just get through this," he went on. "And find the

person responsible. Find those babies, too, so we can get them back where they belong."

Again, on the same page.

So why did it feel as if she were about to step off a cliff?

"What happens now?" she asked. And Maya hoped she didn't have to clarify that she was talking about the investigation and their current situation. They couldn't stay at the sheriff's office much longer, because she didn't have any additional formula for Evan.

"You'll need to go to a safe house." Slade checked the time. "My brother's working on that. The sheriff will continue to press Gambill and hope he spills something. I don't think Gambill's an innocent as he's claiming, but he's not smart enough to put together something like this."

"What about Randall Martin, the owner of the green SUV?" she asked.

"I talked to him on the phone, and he's coming in for an interview, but he claims someone stole his SUV and that he reported it stolen before the attack."

"You believe him?"

Slade lifted his shoulder. "He knew about the kidnappings. Said he heard about them on the news." He scrubbed his hand over his face. "Maybe he did. But he doesn't have an alibi for the time of the kidnapping attempt. He claims he's been home alone."

So he could be the person responsible and could have reported his vehicle stolen to cover his tracks. "What about the missing nanny, Andrea Culberson? Are the cops still looking for her?"

He nodded. "Looking but with no luck finding her. She's left no money or paper trail."

Maya couldn't dismiss the nanny as a suspect, but there was something about her situation that didn't make sense.

"If Andrea took her employers' baby, then why would she take another child and then attempt to kidnap Evan?"

"She had some mental problems," Slade reminded her. "Maybe this is just overkill." He paused. "Or she could be dead. The kidnapper could have murdered her when he took the baby."

Despite the bone-weary fatigue, that sent a spike of panic through her. Maya wanted to get out of there, fast, so that her baby wouldn't be in danger.

As if he knew exactly what she was thinking, Slade cupped his hand around her wrist. Not a rough grip. A barely there touch, something she wouldn't have thought him capable of, not with that strongman's body.

"Breathe," he insisted.

Only then did Maya realize that she'd sucked in her breath and held it. She released it and shook off his grip. But it didn't matter. Just that brief anchor had been enough to help her settle the panic.

"Andrea's employers, Nadine and Chase Collier, have hired a P.I. to look for her," Slade added. "And their baby, of course."

She looked down at her son and couldn't imagine losing him. A parent's worst nightmare. One that Slade had been through himself. No doubt that was the reason for the pain she now saw in his eyes when he stared at Evan.

The sound shot through the room, and because Maya's nerves were right there at the surface, she gasped. It took her a moment to realize someone had knocked on the door. Slade jumped to his feet, moving in front of her, but she saw his shoulders relax when the door opened.

But Maya didn't relax.

The man in the doorway looked just as intense as Slade.

"My brother," Slade said to her. "Marshal Declan O'Malley."

The lanky dark-haired man slipped off his Stetson, caught her gaze and nodded a greeting. Maya noticed not only the lack of resemblance but the different surnames.

"Your brother?" she questioned.

"Foster brother," Marshal O'Malley explained. Like Slade, he had an easy Texas drawl, but there was a hint of some other accent. His gray-green eyes went from her to Slade and then to Evan.

"The safe house is ready." Declan handed the papers he was holding to Slade. "The background checks you wanted."

Slade took them, and Maya went closer to him so she could see what had captured his complete attention. Randall Martin's name was on the first line. Before she could even scan through the personal info about his address, age, etc., Slade mumbled some profanity.

"Yeah," his brother concurred. "You need to question him."

Maya saw it then. In the paragraph of comments. Randall's girlfriend, Gina Blackwell, had left him several months earlier, and apparently it hadn't been a peaceful split, because she'd filed a restraining order against him.

The restraining order didn't prove that Randall could be involved in the kidnappings, but it was a clue that he could be violent. However, there was nothing to indicate that Randall had believed a baby would help bring his ex back to him. But maybe that was exactly what'd happened.

"Might be best if I take Randall into Maverick Springs for questioning," Declan explained. "This is already federal anyway, since the FBI was called in."

She shook her head. "Does that mean the marshals would handle the case?"

"We already are." Slade's tone wasn't as bossy as usual, but he certainly wasn't asking for permission.

"Before you take Maya to the safe house, you can question Randall at the marshals' office," Declan went on. "And talk to Ranger Morris." He paused, met his brother's gaze. "There's been a...development."

Both men glanced at her, and she didn't think it was her imagination they were considering if they should take this conversation out of the room. But then Slade looked at the baby.

"What development?" he asked Declan.

Even though Slade had obviously just given him the green light to continue, Declan hesitated. Mumbled some profanity. "The Rangers claim they found an eyewitness who puts you near Webb's office at the time of the murder."

Of all the things she'd thought he might say, that wasn't one of them. "You're a suspect in a murder investigation?"

Slade's mouth tightened. "I'm a suspect in a witch hunt," he huffed, putting his hands on his hips. "I was raised at the Rocky Creek Children's Facility."

Oh. Now, that was a place she recognized because it'd been in the news for months. The facility was closed now, but it had a less than stellar reputation. As had the headmaster, Jonah Webb, and about six months ago Webb's body had been found in a shallow grave near Rocky Creek.

But she recalled other facts. Ones that had her shaking her head. "Webb's wife confessed to the murder."

Declan nodded. "But before she went into a coma, she said she had an accomplice."

She turned toward Slade so quickly that she accidentally bumped into Evan's carrier. Startled, her son's hands flew up, and he started to cry. Maya picked him up to try and soothe him, but she needed some reassurance of her own.

"The Rangers believe you helped murder Webb." And it wasn't exactly a question.

Maya hadn't thought it possible, but Slade's jaw tightened even more. "For the record, Webb deserved to spend an eternity in hell, and whoever sent him there should be given a medal. Not jail time."

It wasn't the declaration of innocence she'd been hoping for, but Maya decided to withhold judgment. About that anyway. From what she'd read about Webb, he had been physically abusing the children at the facility he ran. A man who preyed on someone weaker than himself.

Something Maya had some experience with.

And that was the reason she was willing to cut Slade some slack.

She hoped that was the only reason.

Maya was so deep in her own thoughts that she nearly missed the look that Slade and Declan gave each other. Something passed between them, maybe an entire conversation, and at the end of it, Slade and Declan moved away from her and closer to the door. With their backs to her, Declan whispered something.

"Is this personal?" she thought she heard Declan say. But what she didn't hear was Slade's response. Declan handed Slade something, and when he turned back around to face her, she saw the small plastic bag in his hand.

"It's a DNA test kit." Slade's attention went straight to Evan. So did he. Slade walked back toward her, reached out and touched Evan's cheek.

Evan stopped whimpering and turned his head toward Slade. Her baby studied the dark and brooding man who'd deemed himself their guardian-protector.

"DNA?" Maya shook her head. "You didn't answer my question earlier when I asked about it. You don't think I had something to do with the kidnappings?"

"It's for the baby. For Evan." He paused, kept touching Evan. "You'll need to swab the inside of his mouth so we can see if there's some kind of genetic connection to any of our suspects. Or someone else in the criminal database. It could give us answers as to who the kidnapper is."

Oh.

She took a moment to let that settle in, and it didn't settle in well. A chill went through her, and Maya turned her body so that Slade's fingers were no longer on Evan's cheek.

"We already have the DNA from one of the missing babies—the second one taken. The lab got it from the baby's pacifier. Now we're working on getting samples for the first baby, his parents and from Evan's birth mother and father."

Again Maya had to shake her head. "The birth mother didn't want her identity known. And my adoption attorney said the mother couldn't name the father. She apparently had multiple partners and wasn't even sure who the father was."

"The DNA might tell us that," Declan volunteered. "And if the birth father has a criminal history. It's possible that he heard about the baby and is now trying to find his son."

That chill in her body turned to ice, and because she was afraid her legs might give way, Maya hugged Evan closer to her and sank back down into the chair. As bad as that scenario was, maybe it meant the other babies were safe, that the kidnapper would release them as soon as he learned they weren't his child.

But what would he do with the child that was his?

Maya hugged Evan even tighter.

Declan looked down at some notes he was holding. "I went through hospital records, and Evan's birth mother is Crystal Hanson. We're searching for her so she can give us a sample, but she has a do-not-contact order regarding anything about the baby. We're also hoping that someone who knew her will be able to tell us the identity of the father." He looked up from the notes and at her. "You never met Ms. Hanson?"

"Never. Evan was actually supposed to go to another family, but they had to back out at the last minute. I was the next one on the list at the adoption agency, so two days after he was born, I got the call."

The best call of her life. Of course, now the danger and fear of the unknown were overshadowing her happiness. Maya resented it, too. Yes, it seemed a small complaint in the grand scheme of things, but she wanted to be able to enjoy every precious moment with her son, and this kidnapper was taking that away from her and from Evan.

Slade opened the test kit and handed her the swab. Part of her wanted to refuse the test and bury her head in the sand, but that wouldn't make the danger go away. And besides, this might just be the first step into stopping the danger so they could get on with their lives.

"Just rub it on the sides of his mouth," Slade instructed.

Maya did it as quickly as she could and handed it back to Slade, who put it back into the plastic bag before he gave it to Declan. "I want preliminary results back ASAP."

Declan nodded and opened his mouth to say something. However, the knock at the door stopped him. Again Slade stepped protectively in front of her, and she had to peer around him to see who was in the doorway when Declan opened it.

Sheriff Monroe.

The sheriff looked at Slade. "You know that missing nanny—Andrea Culberson?"

Slade nodded. "Yeah. The one who might be the kidnapper. What about her?"

Sheriff Monroe hitched his thumb in the direction of the dispatch-reception area. "Well, she just walked in."

"She's here?" Maya couldn't believe it. According to

Slade, every law enforcement agency in the state was looking for her and even thought that she might be dead.

"She's here," the sheriff verified, then turned to Maya. "And she's asking to see the marshal and you."

Chapter Six

Slade groaned.

Yeah, he wanted this meeting with Andrea Culberson, especially if she could tell him what the heck was going on with these kidnappings. But he hadn't wanted this to happen until he'd had Maya and the baby tucked away someplace safe. Meeting face-to-face with a suspect didn't qualify in any way as *safe*.

"I'll take Ms. Culberson in the interview room," the sheriff said as he left.

Declan paused a moment, no doubt silently asking Slade if he should hang around. "Get those results to the lab," Slade insisted. "And as soon as you can, I need all you can find out about our visitor, her employers and their missing baby."

His brother didn't question any of that. Declan hurried out. Maya might have hurried out, too, probably so she could confront Andrea, but Slade stepped in front of her and shut the door.

She stopped but not before brushing against him. Not exactly body-to-body contact, but it was enough for him to feel the heat knife right through him. Heat he darn sure shouldn't be feeling, at least not until he'd settled some things with her.

Like the paternity of the child in her arms.

If that was his son, he would challenge her for custody. And he'd win because he had the law on his side. Best not to allow something stupid like attraction to get in the way of that. Besides, once Maya learned that he was hiding the possible paternity from her, any and all heat between them would vanish in a heartbeat.

"I want to talk to Andrea," Maya said, but then she stepped back, swallowed hard.

"Do you really want Evan in the same room with a possible kidnapper? Because I don't," Slade added before she could answer.

Maya looked ready to start a big-time argument about that, but he saw the fight leave her eyes. "I just want this to be over." Her words were mostly breath, and the weary sigh turned to a slight tremble of her bottom lip. Heck, her eyes even watered.

She'd been strong so far. A real fighter. But this had to be getting to her.

Slade did the exact opposite of what he'd told himself to do. He didn't stay away from her. He slipped his arm around Maya's waist. "Let me question her, and I promise I'll tell you everything she says."

She looked up at him, maybe to see if there was something he wasn't telling her. Or maybe she was just looking, but either way, Slade was glad she had Evan in her arms or he might have been tempted to ease her closer.

Correction.

He would have been tempted to kiss her, and he wasn't a man who was easily tempted. Still, Maya seemed to have his number when it came to reactions he'd rather not have.

Slade moved her back across the room and eased her into the chair. "Wait here, and I'll make sure a deputy or someone is guarding the door. As soon as I'm done, I'll get you to the safe house so you can get some rest."

Again, she didn't argue, though that might come later, when she'd gotten a second wind. Maybe the safe house wouldn't even be necessary if he got a confession from Andrea and located the missing babies. Of course, that would only be the start of it for Slade.

The results of that DNA test would be critical.

Slade had no proof that Evan was actually his even if he had felt that connection to him. He only knew that he had *a* son out there somewhere, a baby who had likely been stolen from his ex. If Evan wasn't his, then maybe one of the others would be, but he had to wonder how Maya would deal with the tests results if they confirmed that he was indeed Evan's father.

That was the thought he had on his mind when he leaned down and brushed a kiss on Evan's head. Bad idea. Real bad. Because something flashed through Maya's eyes, and it wasn't tears.

It was suspicion.

"Stay put," he warned her. And because of that suspicion, the moment Slade walked out and shut the door, he didn't head to the interview room but rather to the dispatch desk, where he found Sheriff Monroe.

"I need someone to watch Maya and the baby," Slade explained. He didn't want to get into a lengthy explanation about suspicious eyes, so Slade went with something faster. "She's on the verge of panicking and might think she'd be better off on her own. She won't be. If Andrea isn't the kidnapper, then Maya could be taking the baby right into the path of danger."

No suspicion in the sheriff's eyes. Just concern. He nodded. "I'll keep an eye on her."

With that box ticked, Slade went back down the hall. Andrea was already in the interview room, clearly waiting for him. And pacing. He instantly recognized the tall, thin blonde because he'd studied her photo. Even dressed in jeans and a simple gray jacket, she looked more like the person who'd hire a nanny than someone who'd be one. Probably because she came from rich roots and had only taken the nanny job after being disinherited by her wealthy folks.

"Marshal Becker?" she asked, her eyes wide. She was also nibbling on her bottom lip.

He nodded. "You asked to see me."

"And the woman whose baby was nearly kidnapped." Andrea's words came out so fast that they practically ran together. "I need you to understand I'm not guilty, that I didn't take Will."

Will, short for William Chase Collier, the adopted baby boy who'd been in her care when both the baby and she had disappeared two days ago.

"Where's Will?" Slade asked, and he didn't bother to sound friendly. In his experience, a badass attitude made things move a lot faster.

"I don't know." Her voice broke, and she caught onto the side of the table as if to steady herself. The tears came. Man, did they. They started streaking down her cheeks, and while they looked genuine, Slade knew that sort of thing could be faked.

"Start from the beginning. Give me your version of what happened, because your employers, Nadine and Chase Collier, insist you kidnapped their child. And for the record, that makes you a suspect in a subsequent kidnapping and another attempt that happened just a short while ago."

She didn't seem surprised about that, only more distressed. Her chest began to pump for air, and Slade was thankful that she sat down because she looked ready to fall.

"It started two days ago." Her words no longer came out at breakneck pace. She spoke in a ragged whisper. "I put Will down for a nap after his afternoon bottle and then went to grab something to eat from the kitchen. I had the baby monitor with me and was gone a half hour, tops. When I got back, Will wasn't in his crib."

"You didn't hear anyone?" Slade asked.

She shook her head and shoved her hair from her face. "It's a big house. Twenty rooms, and it was also cleaning day. Three maids were coming and going. A crew of handymen, too. None of them saw anything, either."

"There's been no ransom demand," Slade reminded her.

"I know." Her teary gaze came to his. "The kidnapper planned it that way so I'd look guilty." She reached in her pocket, took out her phone and scrolled through the numbers. "He called me just seconds after I realized Will was missing. The number isn't working now. Believe me, I've tried."

The kidnapper had probably used a prepaid cell. Or Andrea could have used one to call herself. Still, if she'd planned this kidnapping, then why was she here? She had to know that she'd be a suspect. Better yet, where was the baby?

"What'd the kidnapper say to you?" And Slade didn't bother to take the skepticism out of his voice.

What little color Andrea had drained from her face. "He said to meet him at the park and to bring money, and if I called the cops, the baby would die." She paused, mumbled a string of *oh, Gods*. "He insisted he had the place bugged, and he'd know if I called anyone."

That wasn't a new ploy. Slade had heard of other kidnappers doing the same. Maybe it was true, maybe not. One of the maids or someone on the work crew could have planted a bug and then even set the fire.

"I told him I didn't have much cash," Andrea went on, "and he said for me to bring him some of Nadine's jewelry. He gave me thirty minutes to get there." She shook her head. "I had to drive like crazy to make it, and I was terrified. I love that baby like he is my own."

Slade got an uneasy feeling of how he would have reacted if it'd been his child being held hostage. Not a good time for that. And he forced his mind back on the interview. "What happened when you arrived at the park?"

"The kidnapper wasn't there, but he called me again." She showed him the second number on her phone. "He said the cops had been alerted that I'd kidnapped Will. I didn't tell them," Andrea insisted.

Slade lifted his shoulder. "If you're innocent, why'd you run?"

"Because the kidnapper threatened to hurt Will again. He said for me to leave, to get far away from the Colliers' estate and that he'd contact me soon. But he hasn't." She pressed her hand to her mouth. "And I heard someone burned the place down right after Will was taken. I couldn't stay in hiding even if I figured I looked guilty. I didn't know what else to do."

Slade caught movement from the corner of his eye and turned to find the sheriff motioning for him to step out of the room.

"Stay put," Slade warned Andrea first, and he went back into the hall, where he would have asked what Sheriff Monroe wanted if he hadn't seen the open door. Not just any door, but the one to the office where he'd left Maya and the baby. And clearly no one was guarding it.

Slade practically pushed the sheriff aside so he could get to the room and see what was going on.

No Maya.

No baby.

"They're in the break room," the sheriff explained, pointing toward the back of the building. He also handed

Slade a grocery bag. "It's formula and diapers. I had my wife run to the store and get it."

Slade mumbled a thanks and started to move again, but the sheriff stopped him. "You should know that Maya's upset," the sheriff said. "She got a phone call that seemed to shake her up, and she said she needed to stretch her legs." Maybe because Slade was cursing a blue streak, Monroe added, "There's no exit off the break room, just some windows."

Windows could easily turn into an exit for someone desperate. He ran, practically knocking into one of the deputies, and he skidded to a stop in front of the door. It took him a moment—a bad, heart-stopping moment—to pick through the furniture and appliances cluttering the room and locate Maya on the sofa. She had Evan in the crook on her arm and a death grip on her phone.

She looked up, her gaze connecting with Slade's, and he immediately saw the tears. Unlike Andrea's tears, these punched him hard in the gut.

"He said he'd kill us," Maya whispered.

That was another punch. "Who said that?" Slade went to her, set down the bag of supplies and looked at her phone when she held it up for him to see the number of the person who'd called fewer than five minutes earlier.

"He didn't tell me his name." Her voice was shaking as much as she was. "Only that if I didn't hand over Evan, he'd kill all of us, including you. He also said he'd kill us if I told the sheriff, that he'd shoot up the place and he'd know if I'd told him."

Hell.

Things were escalating faster than he could keep up. And it was having a bad effect on Maya. Thankfully, not Evan. The baby had fallen back to sleep.

Slade wasn't good at providing a shoulder to lean on,

but he figured Maya needed something. He slipped his arm around her and pulled her to him.

It felt better than it should have.

Far better.

"Think hard." He tried to keep his voice level. Hard to do with the emotions and anger firing on all cylinders. "What else did he say?"

"That I was to sneak out of the sheriff's office and meet him at an abandoned gas station at the edge of town. That's when he said he'd kill us all if I didn't come."

He'd probably try to kill them all if they did show up at the gas station. A Catch-22. Whoever was behind this was getting desperate. Or maybe the guy was just stupid. Either way, Maya and Evan weren't getting close to that gas station.

Too bad Slade couldn't, either.

He wanted to meet this SOB face-to-face, but it was too big of a risk to take because this could be some kind of ploy to lure him away from Maya.

But why?

The kidnapper had to know that Slade wouldn't leave them unprotected. But there was the other possibility. A bad one. That maybe the guy had some contact inside the sheriff's office and would indeed know that Maya had told him about the call.

"Come on," Slade said, and he helped her to her feet so he could lead her to the far side of the room, where there were no windows. He also shut the break room door. There was no lock, but at least it would stop someone from walking right in on them.

"What should I do?" Maya asked.

"Nothing. I'll handle this." He moved the car seat and supplies closer to them, too, in case they had to make a quick exit, and he called his brother Harlan at the marshals' office in Maverick Springs.

"Declan just filled me in," Harlan greeted him. "I've been working on those background checks you wanted."

Good. He'd need that information later, after he'd taken some other measures. "Maya got a call from the possible kidnapper." Slade took her phone and read off the number.

Almost immediately, he heard Harlan's fingers clicking on the computer keyboard. "It's a burner," Harlan said several moments later.

"A burner?" Maya asked.

Slade hadn't realized she could hear the conversation, but then, he had her plastered right against him. She was no doubt as desperate for answers as Slade was, and that was the reason he clicked the speaker button.

"A burner is a prepaid cell. Can't be traced," Slade explained. Then he added, "Harlan, Maya's listening in now, but the person who called from the burner threatened to kill her if she didn't meet him at an abandoned gas station here in Spring Hill. He wants her to turn over the baby to him."

"I'm not doing that," she insisted, the tears spilling down her cheeks again.

There was the sound of more keyboard clicks. "The name of the gas station is Jasper's. It's been closed for nearly a year now. You want me to get someone out there?"

Slade knew this would alarm her, but he had to say it. "Yeah. But not the locals. Judging from the threat this guy made, he could have a *friend* in the sheriff's office. It's just a precaution," Slade added when her eyes widened, and she stared at him.

"Hold on a sec," Harlan said, and Slade heard him make a call to arrange for some marshals to drive out to Spring Hill.

Those marshals would likely be more of Slade's foster

brothers. There were some huge advantages to having five brothers who were all federal marshals, and this was one of them. Slade trusted them with his life.

"Done," Harlan verified. "Now for those background checks." He paused. "You want them now?"

That was Harlan's way of asking if Slade wanted Maya to hear. Slade didn't, not really. She was already too close to falling apart, but Maya's gaze suddenly steeled up.

"I want to hear," she insisted.

Slade mentally debated it but knew whatever he learned from Harlan, he'd eventually have to tell her anyway. "Go ahead," he told his brother.

"You still got Andrea Culberson there in custody?" Harlan asked.

That wasn't the question Slade expected. "Yeah. Why?"

"Because you need to ask her about her employers. She could be innocent in all of this." More keyboard clicks. "I just found out that her boss Nadine Collier is up to her Botoxed forehead in gambling debts. The woman loves betting on the horses, but she's apparently not very good at it. She owes a cool million, and she owes it to the wrong people."

A million. Good grief. That was a big motive for plenty of things. "You think Nadine could have set up the kidnappings to collect the ransoms and pay off her debts?"

"It's possible, especially since her husband, Chase, doesn't seem to know about those debts." Harlan paused again. "The Colliers got a ransom demand about five minutes before you called me."

The demand was actually a relief because until now Slade hadn't known the kidnapper's plans for the missing babies. Maybe this meant the kidnapper wouldn't harm the babies.

Unless...

"Perhaps Nadine didn't kidnap the other baby, only her own adopted son," Slade suggested.

"Yeah." And that's all Harlan said for several moments. "I'm working on it, and if Nadine has her son hidden away, then I'll find him."

Maya shook her head. "So this might have nothing to do with fact that the babies are adopted?"

"We'll piece this together," he settled for saying. Especially since Nadine could still be responsible for all the kidnappings. "How soon can you question Nadine?"

"She's coming in for an interview first thing in the morning."

That wasn't soon enough for Slade. He didn't want Maya to have to go through a night with the danger looming over them. But then, even if Harlan pressed Nadine hard, the woman probably wouldn't confess to kidnapping. She'd no doubt have some well-paid lawyers who would keep her quiet, too.

"Talk to her husband," Slade insisted. "See how he reacts when you tell him about his wife's gambling debts."

"Will do. I'll set up the interview so you can watch it from a laptop. Didn't figure you'd want to bring Maya and the baby here to Maverick Springs to hear the interview in person."

He didn't. It was too big a risk to be on the road with them, and yet he had no choice. Slade had to get her to the safe house. And away from the sheriff's office. Yeah, there was only a slim chance that the kidnapper had an ally here, but a slim chance was still too big of a risk.

"I'll wrap up the interview with Andrea," Slade told his brother. "Better yet, can you send someone out here to finish things with her?"

"Sure. The sheriff does plan to hold her, right?"

"He does. She's a kidnapping suspect."

Of course, if she was the actual kidnapper, she had help since there was no way Andrea could have made that call to Maya. There was also the question of a mole in the sheriff's office and maybe that was the person who'd made the call.

"I know I've loaded you down with stuff, but I have to add one more thing," Slade continued. "Have someone run a check on the sheriff and his whole department. Just in case the caller was telling the truth about that."

"If he was, you shouldn't be there," Harlan insisted.

"I won't be much longer. Call me—"

"Wait," Harlan interrupted. But he was the one who paused. "I need to go over one more thing with you. In private," he added.

Slade groaned. This couldn't be good.

"I want to hear whatever he has to say," Maya insisted.

No doubt. But that didn't mean she should hear it. Slade clicked the button to take the call off speaker, and he put the phone to his ear.

"What's going on?" Slade asked his brother.

"Declan just dropped off the swab kit with the baby's DNA at the lab, and he said the results are for our eyes only."

"That's right." But he knew what his brother was really asking—why did the results need to stay secret? After all, this baby had been involved in a kidnapping attempt.

"So you want some kind of DNA comparison to prove what—the identity of the birth parents?"

"Yeah."

Another pause. "That's a short answer for a big question. I'll do an entire database search to see if there's a DNA match. But who's the specific DNA comparison we're looking for?" Harlan came right out and asked.

"Mine." He waited for his brother to question that, but

Harlan didn't say anything. "Call me when you have the results."

Slade ended the call, shoved his phone back in his pocket so he could carry the car seat and baby supplies but still have his right hand free for his weapon. He prayed he didn't have to pull it, but with everything going on, Slade wasn't going to trust anyone who wasn't family.

"We're leaving," Slade told her. "We'll go out the side exit, and once we're outside, move as fast as you can to my truck."

She nodded but didn't budge. Maya looked up at him. "I heard," she said in a whisper.

"Heard what?"

Maya swallowed hard. "I heard," she repeated. "Why do you want Evan's DNA compared to yours?"

Oh, hell.

Slade should have remembered that she'd heard the earlier comment made in a phone conversation. The woman had excellent hearing.

And bad timing.

This wasn't something he wanted to take the time to explain. "We'll talk about it later."

Maya caught onto his arm when he opened the door. "No. We'll talk about it now."

He didn't like that determined look in her eyes, but it faded just a bit when they heard the movement. Sheriff Monroe was making a beeline toward them, and he was moving darn fast.

"We have to get out of the building now!" the sheriff insisted. "Someone just called in a bomb threat."

Chapter Seven

The bad news just kept coming, and Maya was afraid it would even get worse. Judging from Slade's body language and his sharp replies to the person on the other end of his phone conversation, he felt the same way.

Slade had taken or made multiple calls every second since they'd evacuated the sheriff's office in a mad rush. The ride was equally mad, but that hadn't stopped Slade from keeping watch of their surroundings as they'd first gone to the marshals' office in Maverick Springs so he could get a "clean" vehicle. A truck that couldn't be traced back to him or the Marshals. One that he was now driving down the rural road.

Maya had kept watch, too, because she knew this could all be some kind of ploy to get them out in the open so that the kidnapper could try to take Evan.

"I want him found," Slade snapped, and he jabbed the end-call button as if it were the cause of their problems. "They didn't find a bomb, but during the evacuation, Morgan Gambill disappeared."

Mercy. No wonder Slade had jabbed the phone button so hard. "How the heck could that have happened?"

Slade shook his head and looked on the verge of cursing, but he glanced down at the car seat they'd strapped in between them. Evan was wide-awake and appeared to be hanging on every word.

"The deputy said he just lost sight of him," Slade settled for saying.

Great. Now one of their suspects was on the loose. Even if Gambill wasn't the kidnapper, it was entirely possible he was working for the very person who'd tried to take Evan. "Please tell me they managed to hang on to Andrea."

"They did, and my brother Dallas is personally transporting her to the Maverick Springs marshals' office. I'll question her again tomorrow. Along with Nadine and Chase Collier." His gaze met hers. "That means you'll need to stay at the safe house with one of my brothers."

There was a lot he left unsaid in that last part. Slade seemed to be waiting for her to object. And maybe she would.

Slade was keeping something from her, and she wanted to know what. But first things first. Since he'd been on the phone during their entire hour-long drive, she hadn't had a chance to ask some much-needed questions.

"What about the meeting at the abandoned gas station?" she asked. "Did anyone show?"

"No one. That could mean the guy had us under surveillance and wanted to see what we'd do."

She waited but he didn't add anything. "There seems to be an *or* at the end of that."

Slade lifted his shoulder. "He could just be crazy. Or maybe he wants to torment us as much as he can."

Maya had to groan. Neither of those were *ors* she wanted to consider. "How safe is this safe house where you're taking us?"

"As safe as my brother could make it."

For him, that probably meant it was *safe,* but again, she would decide once they were there. "How much longer before we get there, because I'll have to feed and change Evan soon?" Besides, it was getting dark, and she didn't want to be on the roads if she couldn't see if someone was following them.

Slade checked his GPS. "We're only about two miles away."

Good. But there was a downside to that—it wasn't nearly enough time to press him on the part of the conversation that she'd overheard with his brother Harlan.

"My brother learned more about the Colliers," Slade continued before she could say anything. "First of all, the ransom demand didn't pan out. They claim the kidnapper told them that he'd be calling them back, and it hasn't happened."

Maybe the kidnapper would call, though. And soon. "Did your brother learn anything else about the Colliers?"

"Some. Nothing good, though. According to an acquaintance, their marriage has been rocky for a while, and it was Chase who pressed for the adoption because he thought it would make things better."

She thought about that, shook her head. "How could any agency let them adopt under those circumstances?"

"It was a private adoption, and a lot of money changed hands. This acquaintance also said that Nadine wasn't happy about any aspect of the adoption, that she didn't want to be a parent and resented Chase for dumping the baby on her."

Maya actually shivered and silently cursed the fact that money had put that innocent baby in what seemed to be a toxic home. When the children were found—and she had to hold out hope that they would be—maybe someone would rescind the petition for adoption.

Slade took a turn off the rural road, and she spotted the one-story house just ahead. Other than a barn, there was nothing nearby, and the pastures stretched out on both sides.

"The town is a good ten miles away," Slade explained, "and the locals believe the owner is a city businessman who lends the place out to clients."

That would provide good cover as to why people would be coming and going, but it looked like an ordinary Craftsman-style house, not a fortress.

Slade didn't stop in front of the house. He drove to the back, parked directly next to the porch and began to unhook the car seat at the same time Maya reached for it. Their hands touched.

Gazes met, too.

She hated the warmth that pooled in her body. Obviously, her past hadn't taught her anything, and she pulled back her hand so she could touch one of the scars on her stomach. Her clothes concealed them, but she could always see them in her mind. And it was the reminder of the scars that gave her the attitude adjustment she needed.

"Once we're inside, I'll want an explanation about the DNA," she said.

He didn't dodge her gaze. In fact, Slade didn't have any reaction other than the barely audible sigh that left his mouth. He lifted the car seat, Maya grabbed her diaper bag and the plastic bag with diapers and formula that the sheriff had given them, and they hurried out of the truck. Slade also didn't waste any time using the electronic keypad to open the door.

The moment they stepped into the house, the security system started to beep.

"Is that you, Slade?" someone asked.

The sound of the man's voice caused Maya to gasp, and it took her one breath-stopping moment to realize the person wasn't inside the house but rather had spoken through the speaker mounted on the wall next to the keypad.

"It's me," Slade verified.

The buzzing stopped, and she saw the keypad lights go from red to green. "The security system is armed," the man said. "If you need anything, just hit the panic button. There's one on the wall in every room next to the light switches."

"Will do. What other measures have been taken?"

"There's perimeter security. If someone turns onto the road that leads to the house, it'll trigger the sensor and that'll give you at least ten minutes' notice that someone's coming."

"What if someone tries to reach this place on foot?" Slade asked.

"No sensors for that. We tried it, but the deer kept tripping it. But the windows are bullet resistant. And in case you have to get out in a hurry, the road curves around, so you could leave out back if you had to."

Maya prayed it wouldn't come to that.

"Call if you need anything," the man added.

Slade assured him that he would, and he pressed another button on the keypad before he walked across the hardwood floor and set the baby on the coffee table in the modestly furnished living room.

Modest described what she could see of the rest of the place, too. There was a dining room directly across from them and the kitchen behind them. She figured the three doors on the right led to the bedrooms. Well, hopefully there were at least two because she had no intentions of sharing a bed with Slade.

Without asking her permission, Slade undid the safety belts and took Evan into his arms. Her son didn't fuss.

In fact, he stared at the stranger holding him. And Evan smiled.

Yes, smiled!

Maya figured it had to be gas. From all the books she'd read, Evan was still too young for a real smile, but she felt the tightening in her chest. Not jealousy that someone other than her had been on the receiving end of a smile. No. This was something much stronger than jealousy.

It was fear.

"I want answers," Maya managed to say, though she wasn't sure how. In addition to the tightening in her chest, every part of her seemed frozen in place.

He didn't jump to say anything. In fact, he took his time, and he kept his attention pinned to Evan. No smile for Slade, just the raw intensity that had stirred the muscles in his jaw.

"Remember when I told you about my ex-girlfriend?" he finally asked.

Maya nodded. "The one who was pregnant and disappeared."

"Yeah." And that was all he said for several moments. "Well, it wasn't a relationship, more like a one-night stand, but months afterward she called to tell me she was pregnant with my baby. She said she was within days of her due date, and she wanted me to meet her. She was scared and said someone was trying to kill her."

Evan cooed, the sweet sound drifting through the room, and despite the pained look in his eyes, the corner of Slade's mouth lifted. Not exactly a smile, but she thought maybe that was the nearest he came to that particular expression.

"I wasn't sure it was a real threat," Slade continued, "but I drove to her place in Austin only to find it ransacked. And she was missing."

Oh, mercy. Maya didn't like the sound of this at all. "What happened?"

Slade lifted his shoulder, but there was nothing casual about the reaction. There was a storm raging just beneath the surface. "Deidre's body was found a few hours later."

Maya put her hand on her chest to steady her heart. It was racing now, and she wasn't sure she wanted to hear the answer to her next question. Still, she had to know. "And the baby?"

"Missing. He wasn't with her body."

Her heart pounded even harder. "*He?* She had a son?"

Slade nodded. "I managed to learn that from the doctor who delivered the baby. Deidre had paid him to keep the delivery secret."

"From you?"

"Maybe." Another pause. "But she was in trouble, had gotten involved with the wrong man—a guy named Damien Waters—who was jealous that she was carrying another man's child." He mumbled something that she didn't catch. "Deidre had this thing for bad boys."

Something Maya could understand. She, too, had once been there, done that. And yes, she had the scars to prove it.

"From what I've been able to piece together, Waters was verbally abusive. Maybe physically, too," Slade added like profanity. "He's dead now, so I can't get answers from him."

Maya wanted to ask if Slade had been the one to kill this abusive man, but again, it wasn't an answer she wanted to hear.

She waited, breath held, but she had the sickening feeling that she knew where this was going. "This happened a long time ago?"

Now Slade's gaze came to hers. "September 16 of this year."

Evan's birthday.

And the birthdays of the missing babies.

Her heart slammed against her chest. Her breath stalled, only to start gusting in and out. And because she had no choice, she sank down onto the sofa. Everything hit her at once. The realization. The tornado of emotions.

And, yes, the fear.

"You think Evan is your son." Maya didn't wait for him to confirm it. She would have grabbed Evan right out of his hands, but Slade moved, turning his body so she couldn't do that.

"No need for that." Slade's voice sounded like a warning, and she thought for a moment he might use physical force to take Evan.

But he didn't.

He calmly shifted Evan back toward her and eased him into her arms.

"Oh, God," she mumbled, and she just kept repeating it. Maya was aware that she sounded crazy, but considering the circumstances, she had a right to snap. "I thought that happened a long time ago."

"No." His gaze came back to hers. "Put yourself in my place. The doctor who delivered my son confirmed that he was born on September 16, and three baby boys born that same day were put up for adoption. If Evan's not mine, then it means my child is likely one of the other two, and he's already been taken."

Or worse.

Slade didn't say the words aloud, but she heard it in his voice. Saw it in his face.

She swallowed hard so she could speak. "Evan's birth mother wasn't named Deidre. It was Crystal Hanson."

"Deidre gave the doctor a fake name, too. Besides, if Waters killed her, took the baby and put him up for adoption, he wouldn't have used her real name."

Maya jumped right on that. "But there was a birth certificate for Evan, and the mother was barely twenty. Deidre was older than that, right?"

"Yeah. But Waters could have faked the name, the age, everything. He was into all sorts of illegal things, including a few forgeries. If he didn't do the paperwork himself, I'm sure he knew where to find someone to do it for him."

She wasn't giving up. Maya wasn't ready to buy any of this, because if she did, that changed *everything*. "How can you be sure Deidre was even carrying your child? From the sound of it, she wasn't a very reliable woman."

"She wasn't," he readily admitted. "But the timing is right for her to have conceived my baby. And she wouldn't have voluntarily given him up for adoption. Deidre could be flighty, but the one thing she wanted most was to have a baby." His jaw muscles stirred again. "In fact, she could have gotten pregnant on purpose."

"And not told you?" she snapped.

He gave her a flat look. "Deidre and I had sex. Nothing more on her part or mine. We weren't in love, not by a long shot. I figure the only reason she called me to tell me about the pregnancy was because she knew she was in danger and that I'd protect her."

Maya wanted to scream for him to stop. She didn't want all these pieces lining up like this. Especially when the pieces kept pointing to a conclusion that couldn't be reached.

"I'm sorry. But you can't have Evan. He's my son." And she hugged him close to her.

Slade didn't challenge that. In fact, for several snail-crawling moments he just sat there. "There'll be toiletries in the bathroom. Extra clothes in the bedroom closets. Oh, and the fridge will be stocked. You should eat, feed Evan, change him and then try to get some rest. You need any help?"

She shook her head so fast that her neck popped. Maya didn't want him touching Evan. And as for eating, that wouldn't happen. Her stomach was churning, but thankfully she had enough formula for Evan. Also, thankfully, her baby seemed to be totally unaware of the nightmare going on around him.

Slade got up and first opened the doors off the living room. She'd been right about them being bedrooms. Well, two were. The center one was a bathroom.

"I'll take the bedroom at the front of the house," Slade said, and walked into the kitchen.

Maya tried to level her breathing. Tried to think. But most of all she forced herself not to run. Slade had the truck keys—she'd seen him slip them into his jeans pocket—so she literally had no way out of here except on foot.

But she did have a phone.

She hurried to the diaper bag to get it but then froze when she looked at the phone screen. Who could she call?

Sheriff Monroe, maybe.

Then she remembered Slade saying something about the kidnapper perhaps having a *friend* in the sheriff's office. She didn't want to do anything to lead the kidnapper right to Evan.

Frantically, she scrolled through the numbers she had stored. Her parents had been killed in a car accident when she was in high school. She had no family except for distant cousins who she rarely saw, but she had friends and coworkers.

And one by one she excluded them.

Anyone she called would automatically be put in danger. And besides, she didn't personally know anyone with the physical skills to help protect Evan.

Sweet heaven, what was she going to do?

Maya caught the movement from the corner of her eye and whirled around. Slade was in the doorway of the kitchen, his shoulder propped against the jamb, and he was eating a sandwich. He was also watching her. Or rather watching her hold Evan while she panicked. But Slade wasn't panicking. He looked much as he had when she'd first seen him lounging against her car.

Well, the same except for his eyes.

Those deep blue eyes were still intense. As was the rest of him. But there was something else there, too. Something she couldn't quite put her finger on.

Wait, she could.

It was the kind of look a father might give a child he loved with all his heart. And that broke Maya's own heart. Because his love might be warranted if Evan was his son.

Slade pushed himself away from the jamb and walked closer. "Keep away from the windows," he said. Not one of his growled warnings that she'd become accustomed to. There was a gentleness in his voice.

He reached in the back waist of his jeans and took out a gun. For one terrifying moment she thought he might aim it at her and demand that she hand over Evan.

But he put it on the coffee table.

"There's no safety on this weapon," he said, "and if you call anyone, don't use your cell. It can be traced. Besides, service out here sucks anyway. Use the landline in the kitchen instead."

Maya shook her head. Was he giving her permission to call someone else for help?

He took out the truck keys from his pocket. They jangled when he dropped them on the table next to the gun. "I'm asking you to trust me, but I won't force you to stay under my protection against your will. Just be smart about it and make sure anyone you involve in this will put Evan's safety first."

It was an out. A surprising one. "You care whether I trust you or not?" she asked.

"Yeah." He didn't sound very happy about that. "Let me know what you decide to do."

And with that, Slade walked away from her and disappeared into the bedroom.

Chapter Eight

Slade sat on the bed and watched the line of light seep through the edges of the blinds. It was both a welcome sight and not so much of one.

Yeah, they'd survived the night without someone coming after them, but that sun was rising on what no doubt would be a hell of a day.

There'd been a steady flow of emails and text messages throughout the night. Some were updates on the case. Others were details for the security arrangements for the interrogation of their suspects—Andrea and Chase and Nadine Collier. Slade hadn't considered Chase an actual suspect, but then Declan had added a strange note to the arrangements: "Wait until you get a load of this guy."

Clearly, his brother had seen a red flag or two in the man's demeanor, and that was good enough for Chase to land on Slade's suspect list. But that list, and the interrogations, were just the tip of the iceberg.

Morgan Gambill, the guy who'd escaped during the bomb scare, was still missing. Definitely not good. Because his escape alone was enough to prove guilt of something.

But what?

Slade needed to find out.

Then there was the added annoyance of Randall Martin, the owner of that green SUV, who still hadn't been brought in for questioning. Randall had stonewalled pretty much every agency involved and, fed up, Slade had ordered the man arrested. And it would happen, as soon as he was located. Yeah, Randall had indeed filed a stolen-vehicle report hours before the kidnapping attempt, but Slade was tired of having no answers. Because no answers meant Evan was in danger.

That thought snaked through his head just as he heard the movement. He'd been expecting it but didn't reach for the gun he had on the nightstand beside him. The footsteps belonged to Maya. He'd gotten very familiar with their sound because he'd listened for them during the entire night.

And there'd been a lot of them to hear.

When she'd taken Evan in the bathroom so she could bathe him and then take a shower herself. When she had gotten something to eat from the fridge. And when she had fixed Evan a bottle in the middle of the night and then another just a half hour earlier.

Plenty of opportunities to hear footsteps.

And an equal number of opportunities to worry that he'd made an idiot of a mistake by leaving her those keys and that gun. It'd been a gamble. But it had obviously paid off. The proof of that was when Maya stepped into the open doorway of his bedroom.

She'd changed her clothes. A loose green skirt and sweater top. Nondescript clothes provided by the U.S. Marshals Service, but on Maya no clothes were nondescript. The woman managed to make even baggy attractive.

Something he cursed himself for noticing.

"How's Evan?" he asked.

"Fine. He just finished his bottle and will probably sleep for an hour or two." She stretched out her arms, caught onto the doorframe with both hands. "You knew I wouldn't leave even if I could come up with my own safe house and body-guard. You knew I wouldn't risk taking Evan away from you. Away from the security you've already put in place."

It sounded exactly like what it was—an accusation. He moved the laptop to the bed and eased his legs off the side. He didn't get up, because he didn't want to give Maya any reason to back out of that doorway. This conversation was necessary, though it wouldn't be pleasant.

Slade lifted his shoulder. "You love Evan, and I figured you'd do whatever it took to keep him safe."

Her mouth tightened, and she looked ready to curse him out. "I wanted to leave."

"Yeah," Slade settled for saying.

The silence came. Man, did it, and it was even more uncomfortable than the stare she was giving him.

"There was a laptop in the bedroom, and I did an internet search on you," she finally said. And that sounded like an accusation, too.

"I bet there was nothing in that search about me being in reform school when I was fourteen. I was pretty much a renegade in those days. Still am."

She flinched. But maybe not from surprise. "No. But there was a lot of info about you and your five foster brothers being raised at the Rocky Creek Children's Facility."

Slade couldn't help it. The name of the place always made him scowl. It was too pretty of a name for a hellhole.

"Your foster father, Kirby Granger, was a marshal, and he got custody of all six of you."

He nodded. "Kirby saved us."

And now someone had to save Kirby. His foster father was going through cancer treatments, and it wasn't clear if the treatments or the cancer would kill him. But added to that, Kirby was suspected of murdering the Rocky Creek headmaster, Jonah Webb.

Yet another name that always caused Slade to scowl.

So did the fact that Kirby wasn't the only suspect. Slade and all his brothers were, too. "I cleared up the question the Ranger had about where I was that night," Slade volunteered. "I was with someone." Angelica Sanchez. Angel for short. And she wasn't nearly as spiritual as her name implied.

"*She* was able to give you an alibi?"

Even though he hadn't said he'd been with a girl, Maya had obviously guessed. Slade nodded. "There's still a window of opportunity where I was unaccounted for, but she managed to make that window very narrow by corroborating the time we were together."

He paused. "Are you going to ask me if I killed Jonah Webb?" Slade tossed out there.

She opened her mouth, closed it and shook her head. "From everything I read about him, Webb deserved to die. I don't have any warm fuzzy feelings for a brute of a man who would abuse children under his care."

No surprise there, but Slade hadn't expected her to cut him even an inch of slack.

He tipped his head to the laptop on his bed. "I did a search on you, too." But he hadn't used just the internet. He'd also gotten a thorough background using some law enforcement contacts.

Even in the dim light, he saw the color blanch from her face. "Like Deidre, I had a thing for bad boys."

He shook his head. "Dominic Luker wasn't a bad boy."

Slade hadn't thought it possible, but she lost even more color with the mention of her attacker/ex-lover's name. He heard the shivery sound her breath made.

"He was a sociopath," Slade clarified, and decided to end it with that dime-store diagnosis. He seriously doubted that Maya wanted to discuss the details of the attack that had nearly left her dead.

And unable to have children.

Several of the sixteen knife wounds Luker had given her had seen to that. But she hadn't given up. She'd recovered, finished law school and started a nonprofit victims' rights group.

Except recovery maybe wasn't the right word.

Yes, Luker was out of her life permanently since he'd been killed in a prison shank fight. Ironic for a man who loved knifing women.

But Luker had left his mark on Maya.

She had no close friends. Hadn't been in a real relationship since the attack and had basically thrown herself into work. Well, until she'd adopted Evan. According to her coworkers, she had no immediate plans to return to work but would instead live off the modest inheritance her late grandmother had left Maya when she was a toddler.

"So we know each other's secrets," she concluded. She walked closer. Slow, tentative steps. But that wasn't a tentative look on her face. "On paper I suspect neither of us looks like a parent-of-the-year candidate. But given the chance, I'll be a good mother."

Her voice cracked, and there was just enough light now for him to see the shine in her eyes. From tears that were threatening to spill.

There it was again. That punch. And this time, it wasn't from heat between them but from that need deep inside him to comfort a damsel. Not that she was exactly the damsel type, but he'd just brought up some of the worst memories of her life and his sheer presence was a reminder that she might lose her son.

Slade went to her, but when he reached for her, she batted his hands away. "Don't. If you touch me, I'll fall apart."

He had his own reasons why he shouldn't touch, but Slade touched her anyway. He pulled Maya into his arms and braced himself for the tears.

But she didn't break into a sob.

Nor did she move.

She stood there, seemingly frozen in place with her arms down by her side while he held her. It took him a couple of seconds for the *oh, hell* to dance through his head. For her, being held by a man might bring back the memories of her attack, and Slade would have jerked away from her.

If she hadn't lifted her hands.

First one, then the other. And she put them on his waist. Definitely not pushing him away.

Just the opposite.

She inched closer to him until they were body-to-body.

"I hate the danger," she said. "It's broken down a barrier that I've spent years putting up."

He knew all about barriers. Knew that sometimes, like now, they were a good thing. But danger, especially shared danger, could indeed bring down walls and forge bonds that could get them in all sorts of trouble.

And maybe even save them.

The best way to keep Evan safe was for them to work together.

"This has nothing to do with Evan." Her voice was a breathy whisper, so soft. Like the rest of her body. And that scent of hers that dulled his mind just enough that it took a second or two for that to sink in.

"I never thought it did."

"I don't want you to think I'm trying to get close to you," she clarified.

But no clarification was needed. That wasn't the grip of a woman planning to seduce a man to get him to back off.

Or even to soften him up. Her touch was tentative, but the tentativeness didn't make it to her eyes.

Her grip tightened slightly. She inched even closer. "And this has nothing to do with you being a bad boy."

"Good thing. Because I lost my bad-boy status years ago." Yeah, it was a poor attempt to lighten things up, but since she looked ready to shatter into a thousand little pieces, he thought she could use the levity.

It worked.

The corner of her mouth lifted just a fraction. "I don't think it's a status you can lose. It comes with the looks and the attitude."

Her gaze combed over his face. Lingered on the dark stubble that was there. Before her attention went lower, to his chest. Only then did he remember his shirt was wide open.

Oh, man.

He was in trouble here. Yeah, she might not be trying to seduce him, but she was doing it anyway. And for multiple reasons he wanted to keep his hands off her. After all, they might end up in a custody battle.

Or together on the receiving end of another attack.

But that didn't stop him.

Hell, maybe she was right. Once bad, always bad. That was the only explanation Slade could come up with as to why he lowered his head and brushed his mouth over hers.

Maya made a sound of startled surprise. Now she'd pull back. Maybe even slap him into the next county.

She didn't do that, either.

She stared at him as if trying to decide what to do, and while she was deciding, Slade took a nosedive off a cliff. He snapped her to him and kissed her the way his body was begging for him to kiss her.

The taste of her slammed right through him, and it evaporated what little common sense he had left. But it wasn't the taste that made things escalate. It was that little sound she made. A little catch in her throat. The sound not of surprise or protest.

But of pleasure.

She slid her arms around his waist and upped the already bad situation when her breasts landed against his chest. Yeah, she had on that skirt and top, but since his chest was bare and also since she seemed to be wearing the thinnest bra ever, he could feel parts of her that he shouldn't have been feeling.

That didn't stop him from feeling anyway.

It'd been a while since the slow burn had turned into an ache. He generally liked to dive right into sex so he could, well, find relief and then leave. Of course, the leaving didn't happen right away, and despite his badass reputation, he didn't fall into bed with many women.

But there'd be no leaving with Maya.

Nope. He had to stay with her until the danger was finished. Until they had the results of the DNA test.

And maybe even after that, if Evan was his son.

That finally sank into his hard head—his quickly hardening body, too—and Slade moved away from her.

"I don't do things like this," she mumbled, and she made his body beg when she flicked her tongue over her bottom lip.

"Ditto."

She gave him a flat stare that was somewhat diminished because she was flushed with arousal.

"Ditto," he repeated.

"Not with those looks," she added, also in a mumble.

He took her by the arm and put her in front of the mirror. "Look at yourself. You're a knockout."

Maya laughed, but it wasn't from humor. She pulled up

her sweater top, and the first thing that caught his attention was her barely there bra and her breasts that seemed ready to spill right out of it.

But then he saw the scars.

They were thin white lines, barely visible in the thready morning light. But he figured this was a case of more than skin-deep. Those scars had cut her to the core.

There was nothing he could say or do to lessen the pain she'd always feel, but Slade wished Luker were alive so he could hurt him for what he'd done to Maya.

Slade reached out and ran his index finger over one of the scars. He barely touched Maya, but she shivered. Not from heat this time.

"It's not exactly a *ditto,* but since you've shown me yours, I'll show you mine." He pushed back the side of his shirt, unzipped his jeans and lowered them and his boxers.

Maya's eyes widened. "What are you doing?"

"Not *that,*" he assured her. Though with the taste of her still in his mouth, getting naked with her held plenty of appeal. Thankfully, he did have some shred of common sense and control left.

Some.

"My scar." He stopped lowering his clothes at about the midhip-bone point so she could see the healed wound.

She leaned down for a closer look. "You were shot?"

"Yep. By a meth-head federal fugitive I was trying to arrest. She said she was aiming for my...family jewels," Slade settled for saying.

"She nearly succeeded." Maya reached out as if to touch the scar but jerked back her hand. No doubt because she realized it was indeed just inches away from a still-very-aroused part of him.

"My injury was paltry compared to yours," he went on, "and it didn't come at the hands of someone I thought I could trust. I just wanted you to see that scars are just that. Scars. They don't lessen the rest of you."

She swallowed hard, and the moment turned to something else. Probably because he was standing there with his jeans and boxers hiked down to R-rated level, and the air and his body were still sizzling.

"Slade?" The voice whipped through the room and sent Maya and him flying even farther apart.

He fixed his jeans and pressed the button on the intercom mounted near the light switch so it would allow Declan to hear him.

"I'm here," Slade told his brother. "What's wrong?" And he figured something had to be wrong for Declan to contact him at this hour.

"A vehicle just triggered the motion detector at the end of the road. No one should be out there."

That was *not* what Slade wanted to hear. He grabbed his gun and hurried to the window. The sun was up, barely, but he couldn't see the end of the road because of the wide curve and some trees.

"I need to get Evan," Maya said on a rise of breath, and she rushed out and back into the other bedroom.

"Stay down and away from the windows," Slade reminded her, but he figured it was unnecessary.

"Backup's been alerted," Declan added. But Slade heard what his brother didn't add. That backup wouldn't be nearly fast enough. "My advice? You've got a couple of minutes before that vehicle reaches you, so you should get the heck out of there."

Slade had already decided the same thing. "We're leaving," he shouted to Maya, and he hurried out of the room, nearly running right into her.

She had Evan in her arms, his bottle, too, and she reached down to grab the diaper bag.

But Slade stopped her.

Even though his mind was racing with the need to escape, he had to consider all angles. The location of the safe house was secret, only known to his brothers, and they wouldn't have told anyone.

"Leave the bag. The plastic one with the formula, too," Slade insisted when she shook her head.

Thankfully, she didn't ask why. Maya just ran with him, first to get the keys and his backup weapon from the coffee table and then to the back door. Slade got them into the truck as fast as possible and drove away.

Even in the dim light he could see that Maya's hands were shaking as she strapped Evan into the car seat. "How did he find us?"

Slade didn't know, and he didn't have time to answer. He saw the blur of movement in his side mirror. And the glint of sunlight on metal.

"Get down!" he shouted.

Just as the sound of the shot cracked through the air.

Chapter Nine

Maya threw herself over Evan, and praying, she tried to brace herself for the worst, for the bullet to rip through the truck and into one of them. Thank God that didn't happen. The gunman must have missed.

But he immediately fired off another shot.

Slade cursed but didn't return fire. He kept his gun ready in his right hand, but he slammed his foot on the accelerator.

The road was little more than a dirt path, uneven and littered with potholes. The truck bobbled over the surface, slinging them back and forth. Except for Evan. Somehow, she'd managed to get him buckled in. Maya didn't want to think how bad this could be if she hadn't done that.

Another shot came.

Then another.

She put her hands over Evan's ears to shut out the noise. "Who's trying to kill us?" she asked, not really expecting an answer from Slade.

"He's not shooting at us. He's trying to shoot out the tires."

Mercy, that couldn't happen. Because if the gunman managed to disable the vehicle, he could kidnap Evan. Or at least try. Slade and she would do whatever it took to make sure that didn't happen, but they couldn't risk getting into a gunfight with this man.

Or *men*.

It hit her then. There was no way the driver of the vehicle on the other road could have made it back here ahead of them. So there were two attackers.

Maybe more.

And that sent another jolt of terror through her.

The gunman got off two more shots, but the truck didn't jerk or move as if the tires had been hit. Maya said another prayer of thanks for that and yet another prayer when Slade turned off the trail and onto a road.

"Keep low but try to keep watch," Slade told her. "There could be someone out here waiting for us."

Oh, God. He was right. Whoever was behind these kidnappings was determined to get his or her hands on Evan, but Maya was equally determined to keep her baby safe.

Slade kept watch, too, his gaze slashing back and forth from the side and rearview mirrors. Maya did the same, but she didn't see anyone, only the empty country road. She hoped it stayed that way.

"Any chance someone could have broken into your car and planted a tracking device on Evan's car seat?" Slade asked.

That sent yet another slam of fear through her, and Maya's first reaction was to say no, that there wasn't a chance of something like that happening in Spring Hill. But the first kidnapping attempt had happened there, so she couldn't be sure.

"Where would someone put a device like that?" Maya frantically ran her hands around the seat, lifted it a fraction and felt there, too.

Nothing.

Evan was awake, his eyes trained on Slade again, but

she lifted the baby as much as the straps would allow and felt around the padding beneath him.

"Some are as small as a box of matches." Slade glanced over at her search just as Maya looked at him to say she hadn't found anything.

She saw the worry that was no doubt mirrored in her own eyes. But she saw something else. For just a second or two, Slade's expression changed when his gaze landed on Evan. Of course, Maya had already known that he looked at her son with affection, but this was different.

He was looking at Evan as if the baby were *his*.

That didn't help with the adrenaline that was spiking through her. Didn't help with the memories of that kiss that she was trying to forget. That look only made things much, much worse. Because she might be saving Evan only to lose him to the very man who could keep him safe.

"What's wrong?" Slade asked. "Did you find something?"

Maya realized she was staring at him, and she shook her head to answer his question. No, she hadn't found a tracking device, but that look had drilled home something she was terrified to accept.

Slade huffed. Maybe because he was frustrated from the attack. Or from everything else about their situation.

"Don't borrow more trouble," he mumbled.

He didn't add more, because he took the turn off the rural road and onto the one that led to the interstate. At the same time, his phone rang, and he pulled it out and put it on speaker.

"Are you out of the house?" Declan asked the moment Slade answered.

"Yeah. Any idea who just fired shots at us?"

"Not yet, but someone should be out there in the next

twenty minutes. If there's anything left to find, we'll find it."

Good. Maya held on to the hope that something would link this to the person behind the attacks and kidnappings.

"What's your situation now?" Declan asked. "Anyone in pursuit?"

Slade checked the mirrors again. "Not that I can tell. But there might be a tracker on one of the items we brought with us. Unless you have some other idea as to how this SOB found us."

"None, but we'll search for the tracker. Where are you now?"

Slade pushed some buttons on the GPS and turned on the ramp to the interstate. Instant traffic. Maya wasn't sure if that was good or bad. Obviously, the shooter knew which vehicle they were in, so even if he wasn't personally in pursuit, that didn't mean he hadn't phoned for help.

"We're about twenty minutes from Maverick Springs," Slade told his brother. "I'm heading to the marshals' office, but I'll need to have someone pick up some supplies for the baby."

Maya blinked. "Aren't the suspects there?"

"They are," Declan confirmed. "Well, Andrea, Nadine and Chase are anyway. Still no sign of Morgan Gambill, the guy who escaped during the bomb scare."

Too bad he was still missing, because Maya figured he had important info. Judging from Slade's scowl, he believed it, too.

"But I do have some news on Randall Martin's missing green SUV," Declan added. "The San Antonio police found it in the parking lot of an abandoned warehouse."

Maya held her breath, hoping this would be the break in the case they needed. But obviously Slade wasn't so hopeful. He looked on the verge of mumbling some profanity. "What's wrong?" he asked his brother.

"Pretty much everything. The person behind the wheel was a thug, Clifford Atwood."

Not Randall, the owner. Maybe he'd been telling the truth about his vehicle being stolen.

"Atwood has a long history of drug-related crimes," Declan added.

Slade repeated the man's name. So did Maya, but it wasn't a name she recognized. "Why would a druggie want to kidnap my son?"

"I think Atwood was just a lackey," Declan explained. "Now he's a dead one. Someone shot him at point-blank range on the left side of his head."

Maya couldn't stop the images from coming. Not images of a man she didn't know but those from her own attack.

It wasn't logical, but violence always brought back memories. Of course, in this case Atwood deserved to die because he'd tried to kidnap Evan. Or worse. The way he'd bashed into her car with the SUV, he could have killed Slade, Evan and her.

Slade's jaw muscles tightened and stirred. "Please tell me there's some evidence in the SUV that points to the missing babies or whoever hired Atwood."

"Nothing," Declan answered right away. "SAPD will keep looking, though. We might get lucky."

Might. But it sounded like a dead end—literally.

"You want me to get started on another safe house?" Declan asked.

Maya groaned softly. They definitely needed a safe place to go, but the thought of being discovered again made her feel sick. She brushed a kiss on Evan's forehead. Then his cheek. And wished she could do more to keep her baby out of this dangerous mess.

"Hold off on the safe house," Slade answered. "I'm thinking about taking them to the ranch."

Even though she couldn't see Declan's face, Maya could feel his surprise. He paused a long time. "Let me know what you decide. I'll see you in a few." And Declan ended the call.

"The ranch?" she challenged. "As in the one you and your brothers run?"

Slade nodded. "Yeah, and I know what you're thinking. The kidnapper will know to look for us there, but it won't be his first choice of places to launch another attack."

Maybe. After all, from what she'd gathered in her internet search, all five of his brothers were marshals and lived at the ranch. It no doubt had some kind of security along with ranch hands who could keep watch for a kidnapper. But there was another side to going there. A bad one.

"Your family could be hurt in an attack."

Slade didn't jump to deny that. "We'll have to take precautions."

He didn't have time to say what those might be, because his phone rang again, and Evan started to fuss. It wasn't time for his bottle, but it was possible he needed a diaper change. Unfortunately, she didn't have any way of doing that. She didn't even have a pacifier, but Maya tried to gently rock the car seat. It didn't help. Evan's whimpers turned to cries.

"We're almost there," Slade let her know. And he took the turn off the highway and toward Maverick Springs.

Probably because her nerves were already at the breaking point, Evan's cries only made it worse. Maya wanted nothing more than to pull him into her arms and try to comfort him, but she couldn't risk taking him from the seat.

It seemed to take an eternity for Slade to turn into the

parking lot of the Marshals Service, and the moment they came to a stop, she picked up her baby. He just kept crying.

"I know how you feel, little man," Slade mumbled, and he hooked his arm around both of them to help them from the truck.

And just like that, Evan hushed.

It seemed like such a petty thing, for her to be upset that Evan was responding better to Slade than to her. But it was worse than pettiness. Was Slade's ability to soothe the baby some kind of proof of a genetic connection?

She silently groaned.

You're losing it.

Slade got them inside the building and up the stairs, past the reception-security and to the sprawling office that was jammed with desks and cubicles.

And people.

All those people were chatting, and the room was a bee-hive of activity. But then everything stopped when Slade and she stepped inside.

"Are you okay?" a woman immediately asked. The jeans-wearing blonde rushed toward them, and even though she didn't pull Slade into her arms for a hug, she looked as if that's what she wanted to do.

"We're fine." Slade's tone was slightly warmer than usual, and the woman seemed surprised when Slade brushed his hand over her arm.

The blonde's attention went to Maya, then Evan. "I'm Caitlyn Barnes."

"Maya Ellison."

Caitlyn hitched her thumb in the direction of a wide-shouldered man at one of the desks. "That's Slade's brother Marshal Harlan McKinney, my fiancé."

Maya recalled the name from her internet search and Slade's earlier conversation. Harlan clicked a button on his phone and came closer. His dark eyebrow lifted when his attention landed on Slade's unbuttoned shirt. Only then did Maya realize just how disheveled she probably looked. And maybe he thought that dishevelment wasn't all from the quick escape they'd made from the safe house.

"I've arranged to have formula and diapers delivered," another man said.

"My brother Clayton," Slade clarified. "You remember Declan and that's Wyatt."

Marshal Wyatt McCabe.

If she were putting labels on them, Harlan looked like a pro-football linebacker. Declan, a rodeo rider. Clayton, a jeans-wearing lawyer. Slade, a vampire and not one with friendly intentions, either. But Wyatt, well, his looks seemed more like the kind a lead singer in a rock band would have. Except his clothes were pure cowboy. He even wore his gun in an old-fashioned hip holster.

Wyatt's mouth bent as if he might smile, but when he looked at Evan, the smile went south. He mumbled something about it being nice to meet her and strolled out.

"Does he have a problem with me?" Maya whispered to Slade.

He glanced at Wyatt, who was disappearing down the hall. "No. It's the baby. Wyatt's always wanted to be a father, and he hired a surrogate but something went wrong with the deal, I think. Nothing that he's ready to talk about, though."

She gathered that wasn't usual. Probably because they were family and discussed their lives with each other, but judging from Wyatt's sullen reaction, something more than just *wrong* had happened.

"It doesn't help that the ranch is going through a mini baby boom," Clayton said, taking up the explanation. "My son is due any day now. And our other brother, Dallas, and his wife, Joelle, are expecting."

Maya glanced at their faces and then around the room. "They all believe Evan's your son?"

Slade did some glancing, too. "Probably."

There it was. That unruffled response she was starting to know so well. But his answer didn't need the heavy emotion for it to hit her hard. If Evan was indeed his child, Slade would have plenty of moral support. He had a family already in place to help him win a custody battle.

Something she didn't.

Slade hesitated a moment. Looked down at Evan. "Come on."

He led her down the hall where Wyatt had disappeared minutes earlier. They passed several rooms, all with the doors closed, and she figured their suspects were in those rooms. Nadine and Chase Collier. Andrea, too. The two people who weren't there were Randall Martin and Morgan Gambill, but Maya hoped that with Slade's entire family seemingly working on this, it wouldn't be long before they could bring them in.

And get answers.

Of course, those answers were just the beginning. Stopping the danger was a must. Finding the missing babies, too. Then she'd have to deal with the results of the DNA test Slade had ordered.

Slade took her into what appeared to be a break room and had her sit in one of the chairs. "It won't be long before the diapers and formula arrive." His stare stayed fixed on Evan for several long moments.

Maya also looked at her son, to try to see what Slade was seeing. "Does he look like Deidre?" But she didn't want to hear any answer other than *no*.

"Truth is, I don't know. I never saw a picture of Deidre

as a baby. Nor one of me, either. And I have no idea who my birth parents were. My mother was supposedly an addict and a prostitute who sneaked out of the hospital right after I was born."

Maya pulled in her breath. That sort of thing probably happened all the time, but it tugged at her heart to know that Slade's start in life had begun at what was essentially rock bottom.

"Your adopted parents didn't take pictures of you?" Because she'd already taken dozens of Evan and couldn't imagine an adoptive parent who wouldn't do the same.

"My adoption was…complicated." He sank down in the chair beside her and rubbed his index finger over the back of Evan's hand. Her son's eyes were already drifting down, but he opened them and stared at Slade. "I was given to a family when I was a couple of months old, but before the adoption was final, the woman got cancer and died. I ended up with another family. Then another."

She'd been a victims' rights advocate long enough to know that probably meant Slade had been removed from an abusive environment.

"I don't remember a lot of it," he said as if he knew exactly what she was thinking. "And by the time I was old enough to remember, I was strong enough to fight back."

That created more of a tug in her heart. No child should have to fight back anyone or anything.

"And then you landed in Rocky Creek Children's Facility," she mumbled.

He nodded, but other than a flex of his jaw muscles, he had no reaction. She was betting inside, though, he had enough bad memories to last a lifetime or two. Thankfully, Kirby Granger had rescued him, and if Kirby had had to kill Jonah Webb to do that, then maybe it was justified.

Maya winced at that thought.

Until now, until this whole ordeal, she'd never thought of violence as justified. Still, maybe it had been in that case. And it was certainly warranted if it would keep Evan safe.

"At least Kirby gave you a home," Maya said.

But he didn't jump to agree with her. "He gave me the attention a father gives a son. And he made me a part of the ranch."

No mention of family. "He gave you your brothers," Maya reminded him.

"Yeah." And he hesitated again. "For the record, I didn't kill Deidre's lover," Slade volunteered. "The guy committed suicide before he could tell the cops what he'd done with Deidre's baby."

That ate away at her, too. Maya prayed the man hadn't done anything to hurt the newborn. Of course, maybe the only reason she had Evan was because this now-dead man had taken his estranged lover's child that she'd conceived with Slade.

"Good thing he killed himself," Slade said under his breath. "Because after seeing what he'd done to Deidre, there's no way I could have held myself back."

Maya swallowed hard, and though she knew this would complicate the heck out of things, she leaned over and brushed a kiss on Slade's cheek. It seemed far more intimate than the scalding-hot kiss they'd shared in the bedroom at the safe house. More dangerous, too.

Because she was falling for him.

And that couldn't happen.

"Flashbacks?" he asked. Maya must have looked as confused as she felt, because he added, "You made a face after you kissed me. I figured maybe it was causing flashbacks."

Of her attack.

She understood then. Slade probably thought any intimacy would trigger flashbacks. Probably should have, too. It had the couple of times she'd tried to go on dates. But with Slade it hadn't been flashbacks and nightmarish memories going through her head.

That didn't make her feel better.

Just the opposite.

"Oh," he mumbled, and he had a split-second smile. He probably didn't know he had a killer smile to go along with those killer good looks.

"I don't want to want you," she let him know.

Slade nodded. "Ditto." His gaze met hers. "You're the worst kind of complication. The kind that could cause me to lose focus. And I never lose focus."

It sounded as if he was trying to convince himself. Or maybe it was just a reminder. Either way, she didn't feel herself pulling away from him. Maya leaned against him, her arm pressed to his, knowing it was a mistake but not doing anything to correct it.

And that's how Declan found them when he appeared in the doorway.

Slade and she eased away from each other, but coupled with the fact that Slade had shown up with an unbuttoned shirt, Declan probably thought Slade and she were well on their way to becoming lovers. Or already had.

Declan came into the room and set down a bag near her chair. The diapers and formula, no doubt.

"The Colliers' lawyer is here," Declan told his brother. He handed Slade some papers. "That's the background check on them."

Slade glanced over the pages, scowled.

"Yeah," his brother verified. Obviously, Declan had read it, too. "We're not looking at parents of the year here."

Maya wasn't sure what had caused Declan to say that, but she hoped she got a chance to read the background check that had created Slade's scowl.

"Andrea's lawyer is here, too," Declan added, "so we can start the interviews."

Good. Maybe one of them would confess and this would be over soon.

Slade and Declan's gazes stayed locked. "What's wrong?" Slade asked.

Maya's head whipped up, and even though she hardly knew Declan, she saw it then. The troubled look in his eyes.

"I had someone go through the safe house," Declan explained, "and they found a GPS tracking device. That's how the kidnapper knew where to find you."

Maya adjusted Evan in her arms and slowly rose to her feet. "So the house wasn't safe after all."

Declan shook his head. "The house was fine, but the GPS device was in the plastic grocery bag you'd brought with you. Where did you get the bag?"

Maya groaned. "From Sheriff Monroe."

Declan scrubbed his hand over his face, cursed. "I'll get him out here so we can question him."

Chapter Ten

Yet one more thing to add to the list—make sure Sheriff Monroe hadn't aided and abetted the kidnapper by placing a tracking device in the bag he'd given Maya and Slade. He figured the sheriff was innocent, that someone else had planted the bug, but the whole mess would have to be cleared up.

Along with the other messes on the ever-growing list.

First and foremost was keeping Evan and Maya safe, but the missing babies were equally important. After all, one of those baby boys might be his son, and even if they weren't, if Evan was his child, Slade still wanted the babies back safe and sound.

Declan's phone buzzed, and he stepped back into the hall to answer it.

Evan's whimpers pulled Slade from his thoughts, and he checked the time. The baby was probably hungry, wet or both, and while the marshals' building wasn't the most convenient place to tend to a baby's needs, it was safe.

Well, hopefully.

After everything else that'd happened, he wasn't letting Maya and Evan out of his sight. Unfortunately, that meant they were stuck there until he or one of his brothers had interviewed their suspects.

"I need one of the diapers," she told Slade. She set the

bottle she'd brought with them on the floor next to the chair. "And wipes if there are any in the bag."

There were, which made him suspect that his very pregnant sister-in-law, Lenora, had been the one to buy the items. He seriously doubted any of his brothers would know to include such things.

Maya repositioned Evan on her lap so that his feet were against her stomach, and she pulled open the blanket. He wasn't sure how she managed it, but she unsnapped the stretchy blue one-piece outfit and changed Evan's diaper. Evan wasn't happy about the maneuvering, though, because his cries got louder.

"I have to warm the formula," Maya said, tipping her head to the microwave on the counter. She glanced around as if trying to figure out how to accomplish that.

Slade solved the problem for her. He scooped Evan into his arms. Like the night before, he got that punch of emotion and something he rarely felt.

Peace.

Yeah, he was surrounded by family. Five brothers and a foster father he'd take a bullet for. But truth was, he'd never felt as much of a part of the family as the others obviously did. Maybe because they'd figured out a way to put their pasts behind them.

Something Slade had never quite managed.

For the first time, it felt, well, possible.

What would it be like to be a father to his child? To any child? To have that unconditional love that he hadn't experienced from anyone but Kirby? It was something he'd never allowed himself to consider.

But he considered it now.

If Evan was his, then he might have to consider joint custody. Or something. He couldn't just rip this baby from Maya's life.

And that made him one sick puppy.

Because he was thinking with his heart now, and he was pretty sure that wouldn't send him down the best path. Nope. In addition to the distraction it'd cause, it might become the worst hurt of his life.

Maya cleared her throat, and when Slade looked up at her, she had her attention fastened not on Evan but on the hall. He looked past Declan, who was still on the phone, and saw the blond-haired couple making a beeline toward them.

Slade recognized them from their photos—Nadine and Chase Collier. The tall dark-haired guy in a suit behind them was no doubt their lawyer. Slade automatically stood and handed Maya the baby so he could put his hand over the butt of his gun.

"Marshal Becker?" Nadine asked. There was nothing friendly about her tone. Or her eyes. Ice-blue, the same color as the body-hugging skirt and top she was wearing. Everything about her screamed trophy wife, including the fact that she was nearly twenty years younger than her husband.

Declan ended his call and would have stepped between the Colliers and them, but Slade did the stepping first. He moved into the doorway so that he was in front of Maya and the baby.

"I'm Becker," Slade let her know.

He hadn't thought it possible but Nadine's ice-blue eyes narrowed even more. She had on so much makeup that he was surprised her lashes didn't gunk together.

"You're the one accusing us of stealing our own child," she snapped.

Chase didn't acknowledge her comment, but he did extend his hand. Slade shook it, eventually.

"Marshal, we're hoping you have a lead on our son's kidnapper," Chase said to Slade.

It wasn't just his tone that made him seem different from his wife. The Colliers were definitely an odd couple. Chase looked more like an aging rocker with his cargo pants, black T-shirt and spiked blond hair. Plus, there was the nose ring. Slade wasn't opposed to body piercings and such, but on Chase it made him look like a man who was clinging to his youth.

And failing miserably at it.

"I was hoping you had a lead," Slade fired back.

"See?" Nadine grumbled. "He thinks we took Will." She folded her arms over her ample chest. "Why in the name of God would you believe we'd do that?"

Slade lifted his shoulder. "People do all sorts of things for reasons that don't make sense to me. Like gambling, for instance." He waited because he figured that would strike a nerve.

It did.

Nadine cursed him, but Chase only huffed. "My wife has control issues," he volunteered. "She loves flying to Vegas and dropping a bundle of my money." Chase paused, his mud-brown eyes fixed on Slade. "But, of course, you're referring to the questionable loans she took out to try to hide her debts from me."

"My debts have nothing to do with this." Nadine jabbed her perfectly manicured index finger at Slade. "And I resent the implication. If you want to accuse someone of stealing Will, then look at Chase."

Slade did indeed look at the man, but Chase was now glaring at his wife. "Nadine gets things mixed up in her head. She seems to believe I'd steal Will to punish her. But there's one problem with that. Nadine didn't want a child to begin with. The only reason she agreed was because she thought it would stop me from divorcing her. It won't."

"And if you think I'll just hand you a divorce, then think

again," Nadine fired back. "There was no prenup, which means I'm entitled to half of the Collier estate. Besides, you cheated on me, and I'm betting I can convince a judge to give me a lot more than half."

Chase moved in so close to his wife that he was practically in her face. "Prove the cheating." His mouth twisted in a sick smile. "Oh, but you can't, can you? Maybe because you were too busy climbing between the sheets with the pool boy or that dealer in Vegas."

Oh, man. Under the definition of toxic marriage, there was probably a picture of those two clowns. Slade had spent just minutes with them and wanted to knock some sense into both of them.

"I didn't take Will," Slade heard someone say a split second before he saw the speaker. It was Andrea, and she was making a beeline for them.

Great. Now the gang was all here. Their lawyers, too, since Andrea's was trailing along right behind her.

"Why don't we just make this easy on everyone?" Slade suggested. "One of you just confess so we can get those babies to a safe place."

He watched their reactions.

Nadine started to howl about her innocence. Andrea began crying again. And Chase's attention went over Slade's shoulder and to Evan. Chase might have even gone over to Evan if Slade hadn't stepped in front of the man.

Chase shook his head as if pulling himself out of a trance. "Sorry. He just reminds me of Will."

There was the emotion that Slade had been looking for.

Maybe it was genuine. Maybe not.

But at least Chase appeared to be the concerned father of a missing child. Andrea was making a show of being the wrongfully accused, worried nanny. The only one of the lot who was spouting the poor-pitiful-me act was Nadine.

Slade glanced back at Maya. She was standing, feeding Evan his bottle, but he also saw the weariness in her eyes. It'd already been a hellishly long day, and he wanted to cut this little visit short so he could make plans to get them out of there.

He turned to Nadine, though it put a knot in his gut just to look at her. "Give me your best guess as to who took Will."

Nadine blinked, maybe because she hadn't expected the direct question. "If I knew, I'd tell you. Just because I didn't want a child, it doesn't mean I want Will to get hurt."

Okay. More of what he was looking for. At this point he'd take even fake emotion.

Slade turned to Andrea, who was staring at Nadine. "I think she took Will and hid him somewhere," Andrea said.

Nadine huffed. "If I'd done that, I damn sure wouldn't have burned down the house." Her gaze came back to Slade. "Any idea how long it'll take me to replace all the things that fire destroyed?"

Slade didn't even attempt to answer that, because it would require him to get his jaw unlocked. Instead he looked at Chase. "Give me the name of the person you suspect."

"Nadine," he said without hesitation.

So two votes for Nadine, and she was looking like a top suspect in his eyes, too.

"Well, I suspect you!" Nadine fired back at her husband. She whirled around toward Slade. "And he'll claim he doesn't have motive, but he does. If he can get me locked up for kidnapping, it'll save him millions because he won't have to pay up when I divorce him."

Slade groaned. His head was starting to throb, and it only proved what he already knew. All three of them were suspects.

"Who's interviewing them?" Slade asked Declan.

"Harlan's taking the Colliers, and Wyatt will be with Andrea."

Good choices. Harlan was big and intimidating. Not that intimidation would work on Nadine, but Harlan had a poker player's patience, and he could maybe spur them into an incriminating argument. And as for Andrea, well, Wyatt was a first-class charmer, so perhaps he could work his magic on the young woman.

"This way," Declan told the trio, and he got them moving back to their respective interview rooms.

"You okay?" Slade asked Maya, and because she looked ready to collapse, he took her by the arm.

"Please tell me when you find that baby, you won't give him back to those people."

It was a promise he had no trouble keeping. "The adoption isn't final, and I'll make sure it never is."

Maya was no doubt thinking he'd do the same to her if he found out Evan was his. Soon they were going to have to talk about that.

Once Declan had deposited their suspects in the interview rooms, Slade motioned for his brother to come back to the break room. He had a plan, but he couldn't do it alone.

"I need a decoy vehicle," he explained to Declan. "Because I'm pretty sure that the kidnapper has a hired gun who'll try to follow us."

And now here was the hard part. Slade turned to Maya. "I want Declan and my brother's fiancée, Caitlyn, to take the baby to the ranch."

"No," Maya said before he could even finish. She pulled Evan closer to her.

"It's the safest thing for Evan." Yeah, that was playing dirty, but it was true. "You and I'll leave together, and you'll pretend to be carrying Evan in your arms."

Slade wished he had a way to keep Maya out of this, but the kidnapper's lackey would zoom in on her, figuring that wherever she went, so would the baby.

"What if the kidnapper comes after Declan and Caitlyn?" she asked.

"They'll leave out back at the exact moment we leave through the front. The kidnapper will want us followed."

As Slade had expected, tears shimmered in her eyes. "But how long will I be away from Evan?"

"Not long." He hoped. "We'll have to drive around until we lose this guy, and then I'll take you back to the ranch."

"The kidnapper will guess that's where we're going."

"Even if he does, he might not want to go barreling onto the ranch with my brothers. Declan, Dallas and Clayton will all be there. Plus the ranch hands."

Maya was still shaking her head, and those tears were now spilling down her cheeks.

"I'll get things ready," Declan said. He scribbled something on a piece of paper and handed it to Slade before he walked away: "Distract her."

Declan had no doubt noticed those tears and probably thought Maya was about to bolt. She wasn't. But that didn't mean Declan's tactics were wrong. A distraction might help. Well, with the tears anyway.

"I hate feeling this way." Maya's voice was a hoarse whisper.

Slade touched his fingers to her waist, urged her closer. "You're scared. And you hate having to rely on me."

Her forehead bunched up. Clearly, she wasn't pleased he knew that about her or with his attempt to distract her.

He brushed a kiss on her temple. "Don't worry. Soon you can rely on yourself again."

She didn't say anything, but he wished he had a way of reading her mind. Because this time, he couldn't figure out what was going on in her head. There was something in her expression. A different kind of fear, maybe. Or else he was just projecting his own fear.

"For the record, I'm not used to relying on anybody, either," he let her know.

She huffed. "You're not relying on anyone now. Certainly not me."

"Wrong." He shook his head and tapped his temple. "You're here now. I don't want you there, and I'm pretty sure you feel the same."

"I do," she readily admitted. But she, too, shook her head. "I can't get involved with you like that, Slade."

"Yeah." He leaned in, brushed his mouth over hers and felt the kick of heat when her breath shuddered against his lips.

"*Yeah* as in you agree?" she asked.

"*Like that* as in sex?" he countered.

No answer was necessary, because they both knew they were just blowing smoke with this conversation. Both were hell-bent on stopping something that it wasn't in their power to stop. He didn't believe in soul mates or love at first sight, but Slade did believe in basic attraction.

Slade moved in closer, put his mouth to her ear. "Sooner or later this pull between us will make it darn near impossible to remember just how bad this'll screw things up."

Maya pulled back, swallowed hard, but she didn't move away when Slade kissed her again.

"That's your idea of a distraction?" someone mumbled.

Slade snapped in the direction of the speaker and saw Declan just a few feet away. Hell. Slade hadn't even heard his little brother's approach.

Maya wasn't the only one in distraction mode.

"The vehicles are almost ready," Declan said, thankfully not lingering on the kiss he'd just witnessed. "And I spoke with Sheriff Monroe. He claims he didn't put a tracking device in the bag. His wife picked up the formula and diapers, and she says she didn't do it, either."

"Well, someone sure as heck did," Slade snarled.

Declan mumbled an agreement. "That's why I faxed the sheriff a photo of Clifford Atwood, the dead guy we found behind the wheel of the SUV used to attack you. The sheriff's wife says she's almost positive she saw him in the grocery store when she was shopping for the baby things."

"But how could he have managed to put the GPS in the bag without her noticing?" Maya asked.

Slade didn't have any trouble coming up with an answer. A plausible one that could mean both the sheriff and his wife were innocent. "Atwood could have bumped into her and dropped it into the bag. Atwood was a career criminal, so it probably wouldn't have been much of a challenge to do something like this. Especially since the sheriff's wife was likely in a hurry."

"What about fingerprints?" Maya asked. "Were there any on the GPS?"

Declan shook his head. "Nothing. No prints or trace. But we might get something from the area around the safe house. The CSIs out there found footprints along the trail where the guy took shots at you. Spent casings, too."

And sometimes fingerprints could be recovered from those. Any prints could lead them to the hired guns, which in turn could lead them to the kidnapper.

Declan glanced around as if making sure no one was close enough to hear what he had to say. "There's a truck out back, and I figure that's the way Caitlyn, Dallas and I will leave with the baby—minus the blanket you have him wrapped in. You can stuff that blanket with something and leave through the front of the building with Clayton. I've had Evan's car seat moved to the vehicle you'll be taking so if anyone is watching, they'll believe you really have the baby with you. We have another car seat in the truck thanks to Clayton and Lenora."

"Get Caitlyn," Slade said before Maya had a chance to change her mind about this plan. And before he had a chance to change his.

Declan turned, but he only made it one step before he stopped in his tracks. He didn't draw his gun, but he did put his hand over it, and Slade did the same.

"What's wrong?" Maya asked. Thankfully, she moved behind him, because Slade's attention was on the man who'd just stepped into the hall.

A man he recognized from photos. And a man he very much wanted to see. Just not with Maya and Evan around.

Their suspect Randall Martin.

Chapter Eleven

It took several heart-slamming moments before Maya could see the man who'd caused Slade and Declan to go on full alert. And even after seeing him she had no idea who he was until Slade mumbled his name like profanity.

Randall Martin.

Declan took out his phone and pressed some buttons. "We just got a visitor. How the heck did he get in, and was he armed when he went through the metal detector?"

She couldn't hear the answer, but Declan looked at Slade, shook his head and put his phone away. "The dispatcher's new, and when Randall said he was a visitor, she processed him through. He didn't set off the alarms, but he could have some kind of nonmetal weapon on him."

"I don't. I carry a gun, usually concealed, and yes, I have a permit to do that," Randall volunteered. "But I left it in my car. Didn't figure I should give you boys any more reason for concern."

"We've been looking for you," Slade said. His voice was all lawman, and there was zero trace of the heat that had been there just seconds earlier.

"I heard." Randall walked closer, and she got a better look at him. Late thirties, pasty white skin and hair that seemed way too black to be natural. He wore an expensive-looking linen suit, not at all what she'd expected from the owner of a bowling alley. Judging from the clothes, the business was very successful.

"I also heard that you plan to accuse me of trying to kill you," Randall added. He was a big man, even bigger than Slade, and he met their stony glare with one of his own. "I didn't." He reached in his pocket, causing both Declan and Slade to draw their guns.

Randall rolled his eyes in a dramatic fashion. "It's a copy of the surveillance footage from the parking lot of the bowling alley." He pulled out a disk and offered it to Slade.

Slade took it, but he didn't reholster his gun as Declan did.

"When you watch the footage," Randall went on, "you'll see that I was telling the truth about someone stealing my SUV. It's not my primary vehicle. I use it mainly for employees to do pick-ups and deliveries, so I didn't notice it missing right away."

Declan and Slade exchanged glances before Slade looked back at her. "Stay behind me."

She had no intention of facing this man head-on, not with Evan in her arms. They went up the hall to an office, Slade staying between Randall and her, but that didn't stop the man from peering around Slade to look first at her.

Then at Evan.

"Glad he's safe," Randall told her. "I'll bet this has you rattled. Sorry about that, but I didn't have anything to do with it."

Maya wasn't certain she believed him. Judging from Slade's body language, neither did he.

Declan put the disk into a laptop on the desk in the office, and it didn't take long before the images appeared on the screen. A dimly lit parking lot at night with only two vehicles—a BMW and the green SUV. She could see the neon sign for the Perfect Strike bowling alley.

"Fast-forward to just past midnight," Randall instructed. "The place was closed, but I was still there working in my office."

Declan moved the footage to midnight, and a man appeared on the screen. He walked—no, he skulked—from the back of the building and straight to the SUV. She couldn't see the device he used to unlock the door, but it took him only a few seconds to get in.

"I don't use my car alarms," Randall explained. "I got tired of having to turn them off when someone would accidentally trip it just by getting too close. Wish it'd been on in this case, though, so I could have caught this moron."

Declan zoomed in on the car thief's face, and even with the grainy texture of the footage, Maya had no trouble recognizing the guy.

"Clifford Atwood," Slade and she mumbled in unison.

Of course, they'd known Atwood had been in the vehicle because he'd been found dead behind the wheel. She also didn't have any trouble believing Atwood had attacked them.

Or rather had been hired to attack them.

"Atwood has a connection to Nadine Collier." Randall paused and looked a little smug after tossing that out there. "I'm sure you would have found it soon enough, but I hired several P.I.s to get to the bottom of this. And to do something else," he added in a mumble. The smugness vanished, and he didn't volunteer any more about that "something else."

"What connection?" Slade snapped.

"He was her bookie for a lot of her horse betting. And I'd rather not say how I came by this information, but if you ask around, you'll eventually find someone who'll squeal."

Declan cursed. "But not you?"

Randall gave him a flat look. "Someone put a bullet in Atwood's head, and I'd rather not meet the same fate."

Maya couldn't fault him for that, but Randall was holding something back. "You think Atwood and Nadine are connected to the kidnappings?" she asked.

He shifted his position so that he could better see her. But he didn't answer. He looked at Evan again, squeezed his eyes shut and groaned.

"I don't know about Atwood and Nadine," Randall finally said. His attention shifted to Slade. "But I got something to tell you that's going to make me look guilty."

Maya certainly hadn't expected that, and she held her breath, waiting.

"My girlfriend, Gina Blackwell, and I split up a few months ago." He paused again, cleared his throat. "She was pregnant, and I told her when she had the baby to contact me. If the kid turned out to be mine, I was more than willing to pay child support. But she didn't call me. I found out a few days ago that she'd delivered a baby boy."

Oh, mercy. Maya didn't like where this appeared to be going.

Slade eased his gun back in his holster. "Are you saying one of the kidnapped adopted babies is your son?"

Randall dragged in a long, weary breath. "It's possible. That's why I hired the P.I.s. I've been looking for both Gina and the baby, but then I just found out this morning that Gina had given the child up for adoption."

"How'd you learn that?" Slade pressed.

He handed Slade a business card that he took from his pocket. "From a waitress friend of Gina's. Her name and contact info are on the back of the card. According to this woman, she and Gina worked together, and she was with Gina when she went into labor. She claims she drove Gina to the hospital but that both Gina and the baby were gone when she went back later to check on them." Randall stopped again. "I'm pretty sure the birth date of Gina's kid matches those of the kidnapped babies. And *him*."

Maya dropped back a step when Randall's gaze snapped to Evan. She pulled the bottle from her son's mouth and put him against her chest and shoulder so that Randall couldn't see his face.

"You have a strong motive to be the kidnapper," Maya managed to say.

The anger was instant, and it shot through Randall's already dark eyes. "Would I have told you all of this if I was guilty of kidnapping those babies?" He groaned again, scrubbed his hand over his face. "Besides, Gina might not have even been pregnant with my kid. She slept around a lot."

"Any chance Gina ever used a fake name? Like maybe Crystal Hanson?" Slade asked.

Randall shook his head. "I don't think so."

Despite the dread and fear rushing through her, that gave Maya some hope. Maybe Evan wasn't Randall's. Or Slade's, for that matter. Maybe when the danger was over, no one but she would have a claim to this child whom she loved more than life itself.

"Who would have known any details about Gina's baby?" Slade asked.

"I don't know. But I intend to find out. Finding Gina and the baby is the fastest way to clear my name. That's why I need your help." Randall tipped his head to the business card he'd given Slade. "My numbers are on there. Call me the second you find out anything."

Randall started to walk out but then stopped. "May I leave, or do you plan to arrest me?"

Slade met him eye-to-eye. "No plans. *Yet*."

The anger returned to Randall's eyes, but Maya only saw a flash of that before he strolled away.

"I'll call in some favors to get someone started on finding Gina Blackwell," Declan said. He looked at her. "You need to get the baby ready to leave."

Just like that, it felt as if her heart were being crushed in her chest, and she might not have been able to move if Slade hadn't helped her. He led her by the arm back to the break room, and together they took the blanket off Evan. Slade wrapped him in a jacket that he took from the closet.

And he kissed Evan's cheek.

Just as a father would kiss his son.

That crushed her heart, too, not just because Slade was obviously growing closer to Evan. But because Maya was already starting to spin a fantasy that shouldn't be spun. Of Slade and she raising Evan together.

As a family.

It was a dangerous fantasy, and she reminded herself that Slade could crush her dream world by being Evan's father and taking him from her.

Just as he was doing now.

He eased Evan from her arms when his brothers Declan, Clayton and Dallas and then Caitlyn came into the room.

"Harlan and Wyatt are still doing the interviews," Clayton let them know. "They'll call us if they get anything."

That was a glimmer of good news in what would be a horrible next few minutes. Maybe even hours, since Maya had no idea how long it would take them to get to the ranch.

"I'll take good care of him, I promise," Caitlyn said softly to her.

Maya hated trusting these strangers with her baby's safety, but there were few choices here. They couldn't live at the marshals' office, and this way they might even catch the kidnapper. After all, this was essentially a trap.

Slade took Evan's blanket and grabbed another jacket from the closet. Maya didn't have time for a long goodbye. Just a kiss and a prayer before Slade handed Evan over to Caitlyn and put the blanket and jacket in her arms. Maya used the two items to make the fake baby.

"Move fast and keep watch," Slade said to Declan. "We'll do the same."

"The windows of the vehicles are bullet resistant," Slade told her. He took her arm again and headed to the front of the building. Clayton followed along right behind them.

Maya tried to give Evan one last look but she couldn't see him, because the coat was wrapped around him. Slade led her down the stairs and to the door. He looked out, his lawman's eyes combing over the area before they went outside. They moved fast to the black four-door car. Clayton got behind the wheel, and Slade and she climbed into the backseat.

"Pretend you're strapping the baby into the car seat," Slade instructed.

Somehow Maya got her hands to move, and she put the bundle into the seat as Clayton sped away.

And the waiting and watching began.

She glanced around but didn't see Declan and the others. That probably wouldn't happen until they reached the ranch.

Without taking his attention off their surroundings, Slade reached over and slid his hand around the back of her neck. It was such a simple gesture, but it gave her far more comfort than it should have.

Clayton's phone buzzed, and while he took the call, he drove them out of town. Maya tried to make sense of the nightmare. She wanted to think about anything but Evan and how much she missed him.

"I feel lost without him," she mumbled, looking at the empty car seat.

"Yeah." Slade gave her a quick glance, and she realized it wasn't just a response. It was the truth. In this short period of time, he'd become attached to Evan. Maybe even more than attached. He might even love her son. Maya knew that was possible because she'd loved Evan the first time she'd seen him.

Clayton kept driving, taking one turn right after the other while he talked on the phone that he had sandwiched between his ear and shoulder. Each car around them got Slade's attention. Hers, too, but no vehicle seemed to be following them as they meandered away from town.

"That was the initial report on Gina Blackwell," Clayton relayed to them the moment he ended the call. "She's twenty-four, a waitress and she worked at Randall's bowling alley until about four months ago, but she's been off the radar since."

"Any confirmation that she was pregnant?" Slade asked.

"Yeah. She used one of those free medical clinics, so her name's in the database. She was seeing an obstetrician, but he didn't deliver the baby. Saul's sending someone over there now to try to get her records and interview the doc. Her former coworkers, too."

"Saul Warner," Slade explained to her. "Our boss. You talked to him on the phone yesterday."

She remembered. Maybe the head marshal would get somewhere, but she knew from experience that doctors were often bound by law and privacy acts. Still, they might learn something they could use to find the woman.

"You think Randall was lying about being the kidnapper?" she asked.

Slade lifted his shoulder. "He could have volunteered all that info about his ex just so he wouldn't look guilty."

Yes, and maybe he faked his lack of emotion for the child who might be his. Randall had certainly seemed more concerned about clearing his name than finding the babies.

Clayton continued to drive, and even though he didn't have on the GPS, Maya sensed they were circling Maverick Springs. The minutes just crawled by, but no car came into view. Which meant their plan had failed. The kidnapper hadn't come after them.

"Maybe the kidnapper went after Evan," she mumbled.

"No," he quickly assured her. "Declan would have called us if that'd happened."

The words had no sooner left his mouth than his phone rang, and her heart slammed against her chest. Maya moved closer, trying to hear what the caller was saying. Thankfully, the call was short, and as soon as he finished it, Slade turned to her.

"They made it safely to the ranch."

The relief was instant and overwhelming, and even though Slade didn't make a sound, his fingers tensed slightly on the back of her neck, reminding her that he was there. Of course, she hadn't needed such a reminder. Slade had a way of making sure his presence was known.

Clayton took several more turns, both Slade and he checking the mirrors, but no one was following them when he made the turn for the Blue Creek Ranch. Maya had been worried about going to Slade's home. Like walking into the lion's den. But now that Evan was there, she couldn't wait to arrive.

The place was huge, with acres of pastures still green despite it being late fall. They passed by two houses; one looked decades old and the other was much newer.

"Harlan and Caitlyn live there." Slade tipped his head to the older house. "Dallas and his wife, Joelle, live in the other. Clayton and Lenora's house is on the back part of the property."

"How secure are the grounds?" she asked.

"The ranch hands are keeping watch for anyone. Plus, we've moved Lenora to the main house with my foster father, Kirby."

Lenora, the pregnant sister-in-law, and Kirby, who was apparently battling cancer. Maya hated that both could be in danger, and she prayed all the security measures would be enough to keep everyone safe.

Clayton pulled into a circular drive and stopped directly in front of the sprawling house. Maya didn't wait for Slade. She got out and practically ran up the porch steps to the front door. It was locked, but before she could ring the bell, Slade came up from behind her and punched in some numbers on the keypad.

The moment she was inside, Maya heard the voices, and she followed them through the foyer and toward the back of the house to the huge eat-in kitchen. She immediately spotted Declan, Caitlyn and another man wearing a badge.

But Evan wasn't there.

"The baby's upstairs with Stella," Caitlyn jumped to say, probably because Maya looked on the verge of panicking.

"Stella?" That wasn't a name she'd heard before.

"A friend of the family," Slade supplied. "This way." He led her to some back stairs and to the second floor.

There seemed to be dozens of rooms, but Slade took her to one toward the center. A woman with graying auburn hair was standing in front of a crib, and she put her finger to her mouth in a be-quiet gesture.

Stella, no doubt.

Maya probably made more noise than the woman wanted when she raced to the crib. She wanted to scoop him into her arms and kiss him, but Evan was sound asleep, snuggled beneath a pale blue blanket.

"He was just tuckered out," Stella whispered. She smiled when she looked at Maya. "You appear to be, too. I'm Stella Doyle."

"Maya Ellison." She shook hands with the woman. "You have children of your own?" Because she'd obviously done a good job putting Evan to bed. Her baby was on his side and with nothing near his face to interfere with his breathing.

Stella shook her head, and some kind of pained look went through her eyes. "Wasn't blessed with ones of my own, but I did enough of caring for this lot when they were at Rocky Creek. I was the cook there."

The horrible place where Slade had been raised. But apparently she hadn't been responsible for any of that horror or she wouldn't be here. Yet more family. And Maya was beginning to feel as if she was up against an entire united clan who could challenge her for custody of Evan.

Stella hitched her thumb to the king-size bed on the opposite side of the room. "You could probably do with a nap yourself. If you need to freshen up a bit, you'll find everything you need in the bathroom. The housekeeper, Loretta, keeps this room all fixed up for guests."

Obviously, guests with children. Maya hadn't expected the ranch to even have a crib, but she was thankful for it. Especially since she wasn't sure how long they'd be staying.

Hopefully not long.

Stella's attention landed on Slade when he slipped his arm around Maya's waist and looked down at Evan. The woman made a soft sound of surprise and gave Slade's arm a gentle pat.

"Never figured fatherhood would settle this good on

you." Stella didn't wait for Slade to say anything. She walked out and eased the door shut behind her.

"I'm sure Stella can get some extra clothes and baby supplies for Evan and you." Slade kept his gaze nailed to Evan and his voice at a whisper.

That was good to know, but it was Stella's fatherhood comment that Maya needed to discuss.

"No," Slade said before she could utter a word.

Maya's eyebrow lifted, challenging that he didn't know what she'd been about to say.

"I didn't bring Evan here so I could shut you out," Slade clarified.

Oh. So he'd known what was racing like wildfire through her head. "But you have so many people on your side."

He still had his arm around her and pulled her closer until she was right against him. "There's only one side here, and it belongs to him." He glanced down at Evan.

It was the perfect thing to say to lessen her fears, and that was a Texas-size red flag. "Careful," she mumbled, "or you'll really lose your bad-boy image."

The corner of his mouth lifted, and she felt the jolt of that blasted smile again. If Slade knew just how much it weakened her defenses and made her go all warm, he would probably use it more often.

But she rethought that.

Slade didn't need to do anything to make her go all warm, and he wasn't a man to resort to tricks to seduce a woman. She came up on her toes, intending to give him a quick brush of her lips. But he made a rumbling sound deep within his throat, turned and snapped her to him.

Definitely not a touch of lips.

He put his mouth to hers and kissed her as only Slade could do. Gently but somehow thoroughly at the same time.

And the kiss was just for starters. The taste of him slid through her, easing away all the stress caused by the danger and revving up a different kind of tension.

Sizzling heat.

Before she'd met Slade, it'd been so long since she'd been in a man's arms, and this particular man's arms felt as if they were right where she belonged. Against his body, too, and Slade made sure she could feel every last inch of him when he repositioned her, bringing her breasts against his chest.

"If this makes you feel like panicking, let me know," he mumbled before he took her mouth again.

It took her a moment to cut through the hot haze in her head and realize he was talking about the attack. The last thing that'd been on her mind. Mercy. How could Slade do that? With just a few kisses, he could make her forget something that had been forever branded in her memory.

He shifted again, moving her away from the crib and to a recessed area on the other side of the wall. At first she didn't know why he'd done that, but she soon figured it out. He pinned her hands to the wall and took his clever mouth to her neck.

Maya melted.

Worse, she wanted to melt. She fought to get her hands from his grip, and Slade met her gaze as if he were about to stop. But stopping was the last thing she wanted. This kiss, *this,* made her feel something she was desperate to feel. And not with just any man.

Only with Slade.

That was another red flag. She couldn't think of him that way. As a lover. But her body was in control of those thoughts now. In control of her. And the second she got her hands free from Slade's grip, she wrapped her arms around him and pulled him even closer. Until his sex was aligned with hers.

She didn't just melt. She saw stars.

"You want me to do something about this?" Slade asked, but he didn't ask permission to slide his hand beneath her top and into her bra.

He pulled back, obviously waiting, but not just waiting. He dampened his fingers with his mouth and slid all that dampness over her now exposed right nipple.

Maya heard the sound she made. Pure need. The sound of a woman ready to be dragged off to bed.

"Well?" he prompted. And he gave her left nipple the same treatment. "Let me know what you decide."

He pushed up her top, lowered his head and tongue-kissed her breasts. More fire. More ache. More everything.

"We can't," she managed to say. "Not here, not in the same room with Evan. And the door isn't locked."

He was already lowering himself to her stomach, but that stopped him, and he gave her a flat look. "That's a mixed signal."

"I know." She groaned. "It's because I really, really want you to lock that door, but Evan's here. And your family's downstairs. And we have other things we should be doing." Though she couldn't have named one other thing that didn't involve getting into bed with Slade.

It took him a moment and some mumbled profanity, but he finally eased back up, dropping a few more kisses on her breasts before he fixed her clothes. What he didn't do was move away. Slade stayed right there, his body pressed to hers and with every part of her wanting every part of him.

"I'm used to sex meaning little or nothing." He pushed her hair from her face. "I'm guessing it can't be that way with you?"

She wanted to lie, to say that she could let him satisfy

this ache he'd built inside her. But Maya had to shake her head.

"That's what I thought." Slade still didn't step back. And his erection was still pressed against her, making her body rethink that head shake.

"Does that mean you'll never have sex with me?" she came right out and asked.

Now he shook his head and brushed one of those mind-blowing kisses over her mouth. "It just means I'll know beforehand that it'll be screwing things up." Another kiss. "Right now you're starting to trust me. You don't tremble when I touch you."

Maya checked. "I'm trembling now."

"Not a bad tremble." No kiss, just a deep-down gaze that seemed to slide right into her soul. "But I don't want you trembling for all the wrong reasons when I'm inside you."

That pretty much stole her breath. Mainly because she could practically feel him inside her. She could feel all the touching, the kissing and the pleasure he would give her. And Slade was right—it'd screw things up.

Still, she wanted it but clamped her teeth over her bottom lip so she wouldn't blurt it out.

It took her a moment to realize the buzzing sound wasn't in her head but that it was Slade's phone. He reached in his pocket. Not easily. Because his erection had made his jeans a very tight fit. And he extracted his phone.

"It's Declan," he said, and Slade hit the speaker button.

Just like that, the heat vanished, and she knew this call could be a warning that someone had come to the ranch looking for them.

"I hope to hell this isn't bad news," Slade growled.

"It's news. Not sure if you'll consider it good or bad." Declan paused. "I got the result from the DNA test."

Chapter Twelve

Slade felt as if someone had punched him. Not because he'd forgotten about the DNA tests. He hadn't. But with everything else going on, it hadn't been foremost in his mind.

Even though it could change everything.

Maya sucked in her breath and held it. "Breathe," Slade reminded her. "We're listening," he said to Declan.

"This is the result on the second kidnapped baby, Caleb Rand. He's not a match to you or any of our suspects."

Maya finally let out the breath she'd been holding, but then the renewed fear flashed through her eyes. With one baby ruled out, that meant either Will Collier or Evan was likely to be Slade's son.

Fifty-fifty.

Odds that Maya no doubt hated.

"We did get a match for the baby's birth father. He's barely sixteen and spent some time in juvie lockup for an attempted B and E. Definitely not a suspect for the kidnappings. He hasn't got the money, the connections or the motive."

So the birth father hadn't given up the child and then tried to reclaim him. That really narrowed their suspects, and that meant they were back to the Colliers, Randall or Andrea.

"When will we have Evan's results?" Slade asked.

"Soon. And we might also have Will Collier's DNA."

Slade shook his head. "The estate burned to the ground. I didn't think there was any recoverable DNA."

"There wasn't in the house. But we had CSIs go through the vehicles, and they found a blanket that had fallen under the seat. They managed to get a sample, but they're not sure it's enough to run a comparison." Declan paused. "If it is, we'll compare it to yours."

"And Randall's," Slade insisted.

"Yeah. We have someone headed over to see Randall now to get a sample. And we have a court order in case he refuses."

Good. Well, it was *good* if this gave them some answers, but Slade had to consider that neither baby could be his son. Even though Deidre's doctor had said he was certain, he could have been wrong about the exact delivery date. And if that was the way the tests panned out, then his investigation was just getting started. His baby was out there somewhere. Hopefully, alive and well.

And Slade would find him.

"I'm sorry," Maya said to him the moment he ended the call with Declan.

"Thanks." He looked at her kiss-swollen mouth. Then at Evan. He could stay here with Maya in his arms, but that wouldn't do either of them much good. He had work to do, and Maya needed some rest.

"Why don't you take a nap?" And just in case she objected, he scooped her up and took her to the bed. His stupid body got an equally stupid notion that this was to continue the kissing session, so Slade made it quick. He deposited her onto the bed, gave her a chaste kiss on the cheek and headed for the door. "If you get hungry, just use the phone next to the bed, and I'll bring you up something."

"Slade?" she said just before he could leave. "Don't withhold any news from me, okay? Whether it's good or bad, I want to know."

It was a tall order because there was potentially some really bad news out there, but he nodded. And he meant it. It was hard to hold back with a woman he wanted more than his next breath.

Slade went back downstairs to find both Declan and Clayton on their phones. Stella was at the stove fixing what smelled like a pot of chili. There was corn bread baking in the oven. Dallas was seated at the table, on the phone as well, but he had his wife, Joelle, on his lap, and despite what sounded like a serious conversation about the investigation, Joelle was nuzzling his neck. Caitlyn was helping Stella but was also on the phone with her fiancé, Harlan, and it was clear from what she was saying that she missed him.

All the smells and sounds of home and all the things that usually would have sent Slade heading off to his bedroom. Even though this was his family in every sense of the word, he'd never actually felt part of it like the others. But it was good to have them all on his side because that meant they were helping Evan, too. Even if it turned out that Evan wasn't his, he wanted to do everything humanly possible to keep the baby safe.

Joelle got up from Dallas's lap and went to him. "How's Maya holding up? How are *you* holding up?" she added when their eyes met.

Since Joelle had been with him and all of his foster brothers at the Rocky Creek facility, she knew him a little better than Slade liked people knowing him. She must have seen the stress and worry all over his face. He tried to adjust his expression so it wouldn't show.

"It'll be better once we have some answers," Slade settled for saying.

Joelle gave a soft sigh, probably because he hadn't bared

his heart and soul, and she kissed his cheek. Slade frowned, not because it wasn't a nice gesture. It was. But since it was a first, Joelle must have figured things were pretty darn bad to try to comfort him with a sisterly kiss.

"Hungry?" Caitlyn asked, holding up a spoon of chili for him to sample.

But before Slade could decline, his phone rang, and he saw Randall's name on the screen.

"My P.I.s found a lead on Gina," Randall greeted. His words were rushed, and he sounded excited. "The doctor at the free clinic that Gina used decided to talk since he's worried for her safety. He admitted to delivering the baby. A boy. On September 16, the same birthday as the kidnapped babies." Randall finally paused. "That could be my son."

Yeah. And it could be the reason why these kidnappings were happening if Randall had known about the child days earlier.

"Gina used a fake ID when she had the baby, and the doctor admitted she had made plans for a private adoption. He claims he doesn't know the name of the adoptive parents."

Or maybe he wasn't saying.

Declan had already said they were sending someone over to chat with the doc, so maybe he'd spill more to the marshals than he would to P.I.s hired by the prospective birth father. Who was also a suspect in two kidnappings, two more kidnapping attempts and the murder of a hired gun who'd stolen an SUV.

"Where's Gina?" Slade asked.

"The doctor didn't know. He claims he hasn't seen her since she gave birth, and none of her friends have, either. Not that she has many friends, and they could be lying. Like Gina, her friends don't tend to be reliable."

There it was again, that jab at his ex. Ironically, Randall and he were in similar situations with an ex who'd possibly given birth to their child. And that led Slade to his next question.

"You think Gina could be dead?"

"Not a chance. I think she's laying low so I won't find her and demand to know if she stole money from me."

"Money? This is the first I'm hearing about possible stolen money."

"Because I just found out about it. My accountant was going through my books, and he found the discrepancies. If he's right, Gina might have stolen ten grand from me."

That was a good-size chunk of money, but it wouldn't go far if Gina was trying to disappear. "So you think Gina's in hiding because she stole money?"

"Why else?"

"Maybe because she's afraid of you." And Slade made sure it sounded like the accusation that it was.

Randall cursed. "So we're back to that. Look, I just want to get to the bottom of this so I can clear my name. I have no interest in Gina herself or the kid she gave up for adoption."

Which was another reason for Slade to dislike Randall. It took a special piece of slime not to care about his own child.

"I've instructed my P.I.s to keep looking for Gina for another twenty-four hours," Randall continued, "but if she hasn't turned up by then, I want this investigation to end. I'm a businessman, and something like this could hurt my reputation beyond repair."

"So would your being arrested for murder." Yeah, it was a cheap dig, but Slade was tired of this. Of this investigation. And especially tired of not having answers. He clicked the end-call button just as Declan finished his call.

"The DNA sample from Will Collier was good to go. They're already running a preliminary test, and we might have something by tomorrow."

That soon? Slade figured either way the test went, it could pose new problems, but he decided to put those on the back burner. He already had enough to deal with.

He heard the footsteps behind him and knew they belonged to Maya before he even turned around. She had Evan in her arms, and the baby was wide-awake.

"No nap, huh?" Slade went to her, took the baby and motioned for her to sit at the table. "You need to eat something anyway."

He didn't miss the shocked looks on his brothers' faces, probably because it was the first time they'd seen him voluntarily hold a child. He'd had some cases that'd involved babies and children, but Slade had been careful to avoid being hands-on with them.

Maya was nibbling on her lip when she sat down, but Caitlyn, God bless her, came to the rescue with a smile and a bowl of chili.

Joelle smiled, too. "So what's it like to be a mom?" She patted her own stomach. "Dallas and I have one on the way."

"It's amazing," Maya said without hesitation. She didn't sample the chili until Stella, Clayton and Joelle had dished up some for everyone. "Exhausting, though. You won't get much sleep."

"After you eat, go ahead and take a nap," Slade offered. "I'll watch Evan."

Again that earned him some shocked looks, and Declan's was so bad that Slade scowled at him. The scowl was still on his face when Slade's phone rang again. Not Randall this time but another of their suspects.

"Nadine Collier," he mumbled. Since this call probably involved the investigation they were all a part of, Slade put it on speaker.

"I need your help," Nadine said the second that Slade

answered. "Look at the two pictures I'm sending you. Do it *now*."

That brought the others hurrying to his side so they could see it, as well. The photos took a while to load, and they were grainy, but he had no trouble spotting the man.

The guy was wearing a ski mask.

And he was holding something in his arms.

The second photo showed exactly what he was holding.

"He has the baby." Nadine's voice cracked. "He has us both at gunpoint."

Maya took Evan from his arms, and Slade got to his feet. "Who's holding you at gunpoint and who's the baby?"

"I don't know." It sounded as if she was crying. "On both counts. He won't let me see his or the baby's face, and he had the baby's head covered with a cap so I can't even tell the hair color. He used a stun gun on me when I was in the parking lot, and he drove me to this place. I don't know where we are, but he's holding me in a barn."

None of this could be good. Or the truth. "What does he want?"

"Money." A hoarse sob tore from Nadine's mouth.

A ransom demand. Slade had been waiting for another of those, but he hadn't expected it to come like this. "Put the man on the phone."

"He won't talk to you. I already tried. If you don't come, if you don't help, he says he'll kill me, and no one will ever see the baby again."

Hell. This was not what Slade wanted to hear.

"You have to come," Nadine insisted. "You and Maya, and you have to bring as much cash as you can get your hands—"

"Wait a minute," Slade interrupted. "Why does he want Maya?"

"He won't say."

The color drained from Maya's face, and he probably went a little pale, too. The last place he wanted her was in the middle of a ransom exchange. It was bad enough that Nadine was there. Of course, Nadine could have orchestrated all of this, so maybe the only danger was this plan to get Maya and him out in the open.

Slade cursed. "Give your phone to our masked friend."

Nadine repeated that the man wouldn't talk to Slade, but he could hear the movement. "I got my orders," the man snarled into the phone. "If Maya Ellison doesn't come with you and if you don't have a boatload of cash, this kid is on the next flight to Mexico."

Slade tried not to react, but he wasn't immune to that threat. Even if this wasn't his baby, the infant was still in danger, and God knows what would happen to him.

"Meet me at the old Weston ranch," the man said. "You know the place?"

"Yeah." It'd been abandoned for several years, and there was only one road in and out. It was a good fifteen-minute drive from their own ranch.

"I'll go," Maya said.

"No, you won't," Slade insisted. He had to try again to bargain with the devil in the picture holding that baby. "I'll come alone." A lie. He'd have at least one of his brothers hidden away as backup. "And I can bring $20,000." They probably had that much in the safe in the ranch's office.

"Bring more," the man countered. "And don't come alone. If Maya's not with you, then the deal is off. It's the same if you bring any of your law enforcement buddies. Just Maya and you. You've got thirty minutes, or I start shooting."

"No. I need a different plan," Slade said, but he was talking to himself because the kidnapper had hung up.

Chapter Thirteen

"You're not doing this," Slade snarled.

Maya had lost count of how many times he'd already said that, and she figured she would hear it plenty more before this was over and done.

But that wouldn't change things.

She didn't consider herself a brave person. Not with her brutal past. This had nothing to do with bravery but had everything to do with a child's survival.

"What if the kidnapper had Evan?" she tossed back at Slade. She didn't add *What if this is your child?* but she figured they were both thinking it.

"It's too dangerous." Slade finished shoving the money from the safe into a bank bag. It looked to be significantly more than $20,000, and she prayed that it'd be enough.

"It's more dangerous for the baby if I don't go."

That silenced everyone in the room. Declan, Clayton, Dallas, Caitlyn, Joelle and Stella. They were obviously all waiting for Slade to respond, but he stood there, mumbling profanity and closing the bank bag as if he might rip it to pieces at any moment.

"She's right," Declan finally spoke up. He went to the closet in the office and hauled out an equipment bag. "If it were just Nadine's life at stake, I'd never agree to this. But it's a baby, Slade."

But Slade shook his head. "A baby this kidnapper could be using as bait to draw out Maya."

"There's no reason for him to draw me out," she argued. "He could just want me there because he might think it'll keep you from firing shots at him."

"The baby would prevent me from doing that." Slade cursed again. "And maybe he's doing this to get us away from Evan so he can be kidnapped, too."

Maya pressed Evan closer to her heart to try to steady it. Her son had already spent too much time in danger, and it wasn't over.

But maybe this was the beginning of the end.

Dallas stepped forward. "You know there's no way we'd allow anyone to take Evan. You and Maya go out to the Weston ranch, and the rest of us will stay here and guard him. You can take the infrared scanner so you can see who's in that barn and anywhere else on the grounds before you go in. Harlan, Wyatt and one of the deputies can follow you and stay close in case you need backup."

"That still leaves Maya in danger." Slade's voice was so loud that it startled Evan, and he began to cry. "Sorry," he grumbled.

"It's okay." She went closer and gave Slade's arm a gentle touch. It didn't soothe him one bit, but that was asking a lot of an arm rub.

"I can go in the truck with Maya and you," Declan volunteered. "I'll stay down so the kidnapper doesn't see me. We'll all have on Kevlar vests. And when we get there, you can go in for the money drop. If the kidnapper insists on seeing Maya, he can get a glimpse of her in the truck."

Slade was still shaking his head.

"If things don't look right, we'll get out of there fast," Declan added.

"And what if things go wrong here?" Slade asked.

Maya's breath caught in her throat. The idea of her son being in more danger was terrifying, but the danger existed no matter where he was. And this might be a way to stop it. Because if they got lucky, this wouldn't be just a money drop—they might be able to rescue the baby and capture the kidnapper.

"I'll have Sheriff Geary come out here," Dallas explained. "Plus, every ranch hand will be armed and ready."

"I can watch the baby," Stella said, stepping forward.

"I'll help," Joelle and Caitlyn offered in unison.

Maya looked down at her son. Then at Slade. She wanted nothing more than for them all to stay put at the ranch, surrounded by his family, who would protect them at all cost. But the kidnapper had made that impossible.

"There, there," Stella whispered to Evan as she took him from Maya. She nuzzled Evan's cheek and gently rocked him. His whimpers stopped almost immediately.

"You need to put this on." Declan took several vests from the equipment bag and handed Maya one. "It's Kevlar. It'll stop a bullet."

"Yeah, but not if this SOB aims at her head." Slade snatched one of the other vests from Declan, and both Declan and he put them on.

"The kidnapper will have to go through me to get to Maya's head," Declan snarled back. "Or any other part of her, for that matter. Look, I'm not happy about this, either, but we don't have a choice."

Maya agreed, though the thought of all of them in direct danger made her sick to her stomach. At least Declan and she would be in the truck. Or that was the plan anyway. But Slade would be the one to walk inside the barn and try to negotiate the release of the baby.

"Let's go," Declan added. "I can call Harlan and Wyatt to get them headed out there."

"And I'll call Sheriff Geary and the ranch hands," Dallas volunteered.

Still, Slade didn't budge for several long moments. He finally aimed his index finger at Maya. "You'll stay down, and you won't take any chances."

It seemed as if they all made a collective sigh of relief, but there was no real relief and wouldn't be until they got the baby safely out of there.

Slade grabbed the equipment bag and some extra guns from the closet. He handed her one before they headed out. However, he paused to brush his hand over the top of Evan's head, and Maya kissed her son again.

"I'll take good care of him, I promise," Stella said. And even though Maya hardly knew this woman, she believed her.

With Declan on the phone to Harlan and Wyatt, they hurried to one of the trucks parked at the back of the house. Slade got behind the wheel, and Maya slid into the center so that Declan could take the window and keep watch. At least it was during daylight, unlike the ordeal that'd gone on at the safe house, so they'd be able to see a threat before it was too late.

Well, maybe.

"What if Nadine is behind this?" she asked. "What if she's doing this to cover up the fact that she had her adopted child kidnapped, maybe to get back at her husband? Or maybe just for the ransom?"

"If she's behind this, she'll probably have more than one hired gun with her." Slade responded so quickly it was clear he'd already given this some thought.

However, Maya had to shake her head. "But Nadine's motive would be money to pay her gambling debts. Why demand cash from you when she could make a much larger ransom demand from her husband?"

"Because maybe that's too obvious. It'd make us key in on her even more as a suspect. This way she looks like a victim and not a perpetrator. Besides, this is just one of the babies. She could be planning to hit up Chase for a ransom for the second."

True. And maybe she hadn't asked ransom of the adopted parents of the second missing baby, Caleb, because they wouldn't have had much cash to give. Maya remembered that Slade had told her they were both schoolteachers.

Slade's attention volleyed between the side- and rearview mirrors, but he also sent one of those glances her way. "Hell," he mumbled.

That sent a jolt of alarm through her. "What?"

"This," he snarled.

And when she looked into his eyes, she knew exactly what *this* meant. This attraction between them was rearing its head again and not in a heated I-want-you-now sort of way. It was creating a distraction because Slade wasn't thinking like a lawman.

"Harlan and Wyatt will get there ahead of us," Declan relayed the moment he finished his call. "They have infrared, too," he added, fishing the handheld machine from the equipment bag. "The plan is for them to move into position at the back of the barn. Deputy Randy Wells will be coming in behind us."

So there'd be five lawmen and her. Since Maya had never fired a gun, she wouldn't be much help, but she was glad she had something in case things turned bad.

"Don't you dare get shot," she mumbled to Slade.

"Same to you," he mumbled back, and he turned onto a gravel-and-dirt road.

"Fresh tracks," Declan pointed out.

The tracks didn't exactly confirm Nadine's story, but it was clear someone had recently driven out here.

With each passing second, Maya's heart beat even faster, and by the time the ranch came into view, she was fighting just to keep her breath level. It wouldn't help matters if she hyperventilated, and the last thing Slade needed was to babysit her.

"Time for you two to get down," Slade warned them. He stopped at the rust-scabbed cattle gate about two hundred yards from the house.

Maya made a sweeping glance of the house and grounds. It was nowhere near as large as Slade's family ranch, and the pasture fence was falling down in spots. The weeds and grass were at least knee-high in places, the trees and shrubs overgrown as well, and maybe that overgrowth would give Harlan, Wyatt and the deputy some cover as they made their way to the barn.

Maya got on the floor of the truck and Declan dropped down across the seat just as his phone buzzed. "Harlan," Declan greeted, but she couldn't hear the other end of the conversation.

While Declan was talking with his brother, Slade took the infrared, turned it on and aimed it at the house, then the barn. Maya levered herself up just enough to see the screen and the three colored splotches in the barn.

"He definitely has the baby," Slade commented. "And it appears to be in some kind of carrier on the floor next to the kidnapper." He tapped the other splotch. "That's probably Nadine. It looks as if her hands are tied behind her back."

That didn't mean this wasn't still a setup, but it was looking more and more as if Nadine had been telling the truth.

"Harlan and the others are coming across the back pasture now," Declan explained when he finished his call. "There's a van behind the barn, but according to infrared, no one is inside."

She didn't miss the look that passed between Slade and Declan.

"Is that bad?" she asked.

"Strange," Slade clarified. "The kidnapper must have anticipated that I'd bring in backup, so why would he come alone?"

True, and Maya could see where this was going. "Maybe he didn't come alone. Maybe Nadine isn't really tied up."

"Yeah." And that's all Slade said for several seconds before he took out his phone and redialed Nadine's number. He put the call on speaker.

But it wasn't Nadine who answered. It was the man in the barn with her. Maya could see enough of the man's movements on the screen to determine that.

"I don't see Maya with you," the man said.

Slade mumbled some profanity, squinted against the afternoon sun and pointed toward the front of the barn. *Camera,* he mouthed.

Declan mouthed some profanity, too, and fired off a text message to Harlan to warn him that there might be a camera at the rear of the building, too.

"Maya's on the seat," Slade told the man. "I don't want her in the line of fire."

"The only way I fire is if I don't see her."

The muscles in Slade's jaw stirred. "Sit up for just a second," he told her.

Maya made her way off the floor, but she barely had time to look over the dash before Slade pushed her back on the floor.

"There," Slade snarled. "You've seen her."

"Who else you got in that truck with you?" the man asked.

Maya's heart nearly stopped, but she reminded herself

that the camera hadn't spotted her, so it wouldn't spot De-clan. Unless the kidnapper had infrared, too.

"It's just Maya and me," Slade lied.

The kidnapper didn't say anything for several moments, but the baby started to cry. "All right, then. Now call your brothers or whoever you've got hiding in the back pasture and tell them to stop in their tracks. Do it."

Oh, God. So there'd probably been a camera back there after all. She prayed the three had gotten close enough to the barn to help if things started to unravel.

"What part of that didn't you understand?" the kidnap-per taunted over the cries of the baby. "Call your backup and tell them to stop. If they move another inch forward, I shoot Mrs. Collier and hightail it out of here with the kid. Remember what I said about sending the brat to Mexico. And trust me, I don't care what kind of *family* he ends up with."

Slade mumbled some profanity, but he made the call and told his brothers and the sheriff to hold their position. "What now?" he snapped to the kidnapper.

"You drive to the barn. Stop directly in front of the door and wait until you hear from me."

"Don't let him shoot me!" she heard Nadine yell.

The woman genuinely sounded terrified, but Maya wasn't ready to trust anyone other than Slade and his fam-ily.

"Stay down," Slade repeated to her, and he did as the kidnapper had asked. He pulled the truck to a stop and waited. They didn't have to wait long. His phone rang just a few seconds later.

"Don't think about trying to take me out," the kidnapper warned, "because I got the kid in my arms. And I've put a few security measures in place to make sure you don't try to blow off my head."

He's up and moving, Declan mouthed.

Even though Maya couldn't see what was happening, from the sound of it, the barn door opened and the baby's cries got louder. That cut her to the core. Even though the child was too young to understand what was going on, he might be hungry or worse. God knows what kind of care this monster had given the precious baby.

"How much money did you bring?" the kidnapper asked Slade.

"At least thirty grand. It was everything we had in the safe."

The man made a sound of disapproval. "I wanted more, but I guess that'll have to do. The next kid will cost you a lot more."

Maya wasn't sure whether to be relieved or terrified that he had both babies and was willing to ransom them. Maybe this meant they'd soon recover both children. And maybe it also meant the threat to Evan was over.

"Where's the other baby?" Slade snapped.

"That's a secret." It sounded as if the guy was smiling, and Maya wished she could slap him for that. Or better yet, get Slade to beat him to a pulp. She hated this monster for putting the babies in danger.

"Just focus on getting this kid for now. We'll work out the details of the other later. Oh, and if you or your marshal brothers decide to put a bullet in me, I think you should know that'd be like putting a bullet in both kids. As you can see, I'm holding this one, and if I'm dead and gone, the other kid will just disappear."

That caused Maya's stomach to clench. This had to end. They had to recover those babies.

"Plus, there's that security measure I talked about," the man continued. "There are two assault rifles aimed at right about the spot where you've parked, and they're rigged with a sound sensor and detonators. If someone fires a shot, the assault rifles start firing, too. I'm not exactly sure where the bullets will go, and I don't think you want to find out."

Maya couldn't see the guns from her angle, but there were holes in the upper part of the barn. The guns could be positioned behind there.

"You and Maya need to step out of the truck," the kidnapper instructed. "I want the money in Maya's hands. You can keep your gun because I suspect you've got one hidden away as backup anyway. Just remember that part about bullets flying. Not a good idea."

"There's no reason for Maya to get out," Slade argued. "I can bring you the money."

"You could if that's what I'd told you to do. I didn't. I said for Maya to bring it. Or maybe you want this kid sent off to Mexico."

"I'll do it," Maya insisted. Their gazes met, and she hoped that her expression was a reminder that they had backup in place and there was no reason for the kidnapper to shoot them.

Well, no reason she could think of.

She prayed she was right about that.

Slade mumbled some profanity, and she could see the struggle going on behind those steely muscles. But there was no other option here. They couldn't risk a shootout with the baby and Nadine as hostages.

"Stay behind me," Slade insisted, and he scooped up the money bag and handed it to her. "Get out on this side."

Of course, that meant her crawling over Declan, but somehow they managed to reposition themselves so that she could exit on the driver's side behind Slade.

Maya finally got a good look at the kidnapper, who was indeed wearing a ski mask, and he had a gun in his right hand. The baby in his arms was crying nonstop now. That didn't help settle her nerves. Of course, nothing would at this point except getting the baby out of there.

Was it Morgan Gambill behind that mask?

It was possible.

He'd escaped from the sheriff's office during that fake bomb scare, and she had no doubt that he worked for the kidnapper. That slight bulge beneath the mask near his right ear also told her that he was probably wearing some kind of communicator. Maybe so the man who'd orchestrated this could give him orders.

"Is the baby Will?" Nadine called out. "I can't see his face, but I need to know if it's Will."

Maya was surprised she couldn't tell from the baby's cries. She certainly would have been able to tell if it was Evan. Of course, Nadine probably hadn't spent a lot of time with the baby she'd intended to adopt since the adoption had been Chase's idea.

"Open the money bag and drop it in front of me," the kidnapper instructed, drowning out Nadine when she repeated her question.

Even though her hands were shaking, Maya managed to open it, and Slade and she walked forward with him staying in front of her. She saw Nadine sitting on the hay-strewn floor. Her hands had been tied to a support post, and she looked as terrified as Maya felt. If this was an act, then Nadine was doing a very good job of playing the hostage victim.

"Come closer," the man ordered. They took another step just as Slade's phone rang. "Go ahead. Answer it."

That was a surprise, and Maya was instantly suspicious. Slade didn't take his eyes off the kidnapper, but he used his left hand to ease his phone from his pocket, and he handed it to Maya. She saw Declan's name on the screen and figured this wasn't good news.

"We got a problem," Declan said the moment she answered. "There are two vehicles approaching the ranch. Slade and you need to get out of there *now*."

Chapter Fourteen

Slade couldn't hear what the caller had said to Maya, but it had her turning, and her attention zoomed to the road leading to the ranch.

"I guess that was one of your brothers letting you know we have visitors," the kidnapper calmly said.

Hell. This couldn't be good. Even though his gun was ready, Slade turned slightly so he could try to better protect Maya.

"No reason for concern," the man added. "Our visitors are just like you. They're here to bring money so you can bring this squalling kid back where he belongs."

Slade glanced at the two approaching vehicles. There was no way Declan could have seen them from his position in the truck, so that meant his brother must have used the infrared.

"Are they armed?" Slade said loud enough that Declan would hear.

Maya still had his phone pressed to her ear, and she shook her head. "He can't tell."

So that meant Declan was no doubt positioning himself in case this went from bad to worse.

"Remember, keep your fingers off those triggers," the kidnapper growled.

As if Slade needed the warning. The baby's cries were

plenty enough for him to know this couldn't turn into a shooting match. Well, not unless Slade could get the baby and Maya to safety first. Then he'd like nothing more than to take this guy out.

Of course, there was the threat of the assault rifles.

It was possible to rig the rifles to fire with some kind of trigger device, but there was no way to predict the path of the bullets. That only made things more dangerous.

The two cars pulled to a stop on each side of his truck, and Slade maneuvered Maya so that she was closer to the door in case she had to run for cover and get back inside with Declan.

"It's Randall," Maya mumbled.

Yeah, it was. Randall stepped from the first car. He had a gym bag in his left hand and lifted his right hand in the air as if surrendering.

"Welcome, Mr. Martin," the kidnapper said. "Hope you brought me lots of cash."

Randall scowled at Slade and Maya as if this were somehow all their fault. "I brought what I had from my business. About $11,000." It wasn't just his expression that was hostile. His tone was, too. "Now, where the hell is Gina? And is that her kid?"

The kidnapper shook his head, and though Slade couldn't see his face, he could have sworn the guy smiled. "Sorry, no Gina."

"You bastard! You said you had her and would release her if I paid you." Randall charged forward but came to a skidding stop when the kidnapper pointed the gun at him.

"Hey, I had to say something to get you here," the kidnapper calmly answered. "And it worked. Besides, this kid *could* be hers. Trust me, I'll be more than happy to turn him over to you just as soon as I have all the money."

Randall made a sound of outrage. "I don't want the baby. I want Gina!"

"Oh, your poor thing," he mocked, but his voice took on a harder edge. "Just drop the money bag in front of me and shut the hell up."

"I want to know where Gina is," Randall fired back.

"You'll learn that *after* I have the money from all of you. Now put it on the ground and then step back by the marshal."

Slade wasn't at all sure Randall would do that, but he finally went forward. That was when Slade saw the gun tucked in the back waist of Randall's pants. He hoped to hell Randall didn't start shooting.

"He says he's got assault rifles rigged to a sensor," Slade explained to Randall. "If any of us fires, he says the rifles go off."

Randall's eyes widened, and he glanced nervously around the barn. He gave a shaky nod, dumped the bag on the ground and then went to stand beside Slade. Not the best position as far as Slade was concerned. He didn't want any of the suspects this close, but at least he could see Randall this way. The more immediate concern was the person in the other car.

"Maya, it's your turn now," the kidnapper said. "Put the money bag next to Randall's."

"Not until I know who's in the other car," Slade countered.

"I figured you'd already guessed."

Yeah, he had. "Chase Collier?"

"And the nanny, Andrea whatever-her-name-is." He made a motion with his hand, and the two stepped out. Both put their hands in the air as well, and Chase was carrying what appeared to be yet another bag of money.

Both Andrea and Chase looked terrified, normal for

the situation, but there was nothing about this situation or their reactions that Slade trusted. After all, they were both suspects. As were Randall and Nadine. For all he knew, Nadine wasn't even tied up.

"Chase!" Nadine yelled. "Help me. Get me out of here."

But Chase barely spared his wife a glance. His attention went to the baby. "Is it Will?"

"We don't know, and he won't say," Slade answered.

"You can't tell from the cries?" Maya asked.

Both Andrea and Chase listened, and Andrea finally shook her head. "It doesn't sound like Will."

Then it could be the other baby, Caleb Rand. Or another baby the guy had kidnapped. It could even be Slade's child. But he forced the thought aside. The only thing that mattered now was that a baby needed to be rescued.

"How'd you know to come here?" Slade asked Randall and the others.

"I got a call from this bozo," Randall snapped. "He said he had Gina and that he was holding her hostage."

"He called me, too," Chase answered.

Andrea's attention was glued to the baby. "I was with Chase when he got the call, and I insisted on coming with him. I had to make sure Will was okay."

Later Slade would want to know why they were together, but he had bigger fish to fry—mainly getting them all out of there alive.

"Toss the money bag next to Randall's," he told Maya.

She reached around him and slung the bag in that direction. It landed practically at the kidnapper's feet.

"And what about you, Mr. Collier?" the kidnapper asked. "How much did you bring me?"

"Fifty thousand. It'd better be enough. Now hand over the baby. And Nadine." But it certainly sounded as if he'd added his wife as an afterthought.

Nadine obviously felt the same way. Her mouth tightened to the point of looking painful.

Chase put the money next to the others, and by Slade's calculations, it was about a hundred grand. Not chump change but still not as much as the kidnapper could have gotten from a man like Chase. Of course, if the kidnapper had guessed the child might be Slade's, he could have demanded more, too. Slade himself wasn't a rich man, but since Kirby had given him and each of his brothers part ownership of the ranch, they were all doing a lot better than just okay.

So why this hasty demand?

Had something gone wrong and this guy's boss had told him to unload the baby? Or was something else going on? It was the possibility of something else that worried him most.

"You've got your money," Slade reminded the guy. "Now give us Nadine and the baby."

"I think I'll keep Nadine for a while," the man said. "But Maya can take the kid, and the rest of you can go."

Slade wasn't sure who howled the loudest—Nadine or Randall. "I'm not leaving without Gina," Randall said at the same time that Nadine yelled out, "Chase! Don't let him do this."

"You want Gina," the kidnapper said to Randall. "You need to look in Houston. A little bird told me she was in at one of those extended-stay motels called the Bluebonnet."

Randall turned and started to bolt, but Slade caught onto his arm. "Best if we all leave together," he warned Randall in a whisper. "The kidnapper could have gunmen somewhere on the road to pick us off one by one."

Randall mumbled some profanity, but he stayed put.

"Let's get the baby," Slade whispered to Maya, and he walked with her over to the kidnapper.

"No way," the guy snarled, turning his gun on Slade. "You stay put. I figure if you get hold of me, you can kick my butt six ways to Sunday. So stay back."

And the kidnapper did some moving, too. He positioned himself in front of Nadine and crouched down so that it would make it next to impossible for one of his brothers to use infrared to pinpoint the kidnapper's location and send a kill shot right at him.

That new position didn't please Slade, nor did the man's order for him to stay back, but he stopped. "Move fast," he told Maya. "Get the baby and then get inside the truck."

Maya did exactly as he asked, and Slade knew she was moving fast, but time seemed to stop. It sent his heart crashing when he saw the kidnapper point the gun within just a few inches of Maya's head.

She wasn't faring much better.

Her hands were shaking, but she managed to take the crying baby and pulled it close to her chest as she raced toward the truck. Slade held his breath until she was inside, but he figured his breathing wouldn't return to normal until they were out of there.

"Is that Will?" Andrea called out. She rushed forward and probably would have jumped in the truck if the kidnapper hadn't pointed his gun at her.

"I don't want anybody moving. And here's what's gonna happen next. Maya, you put the baby on the seat and drive out of here. I'll keep the marshal and the others a little while longer."

"No!" Maya said, lifting her head. Nadine and Andrea shouted the same, and Nadine began to struggle even harder with the ropes.

"Yes," the kidnapper argued, his gun still aimed at Andrea. "And since I don't think anyone wants to be shot, Maya better get behind the wheel and start that engine now."

"Do it," Slade insisted when she didn't move. "Get the baby out of here," he added. Yeah, it was playing dirty. No way would she hang around an armed man and put the baby's life at risk.

Behind the kidnapper, Nadine tugged and jerked, her shoulders rocking back and forth. If the gunman noticed, he didn't say anything. He volleyed his attention in front of him, specifically at the truck.

Damn it. This could be a ruse to separate Maya from the rest of them. Was she the kidnapper's target? If so, why hadn't he tried to shoot her when she stepped from the truck?

Maybe because the kidnapper needed her alive.

But why?

Slade didn't have time to come up with an answer, because Maya started the engine and began backing out of the drive. She'd barely made it a foot when Nadine broke free of the rope. Instead of ramming her body into the kidnapper, she tried to get to her feet and run.

Not a good idea.

The kidnapper cursed, turned and latched on to her. Slade's instincts were to rush forward, to try and help Nadine, but he had an even greater need to protect Maya and the baby.

Chase and Andrea, however, both shouted and ran toward the front of the barn. Randall drew his gun. Not the best thing to steady Slade's nerves. Because now he had to watch Randall and the kidnapper.

"Try to contain the situation," Slade shouted, and he hoped his brothers could do that.

He turned so he could get into the truck. That way, if this was some kind of ruse to get Maya, both Declan and he could protect her. Besides, they needed to get the baby to the hospital ASAP just in case he'd been injured.

But the sound stopped Slade cold.

The shot blasted through the barn, and he whirled back around to see Nadine's hand on the kidnapper's gun. Judging from her horrified expression, she'd accidentally pulled the trigger in the struggle. Slade couldn't tell if she'd been shot or if she'd managed to shoot the kidnapper.

That's because a new sound snared his attention. Movement from the barn rafters, and before he could even make it to the truck, the bullets started flying.

Hell.

Since Slade knew from infrared there were no other people inside the barn, that meant the kidnapper hadn't lied about the assault rifles being rigged with a sound sensor.

Everyone dived to the ground, but Slade got into the truck. In the same motion, he pushed Maya back to the floor. Declan was still lying on the seat, the crying baby in the crook of his arm, but he handed off the baby to Maya so he could get up. He lifted his gun.

Just as some shots crashed into the front windshield. The bullet-resistant glass stopped them, but the glass cracked and webbed, making it impossible for Slade to see what was happening.

But he could hear the chaos.

Nadine was screaming nonstop. Andrea, too. But the nanny was shouting out Will's name.

"Get in the back of the truck," Slade yelled to whoever could hear him.

It wasn't ideal cover, but it was better than being out in the open. However, none of them took him up on the offer. Randall jumped to the side of his own car, and Chase and Andrea dived to the side of Chase's vehicle.

The bullets continued to smack into the truck, tearing

through the metal and glass, and Slade knew he couldn't wait any longer. He had to get out of there.

He threw the truck into Reverse and slammed on the accelerator, but he had to weave around Randall's and Chase's vehicles so he could get to open space.

"Harlan and the others are closing in on the barn," Declan relayed. Declan had his phone sandwiched against his ear and his attention on the side mirrors.

Good. Maybe they could get Nadine to safety and arrest the kidnapper. They needed the man alive so he could tell them the location of the other baby.

And the name of the person who'd hired him.

Slade especially needed that so he could go after the person who'd put all these babies and Maya in danger.

The bullets continued to come at them, and once Slade was clear of the other vehicles, he turned the truck around so that the shots were going into the back rather than the windshield. The moment he was on the gravel road, he hit the accelerator again to put some distance between them and the bullets.

"Someone might try to take Maya," Slade relayed to Declan.

She gasped, but Declan only nodded. "That's why the kidnapper insisted you bring her."

"But why?" Maya asked.

That was the million-dollar question, but there was the possibility that the kidnapper wanted to use Maya to get them to turn over Evan. That wouldn't happen, but it was clear the kidnapper was desperate or he wouldn't have orchestrated this lethal situation.

"Oh, God," Maya said over the baby's cries. "What if they're at the ranch trying to take Evan?"

"We're headed there now." Slade had already considered this possibility, and even though the ranch was well protected, he didn't want Maya on the road any longer than necessary. Once he had gotten her and the baby to safety, he could call the hospital and arrange for a doctor to check out the baby.

And figure out who the child was.

Slade was hoping it was either Will or Caleb because he didn't want any other kidnapped babies added to this.

Declan's phone buzzed, and he answered the call while he kept watch.

"Harlan says they made it into the barn," Declan relayed. But then he paused, cursed. "And it's not good. They found a dead body."

Chapter Fifteen

The only thing Maya could do was wait and try to soothe the crying baby. His sobs tapered off to whimpers, but there was no tapering off of the emotion on Declan's and Slade's faces.

Declan stayed on the phone just listening to whatever Harlan was telling him, and whatever it was, it wasn't good.

They found a dead body.

If that body belonged to the kidnapper, then they might have lost their main lead to the other missing child.

Perhaps Slade's son.

Of course, the alternative wasn't much better—that Randall, Chase, Nadine or Andrea was dead. Maya wasn't especially fond of any of them, but if one of them happened to be the person behind the kidnapping, then the missing baby might be lost forever.

Mumbling profanity, Declan ended the call and looked over at Slade. "Andrea is dead. And the kidnapper got away with the money."

Oh, mercy. Definitely not good news, and worse—if the kidnapper escaped, did that mean he was on the road behind them? It seemed a selfish thing, considering that a woman was dead, but if the man started shooting again, the baby could be hurt.

"Where's the kidnapper?" Maya managed to ask despite the fact her lip was trembling.

"He got in the van and drove across the pasture. There's probably an old ranch trail back there. But Harlan's in pursuit while Wyatt and the deputy stay with the Colliers and Randall."

Yes, because if the kidnapper returned, one of them could be shot, as well. Of course, that meant Harlan was headed right into the line of fire by trying to chase down this guy.

It seemed to take Slade several moments to get his jaw unclenched. "How'd all of this happen?"

Declan shook his head and continued his watch of their surroundings. "By the time Harlan and the others got to the barn, they found Andrea dead by the side of Chase's car. A single gunshot wound to the head."

The last time Maya had seen Andrea, the woman had been running for cover. With all those bullets flying, though, there'd been no safe place to hide. "What about the others? Were they hurt?"

Declan shook his head again. "Nadine's screaming at Chase for not doing more to save her, and Randall's riled that Wyatt won't let him leave so he can go to Houston to look for his ex-girlfriend. Chase is demanding that he see the baby we have so he'll know if it's Will."

It shouldn't have surprised her that none of them had asked about the child's condition. Or if he was safe. At least Chase was asking something about the baby, but that could all be for show. To make himself look innocent. The truth was he had just as strong of a motive as the others if he was trying to frame Nadine so that he wouldn't have to split his vast estate with her.

"I'll call Dallas and get him to send me a photo of both babies," Declan offered.

Maya looked up at Slade at the exact moment he looked down at her. "I'm sorry. I don't want to know how many bad memories that brought back for you, but I figure it was *bad*."

She saw the worry and guilt practically weighing him down. Not for himself but for her. It was touching, and unnecessary.

"We got out with the baby," she reminded him, and looked down at the little boy. He'd fallen asleep, probably exhausted from all the crying, but with his face relaxed she was able to look at it and compare it to Slade's. She didn't see any resemblance, but then, it was hard to tell with babies.

And the truth was, he looked more like Evan than this baby.

That was a bitter pill to swallow in some ways, but in others, sharing custody with Slade suddenly didn't seem so bad.

If he shared, that is.

Maybe it was the fact they'd come so close to dying again, but she didn't believe he would just take Evan from her. No. Slade cared. She cared for him, too. But it was worse than that.

She was falling in love with him.

Not exactly the best time for that to hit her, but there was no good timing for this.

"We're on the ranch grounds," Declan told her, and he helped her onto the seat with the baby just as the photos of the two missing children appeared on his phone.

Maya looked at both, then eased off the baby's knit cap so she could compare him to the shots. "This is Caleb Rand," Declan and she said at once.

There was no mistaking it. Of course, the photo was probably only a few days old since the adoptive parents likely would have taken many pictures of the child. Well, they would have if they were better parents than the Colliers.

Declan called Dallas and relayed the info so that Dallas could call the child's adoptive parents. It was a relief to know the child's identity, but there it was again. The questions in Slade's eyes.

If this wasn't his child, then where was he?

Slade pulled to a stop in front of the ranch house, and they all hurried up the steps. Slade's family was there waiting for them, and even though the baby was sound asleep, Stella hurried across the foyer to bring her Evan. Caitlyn took the other baby so that Maya could take Evan.

Maya instantly felt her heart rate decrease, and even though it wasn't, it was as if she'd stepped into her home.

She was clearly losing it.

This wasn't her home, but holding Evan put everything in perspective. He was safe, thanks to Slade and his family, and for now she pushed all her other worries aside. Well, she managed it until Dallas finished the phone call he was making and gave his brothers a glance she'd come to know all too well.

He had bad news.

"Harlan lost the kidnapper," Dallas said.

There was a collective groan in the foyer. Without the kidnapper, they didn't have a lead on the other baby, and that meant the danger would continue.

"Wyatt and the others will get statements from Chase, Nadine and Randall," Dallas went on. "They'll take a look at their phones to see what time they got the ransom calls. And there's a CSI crew on the way to the barn to collect any possible evidence."

She could only hope and pray that the kidnapper had left something incriminating behind.

"What about the baby's adoptive parents?" Slade asked. Because he was looking down at Evan, Maya moved closer and eased him into Slade's arms.

Yet something else that felt like home.

"The Rands are on the way here," Dallas answered. "Needless to say, they're very happy about their son being rescued. I told them the doc would have to check him out first, and they agreed." He glanced at his watch. "Dr. Landry should be here within the next half hour."

"How is Mrs. Rand? I remember Slade said the kidnapper clubbed her when he took the baby."

"She's out of the hospital and well enough to travel."

That was something at least. Of course, even a serious injury probably wouldn't have stopped the woman. It wouldn't have stopped Maya.

Caitlyn looked down at the sleeping baby she was holding. "Should I change his diaper or something?"

"Not yet." Slade glanced at Declan. "Want to check the baby for any signs of…anything?"

Because of the fatigue, it took a moment for that to sink in, and then her heart went to the floor. Caitlyn had a similar reaction because the color drained from her face, and she hurried into the living room and eased down on the sofa. They all followed her, and Maya worked herself to the front of them.

She prayed the monster hadn't hurt this child.

Caitlyn turned back the blanket and then lifted the baby's loose blue top and tugged off the stretchy bottom. There wasn't a mark on him, and the relief caused Maya to wobble. Since Slade's hands were occupied with Evan, it was Stella who caught onto her.

"See," Stella said in a soft, comforting whisper, "the little guy's just fine."

"We'll need his clothes and diaper bagged," Dallas insisted. "Especially that diaper. It's easy to leave fingerprints on the adhesive tapes."

That reminder sent them scattering. Dallas said something about getting an evidence bag from his truck. Joelle hurried to the kitchen to grab a fresh diaper from the supplies they'd gotten for Evan. There were extra clothes in that bag, too, and a blanket.

Stella gave Maya's arm a nudge. "You look ready to fall on the floor. A hot bath will help. Some rest, too. And Joelle brought over some clothes and put them in your room. You two are about the same size."

Maya shook her head. "I don't want to leave Evan." Or Slade.

"They'll be just fine," Stella said as if she knew exactly what Maya was thinking. "And if we hear anything about the kidnapper or the case, Slade can come up and tell you all about it."

"She's right." Slade walked closer. "Get some rest, because it could turn out to be a long night. We'll have to make our official statements about what went on in that barn."

Mercy, she'd forgotten all about the administrative mop-up that'd have to be done. With Andrea's death, this was now a murder investigation, and there was still one baby missing.

"I'll have some food brought up in an hour or so," Slade added, and he kissed her cheek. Pulled back. Stared at her. And then kissed her for real.

Just like that, her brain went hazy again, and it wasn't from the adrenaline crash. One kiss from Slade could make her forget all about the fear, danger and uncertainty.

Potent stuff.

And the kisses played with her breath. She couldn't seem to catch it, and when Slade pulled back, his eyebrow lifted.

"Rest," he insisted. His voice was a whisper now. "Better go now before I change my mind about what you should be doing."

She bit back a laugh and then remembered they weren't the only two people in the room. Somehow she'd managed to forget that. But thankfully the others were all caught up in the things that needed to be done for the Rand baby and the investigation. Well, all but Stella, and she was trying not to smile.

Maya gave Evan a kiss and headed up the stairs to the guest room. Her legs got more tired with each step, and by the time she reached the guest room, she wasn't even sure she could make it to the shower. However, she forced herself in there anyway. She stripped down, leaving a trail of clothes, and made her way into the steamy water.

Instant relief.

Well, sort of.

The heat relaxed her muscles anyway, but Slade's kiss was still causing her body to ache for other things.

Especially *him*.

Sex would complicate things. Would blur lines best left clear and untouched, but still she ached. It'd been so long since she'd felt anything like this. And never had the ache been this strong and relentless. It was as if she needed him, and that worried her more than the ache.

When she finished her shower, Maya found the stack of clothes that Joelle had sent her. There was a gown, cotton and a little on the thin side. Since that would only make Maya think of Slade removing the gown, she went with a pair of jeans and a top. She dressed, made her way back into the bedroom and cursed when she felt the disappointment.

Slade wasn't there.

So much for her insane fantasies of having him instead of a much-needed nap.

Maya dropped down on the bed and tried to sleep. She failed but tossed and turned while the bad part of herself wished Slade would appear at her door. She was so caught up in the fantasy of that happening that she gasped when there was a real, soft knock.

A moment later the door opened, and Slade peeked in. "Figured you'd have trouble sleeping, so I brought you something to eat."

He had a tray with a sandwich and what smelled like chicken soup. It was probably delicious and she was hungry. But Maya stood and found herself going for Slade instead of the tray.

He stepped in, closed the door and set the tray on the dresser. "Stella says she'll watch Evan for the night so we can get some rest."

Okay, that brought her back from fantasyland. She hadn't forgotten about Evan, but Stella's offer was a reminder that her son would want to be fed soon, and he'd need to be bathed.

"Her offer's not lip service," Slade added. "Stella loves kids and wants to do this."

Yes, but it was something Maya should be doing. Something she *wanted* to do. And she would.

Soon.

But for now she accepted Stella's offer of some time, and Maya knew exactly what she wanted to do with that time.

Before she could change her mind or remember all the reasons why this was a bad idea, she slid her hand around the back of Slade's neck. Pulled him down to her.

And kissed him.

THE KISS DIDN'T surprise Slade. He'd seen it coming. Hell, it'd been coming since the first time they'd laid eyes on each other. But he wasn't sure he was ready for the timing of this. Clearly, Maya had other ideas.

Nothing about this was right, but it didn't feel wrong. He should be backing away. Should give Maya a chance to catch her breath or think.

But Slade didn't want her thinking.

He wanted her in his arms like this. Wanted that needful look in her eyes. Wanted the taste of her in his mouth.

He got all of those things.

And more.

She kissed him as if she had no doubts. But she had plenty of them, all right. It was just the fire that was drowning them out. The doubts would return, he knew that, and that should have stopped him, too.

It didn't.

He was certain the only thing that would stop him now was Maya saying no. Judging from the heat of the kiss, no wasn't going to come from her lips. So he just went with it and returned the kiss.

Man, did he.

The other times he'd kissed her, he'd tried to hold back. She hadn't needed a full dose of a man she likely feared. But along with the doubts, the fear wasn't there, either.

"Can you take this off?" She ran her hand over his holster and broke the kiss only long enough to ask the question.

Slade kept kissing her when he removed it and dropped it onto the dresser next to her tray of food. He cursed the rough way he pushed her against the wall. The need was burning him to ash, too, and he tried to stave it off with some deep kisses. It worked.

For a little while anyway.

Then the kisses just fueled the fire even more, and they fought to get closer to each other. They succeeded. Her breasts landed against his chest. Her sex against his.

That wasn't enough, either.

Slade shoved up her top, pulled down her bra and kissed her breasts. Despite the hot haze in his head, he listened for any sound of hesitation, but the only sounds she was making were those little moans of need.

Maya surprised him when she caught onto his shoulders, turned him and reversed their positions. His back landed against the wall, and she yanked up his shirt. Not just up but over his head, and she sent it sailing across the room.

"Yes," she said, and her warm, damp breath hit against his chest when she kissed him there. Then, lower. She dropped some kisses on his stomach.

Mercy. It was the purest form of torture.

And it wasn't torture that he'd allow to continue if he wanted this to last long enough to satisfy a few fantasies of his own. Of course, satisfying those with Maya would take more than a time or two.

A truly unsettling thought.

He wasn't the type for long, messy affairs, and he was certain of two things right now. Maya and he would have sex, and it would make their lives messier than they already were.

That still didn't stop him.

Nope.

With her wrapped in his arms, Slade scooped her up and went to the bed. He dropped her onto the mattress a little harder than he'd intended, but suddenly speed seemed to matter. Maya went after his clothes as if this had to happen now.

It sure felt as if it did.

Slade went after her clothes, too, and stripped off first her top, then the jeans. Even in the frenzy, their gazes met. And Maya froze.

"My scars," she said on a rise of breath.

He gave her a few seconds to scramble away and cover herself. Not that it was what he wanted her to do. Nope. He wanted her naked, but he also knew this was the first time she'd been with a man since her attack, and he didn't want to add to the nightmare she already carried with her.

Her eyes stayed wide.

Her breath frozen.

"They're just scars," he reminded her. "And they mean you're not just alive, you're a survivor."

Slade lowered his head and kissed her. Slow and gentle. First her mouth. Then her neck. Her breasts. And the scars.

One by one.

He lingered a bit on the one on her lower stomach, and he kept kissing her there until her breath returned. The soft moans, too, and she slid her fingers into his hair. Not pushing him away.

But urging him closer.

Slade obeyed.

He slid off her panties and moved the kiss even lower to the center of all that heat and need. Within just a few seconds, he could feel her so close to release, and that's how Slade intended to finish her off.

Maya had other ideas.

With her hand still gripped in his hair, she dragged him back up her body until he was on top of her. Again, she froze for just a split second. Maybe she was having flashbacks. But if so, they quickly disappeared, because she kissed him and maneuvered herself so she could help shove off his boots and jeans.

Before his jeans landed on the floor, Slade fumbled in his pocket so he could locate his wallet. "Condom," he growled.

Somehow he managed to get the darn thing on. No thanks to Maya.

Again he tried to go with the gentle approach when he entered her. Again he failed. And Slade just gave up and let Maya's frantic moves set the pace. His own pace soon became frantic, too, and the need for her took over every single thought in his head.

He moved inside her. Faster. Harder. Deeper. Until everything pinpointed to finishing this. The climax hit her, racking her body, but in that moment, with her eyes glazed with passion and her face flush with arousal, her gaze met his.

Slade, she mouthed.

That was it. All that he needed to send him right over the edge. Slade buried his face against her neck and did something he rarely let himself do.

He surrendered.

Chapter Sixteen

Wow.

Maya had expected for sex with Slade to be amazing, but she hadn't expected it to be something well beyond that. Nor had she expected for her mind to be so clear. No flashbacks of the attack. Just the dreamy feel of pleasure sliding through her entire body.

"You're better than years of therapy," she mumbled.

Slade lifted his head, the corner of his mouth lifting, too, and he eased off her and headed to the bathroom. Instant loss of his body heat and weight. She missed both, and even though the room wasn't exactly chilly, she definitely felt cold, and climbed under the covers.

The thoughts came.

Of course they did.

She had no experience in handling sex with a man she hardly knew. But she rethought that. Timewise she hardly knew Slade, but it was weird. It was as if she'd known him her entire life. She was too grounded in reality—boy, was she—to believe something this strong could happen this fast, but that didn't stop the *l* word from going through her mind.

It was probably on Slade's mind, too.

And not in a good way.

He was no doubt ready to panic right now because he'd

be worried that she would see this as some kind of commitment. After all, it'd been years since she'd had sex, and she'd fallen straight into bed with him.

Slade came back into the room, and Maya opened her mouth to tell him that this was a no-commitment kind of sex, but her jaw dropped when she saw him naked. Her mouth went dry. And just like that, she was ready for sex again.

Whatever was better than drop-dead hot, Slade was it.

"This means nothing," she blurted out. Which wasn't at all the way she wanted to word that. "The sex, I mean." His aroused body certainly seemed to mean *something*.

He climbed under the covers with her, pulled her close. "I'm guessing that's your way of giving me an out."

Slade had a way of cutting right to the bottom line, and Maya nodded.

"You want me to give you an out, too?" he asked.

She blinked. Clearly, it was going to be impossible to hide her feelings and insecurities. "I'm not sure."

"Then why don't we let this just be about sex. The next time can be about something else."

Maya didn't think. She just opened her mouth and the words sort of flew out. "There'll be a next time?"

He lifted his head. Gave her a flat look. "What do you think?"

"I think there'll be a next time."

Slade made a sound of agreement and kissed the top of her head.

Even though they could both use a nap, Maya couldn't make her mind rest. The thoughts just kept flying through her head. The worries, too. Slade really didn't know what he was getting into with her and his promises of "next time."

"The condom wasn't necessary." More blurting out. "I

can't get pregnant, and it's been ages since I've had sex. I figure you're tested for anything we could have passed on to each other."

"Tested, yeah. But I've never had sex without a condom, so there's nothing to pass on."

"Never?"

He looked at her again. "Fatherhood scared the hell out of me. I even used a condom with Deidre, but I guess something went wrong." He pulled her back into his arms. "I'm sorry you can't get pregnant."

She almost dismissed it, but it wouldn't do any good. Slade knew when she was lying. "It still hurts. Having Evan helps a lot, though." She winced. "Sorry, I didn't mean that to sound as if I'm asking you to back off. If he's your son…"

What?

It was too painful for Maya to think of losing her baby.

"If he's mine," Slade said, "we'll work it out."

She was about to press, to ask him exactly what he meant by that, but his phone rang. Slade cursed, rolled away from her and without leaving the bed, he located it.

"It's Clayton," he said, glancing at the screen.

Maya groaned. She'd yet to get a call with good news from his brothers, so she braced herself for another nightmare to start. She got up and started gathering her clothes.

"Is Lenora okay?" Slade asked.

That stopped Maya in her tracks, and even though she was naked, she turned back around to face him. If it was bad news, it sure didn't show on Slade's face.

"Call me when you can." Slade hung up, and the corner of his mouth lifted. "Lenora's water broke. Clayton's taking her to the hospital now."

It took a moment for it to sink in that this wasn't just good news, it was wonderful. A baby was about to be born.

"I'll go downstairs and see if anything needs to be done."

Slade started dressing. "Clayton was working on certain parts of the investigation, and I can finish that up for him."

"I can help, too."

Slade shook his head. "Help by getting some rest."

Rest was no doubt impossible anyway, and she was about to tell him that when his phone rang again. Maya glanced at the clock. It'd been less than a minute since Clayton's call, and she prayed nothing had gone wrong on the drive to the hospital. She dressed even faster than she'd planned in case Slade had to leave.

"Hell," Slade said when he glanced at the phone screen. "Blocked number." He pushed the button to answer and put it on speaker.

"Marshal Becker?" the caller said.

With just those two words, Maya's heart slammed against her chest. Because it was a voice she recognized. It was the masked kidnapper who'd gotten away.

Slade grabbed a notepad from the nightstand and scribbled something for her to read: "Call Declan." He tipped his head to the house phone and wrote down Declan's number.

Maya didn't waste any time doing that, but as she dialed the number, she hurried to the other side of the room so the kidnapper wouldn't hear what she was doing.

"The kidnapper's on the phone with Slade," she whispered to Declan.

"I'll be right there," Declan assured her, and Maya quickly finished getting dressed, then ran to open the door.

"You listening, Marshal?" the kidnapper asked.

"Yeah. What do you want?"

"Well, for one thing I'd like to get rid of this other kid. You up for another ransom payment?"

Oh, God. Not another one.

Slade's jaw turned to iron. "That didn't work out so well last time. A woman's dead."

"Not by my hand."

"Then whose?"

"Not really sure, but I'm in this for the money only. Let me make this easy for you. I did some checking, and Maya and you have got some money. Your brothers, too. I'm thinking with just a phone call to the bank, you can have a quarter of a million within the next hour. And that's exactly how long I'm giving you to get out here with the cash."

With his gun drawn and his breath gusting, Declan came rushing into the room and no doubt heard that last part. He spared Slade a glance, slapped off the light switch and hurried to the window.

"We got a problem," Declan mumbled.

Yes, and the problem was on the phone with Slade. But something else had gotten Declan's attention.

Slade looked at his brother, cursed and returned to his call. "Where the hell are you?" he demanded.

"Oh, didn't I mention that? I'm at the ranch. Not the abandoned one. Your family's ranch. I'll call you with further instructions." And he hung up.

"EVAN," MAYA SAID. She would have raced out of the room if Slade hadn't caught onto her.

"Wait here, just a minute or two." Slade shoved his phone into his pocket and grabbed his holster and gun. "Where is this SOB?" He hurried to the window next to Declan and looked out.

"On the way up the stairs, I got a call from Cutter. He said someone broke through the back fence on the west side of the property. It tripped a security sensor, and he's headed back there now to check it out."

Hell. He didn't want Cutter, their head ranch hand, getting shot, and that's exactly what would happen if he hurried out there. "Call Cutter. Tell him to come back to the house so we can regroup."

Slade tried to give Maya a reassuring look, but he was certain he failed. She'd heard every word of his conversation with the kidnapper and knew what they were about to face. The trick was to face it while keeping everyone safe.

Slade looked down at the flurry of activity that was going on around the ranch. There was an ambulance and a car he didn't recognize. The sheriff's truck was there, too.

And he heard the footsteps on the stairs.

A moment later, Stella appeared in the doorway, and she had Evan in her arms. Maya ran to her and took the baby.

"I didn't know where I should go," Stella said. "Cutter called and said for us to all stay away from the windows, that we might have an intruder."

"We do." Slade wished he could temper that with a maybe, but the call from the kidnapper had come just at the time of the security alarm. He figured that wasn't a coincidence.

"So we need to get ready for the worst," Stella mumbled. "What should I tell the others? Dr. Landry's here. She came in an ambulance in case they had to take the baby to the hospital in a hurry. And the baby's adoptive parents just arrived, too."

Slade didn't want to have to deal with anyone other than the kidnapper, but it might not be safe for his family or the others to be on the grounds. "Tell everyone to stay put and away from the windows. Turn off all the lights, too."

Stella gave a shaky nod and headed back out of the room. Maya hugged Evan and climbed on the bed with him. The baby was sleeping, thank goodness, and maybe he'd stay that way. While he was hoping, he added that maybe this would all turn out to be a hoax.

"Cutter's on the way back," Declan relayed the moment

he finished his call. "Should I call the bank and ask them to bring out money ASAP?"

"Yeah." Slade didn't even have to think about that. This guy wanted cash, and Slade wasn't about to risk a baby's life for money.

If there was a baby.

Unlike last time, Slade had no photo. When the kidnapper called back, he would demand proof before he met this moron face-to-face.

His phone rang, and Slade expected to see the blocked number, but this time it was a familiar one. Randall.

"I just got a call from the kidnapper," Randall said the moment Slade answered. "I thought you marshals had arrested him by now."

"He got away. Why'd he call you?" Though Slade could certainly guess.

"Same as before. He wants money, and he's giving me an hour to get it. I'm trying to find Gina, and I don't have time for another game of ransom and rescue."

Slade hated this weasel's attitude, but Slade was just as sick of these dangerous antics as Randall. "Did he tell you who this child is?"

"Didn't tell me anything other than to show up at your place with more money."

"Do it," Slade ordered. "Get out here as fast as you can. Not inside the house. Wait in the driveway." There were already too many people to keep track of, and he didn't want one of their suspects in the house.

And speaking of suspects, Slade ended the call with Randall and phoned the Colliers.

Chase answered on the first ring. "I can't talk now, Marshal."

"Yeah, I know. You got another ransom demand. I got one, too."

"Well, pay it. This has to be Will. He's the only other missing baby."

The only missing baby they knew of. There could be others, but Slade wasn't about to dash Chase's hopes. Well, if that was indeed hope. It was still possible that all of this had been a ruse to get Nadine arrested, and if Chase was behind it, he was also racking up a tidy sum of money.

Of course, the same could be said of Nadine.

"Where's your wife?" Slade asked.

"On the way to the bank to get the money. She was already in town at the hospital getting checked out. Not that was she hurt, but she insisted. So I called the bank manager and authorized her to draw a half million from my account."

"You trust her to do that?"

"I had no choice." Chase cursed, and they were pretty strong words. "I needed to arrange some security. After what happened to Andrea, I'm not taking any chances, and I want a bodyguard with me."

Slade hated to mention the obvious, but… "What if Nadine runs with the money?"

"Then I'll have the pleasure of having her butt arrested, and then I can negotiate a deal with the kidnapper."

Maybe not an easy thing to do, but Slade didn't get a chance to voice that. He got another call, and he saw the blocked number on the screen again.

"Gotta go," he told Chase, and he switched over to the other call. The first thing he heard was a baby crying. Since he'd put the call on speaker, Maya heard it, too, and she sucked in her breath.

"I want a photo," Slade insisted. "Because as far as I know, that could be a recording."

"No recording," the man snarled. "This is the real deal.

He's crying his head off, is probably hungry and doesn't like being with me very much."

Slade wished he could reach through the phone and beat some sense into this man, but he held on to his temper. "A photo," he repeated.

"Yeah, yeah. Hold on to your shorts a sec." There were some clicking sounds. "Not his best angle probably, but you can see that it's a living, breathing kid. For now."

Slade clenched his phone so hard that he was surprised it didn't crush in his hand, and he watched the photo load. Definitely a baby in a carrier next to a ski-mask-wearing man. This baby was also wrapped in a thick blanket and had a cap on his head.

"Satisfied?" the man asked over the baby's cries, but he didn't wait for Slade to answer. "Here's how it'll work this time. Just as soon as the others get there with the money, you and Maya come out to the back west pasture. On horseback. Don't bring the others, just the money."

Slade was shaking his head before the guy finished. "No. I don't want Maya out there. Not after what happened to Andrea."

"As I said, that wasn't me. And it'll be different this time. Less people around. You two will drop off the money, and I'll hand you the kid. Of course, the rule is you gotta come alone. That means no brothers within sniper distance. Because I got a sniper or two of my own, and you wouldn't want the brat caught in the cross fire, would you?"

"I don't want anyone caught in the cross fire," Slade verified. "Especially Maya. That's why I and I alone will bring the money out to you."

"No deal. Maya's my insurance policy. I know as long as she's with you, you won't be planning some kind of attack. Say, I'm thinking this is more than just a protective-custody kind of thing between you two. Am I right?"

"None of your damn business," Slade snapped. "And Maya's not going out there with you."

"Then you got a problem, Marshal. Because without her, you don't get the kid. And this is a special kid you'll definitely want to get. Wanna know why?"

A chill went through Slade. Like blades of ice. "Why?"

"Because this kid is *yours*."

Chapter Seventeen

Maya scrambled off the bed and got to Slade as fast as she could. Every muscle in his body had gone stiff, and he stood there staring at the phone.

"Impossible. What makes you think I even have a kid?" Slade asked the caller. "The baby couldn't be mine."

At first Maya couldn't figure out why he'd lied, but then she realized this could all be a bluff or fishing expedition, and Slade didn't want to give this monster any more ammunition to use against them.

He already had plenty enough.

"Not impossible," the kidnapper fired back. "And once you test his DNA, you'll know."

If this was Will, then the DNA test was already in the works, but that didn't mean the kidnapper had run a test, too.

"You're taking a lot of risks," Slade said to the kidnapper. "You're sure this is just about the money?"

"What else would it be about? And yeah, it's risky. A pain, too, to get three *daddies* to cough up cash at the same time. But hey, this is enough cash to make it worth all the risks." Slade shook his head as if trying to clear it. "I don't want Maya in on this," he repeated.

"Tough. You've got your orders—now follow them. Oh, and I gotta say, this kid looks just like you."

And he hung up.

Slade groaned, scrubbed his hand over his face and looked again at the photo the kidnapper had sent him. It was hard to see the baby's features, and since he was wearing a hat, Maya couldn't tell his hair color.

She touched Slade's arm and rubbed gently. "I don't want to be out there, either, but we don't have a choice."

"I'll find a choice." He cursed and moved away from her. Back to the window.

"What do you want me to do?" Declan asked.

Slade didn't answer. He stood there staring out, with no doubt an avalanche of emotions crushing him.

"We can do this like before," Maya offered. "We'll wear those bulletproof vests—"

"No," Slade mumbled.

Maya huffed, laid a sleeping Evan on the bed and went back to Slade. "I won't let you trade me for your son."

"We don't even know if it is my son. I don't intend to trust a kidnapper."

"He has a baby, Slade. We saw his photo. If it's not your son, it's Will Collier. Either way, we have to do this."

"Maya's right," Declan said, earning a glare from Slade.

But his glare faded, and his groan turned to profanity. He didn't want to do this, but he would. Because it didn't matter whose child was out there; Slade would need to save him. It only made her care for him more.

If that was possible.

"We can't rule out the possibility that this is a trap to get us out of the house," Slade finally said to his brother. "So you, Wyatt, Maya and I will ride out with the money when it arrives. Wyatt and you will hang back, and we'll position some of the ranch hands with rifles on the barns."

"Sheriff Geary's here," Declan reminded him.

"I want him, Dallas and Harlan to stay inside with Evan just in case something goes wrong."

Maya appreciated the protection for Evan and the others even though she wasn't sure the kidnapper still wanted to get to her son. The plan seemed to have changed with Caleb's release. Maybe this was solely about money now, which could point the finger at Nadine. Of course, it didn't eliminate Chase or Randall. Chase could still be trying to set up Nadine, and Randall could be doing this to locate his ex.

In other words, they weren't any closer to learning who was behind this.

However, if they recovered this last missing baby, that was a start. Maya's stomach clenched, though. Without learning the identity of the person behind this, she would always be looking over her shoulder. Always worrying if someone might try to take Evan from her. It seemed too much considering that Slade might have a claim on him, as well.

The phone calls and the planning began. Slade used the house phone next to the bed, and Declan called the ranch hand Cutter so he could alert the other hands as to what was going on. Maya went back to the bed and held her son. Even though he was asleep and had no idea of the danger, it soothed her raw nerves just to have him in her arms.

Time seemed to crawl by, and with each passing second, the fear and doubts came. That wouldn't change anything, and it certainly wouldn't stop her. Slade had put his life on the line several times for her son, and she'd do the same for this baby. Even if it turned out not to be his.

But what if it was?

Slade would have no hold on Evan. And that meant he had no hold on her.

Well, not a legal one anyway.

Her heart had already taken the leap in his direction, but she had no idea if Slade felt the same about her. If he didn't, if this was a walk-away situation between them, then this baby could mean that she'd never see him again.

A truly heartbreaking thought.

She heard footsteps again, and while there'd been no indication that anyone had broken into the house, both Declan and Slade drew their guns. That didn't help the knot in her stomach, but the person who appeared in the doorway was Dallas. He had an equipment bag that he placed on the floor, but not before he glanced at the rumpled covers on the bed and then looked at Slade and her.

Dallas had no doubt figured out what had gone on here, but thankfully he didn't mention it. Neither did Declan when Dallas and he looked at each other.

There were more footsteps, and Stella came into the room. "I can take Evan to the family room so you can get ready. The Rands are down there. Caitlyn and Joelle, too. We'll take good care of him."

That went without saying, but Maya appreciated it anyway. She handed Evan over to Stella and was surprised and warmed when the woman kissed her on the cheek.

"It'll be okay," Stella whispered. "Kirby's boys know what they're doing."

They did, but Maya knew things could go wrong. Maya gave her son a kiss and felt that fist around her heart when Stella walked out with him. Dallas and Declan left, no doubt to get started on the plan they'd come up with to keep everyone safe. Maya busied herself by putting on the Kevlar vest and barely had it on when Slade's phone rang again.

"Company's almost there." The kidnapper's voice poured through the room as soon as Slade put the call on speaker. "I got somebody watching the road, and both the Colliers and Randall will pull up in front of your house in the next couple of minutes. But there's been a change of plans."

Slade cursed. "The only change better be that Maya can stay here."

"Sorry, no can do. But you'll have a little company on the ride out to the pasture. I want you to bring Randall and the Colliers with you."

Mercy. She didn't want those people near her. Or the baby.

"Why the hell would you want those vipers to come?" Slade asked.

"More insurance. You saw what happened the last time when bullets started flying. A woman was killed. Well, I got the same guns rigged, and I figure the more targets, the less likely you or your brothers will take aim at me."

The same setup as last time. Maya could only pray the results would be different. She only wanted the baby and didn't want anyone else dying.

"By the way, did you run any tests on that bullet that killed the nanny?" the kidnapper tossed out there.

"It's in the works, but why don't you tell me what those results will be?" Slade demanded.

The man made a sound of smug amusement. "From my angle, it sure looked like Nadine pulled the trigger."

"Why would she do that?"

"Oh, come on, Marshal. You didn't see the way Chase was drooling all over Andrea? It's my guess they were playing beneath the sheets, and Nadine took the opportunity to do away with her competition."

That might be a solid theory if Nadine loved her husband. She clearly didn't. But that didn't mean Nadine would tolerate having another woman in the picture. Nadine didn't seem to be the sharing type.

"When you do the tests on the bullet, compare them to the gun that Nadine wrestled away from me."

"You mean the gun you *let* her wrestle away," Slade countered.

"That's good, Marshal." More of that gloating taunt. "That could have happened. Or not. I'll tell you what. When this is over and you have the kid and I'm on my way out of the country, why don't you ask her all about that?"

"Trust me, I will."

"Randall and the Colliers are here," Declan relayed from the window.

"Showtime," the kidnapper announced. "You've got fifteen minutes to get everyone and the money out here, or I'm leaving with the baby."

The man made another of those gleeful sounds that sickened Maya. "Didn't I tell you that I have another party interested in buying this kid? Take the call off speaker, Marshal, and I'll tell you all about it. Wouldn't want the details to upset Maya. Women get funny about this kind of thing."

Slade stared at the phone, and for a second Maya thought he wouldn't do it, but he finally clicked the button to end the speaker function, and he brought the phone to his ear.

Maya moved closer, but she couldn't hear what the kidnapper was saying. However, she did see the effect it had on Slade. He cursed and pounded his fist against the wall.

"Don't do that," Slade warned the man, and it was a warning with a dark, dangerous edge to it.

That danger was still in every bit of his expression when he shoved the phone into his pocket and caught onto her. "Come on. We have to leave *now*."

SLADE REMINDED HIMSELF that the kidnapper's threat could be a bluff. An out-and-out lie. But it didn't feel like a lie to his gut. There was an acid pit churning in his stomach, and he wanted to rip this man limb from limb.

And he just might.

After he rescued the baby that this bastard was using like a chess pawn.

"What'd he say to you?" Maya asked. They hurried downstairs and through the house to the back door.

Slade hated to repeat it. Hated that Maya even had to consider a possibility that was almost certainly a lie anyway. But if he didn't tell her, then her worst fears would run wild.

"He said he put out the word that he had a marshal's baby to sell on the black market, and that an old enemy, someone that I'd arrested, said he'd pay top dollar."

Maya sucked in her breath. "Is that possible? Do you have an old enemy who'd do that?"

"I've arrested a lot of scum, and yeah, they're enemies." It hurt to say that and cut him to the core that it might be true. But there was another side to this. "If we're dealing with Gambill, he'd have the contacts to get out the word about the baby, but I don't think he's had enough time for someone from my past to come back with an offer."

Slade opened the door, looked out and saw the beehive of activity. Dallas was there giving out Kevlar vests to Randall, Nadine and Chase. Ironic that one of those vests might protect the very person who'd set up these crimes. Of course, maybe the kidnapper was operating alone. If it was Gambill, he was certainly capable of something like this.

"I'm so sorry." Maya gave him a gentle kiss, and that helped more than Slade had ever expected a kiss to help.

"Let's finish this." He threw open the door and stepped into the middle of the chaos.

Nadine and Chase were bickering, but when the woman

saw them, she stopped and lifted the canvas bag in the air. "I came with the money."

"And she thinks she deserves a medal for it," Chase snarled. "It's my money, and all she had to do was pick it up from the bank. When this is over, one way or another, I'm getting you out of my house and my life."

"You won't, not without paying me half of everything."

"Can we just get on with this?" Randall snapped. He, too, had a bag, and the moment Cutter led two horses out of the barn, Randall went to one and climbed into the saddle.

Chase did the same, and as if it were a chore, he pulled Nadine into the saddle behind him. Slade hadn't even thought to ask any of them if they could ride, but it didn't seem to be an issue.

Slade got on his black gelding, Wolf, which one of the other ranch hands led out. He helped Maya on and then looked down at Dallas.

"Everything's in place," Dallas assured him. He handed Maya a gun and gave Slade another one that he tucked in the back waist of his jeans. "Wyatt and Declan are in the pasture, keeping a safe distance but ready if you need them." He pointed to the trio of barns and stables. "There are at least two men on each, including one of the deputies. We have the house covered, too."

"What about Clayton? Any word about Lenora?" Maya asked.

It surprised Slade that she could think of his brother and sister-in-law at a time like this. They'd been in the back of Slade's mind, too.

Dallas shook his head. "After you're back and this guy's behind bars, we can go to the hospital and wait for the baby to come."

An arrest was being optimistic, but Slade knew that's exactly what had to happen. No way would he let this dirt wad get away with what he'd been doing, and that threat to the baby was the last straw. This moron was going down, and he'd be the one to do it.

It was dark already, but thankfully there were enough security lights on the barns and outbuilding. A decent moon, too, so he should be able to navigate the pasture. It also helped that he knew every nook and cranny, but he also knew there were plenty of places for someone to hide and ambush them.

Chase maneuvered his horse closer to Slade's. "When the kidnapper called me, he said the baby might be your biological child. Is he?"

Maya had her arms around his waist, and her grip tightened. She was probably trying to comfort him, but they were well past that point. "Maybe."

"Yours?" Randall snapped. "How the hell did you get involved in this?"

"Long story," Slade mumbled. And it was one he didn't care to discuss with Randall.

Randall cursed and said something under his breath that Slade didn't catch. "Well, if the kid is mine, I want him."

"Why?" Chase immediately challenged. "Because Gina will come back to you if you have the baby?"

Randall didn't deny, nor did he agree. He eased the mare away from them and looked around as if he expected someone to jump out at them any moment now. That could happen, and that's why Slade kept watch, too.

"The only reason you want the baby is to irritate me," Nadine tossed out there.

"I want a child. An heir," Chase argued.

And that said it all. Again, there was no mention of love or fatherhood. Chase wanted someone to run his business after he was gone, and if he could use the child to get rid of Nadine, even better.

The two started to argue again, making it impossible for Slade to hear what was going on around them.

"Shut up, both of you," he warned them, and he didn't leave room for argument.

Good thing, too, because the moment they hushed Slade could have sworn he heard something. Not the wind, nor the cattle moving around. But something. Maybe his brothers. They were out there somewhere. So maybe he was sensing their movement. Slade hoped that was all there was to it anyway.

The cleared pasture gave way to an area with trees. Oaks and hackberries. The fence was beyond that, which meant the kidnapper had to be close.

Well, unless this was a trap.

So why hadn't the SOB called? And where was the baby? Because Slade certainly wasn't hearing any cries.

Slade reined in and motioned for the others to do the same. He cut off Nadine with a sharp glare when she started to say something. Finally, other than his heartbeat crashing in his ears, he got the quiet he needed.

Still no sounds of the kidnapper.

"What now?" Randall asked.

"We wait until he contacts us." But Slade had no sooner said that when he finally heard something he could identify.

A footstep.

Soft and to his right.

He turned in that direction, looked around but saw nothing. But he didn't miss the sound. No way to miss that.

The bullet went blasting past him.

Chapter Eighteen

Slade moved so fast that Maya didn't even see it coming. He hooked his arm around her waist and pulled her off the horse and to the ground. The gelding reared, the sound of the shot spooking it.

"Stay low," Slade warned her, and gripped her wrist to pull her away from the gelding with one hand and drew his gun with the other. Good thing, too, or she would have been trampled.

She managed to hang on to the gun that Dallas had given her, and Slade started running with her in tow. He didn't stop until they were behind one of the trees. Only then was Maya able to see that Randall and Chase were doing the same—but on the other side of the horses. However, Chase had left Nadine behind, and she was still trying to dismount a horse that was prancing around and ready to buck.

"Hell," Slade grumbled. "I'll have to go out there and help her."

Since that meant him going back in the open, Maya shook off his grip so that she could hold him back. She was about to launch into an argument about why that wouldn't be a good idea, but thankfully Nadine resolved it for them. She practically toppled off the horse, and while still hanging on to the money bag, she ran behind one of the trees.

"What the hell's going on?" Slade shouted.

"False alarm," the kidnapper shouted.

He was close by, but Maya couldn't see him. It was a lot darker here than in the open pasture, and the tree limbs blocked a lot of the moonlight.

"My buddy got a little trigger happy, but everything's okay now," the man added.

That gave Maya no reassurance whatsoever. Neither did the next sound she heard. A baby crying. And not just crying, either. The child started to sob. It broke her heart to think of an innocent baby in the middle of all of this, but maybe they could put a quick, safe end to it.

"You got the money?" the man shouted over the baby's cries. It was hard to pinpoint, but the sounds seemed to be coming from straight ahead, maybe even on the other side of the fence.

Not good.

Because that could mean the kidnapper would have an easier time escaping. Judging from the rock-hard muscles in Slade's body, he was going to do everything to make sure that didn't happen.

"We got the money," Slade answered. "And Maya won't be the one delivering it this time."

"Agreed."

Maya didn't know who was more surprised by that— she or Slade. She'd prepared herself to make the money drop and bring back the baby. So what had changed this time? Maybe Andrea's death had played some part in this?

"Marshal, you'll play delivery boy for this one," the kidnapper added. "And you'll do it unarmed."

Her breath stalled in her throat. Mercy. She didn't want Slade to go out there without a gun. At least if she was the one to do this, he could cover her. Then she remembered that Dallas had given him a backup weapon. Maybe the kidnapper wouldn't see it and make Slade surrender it, too.

"Randall and Chase, throw the bags out from where you're cowering," the kidnapper went on.

Neither man argued. The bags thudded against the ground in the small clearing between the clumps of trees. Slade took out his phone and fired off a text to Declan. You have eyes on us?

It only took a few seconds for Declan to respond: Not you, only the money bags.

I'm headed out there now, Slade responded. Try to watch Maya. He fired off that last text and handed her his phone.

It helped her nerves a little that Declan and Wyatt would be able to see him when he stepped out, but Maya was terrified about the stepping-out part. Also, she wasn't too happy about Slade putting her safety ahead of his.

"Be careful," she whispered, and kissed him. Not some gentle peck. She really kissed him and prayed he'd come back safely to her.

"You, too." He lingered a moment, then glanced down at the gun she had gripped in her hand. "Use it if you need to." He dropped a kiss on her lips.

And that was it. The heart-stopping reminder and the equally heart-stopping kiss.

Slade slung the money bag over his shoulder, and with his gun ready, he stepped out from the trees. The baby's cries tapered off, making it a little easier for her to hear. But she had no idea what to listen for. Clearly, the kidnapper had some kind of backup, and it was possible those men were in the same trees where she and the others were hiding.

"First of all, drop that gun from your holster," the kidnapper shouted. "Then pick up the other bags, and keep walking toward the fence. Drop the gun," he repeated when Slade kept hold of it.

Finally, though, Slade eased the weapon to the ground just inches from him, and he pinned his attention in the direction of the kidnapper's voice, even when he stooped to retrieve the other two bags.

"Now put down the second gun," the kidnapper warned.

Slade shook his head. "I didn't bring one."

Mercy, would he believe Slade?

Maya was breathing through her mouth now, and her heart was beating way too fast. She had no hope of correcting either, and she certainly wouldn't relax until this was over and both Slade and the baby were safe.

"Start walking," the man demanded.

Slade did, and Maya felt each step with a thud of her heart. She felt the relief, too. Well, just a little. At least Slade had that second gun to protect himself. This had to end.

"When you get to the fence," the kidnapper added, "drop the money bags onto the other side."

Slade stopped and shook his head. "Give me the baby first. Then you get the money."

The man didn't answer, and Maya held her breath again. Waiting and praying. When the pain shot through her hand, she realized she had a death grip on the gun, and she loosened her fingers a little.

"How do I know you won't take the kid and the money and run?" the man countered.

"How do I know you won't do the same?" Slade fired back.

The silence came again. Even the baby had stopped crying. And the moments crawled by.

"All right," the kidnapper finally said. "Come to the fence, and I'll hand you the kid at the same moment you hand me the money."

Slade started to walk again, and soon—too soon—Maya could no longer see him unless she leaned out from the tree. Something she was sure Slade wouldn't want her to do. Plus, doing that might obstruct the view that Declan and Wyatt had of him.

She waited again. Until she heard a strange sound. Movement maybe to what would be Slade's right. And it was just the beginning. Suddenly, there were a lot of sounds. Footsteps. Leaves rustling. Even whispers.

Each new sound made her heart race even faster.

She didn't want to call out to Slade, but she had to see what was going on. Maya peeked out from the tree and saw something she didn't want to see.

Her heart went to her knees.

Because, cursing, Slade dived back behind one of the trees near the fence.

"What the hell's going on?" Slade called out.

"Not sure." The kidnapper's voice seemed strained. Definitely not his usual cocky demeanor.

And before Maya could figure out what was happening, the bullets started to fly.

SLADE DREW THE gun from the back waist of his jeans.

All hell was breaking loose. The bullets were flying everywhere, Nadine was screaming at the top of her lungs, and the kidnapper was spewing profanity. Slade tuned that out because he had to do something to stop those shots.

"Stay down, Maya, all the way down on the ground!" he yelled, and he hoped like the devil that she'd listen. The others, too. Slade definitely didn't want Randall or the Colliers in on this.

Whatever *this* was.

One second all seemed to be going as well as it could be going. He'd spotted the ski-mask wearing kidnapper on the other side of the fence, and just as the idiot had said, he had the baby in his arms. Slade had been just seconds away from the exchange when everything turned bad.

The kidnapper had blurted out some profanity and had suddenly dropped to the ground. A second later the bullets started flying. Now the question was why? Obviously, this wasn't part of the kidnapper's plan, but then, things had gone wrong with the last money exchange, too.

Slade looked out at the clearing, at the moonlight glinting off his gun, but there was no one in his line of sight. Definitely no shooter.

"Who's taking shots at us?" Slade asked to no one in particular.

But it was the kidnapper who answered. "I'm figuring your brothers."

"Not a chance." They wouldn't risk one of those bullets hitting the baby.

"It's not Declan or Wyatt firing the shots," Maya called out. "I just got a text from them, and they want to know what's going on."

Welcome to the club. "Nadine? Stop screaming and tell me what's going on where you are."

"I'm not sure," she shouted through the sobs and over the blasts of the bullets. "Chase isn't here. He ran off before the shots started."

That wasn't a good sign, and it could mean Chase was the one doing the shooting. But why? Why would he risk hurting a child he seemed to want?

He could be faking that want, that's why.

Or he could know the baby was safe. Maybe the kidnapper had ducked behind some kind of barrier that he'd put in place before this meeting. Of course, that didn't answer the biggest question of all.

Why would anyone fire shots in the middle of a ransom drop?

"Randall?" Slade called out. He wanted everyone accounted for, but Randall didn't answer.

Slade tried again.

Still no answer.

It was possible that Randall had been shot. There were certainly enough bullets for that to happen, or like Chase, he could be the one shooting.

Or even Nadine.

Slade didn't trust any of them.

He lifted his head a fraction so he could try to pinpoint the direction of the shots, but just like that, they stopped. He waited, the seconds ticking off in his head, but he didn't hear any movement. The baby was a different story. He was crying, and judging from the sound, he was still on the other side of the fence with the kidnapper. So the guy hadn't run after all.

But he likely would run now that the shots had stopped.

"Your money's out here with me," Slade reminded the guy.

"I know." And that's all the kidnapper said for several moments. "Did you see who fired those shots?"

"No. How about your hired guns? Did they see?"

"No."

Whether that was true or not, Slade didn't know. Didn't care at this point. He just wanted to make the transfer so he could get the baby to safety. Because once he had the child, Declan and Wyatt could move in and help him get Maya out of there.

"Declan still doesn't see anyone," Maya relayed.

But his brother would continue to look. That was the advantage of having family as backup. Both Wyatt and Declan would do whatever it took to make this drop work.

"I'm crawling to the edge of the fence right by that

scrawny hackberry," the kidnapper said. "Meet me there with the money."

"Be careful," Maya repeated. And he heard the fear and worry in her voice. There wasn't much Slade could do to make it go away except finish this as fast as he could.

Slade started crawling, and he tried to keep his gun hidden behind the trio of money bags. He heard the movement on the other side of the fence. Exactly where it should be if the kidnapper was going through with this deal.

When Slade made it to the last tree before the fence, he stopped and stood so he could be in a better position to react. He leaned out, looked around.

And spotted the guy.

He was dressed in dark clothes and still wearing the ski mask. The night almost completely camouflaged him, but there was just enough light for Slade to see the gun the guy was holding. He was also nervous. He kept moving his head around, and he looked ready to bolt.

However, what Slade didn't see was the baby.

"Where is he?" Slade demanded.

The guy tipped his head just to his left. "He's in his carrier. All safe and sound."

The baby's cries confirmed the location but not the safe-and-sound part.

"Now toss over the money," he demanded.

"Not until I have the baby."

"You can climb over the fence and get him as soon as I'm out of here."

There was something different in the guy's voice. An urgency no doubt caused by the shots that'd been fired. He glanced around again. Cursed. And then pointed his gun directly at Slade.

"Sorry," he said to Slade, "but I got my orders, and you're to die."

Slade had figured it'd come down to this. He already had his backup weapon in place, and he took full advantage of that. He didn't aim for the guy's chest. The Kevlar would save him, and heaven knows what this guy would do to the baby then.

No. It was a risk Slade couldn't take.

Slade saw the man's hand tense. Ready to fire. But Slade fired first.

Two shots to the head.

A strangled sound ripped from the man's throat, and he dropped to the ground.

"Slade?" Maya shouted.

"I'm okay." Well, maybe. He had to get to the baby, and he was pretty sure the kidnapper had a comrade stashed out there somewhere. After all, someone had fired those shots.

Slade dropped the money bags and vaulted across the fence. He heard the footstep. Just one. And he pivoted in that direction. He caught just a glimpse of the second gunman. Also dressed in black and wearing a ski mask. Slade took aim. Fired and finished him off.

He didn't take the time to unmask either of the men, but he checked to make sure they were dead. They were. Then he hurried to the baby. He wasn't hard to find—Slade just followed his cries. With the sorry luck Maya and he'd been having, Slade halfway expected to see a recording device playing the baby's cries.

But it was the real deal.

The baby was in a carrier seat similar to Evan's, and the kidnapper had positioned it in the center of some limestone boulders. The baby was nestled down in there deep so that he'd be protected from the bullets. That was something at least. The kidnapper had taken some measures to keep the baby safe.

Keeping his gun ready, Slade lifted the seat and glanced

down at the baby. He didn't want to think about this possibly being his child. Didn't want to think of anything but
getting him to safety.

Slade hurried back to the fence and climbed over. Still
using the trees as cover, he opened his mouth to call out to
his brothers so they could move in to help.

But Slade heard a sound that he definitely didn't want to
hear. Not a gunshot this time. Something worse.

Maya's scream tore through the silence.

Chapter Nineteen

Maya heard the movement behind her a split second too late. She whirled around, her gun ready, but something knocked it from her hand.

Not *something,* she amended.

Someone.

She couldn't see who it was, but she definitely felt the blow to the back of her head. The pain exploded through her brain, and even though she tried to catch on to anything to break her fall, she didn't manage it. She dropped straight to the ground.

The fall didn't help. It knocked what little breath she had out of her, and before she could recover and try to figure out what was happening to her, someone latched on to her hair and dragged her back to her feet.

"Maya?" Slade yelled.

He'd no doubt heard her scream, and Maya tried to do it again so he'd know where she was, but she rethought that. Someone had fired those shots, and since Slade was alive, she didn't want him walking into an ambush.

She tried to fight. Hard to do with no breath and the pain stabbing through her head.

Mercy, how badly was she hurt?

Had the person managed to give her a concussion? Or worse? Maya tried not to think of the "worse" part, and she started flailing her arms around, trying to make contact with anything that would get her attacker to release her.

She failed.

The grip on her hair got tighter, and Maya found herself being slammed against someone's chest.

A man.

That barely had time to register when she felt something else add to the pain. Not a gun. But a knife.

Oh, God.

He had a knife.

A thousand flashbacks came. The worst of the worst. They tore through her right along with the pain from the blow to the back of the head. And she relived every slice from the blade that had nearly left her dead all those years ago.

"Maya!" Slade again.

She felt herself go limp, and all the fight left her. Maya couldn't make herself move. Couldn't breathe. Couldn't scream.

Not even when she felt the tip of the knife flick against her throat.

She was going to die. Right here. Right now. He would finish what her ex had started. Maya drew in the last breath she figured she'd ever take.

And then she thought of Evan.

Slade, too.

They were both there, right along with the brutal images of the attack.

Everything inside her went still. An eerie calmness that seemed to reach right down into her soul. But in that calmness, she knew one thing. She had to fight to stay alive not just for herself but for Slade and her baby.

She forced herself to breathe. Relaxed her throat. And focused. Maya gathered every bit of her strength and rammed her elbow into her attacker's stomach. It was risky. He could just cut her throat, but her will to live was the only weapon she had. He staggered back just a fraction, but before she could start running, he latched on to her again.

"Don't make me kill you here," he snarled.

Maya knew that voice, but before she could say his name, Slade came running into the small clearing where she was. He had a baby carrier in his left hand. His gun ready in his right. But obviously he wasn't in a position to fight back, not with the baby in the middle of this.

"Let her go, Randall," Slade ordered.

Even in the darkness, she could see the intense expression on his face. Could hear it in his voice. He would do anything humanly possible to save her, but it might not be enough.

With the knife still at her throat, Randall shook his head and mumbled something. At first Maya thought he was talking to her, but it took her a moment to realize he was speaking into a small communicator that he had in his ear.

"Move in closer," Randall said to the person on the other end of that device. "Let me know when you're in place, and we can get this show on the road—literally."

He was talking to his henchman, no doubt. But what did he want with her? He'd certainly had a chance to kill her and he hadn't taken it.

"My brothers are out there," Slade warned him. "They won't let you get away. *I* won't let you get away," he added through clenched teeth.

"Getting away isn't what I have in mind." Unlike Slade's, Randall's voice was actually calm. Too calm, maybe. "Now that you've killed Gambill and his friend, I have no choice but to use Maya."

So Gambill had been the one behind the mask. That didn't surprise her, but she was shocked to hear that he was dead. And his backup, too. Slade had almost certainly been the one to eliminate them, and despite that it meant two men had died, Maya had no sympathy for them.

Or for Randall.

They'd endangered the lives of those two babies they'd kidnapped, and Andrea was dead. For that matter, Chase and Nadine might be dead, as well.

"Did you kill the Colliers?" Maya asked.

"Not yet. My assistant is holding them at gunpoint so they won't be tempted to help you. I don't want any interference, and I want to make this short and sweet."

"What the hell does that mean?" Slade snapped.

The baby stirred in the carrier, but Slade only turned it so that the child wasn't facing Randall. The carrier wouldn't protect the child if shots were fired, so Maya prayed that his brothers would be there soon.

"Well, the plan was for you to be dead," Randall said, his attention nailed to Slade, "and for Gambill to use the kid there to force Maya to have Evan's DNA tested. Best-laid plans went south again just like at the barn. Gambill set off those damn rifles before I could tell Maya what I needed her to do. After Andrea was shot—an accident, I promise— I had to regroup."

Maya hated to hear the details. Each one made the flash-backs worse. Of course, the knife at her throat didn't help, either, but the worst was having Slade and the baby there in danger.

"Why do you want Evan's DNA?" Slade asked.

"It's obvious, isn't it? If he's my son, then I need to take him. Gina will listen to reason if I have the kid. Even though she gave him up for adoption, she won't want me to raise him without her being around to, well, supervise."

So this was a crazy form of blackmail to get Gina back.

One that might work if Gina knew just how dangerous Randall truly was.

"What if she didn't give him up?" Maya had to do or say whatever it took to give Slade's brothers a chance to stop this. Besides, she might be able to talk Randall out of whatever he was planning. "What if she let you believe she gave him up and then disappeared with the child?"

"Then I'll find her." His voice was no longer calm, and it was laced with emotions she was all too familiar with. Obsession and violence.

A dangerous combination.

"You obviously don't care a thing about your son," Maya tossed at him. "Because if Evan's your son, you could have hurt him when you had your hired gun ram the SUV into my car."

"That wasn't supposed to happen. It was supposed to be a quick smash-and-grab, but when I found out what the idiot had done, he paid for it."

With his life. So Randall had killed him. That was one mystery solved, but Maya hadn't needed to hear it to know he was capable of murder.

"You said this was my son," Slade reminded him, but he also shifted his position and eased the carrier onto the ground. Maybe freeing up his hands for a fight that Maya was certain he wouldn't want to have with the baby so close and the knife at her throat.

"He might be. He sure isn't mine," Randall insisted. "I just got back the DNA results."

"So you lied." Slade shifted again. Inching closer.

"It's only a lie if it turns out to be one. In fact, I wouldn't have even known you were in this DNA lottery if I hadn't been checking for labs running DNA tests on the babies. After a few bribes, I learned the kids' DNA was being compared to yours. Wasn't hard to figure out that you were looking for your kid."

Without warning, Randall jabbed the end of the knife against her neck, cutting into the skin. "Keep moving, Marshal, and the next cut will be a lot deeper."

Slade stopped, and his gaze met hers. He didn't say anything, not with his mouth anyway, but she could almost hear him say he was sorry. This wasn't his fault. He was as much of a victim as the babies, the Rands, Andrea and she were. But he would put this on his shoulders and bear the weight of it.

"We need to end this now," Randall insisted.

"Why the hurry?" Slade tossed back. "You had ample opportunity to kidnap Maya while we were at the safe house after you had someone plant the tracking device in the grocery sack. Yet you waited for hours."

Randall cursed, and she felt the muscles tense in his hand. "I had to regroup then, too. The woman I hired to watch the kids ran out on me, and I had to find someone else."

Maya cringed at the thought of those babies being at the mercy of this monster, but at least Caleb was safe now.

"Good," Randall said into the communicator. He looked at Slade again. "My gunman has your brothers in his sight. Tell them to stay put. Do it now!" he yelled when Slade didn't say anything.

"Randall says his gunman has you in his sight," Slade finally shouted. What Declan and Wyatt would do with that info she didn't know, but Maya prayed they could still help.

"And now we have to get moving," Randall continued. "This is how it'll work. My second assistant will collect the money bags. I need it to pay for this whole kidnapping operation, and then Maya and I will go back to the house. If she makes one wrong move, I'll cut her. It might not kill her, but she'll wish it had. And once we're at the house, I'll get the DNA sample from the kid."

"Then what?" Maya was surprised Slade could speak with his jaw clenched that way.

"Maya and Evan will have to stay with me for a few days. Just until I have the DNA results. If Evan's mine, then I take him. If he's not, then I'll give him back."

She knew it wouldn't be that easy. No. Randall would have to kill her because she was a witness. Slade, too. And that also meant he'd likely given his henchmen orders to kill Slade's brothers and the Colliers.

Maya was afraid to move, but she was more terrified of losing Slade and her son. She wasn't sure what she should do until she heard the scream bubble up in her throat. Her yell blasted through the night.

Randall cursed and moved. No doubt to jab the knife into her, but Maya twisted around, trying to break free.

From the corner of her eye, she saw the movement. A whirl of motion. Slade came right at them, and he shoved her aside as if she weighed nothing. Maya landed on the ground, and Slade rammed right into Randall.

The men went flying.

Oh, God. The knife.

The moonlight hit the blade just right, and she saw Randall swing it at Slade. He was trying to kill him.

Maya didn't have a gun. Randall had knocked hers somewhere on the ground, and it might do more harm than good if she jumped into the middle of the fight.

It was a horrible thing to watch. The life-and-death battle going on right in front of her. She felt around on the ground, feeling for anything she could use, and she found some rocks. It wasn't much, but when Randall rolled on top of Slade, Maya threw the rocks, pelting him in the back.

Randall cursed. It was vicious. As was the look on his

face when he whirled around, ready to launch himself at her.

But Slade didn't let that happen.

He grabbed Randall by the back of the neck, turned and body-slammed him face first into the ground. Even though it must have broken a bone or two, Randall came up fighting. Like a crazed killer.

Slade punched him with his left fist, and Randall's head flopped back. He tried to get up again, but this time Slade put his gun right in the center of Randall's forehead.

"Move, *please,*" Slade growled. "Because I'm looking for an excuse to send you straight to hell."

Randall stopped fighting.

But Maya held her breath. Waiting. Praying this was over. However, she wasn't sure it truly was until she heard the footsteps. She raced to the baby, using her body to shield him just in case this was Randall's henchman.

But it was Declan and Wyatt.

Declan hurried to Slade and hauled Randall to his feet. He took some plastic cuffs from his pocket and restrained the man.

"Are you okay?" Slade asked her, his words rushing out with his breath. "Did he hurt you?"

Maya put her fingers over the trickle of blood running down her neck. It hurt, but she doubted it was serious. Still, Slade cursed and then cursed Randall. Since she was afraid Slade would beat the man to death, she pulled him away.

"I'm fine." That was a lie. Her nerves were a wreck, and she didn't think she'd stop shaking anytime soon.

"Is he okay?" Wyatt asked, looking over her at the baby.

Maya had to see for herself. She didn't know how the baby managed it, but he was still sound asleep. The relief flooded through her.

Well, some relief.

Maya scooped up the carrier and hurried to Slade. Even though they had an audience, she rushed toward him. However, before she could put her arm around him, Slade's attention went to Wyatt.

"How many of Randall's men did you find?" he asked Wyatt.

"Just one. He was holding the Colliers at gunpoint."

Randall laughed, and the sound nearly froze her blood.

Slade cursed and pulled out his phone. "Cutter," he said the second his ranch hand answered. "There's another gunman out there, and he's probably heading to the ranch. Stop him before he can take Evan."

Chapter Twenty

Slade couldn't move fast enough, but thankfully everyone was cooperating.

Maya grabbed the baby and the carrier, and they hurried back to the horses. They had to get back to the ranch because he couldn't risk someone kidnapping Evan.

From the corner of his eye he saw Nadine and Chase. They were arguing, and Chase drew back his hand and slapped her hard. Under normal circumstances, Slade would have intervened, but this was far from normal.

"Arrest them both first chance you get," Slade said to Wyatt and Declan, who were leading Randall back in the direction of the ranch. They couldn't risk putting him on horseback in case he did something to make the horse throw them and escaped. So it wouldn't be a fast journey.

"Call Dallas," Slade said, handing Maya his phone. There wasn't much room in the saddle with both of them and the baby, but she managed to take hold, and she found Dallas's number in his contacts.

"Randall could have a gunman coming to the house," she relayed.

And Slade held his breath, praying the gunman wasn't already there.

"It's under control," Slade heard Dallas say. Maya had put the call on speaker. "We've got the gunman, and the house is secure. The ranch hands are out now looking for anyone else that Randall might have managed to get on the grounds, but there haven't been any other security sensors triggered."

Slade didn't know whose sound of relief was louder, his or Maya's. She dropped her head on the back of his shoulder and mumbled a prayer of thanks. Slade added one of his own.

But they weren't out of the woods yet.

Now that he could slow down, he looked back at her and tried to see how bad her injury was. In the moonlight the streak of blood looked black, but he knew what it was. And it made him want to kill Randall. The acid churned in his stomach at the thought of that bastard putting his hands on Maya.

"Maya needs to go to the hospital," Slade told Dallas. "Randall...cut her." He nearly choked on the words. "And we should have the baby checked out, too.

"Dr. Landry's still here. I didn't want her outside the house with the gunmen at large."

Good. The sooner Maya and the baby were attended to, the better. Slade ended the call and rode toward the ranch.

"The baby is Will Collier," Maya said, easing off his cap so she could look at his hair.

So that meant both missing babies were accounted for. That alone was a miracle. Usually these kinds of cases didn't have happy endings, and here they'd gotten two of them.

And maybe a third.

Because either this baby or Evan could be his son.

Slade took his phone from Maya and called Dallas back. "Randall said he did DNA tests on the babies. Can you track them down and compare the DNA to mine?"

Dallas didn't hesitate. "I'll get right on it."

The ride seemed to take an eternity, but Slade finally saw the lights of the back porch. Even though the threat was over, he couldn't wait to get inside. The moment he reined in, he helped Maya out of the saddle, took the carrier and rushed her into the kitchen.

His attention went right to her neck.

He didn't curse, because there was a roomful of people in the den just off the kitchen. His brothers, sister-in-law, Caitlyn, Stella, who was holding a sleeping Evan, Dr. Landry and the Rands, who were thanking everyone and preparing to leave. They looked eager to get the heck out of there, and Slade didn't blame them. Their lives had been a living hell for the past two days, and they probably wanted to get back to something normal.

Both Dallas and Harlan were on their phones, huddled in the corners of the room. Slade knew that Dallas was working on the DNA tests, and Harlan was no doubt doing mop-up on the dead gunmen and the investigation.

"Evan." Maya made a beeline for him and pulled him into her arms.

"Before he started making some calls, Dallas said you had an injury." Dr. Landry went closer to Maya and started the examination.

"Is she okay?" Slade asked the doc.

"I'm fine," Maya repeated. "But make sure the baby's all right."

Dr. Landry nodded and glanced at the baby. Slade glanced at him, too, and the baby's eyes were wide open now. He was looking around the room as if trying to figure out what the heck was going on.

"He looks pretty healthy to me," the doctor concluded, and she took some supplies from her bag. "Let me just get this wound cleaned first. Don't think stitches are necessary, but I don't want it getting infected." She dabbed away the blood, smeared on some cream she took from her bag and put a bandage over it.

"The baby's yours?" Wyatt asked, looking in the carrier seat at Will.

"Maybe." Slade glanced at Maya. "What if he is?"

The moment the doctor was finished with the bandage, Maya brushed a kiss on Slade's cheek. "Then I'm sure you'll have no trouble stopping the Colliers' adoption and taking custody of him."

Yes on both counts. The Colliers didn't deserve to have a baby.

"How's Lenora doing?" Maya asked, but she had her attention on Will as the doctor took the baby from the carrier and sat on the sofa to examine him.

"It shouldn't be much longer," Stella answered. "Clayton said he'd call as soon as the baby came." She strolled closer, watching Will.

So did the others.

Especially Slade.

He kept volleying his attention from Maya to Evan to Will.

"Got good news," Harlan said when he finished a phone call. "We found Gina, Randall's ex. She's been in hiding because she was scared of him."

Not a surprise. "So is Will her baby?" Slade asked.

Harlan shook his head. "Gina didn't give up her child. She faked the adoption to throw Randall off her trail. I'm guessing she had no idea what kind of hell it'd create."

Hell was a good word for it. But there was a flip side to all of this. If it hadn't been for the hell, he wouldn't have met Maya. Maybe not Evan, either. And even though he didn't want to go back through that, he would go through worse if it meant keeping Maya.

Slade froze.

Mentally repeated that.

And suddenly everything became crystal clear. He knew exactly what he had to do.

With everyone's attention still on Will and his examination, Slade slipped his arm around Maya's waist. "I want you to marry me." He shook his head, mumbled some profanity. That sounded like an order. "Will you marry me?"

Maya blinked. Twice. "Uh, shouldn't you wait until you know if Evan is your son?"

"No. Because it doesn't matter if he is or not." Heck, that didn't sound right, either. "I mean, he already feels like my son, so it won't matter if we have the same DNA. He's my son, and I want you to be wife. Marry me," he repeated.

She stared at him. Licked her lips. Then pushed her hair from her face. "I'll only marry you for love."

Oh. That. Well, heck. He was really putting the cart before the horse. "Easy fix. I love you."

Of course, that didn't mean she felt the same, and Slade held his breath, waiting, hoping and praying that he'd hear the answer he wanted.

Her smile said it all.

And the way she slid her hand around the back of his neck and pulled him closer for a kiss. "I love you, too," she said against his mouth.

Instant relief. Instant heat, too, and Slade deepened the kiss until he remembered where they were. And who was watching. His brothers. His sister-in-law, Harlan's fiancée, the doctor and Stella. All seemed amused.

Even Will was watching them.

The baby was still on the doctor's lap, but he looked up at them. His expression was so intense that it made Slade smile. He picked him up and brushed a kiss on his cheek. Slade was about to press Maya for an answer, but both the doctor's and Stella's phones buzzed.

Slade held his breath, praying this wasn't another dose of bad news, but then he saw both the doctor and Stella smiling.

"Lenora just delivered a baby boy," Stella announced. "Jacob Kirby Caldwell. From the sound of it, he's got a good pair of lungs on him."

"Seven pounds, six ounces," the doctor supplied. "Just got a text from one of the nurses. Both the mom and baby are doing great."

That created a flurry of excitement. His brother had a son. The next generation for Kirby's boys.

Except it wasn't the first, Slade realized, because his son was already six weeks old.

"I'm leaving now," the doctor said. "And I expect an invitation to the wedding. If there is one." She looked at Joelle. "And maybe you'll have a girl. To balance out all this testosterone."

"I'll see what I can do," Joelle said, smiling.

The doctor headed out, and only then did Slade remember that Maya hadn't answered his proposal. She'd said the "I love you" part. He had, too, but he needed the yes.

"Don't say no," Slade insisted.

The corner of Maya's mouth lifted. "Wouldn't dream of it. You're everything I've always wanted, Slade Becker."

Declan groaned. "Not another wedding." But he winked at her.

The others came forward, each hugging Maya and congratulating him. Though it was clear they were all happy for him, no one looked ready to linger. Probably because they figured Maya and he might like a moment alone.

And Slade did.

But he knew the moment would have to wait when Dallas finished his call. Judging from his expression, he had news, but Slade couldn't tell if it was good or bad.

"Evan's not your biological son," Dallas started. "His birth mother is the person on his adoption records, and she voluntarily gave him up. Nothing fishy about the adoption."

"And what about Will?" Slade hadn't intended to hold his breath, but that's exactly what happened.

Dallas nodded. "He's yours."

The emotions slammed through him. The shock. The sheer happiness. Everything. Until Slade remembered they were dealing with Randall. "Could Randall have faked the tests?"

"He didn't. The results match the ones that Declan ran for both babies. Will is your son."

Another slam, but the strongest one of all was the love. It filled every inch of him, and Slade knew it was a love he didn't want to let go of.

Dallas left with the others, and later Slade would thank them for that.

Because he couldn't hold back any longer, Slade kissed Maya. It wasn't easy to do since they were both holding babies.

Their sons.

"You okay with this?" Slade asked.

She smiled, and he could taste that smile in their next kiss. "Better than okay. I get a smokin'-hot husband and two sons. I'm the luckiest person on earth."

No. Slade had that honor. He had Evan, Will and Maya. For the first time in his life, he had something he'd never really had.

A family of his own.

* * * * *

Waves of power and danger had emanated from him and washed over her like some seductive potion.

Their eyes had met across the room and an electric current had zapped her down to her toes. Just like now.

The rough pad of his thumb trailed across her cheek and over her lips, which throbbed at his touch. She dropped her lashes, avoiding the fire in his eyes, afraid of getting scorched once again.

It didn't work.

His palm cradled the side of her head. His lips touched hers, and her bones melted.

She huffed out a breath against his mouth as she hooked an arm around his neck to stay vertical.

God help her. She'd fallen under his spell as quickly as she had in Zurich.

But now she had responsibilities. She planted her palms against his chest, and her fingers tingled to explore the hard slabs of muscle that shifted beneath his flannel shirt.

She pushed him away even as her lips kept contact with his.

CATCH, RELEASE

BY
CAROL ERICSON

MILLS & BOON

First published in Great Britain 2013
by Mills & Boon, an imprint of Harlequin (UK) Limited,
Eton House, 18-24 Paradise Road, Richmond, Surrey TW9 1SR

© Carol Ericson 2013

ISBN: 978 0 263 90381 2

46-1113

Harlequin (UK) policy is to use papers that are natural, renewable and recyclable products and made from wood grown in sustainable forests. The logging and manufacturing processes conform to the legal environmental regulations of the country of origin.

Printed and bound in Spain
by Blackprint CPI, Barcelona

Carol Ericson lives with her husband and two sons in Southern California, home of state-of-the-art cosmetic surgery, wild freeway chases, palm trees bending in the Santa Ana winds and a million amazing stories. These stories, along with hordes of virile men and feisty women, clamor for release from Carol's head. It makes for some interesting headaches until she sets them free to fulfill their destinies and her readers' fantasies. To find out more about Carol, her books and her strange headaches, please visit her website, www.carolericson.com, "where romance flirts with danger."

For all the strong women in my life
who keep it all together.

Chapter One

Deb's eye twitched along with her trigger finger, but she wasn't packing. They'd know. Somehow they knew everything, and they'd warned her if she didn't come alone and unarmed they'd hurt Bobby.

She believed them. Nico Zendaris had made good on every threat so far. Why would she start doubting him now?

Her gaze darted among the faces surging around the frosty Boston street corner. Would someone give her a sign? She clutched her cell phone in the pocket of her coat. She didn't know how they planned to contact her.

One if by land, two if by sea? She was in the right place for signals.

Someone bumped her and mumbled an apology. She stared at the stranger's back, his broad shoulders encased in a puffy down jacket, as he lumbered down the sidewalk. Was that the sign?

She took a few uncertain steps after him, but he turned a corner and disappeared. Stumbling to a stop, she bit her lip. Should she go after him?

The message had ordered her to stand in this spot until further instructions. Was the bump an instruction? Or was the man just a clumsy pedestrian hurrying to his next appointment?

She no longer trusted her instincts since she'd allowed them to snatch Bobby. She should've known. She should've done more.

With a halting gait, she retraced her steps to the lamppost on the corner. If she did everything they asked of her, she'd get Bobby back. Zendaris had promised.

She ground her teeth against the sour bile rising from her gut. She knew better than to trust that man, but what choice did she have?

She'd have to trust him up to the moment he put a bullet in her head. Or she put one in his.

Her cell phone chirped, and she dragged it from her pocket with a hand shaking so badly she almost dropped the phone. She studied the blank display as the phone chirped again. She'd set her phone to vibrate.

She swiveled her head from side to side. Plenty of people with cell phones walked by, but nobody had stopped near her.

The phone chirped again. Gasping, she plunged her hand in her other coat pocket, her fingers colliding with another phone. Not hers.

She grabbed the cell and pulled it from her pocket. It continued its insistent trilling, so she hit the talk button.

"Hello?"

"Hello, Deb. For being a crack Prospero agent, it sure took you long enough to figure out you had a ringing phone in your pocket."

The smooth mocking voice stirred her blood, thick with rage. "That was one of your little minions who bumped into me?"

He chuckled. "Very astute of you—finally."

She didn't even know if the man on the phone was Zendaris. She'd never heard his voice even though Prospero Team Three had disrupted one of his biggest arms deals four years ago.

She growled low in her throat. "I should've dropped him in his tracks."

"Tough talk from the first and only female Prospero agent." He clicked his tongue. "But you wouldn't do that now, would you, Deb? Not while we have Bobby."

His words twisted a knife in her belly and she bit back a sob. She refused to show this scum any sign of weakness. "Let me talk to him. I'm not going to do anything more until you do. I have to know he's okay."

"Deb, Deb, Deb. He's not with me, or I'd gladly put him on the phone. Rest assured he's safe and comfortable. We'll give you proof of life soon enough."

His phrase *proof of life* had her sagging against the lamppost. He'd better show her proof of Bobby's life, or she'd hand Zendaris proof of his own death.

"When? I need something now."

"You have my word, Deb. That's all I can give you at the present time—that and the phone you're using."

She had an urge to toss the thing and the slick voice coming from it into oncoming traffic. But it represented her only connection to Bobby.

She crushed it against her ear. "What's the significance of this phone?"

"It will be our way of communicating with you. It's secure, untraceable, a very special phone. Carry it with you everywhere."

"So what is it, Zendaris? If that's who you really are." Despite the chill in the air, sweat dampened her hairline. She brushed a bead of it away. "What do you want me to do?"

"You Americans, so impatient. You just keep the phone by your side, Deb, and we'll tell you what to do next."

"Why the delay? Tell me what to do now so we can end this game." Silence greeted her plea and she was almost glad of it. A whining, desperate tone had crept into her voice—a tone she didn't want Zendaris to hear.

She examined the phone and pushed a few buttons. There were no contacts, no phone numbers appeared and it didn't seem as if she could make an outgoing call. What other special features did it have? A GPS tracking device? A camera? Were they watching her right now?

Closing her eyes, she rested her forehead against the cold metal of the lamppost and dropped the phone in her coat pocket. What was Zendaris after? What did he want her to do?

She swallowed. Why was she kidding herself? He wanted the plans to the anti-drone. He'd had them first, lost them to her Prospero teammate, Cade Stark, and then the plans had been stolen from Cade.

Neither Zendaris nor Prospero knew the location of the plans, but he must think she knew something. Or he planned to use her to get them.

The phone rang again. That was fast. Now maybe they could get down to business.

"What?"

A different voice greeted her this time, rougher, gruffer. "Face east and take the first right."

She spun around to face the right direction. "Where the man who dropped the phone in my pocket went?"

"Do it."

With the phone clamped to her ear, she strode to the next corner and turned. "What now?"

"Walk two blocks and turn down the alley after the green awning."

She spied a flower shop with a green awning in front and aimed her steps toward it. The man on the other end of the line said nothing, but his heavy breathing kept her moving.

Would they show her some sign that Bobby was okay? Maybe Bobby was down that alley. The thought quickened her steps.

She stopped at the entrance to the alley and braced her hand against the corner of the flower shop building. Her gaze tracked along the length of the alley, stumbling over two Dumpsters but nothing else. No Bobby.

Her shoulders slumped. "I'm in the alley."

"Go to the second Dumpster and take out the black bag."

Her stomach tightened into knots as she crept down the pavement, avoiding the patches of ice that the winter sun hadn't melted. She didn't want to look into that Dumpster. Didn't want to look into any bag.

Fear had her in its grip. Even though she hadn't been acting like it, she was a trained Prospero agent, programmed to laugh in the face of fear.

Without cracking a smile, she pushed up the green lid of the second Dumpster with the heel of her hand. She peered inside and eyed a black duffel bag sitting atop bags of trash and stems, leaves and broken blooms from the flower shop. She gagged at the stench of rotting organic material.

Holding her breath, she balanced one foot on the wheel of the Dumpster and hoisted herself up. She reached into the refuse and snagged the strap of the bag and pulled. It didn't budge.

"I have to put the phone down."

The man grunted in response, and she slid the phone in her pocket. Using both hands, she propelled herself farther into the Dumpster, grabbed the bag with both hands and hauled it out.

She dropped the heavy prize on the ground and crouched beside it. She dipped her hand in her pocket and retrieved the phone. "I have the bag. Should I open it?"

"Yeah, whaddya think?"

She thought if she made one wrong move they'd harm Bobby. It took her two tries to unzip the bag with her trembling hands. When the bag gaped open, she sat back on her heels, her mouth as wide as the opening of the duffel.

"What am I supposed to do with this stuff?"

"Rob a jewelry store."

The shock made her giggle and she toppled over. She sniffed and rubbed her eyes. "What are you talking about?"

"You're robbing a jewelry store. It's a few blocks away."

"Are you crazy? This is what Zendaris wants me to do? Steal some jewels?"

He ignored her questions and began giving her instructions for the robbery. He stopped after every instruction and asked her if she understood. She'd had him repeat the first few directions as the fog slowly cleared from her mind.

Zendaris was serious. He wanted her to rob a store. She knew the consequences if she didn't do it. Was this it? Was this all he'd ask of her?

She might get killed in the attempt, and if she were arrested she would never reveal her motivation. She understood what that would mean for Bobby.

"You got all that?"

"Yes."

"Don't fail."

"I don't plan on it."

She cleared out her own purse and dumped the contents into the big designer bag that was stuffed in the duffel. She pulled the blond wig over her head and clapped the huge sunglasses on her face.

While sitting on the ground with her back against the Dumpster, Deb slipped a pair of high heels onto her feet. Zendaris had told her to dress professionally. The towering heels must've been an afterthought and were more suited to a hooker than the low heels she'd kicked off, but they added to her disguise.

Peering into the mirror Zendaris had thoughtfully provided, she shoved the dark strands of her hair beneath the wig and applied red lipstick.

She crammed the black ski mask into the purse as well, and then tucked the loaded .45 inside—not that she planned on shooting anyone unless Zendaris showed up in the jewelry store.

She pushed to her feet and dropped the duffel bag along with her own empty purse into the Dumpster. She'd put her shoes and everything else from her purse into the designer bag. She tightened the belt of her wool coat and emerged from the alley a new woman.

Maybe blondes did have more fun. A few men cast assessing glances her way as she wobbled down the sidewalk in her high heels.

She passed by the jewelry store once and waited until the lone customer had left. Then she approached the door and stabbed the buzzer. They must've liked what they saw because the door clicked and she pushed through with butterflies taking flight in her belly.

Two clerks. Deb smiled. In her affected Southern accent, she said, "Ahm lookin' for a diamond bracelet?"

One of the clerks, probably a jeweler, looked up from poking at something on a glass table. The magnifying contraption he wore on his head enlarged his eye and Deb felt as if he were staring right through her disguise.

He went back to his work, and the female clerk crossed the room to a velvet-lined case. "We have some beautiful bracelets over here."

"Perfect."

While the clerk bent over the case to unlock it, Deb stepped back and locked the door to the shop, flipping the sign to Closed. She withdrew the gun from her purse as she yanked on the cord to the blinds.

"Excuse me?" The noises had caught the attention of the jeweler and he looked up with his hideously magnified eye.

Before turning around, Deb pulled the ski mask over her head, blond hair and everything, and swung the gun toward him. "Ahm sorry, sir, ahm goin' to have to ask you to move away from the counter."

He dropped his hand from the top of the counter and Deb aimed the gun at his head. "Please don't."

The clerk stood with her mouth open, holding a tray of bracelets in front of her.

"We'll start with those."

While the jeweler kneeled in the middle of the store with his hands behind his head, Deb had the clerk scurrying around the store dumping trays of jewels into her big bag.

Deb apologized repeatedly, but she knew these people would be traumatized. If she could make it up to them one day, she would.

Zendaris never told her how much to steal, so with the bag bulging and half the cases empty, Deb held up her hand. "That's enough. Both of you in the back room. Ahm not goin' to hurt y'all."

She herded them into the back office, which Zendaris had known about. She'd already collected their cell phones, and now she ripped the desk phone out of the wall and smashed it.

"Ahm goin' to lock you in here now, but you should be able to get out soon."

She slammed the door shut and dragged a chair over to wedge it beneath the doorknob. That should hold them until she got away. If she got away.

She pulled the ski mask from her head, shook out her blond hair and replaced her sunglasses. Hoisting the bag with the loot over her shoulder, she slipped from the store, keeping it locked behind her.

Her heels clicked down the sidewalk as she clutched a key chain in her hand and made for the corner. She let out a breath when she saw a blue compact car parked at a meter.

The remote Zendaris had included in the duffel unlocked the car and she slipped inside, her heart pounding unsteadily. She adjusted the rearview mirror and brushed the blond locks from her sweaty brow.

Deb pulled away from the curb. Nice and easy. No hurry. No cops were on her tail. No sirens wailed in her wake.

What did Zendaris want her to do with the jewelry? He didn't need it. Didn't want it. He just wanted her—her total submission. He had that. As long as he had Bobby.

But when she got out of this mess, Zendaris would pay. Unless she wound up dead or in jail.

Following the instructions to a T, she drove across the bridge to Cambridge and pulled into the parking lot of a hotel. She hadn't noticed any cops following her, although she'd seen a couple of possible tails and had lost them.

Maybe Zendaris's guys making sure she got to her destination.

She tilted the mirror down and fluffed up the wig. Then she wiped the lipstick from her mouth with a tissue. Not her color.

Checking in was a breeze with her fake ID and the cash Zendaris had provided.

She hitched the bag stuffed with jewels over her shoulder and made a beeline for the elevator. Once inside, she slumped against the wall and closed her eyes.

What did he have planned for her next? She'd see the fear in that poor jewelry store clerk's eyes before she fell asleep tonight.

When the elevator jostled to a stop on her floor, Deb stepped through the doors and wandered down the hallway looking for her room. A couple passed her, arguing on their way to the elevator, and a maid emerged from one of the rooms.

Deb turned a corner and located her room number. She slid the key card in and out. Red lights blinked at her. She tried again and grasped the handle, bracing her hip against the heavy door.

A soft footfall sounded behind her on the dense carpet. She turned her head to the side. But she was too late.

Something hard and unforgiving prodded the small of her back, and a hoarse whisper grated against her ear.

"Keep moving into the room…and maybe I won't kill you."

Chapter Two

Deb marched in front of him, her long blond hair swaying against her stiff back.

She looked better as a redhead.

"Drop the bag and the coat, and pin your shoulders to the wall next to the bed."

She swung around, her green eyes wide and shooting sparks. "You!"

"Do it, Deb. Right against the wall, and don't try any funny business or you'll be eating carpet."

Her bag and coat fell to the floor. Two red spots formed on her cheeks and her hands clenched into fists, but she backed up to the wall, nearly stumbling in those ridiculously high heels. Who robbed a jewelry store in stilettos?

She lined up against the wall, tucking her hands behind her back. "What are you doing here?"

Beau held up his hand—the one without the gun. "Spread your legs and put your arms out to your sides."

Her nostrils flared, and he could almost see the steam coming out of them.

She widened her stance and flattened her palms against the wall. "I'm not carrying."

"That would be a first."

"The gun's in that pretty designer bag on the floor."

He raised his brows. "At least you're honest." He took

one step back and kicked the bag toward the open bathroom door.

With his weapon still trained on Deb, he reached out and ran his hand down one side of her body and then the other. He lightly cupped each of her breasts, and then slid his hand beneath her straight skirt.

The last time they'd done this it had been a lot more pleasant.

He whipped a plastic tie from his back pocket and twirled his finger in the air. "Turn around and place your hands behind your back."

She complied and he grabbed her wrists with one hand, dragging his gaze away from her rounded derriere. He hadn't bothered to tell Prospero that he'd met Deb before, but he knew he wouldn't let this get personal. He always kept things professional—until the night he'd met her.

Once he had a firm grasp on her arm, he placed his weapon on the bed and cinched the plastic tie around her wrists. He retrieved his weapon and pulled her toward the bed until the back of her knees met the mattress. "Sit."

She dropped to the bed, and her skirt hiked up around her thighs.

Beau shoved his gun in the back of his waistband and yanked down the hem of her skirt. *Keep it professional.*

"Start talking. Why are you in contact with Zendaris and why did you just rob that jewelry store? I'm assuming one is connected to the other."

Her lush lips formed a stubborn line. "So Prospero hired Loki to track me down?"

A muscle in his jaw twitched when she used his code name. He never had told her his real name—even after the night of passion they'd shared.

"Prospero hires the best." He hunched forward, bracing his hands on his knees. "What the hell are you doing, Deb? How did Zendaris get you, of all people, to turn?"

She scooted back on the bed, and her breasts strained against the silky material of her blouse. Her jaw tightened and her eyes narrowed—green cat eyes. They'd captivated him from the moment he'd met her at that gathering of world leaders in Zurich.

He cleared his throat. "Don't think I'm just going to turn you over to the Boston P.D. for that armed robbery. I'm working for Prospero. You do know what Prospero does to traitors, don't you?"

Her Adam's apple bobbed in the delicate column of her throat. "They wouldn't… Jack would never…"

He sliced his hand through the air and straightened to his full height. "Jack Coburn will do whatever necessary to protect the security and interests of this country."

Sniffling, she turned her head away, tucking her cheek against her shoulder.

He'd brought Deb Sinclair to tears? That had to be a first. He'd had her moaning in his arms for one night, but nobody had ever made the first female Prospero agent cry.

Of course, it could all be a ruse.

He grabbed the silky blond strands of the wig and yanked it off her head. Her own dark auburn hair tumbled to her shoulders, catching the sunlight that flooded the room through the open curtains.

"Why'd you do it?"

She puckered her lips and blew at a few strands of hair clinging to her lips. "What are they paying you? I'll give you half of my haul."

Beau reached forward and she flinched, squeezing her eyes shut. Did she really think he'd hit her?

He brushed the hair from her face, his palm making

contact with her smooth skin. He snatched his hand away before the gesture turned into a caress.

Why in the hell did he think he could keep this impersonal? That night with Deb had rocked his world. He'd never forgotten it, or her.

"Make this easy on yourself, Deb. Was it money? I know you never had much growing up. Jack might even understand that motivation. Come clean and give them what you have on Zendaris."

A little smile played across her mouth. "You never told them, did you?"

Warmth burned in his chest and he crossed his arms. "This isn't about me. You're the one with a bag full of stolen jewels."

She threw back her head and laughed so hard her shoulders shook. She fell back on the bed and laughed at the ceiling until tears rolled into her ears.

When she sat up, little black streaks smudged her cheeks. "Loki never told Prospero he bedded the prey, did he?"

"It's irrelevant." Beau ground his teeth together, knowing damned well it wasn't irrelevant.

"Right." She wrinkled her nose and sniffed. "I'm sure Jack wouldn't have hired the great Loki if he'd known his assassin had already gotten intimate with the target."

"That was a long time ago, and I agreed to take the assignment before I knew you were the quarry."

"But once you found out I was the…quarry…you should've come clean. Don't you think so, Loki?" She blinked and raised one dark eyebrow. "I bet you enjoyed that pat-down. Did it bring back fond memories?"

Her emerald gaze dropped below his belt. "Did it excite you?"

He turned his back on her with the blood running hot

in his veins. He snagged the purse by the handle and dumped its contents on the carpet at Deb's feet.

The .45 thudded to the floor—not Deb's usual weapon. As he recalled, she preferred a Glock. Shoes tumbled out along with a ski mask and a tangle of jewelry.

Why would she want this stuff? She'd had a tough life as a kid. Maybe this satisfied some deep psychological need within her. And what did it all have to do with Zendaris?

Could Prospero be wrong? There had been the slimmest of leads linking Deb to Zendaris—that and the fact that she'd dropped below the radar.

Maybe her behavior signaled some kind of breakdown and not a traitorous move to Zendaris's camp.

He ran his fingers through the gems. "Why'd you steal this jewelry, Deb?"

She shrugged and the top button of her blouse popped open. "I wanted it."

"Why are you in contact with Zendaris?" *Come on, Deb. Just deny it.*

Yawning, she flopped back onto the bed.

He drove his fist into the pile of jewelry and hopped onto the bed, his knees straddling her hips, his hands on either side of her head. "Tell me what's going on."

She dropped her dark lashes, still long and lush without the mascara her tears of laughter had washed away. "I'm not telling you anything."

He blew out an exasperated breath, which stirred the tendrils of her hair at her forehead. "I'm taking you in, Deb."

Her body stiffened beneath him, and her eyes flew open. "T-to Prospero?"

"You're their monster. They can deal with you."

She bit her bottom lip but not before he saw it tremble.

"I'll tell them everything, Loki. I'll tell them how you seduced me that night when you were supposed to be guarding the emir's wife."

"Ooh, and you promised you wouldn't kiss and tell."

"I mean it. I'll tell them how we made love all night long and while you were lying there, sated and naked and conked out, I went through your things. You compromised your position and the security of the people you were supposed to be protecting."

And I'd do it all again for one more night with you.

He stared into her eyes, bright with unshed tears. "It's your word against mine, Deb."

"I—I'll ruin your reputation. I'll destroy you."

Tough words, but her voice quavered and cracked when she delivered them.

"Maybe I don't care. Maybe it's time for Loki to die anyway."

She squirmed beneath him and started to bend one of her knees for a well-aimed shot between his legs.

He dropped on top of her, pressing his frame along every line of hers as she huffed out a sigh. Her soft breasts smooshed against his chest. Her sweet scent invaded his pores.

He wanted her, even now. He wanted her traitorous lips against his. He wanted to take her lying tongue into his mouth. He wanted her deceiving hands on his body.

She thrashed from side to side. It only inflamed his desire.

He rolled from her body and stood by the side of the bed, hovering over her. "Sit up."

"That's what I was trying to do before you pinned me."

"You were trying to knee me in the groin."

"A girl has to protect herself." She struggled to a sitting

position. "You'd better think long and hard about turning me in, Loki. I'll bring you down with me."

"What I did was child's play compared to your crimes." He put more distance between them and her sweet scent that lured him to craziness. "Besides, your reputation will be so sullied, I can claim that you seduced and drugged me. Why not? Two can play hardball, sweetheart."

"I don't want to play hardball."

She fluttered her eyelashes in an amateur attempt at flirtation, which fell flat. The Deb Sinclair he knew didn't flirt like some simpering college girl. The Deb Sinclair he knew flirted like a woman—bold, challenging, sexy as hell.

"Let me go, Loki. Stealing a few jewels is not endangering national security. Besides, what do you care about that? You've always gone to the highest bidder and damn the torpedoes."

"I think those claims about me have been greatly exaggerated—maybe even by me. Prospero hired me to do a job, and I'm going to do it. This is Jack Coburn we're talking about. Nobody betrays Jack Coburn, and you're about to find out why."

"He doesn't have to know." She lifted her shoulder to rub the edge of her jaw against it. "Tell him I got away, that you couldn't find me at all. I'm a Prospero agent. That won't be too hard for him to believe."

"And I'm Loki. It'll be hard to believe I didn't run you to ground."

"Nice analogy." She closed her eyes and heaved out a sigh. "Please. I'm begging you. Th-this is not what it seems. Somebody's life depends on this—on my betrayal or at least the appearance of my betrayal."

Narrowing his eyes, he rubbed his knuckles against the stubble on his chin. She'd shifted tactics. "Your life?

Zendaris has threatened to kill the members of Prospero Team Three several times over. He's never gotten the chance."

"Not my life. Much worse than that."

He and Deb had not only had an intense physical connection that night three years ago. When they weren't exploring each other's bodies, they were exploring each other's minds. She'd told him the only family she'd had was the old man who had taken her in as a rebellious teen. Was Zendaris threatening him?

"Your foster father?"

"Robert died last year." A single tear rolled down her cheek, and his heart lurched.

Was she playing him?

He set his jaw and shoved his hands in his pockets. "Sorry to hear it, but if not Robert, who? You told me you had no family other than Robert."

She jerked her head up. "You remembered that?"

He remembered every detail of that night—the musky scent of her perfume, the smooth curves of her body, the low throatiness of her laugh and the taste of her. Sometimes at night that taste still lingered on his tongue.

He squared his shoulders. "I do, so don't try to play some sob story off on me."

"It's not a story, Loki. Zendaris is holding someone I love more than life itself."

A knife twisted in his gut—a husband. Deb had gotten married. And why not? Their connection had been almost three years ago—a one-night stand. Why would that mean anything to her?

He nodded. "You're married."

"No." She shook her head from side to side so vehemently that her hair slipped over one shoulder and then the other. "I'm not talking about a husband. I'm talking about my son. Zendaris kidnapped my son, Bobby. And if I don't do exactly what he tells me to do, he'll kill him."

Chapter Three

Much worse than a husband. Husbands could disappear. Kids stayed with you forever.

That one-night stand had meant less to her than he thought. She must've left him and run to the arms of some other lover.

Unless she was lying. What better way to get off the hook than to play the kid card?

His sharp laugh cut through the confusion. "You're good, Deb. I have to give you that. You're a pro."

"Can you unbind my wrists?" She raised her arms behind her. "I didn't expect you to believe me…at first."

He strolled to the minibar and snatched a bottle of water from the fridge. He downed half of it in one gulp. He didn't want her to see that she'd gotten to him for a minute.

"Unbind you so you can go for your gun? Claw my face off? Make a run for it?"

Her mouth curved up on one side. "You're Loki. I'm not going anywhere. We both know that."

"I'm impervious to flattery."

"Since when?" She tipped her chin at the floor where he'd scattered the contents of her bag. "Then get my wallet. I have a picture of my son."

He wished she'd stop saying that—it sounded so permanent. He slammed the plastic bottle on the credenza. Swooping down, he scooped up the wallet and flipped to the plastic inserts.

A teenaged Deb smiled at him, leaning over a chair, her arms around a grizzled African-American man— Robert, the man who'd taken her in after she'd run away from foster care. He flipped to the next picture and froze.

A towheaded toddler grinned while clutching the handlebars of a red tricycle. He flicked the edge of the picture. The kid didn't even look like her. "This doesn't prove anything."

"Why would I carry a picture of a boy in my wallet? You know I don't have any family, no nephews."

"Doesn't prove anything. Some wallets come with pictures already inserted. Is he even yours?"

"Look at the next picture."

He swallowed as he stared at Deb wearing a hospital gown and cradling a baby. She looked…happy. "Congratulations. I'm sorry for doubting you. It looks like you really do have a child, but there's nothing here to convince me Zendaris has him."

"Well, at least you admitted I'm his mother. Zendaris has him. I'm telling the truth, Loki."

"Stop—" he dropped the wallet on the bed next to her "—calling me that."

"But I don't know your real name. You never told me your real name." She sniffled and her nose reddened.

She was sucking him in again. How was she playing the victim when she hadn't wasted any time replacing him in her bed? Hell, she could've had a boyfriend when they'd hooked up.

If she'd lied about that, how did he know any of this story was true? The picture proved Deb had given birth, but for all he knew the boy could be safe with his father.

"Where is his father?"

She waved her hands. "Out of the picture."

His pulse leapt. At least that was a plus. "I'm sorry if any of this is true, Deb. But if Zendaris has your son, you need to contact Prospero."

Her shoulders sagged. "If I contact Prospero, Zendaris will kill him. You know he tried to do the same thing to one of my team members. He tried to kidnap Cade's son, but Cade was able to protect his son."

The tears ran unabated down her cheeks, and they were just about enough to convince Beau that her story was true. Nobody could fake the anguish he read in her face. And Deb Sinclair didn't cry.

He secured his weapon and hers and sank onto the bed next to her. Reaching behind her back, he released her wrists.

She put her hands in her lap and rubbed the red creases on her skin, but the crying continued.

Slipping an arm around her shoulder, he pulled her flush against his side. Her head dropped to the hollow of his shoulder.

It felt good. He felt good.

"I'm sorry." She rubbed her nose. "I don't think I've cried since the day they snatched him. What's the use of tears?"

She'd discovered early in life that tears didn't solve anything. At least her crying seemed to soften Loki's position.

And she hadn't even had to tell him Bobby was his son.

When she'd heard his voice growl in her ear, hope and fear immediately began to war in her brain. Hope that Loki could help her, especially once she told him Zendaris had his son, too, and fear that he wouldn't believe her and drag her back to Prospero.

If he did that, Bobby would die.

Now was not the time to tell him he had a son. How could she prove to him that Bobby was his anyway? The timing alone wouldn't work. They'd had a one-night stand, and as incredible as it had been for her, he'd had no idea if she'd had a boyfriend or even a husband at that time. Just as she'd had no idea if he'd had a girlfriend or wife. Might even have one now.

He squeezed her closer. "Tell me what happened. How'd Zendaris get Bobby and what does he want? Not someone to rob jewelry stores for him?"

Deb smothered a hiccup with her hand. "One of his thugs impersonated Robert and kidnapped Bobby from daycare. After Robert's death, I stupidly left him on the approved guardian list. When the man claiming to be Robert came to the daycare with ID, they released my son to him."

She crossed her arms across her stomach. Whenever she went back to that day, she got physically ill.

"How long ago was this?"

"Almost a week ago."

"You didn't do a very good job of playing it cool. That's exactly when Prospero pegged your unusual behavior. A little more digging and it was enough for them to call me in."

"I couldn't tell Prospero, couldn't tell Jack. Zendaris warned me that if I called in the police or Prospero, he'd kill Bobby." She ended on a sob despite her efforts to stop the waterworks.

"How did he contact you?"

"He left me a note at the daycare." She pointed to the wallet. "May I?"

Loki may have offered her a shoulder to lean on, but

his lean muscles were still coiled as if on high alert. She didn't want to give him any reason to shoot her.

He nodded and she reached for the wallet. She plucked a folded piece of paper from the billfold and smoothed it out on her thigh. "The pretend Robert left this when he took Bobby."

Leaning over, he read it aloud. "'We have your son. If you call the police or notify Prospero, he's dead.'"

He cursed and jumped up from the bed. "And you knew right away it was Zendaris?"

"Of course. Who else? He'd been trying to get to us through our families for years."

He stopped suddenly and spun around. "How did Robert die?"

"He had a heart attack."

"Are you sure? Heart attacks can be induced."

"Robert had already had one heart attack. His death wasn't completely unexpected."

Shoving his hands in his pockets, he paced in front of the window. "What did they do next? How did they contact you?"

"They sent me another note with instructions to come to Boston, dress a certain way and stand on a busy street corner. While I was waiting, someone bumped into me and slipped a phone in my pocket. Zendaris, or whoever, called me on that phone and told me the plan for the jewelry store robbery."

"Where's the phone now?"

"In the pocket of the coat I dropped by the door."

He picked up the crumpled black coat and shoved his hand in the pocket.

She jumped up, waving her hands. "Don't make any calls on it. It's a special phone."

"Have you looked at this thing yet?" He turned it over

and brought it close to his face. "How do you know it's not bugged with a mic or a camera or a GPS?"

She covered her mouth with her hands. That had flashed across her mind before, but she hadn't found the opportunity to examine the phone. If it had been recording everything she said, she'd just killed Bobby.

In two steps, she was at Loki's side. "I didn't even look. I didn't even think. If Prospero could see me now, they'd fire me for incompetence."

"I think they'd excuse you under the circumstances." He squinted at the back of the phone and rubbed his thumb across it. "I don't see anything that would indicate a camera or a mic, but a GPS is a strong possibility. Did Zendaris tell you what he wanted you to do with the jewelry?"

"No. I don't even understand why he wanted me to hit that store."

"Control."

Deb swallowed and knotted her fingers in front of her as she stepped back from Loki. "I sort of figured that."

"He wants to see how far you'll go to save your son." He slammed the phone against his palm. "What does he really want from you?"

"He wants the plans to the anti-drone."

"The anti-drone? Is that what I think it is?"

"A team of scientists and engineers worked on a weapon to neutralize our fleet of drones. They came up with a set of plans for a prototype and one of our agents stole them. Within a few days, they were stolen from him—from someone inside our organization. Nobody knows where they are now, but Zendaris must think I do or at least he thinks he can use me to find them."

"Then we'd better start thinking of a plan that's going

to make him believe you can do it while we work on finding Bobby."

"We?" She spun around with her arms outstretched.
"You're going to help me, Loki?"

"Only if you stop calling me that ridiculous code
name."

"I'd love to, except that night we didn't get around to
proper introductions."

His mouth quirked. "There was nothing proper about
that night at all."

Her blood stirred. Did he still think about it the way
she did? Did he lie awake some nights and relive every
sensation?

Of course, she'd had a living reminder of their night
together in the form of Bobby. And she didn't regret one
minute of it, then or now.

She thrust out her hand. "I'm Deb Sinclair. It's a pleasure to meet you."

He took her hand. She'd expected a firm handshake,
but his long fingers almost caressed her wrist as he
brushed his palm against hers.

"Beau Slater, and the pleasure is all mine."

"Beau." The name puffed from her lips. *Bobby Slater.*
It worked. "Why are you helping me, Beau Slater? What's
in it for you?"

She had to admit to herself that when she'd first heard
his voice, she'd immediately thought she could get him to
help her by revealing the truth about Bobby's parentage.
A cheap shot, but she wasn't above cheap shots to save
Bobby. But he'd offered to help without even knowing.
Why?

"If I haul you back to Prospero, that's not going to get
anyone any closer to Zendaris. If you're in contact with
him, that's a big step."

She narrowed her eyes. Self-interest—she could believe that. "Has anyone ever sent you on Zendaris's trail?"

"Yes—" he tossed the phone onto the bed "—but I'm not at liberty to reveal the identity of my employer, even now."

"It wasn't the U.S. government, was it?"

He drew a line across his lips. "Not telling. Of course, if you went to Prospero and told Jack Coburn everything you just told me, he'd believe you and probably want to use you as bait."

"No!"

"What about your team members? I know how Prospero works—teams of four agents. Let them in on it. They could help you."

"Are you afraid you're not up to the job?"

His gaze wandered lazily down her body, from her face to the tips of her toes. "Oh, I'm up for the job. I'm just curious why you wouldn't bring your team in on this. Makes me wonder if everything you've told me is the truth."

How could she explain to him her inability to trust her teammates? She had such high regard for them and would help them in a second, but she couldn't dismiss the fact that they were all highly trained professionals—men who wanted nothing more than to get their hands on Zendaris and those plans.

Would they really let a little boy stand between them and those goals? Because if it came down to it, she'd turn over those plans and let Zendaris escape if it meant keeping Bobby safe.

"Everything I told you is the truth." Except for the fact that he was Bobby's father.

"It seems strange, like something's off. I probably should just do my job and deliver you to Prospero."

She straightened her spine and widened her stance. "I'm not going in without a fight."

A fierce light exploded in his blue eyes. Then he lunged at her and tackled her to the floor.

Chapter Four

He was insane. Bobby's father had gone over the edge. But then, what had she ever really known about him?

For the second time since he'd bulldozed back into her life, he had her pinned with his body—and it wasn't as pleasurable as the first time he'd done it three years ago.

"Get off me." She shoved at his chest, which might as well have been crafted from stone. "Are you going to hog-tie me and carry me back? I'm not going anywhere with you."

His heart pounded against her chest, his breath ragged in her hair. His voice rasped. "Stay here."

He rolled from her body and began an army crawl toward the window.

He didn't plan to kill her after all, or haul her back to Prospero—at least not right this minute. She dragged a few breaths of air into her lungs and brought her knees to her chest, rocking forward.

He stopped his crawl and whipped his head around. "Stay down."

"Why? What are you doing?"

"Someone just tried to shoot you."

"What?" She wrapped her arms around her legs, curling into a fetal position.

Beau shimmied to the drapes and yanked them across the windows from the bottom. "Crawl to the bathroom."

Her mouth so dry she couldn't peel her tongue from the roof, Deb mimicked Beau's army crawl until she hit the cold tile of the bathroom floor. Grasping the edge of the tub, she pulled herself onto its edge.

A few seconds later, Beau joined her. He wedged his backside against the vanity and crossed his arms. "What the hell is going on?"

"You're asking me?" The squeak in her voice echoed in the small space. "How do you know someone was trying to shoot me?"

"You had a red laser beam right here." He planted the tip of his index finger in the middle of his forehead.

She gasped and her body sagged. She clutched the edge of the tub to stop her slide into it. "Someone had a scope on me?"

"Well, I don't think it was a light show."

"Did you see anything out the window?"

"I wasn't looking, but there's a building across the way. It must've come from there."

She hoisted herself from the tub and flattened her hands on the vanity, leaning toward the mirror. "It couldn't be Zendaris. That doesn't make any sense. Why would he kill me before putting me to work?"

"My question exactly." Beau turned to face the mirror and caught the eye of her reflection. "Unless he knows I'm here and he's putting the brakes on his plan."

"God, I hope not. If he thinks I called someone in to help me, he'll kill Bobby—before he kills me."

Beau ran a hand up her spine and clasped the back of her neck. "Let's not think the worst. Do you have any way to contact him? The phone?"

"That's a one-way phone. I can't call out on it."

"Who would be after you?"

She met his blue gaze in the mirror and swallowed hard. "Prospero."

"Prospero hired me."

She shrugged away from him and returned to the tub, gripping the plastic shower curtain with one hand. "Maybe Prospero hired two Lokis—one to reel in the catch and one to gut her."

He raised an eyebrow. "If that were the plan, I would've left you in range of the little red dot on your forehead instead of pushing you down."

"Maybe Prospero is using you." She shoved the shower curtain away from her and the silver rings clattered on the rod. "Do you really think Jack Coburn isn't aware that we slept together? He knew all along. That's why he hired you. He figured you were the best person to find me. Figured I might just trust you instead of running away…or killing you."

"I hope he's right." He hooked a thumb in his pocket and a crooked grin played across his face.

"I fail to see the humor." She shoved her hands in her hair, letting it run through her fingers and fall about her shoulders.

"Coburn wouldn't order your execution without listening to what you had to say first. My assignment was to find you and bring you in."

"That was *your* mission." Her gaze tracked to the open bathroom door. "Maybe he gave someone else different orders."

He pushed off the vanity and grabbed her hand. "I think you're looking in the wrong direction, Deb. Prospero doesn't want you dead."

"Someone does, and it's not Zendaris—at least not yet."

"We're getting out of here." He squeezed her hand. "Check out and we'll find another place."

"B-but I'm not supposed to leave."

"Do you think Zendaris would rather have you dead? He has you exactly where he wants you. He's not going to squander this opportunity."

She chewed the inside of her lip. "What if it's all a game? What if Zendaris doesn't even care about those plans? He kidnapped Bobby and now he's torturing me. He has a personal vendetta against us, you know."

"Prospero?"

"Prospero Team Three specifically. One of our members recently discovered that Zendaris's wife may have been a casualty of the raid we conducted on one of his munitions factories. He blames us for killing his wife."

Beau whistled through his teeth. "That puts a different spin on this."

"Exactly. He wants revenge. What better way than to kidnap my son and then toy with me before…before he kills us both."

Beau pulled her against his chest, wrapping both of his strong arms around her. "That's not going to happen. I'm not going to let it happen."

"Why are you helping me, Beau?" She rubbed her nose against the soft flannel of his shirt. "Is it really just to get a crack at Zendaris?"

"That and I have a soft spot for…kids." He tilted her head up with a finger beneath her chin. "Do you take me for some kind of coldhearted killer?"

She blinked her eyes. "I'd heard about you before I ran into you that night in Zurich—the mysterious Loki, Norse god of mischief. I knew all the stories—the hostage rescue in Mali, boarding that Somali pirate ship, taking down the mastermind behind that string of embassy bombings in London, the assassinations."

He put a finger against her lips. "Didn't happen."

"If you say so." She shrugged. She'd been half in love with Loki before she'd ever set eyes on him in the hotel bar where she'd been gathering intelligence at a conference of oil-producing nations.

Of course, she hadn't known the man of steel with the cobalt-blue eyes sipping scotch at the end of the mahogany bar was Loki in the flesh. But on some level, she'd sensed it. Waves of power and danger had emanated from him and washed over her like some seductive potion.

Their eyes met across the room and an electric current had zapped her down to her toes. Just like now.

The rough pad of his thumb trailed across her cheek and over her lips, which throbbed at his touch. She dropped her lashes, avoiding the fire in his eyes, afraid of getting scorched once again.

It didn't work.

His palm cradled the side of her head. His lips touched hers, and her bones melted.

She huffed out a breath against his mouth as she hooked an arm around his neck to stay vertical.

He deepened the kiss, slanting his mouth across hers, sliding his tongue between her teeth.

God help her. She'd bed him as quickly as she had in Zurich. He could have her right here on the bathroom floor and she'd welcome any discomfort, any inconvenience to have him inside her again.

But now she had responsibilities. She planted her palms against his chest, and her fingers tingled to explore the hard slabs of muscle that shifted beneath his flannel shirt.

She pushed him away even as her lips kept contact with his.

Despite her mixed messages, he got the hint and stepped back, ending their heated kiss. He cleared his throat. "Sorry."

"Me, too." She put a hand over her mouth as if to remove the temptation. "It just felt kind of good to share my burden, you know?"

Of course, sharing her burden didn't mean winding up in bed with the first man to offer his help. Not that Loki was just some man. He'd been *the* man for the past three years of her life.

"Let's get out of here." He dropped to the floor again. "I'm going to get that wig for you. Wear it out of here. We're going to have to take the car Zendaris provided or he'll wonder how you're getting around."

"It's parked in the hotel parking lot. Where are we going?"

"Another hotel, but we'll stay in Cambridge just so you can show good faith to Zendaris. We don't want him to think you're trying to escape."

"What if that sniper was a test? What if he wants me to stay put no matter what happens?"

"Even Zendaris is not going to expect you to put yourself in mortal danger. He wouldn't trust someone like that to find the anti-drone plans."

Beau crawled back across the floor and swept the blond wig from the bed along with the phone and dragged the designer bag over the carpet. Once back in the bathroom, he shoved them at her.

"Here you go."

She tucked her hair beneath the wig, punched her arms into the sleeves of the coat and slung the heavy bag over her shoulder. "I'm ready."

Beau poked his head into the hallway and then gestured her through the door. Placing a hand against the small of her back, he guided her toward the stairwell. "Can you navigate the stairs in those shoes? I don't want to be a sitting duck in the elevator."

She kicked off the shoes and shrank five inches, her head barely reaching Beau's chin. "Lead the way."

They ducked into the stairwell. The rubber soles of Beau's running shoes squelched against the steps while her bare feet made her his silent companion.

"We have to go through the lobby to get to the parking garage." She pointed at the metal door on the ground floor.

"Keep your head down." He pushed open the door.

People crisscrossed the lobby on their way back from their business meetings or sightseeing for the day. Deb's gaze darted from group to group, seeing some imagined threat in each one.

Beau hustled her out the side door onto a cement path that led to the garage. He blocked her body with his, his blue eyes wary and alert, his hand nestled in his pocket— the pocket where his gun resided.

He still had her weapon, too. He may be planning to help her rescue Bobby, but he didn't quite trust her.

Should she trust him?

Maybe his willingness to help her was a ploy to get her back to Prospero. And the kiss had been designed to soften her up.

If Beau planned to turn her over to Prospero, he'd learn soon enough she still had a few tricks up her sleeve. She'd fight like a caged animal to save Bobby, even if that meant doing battle against Bobby's father.

She'd put her shoes back on before they hit the lobby and now the clicking sound of the heels echoed on the parking garage's cement floor. "The car's in the next aisle."

She unlocked the car as they approached it. Beau slid into the passenger seat and she tossed the bag into the backseat. Revving the engine, she turned toward him. "Where to?"

He rattled off some directions when they exited the parking structure.

"I wanted to get more info from you before that sniper took aim at your head. Where were you when Bobby was kidnapped? Where do you live?"

"In Virginia, outside of D.C."

"Zendaris sent you to Boston after the kidnapping?"

"Yes. Turn here?"

He nodded. "Is the jewelry heist the first thing he asked of you?"

"After he told me to fly into Logan Airport."

"Do you think Bobby's still in the Virginia area, or do you think he's here?"

"My gut tells me he's here. If the plans are in Boston Zendaris would want to do the swap here, not go back to Virginia." She gripped the steering wheel to stem the tide of panic that washed through her every time she thought about Bobby being held captive by that maniac.

"Any idea what's in Boston?"

"Besides a jewelry store on Beacon Hill? I have no idea. As far as we know, Zendaris doesn't have any connections here."

"Interesting." Beau tapped his chin with his middle finger.

"What's interesting? Boston?"

"The old Deb Sinclair would know that there's a symposium on weapons of the future at MIT this week."

"Really?" Her head jerked his way. She didn't have

the heart to tell him the old Deb Sinclair had melted into a puddle on the floor of her son's daycare the day he went missing.

But this new Deb Sinclair wasn't so unfamiliar. This Deb Sinclair, ruled by fear and anger, had controlled the first sixteen years of her life, until she'd had the good fortune to try to steal from Robert Elder.

"I don't think it's a coincidence that Zendaris sent you to Boston at the same time as this gathering. He wants those anti-drone plans. Maybe he thinks one of the symposium's attendees has them."

"This is an international gathering?"

"It is. Scientists and engineers from all over the world will be there."

She drummed her thumbs against the steering wheel, feeling a spark of life for the first time since Bobby's abduction. Her brain clicked and whirred as if coming to life after a long winter hibernation.

"He could be right. Maybe the woman who stole the plans from Stark sold them to the highest bidder before she died. Maybe she had no intention of giving them back to Zendaris."

"The woman who stole the plans is dead? Did Zendaris kill her?"

"One of ours did, self-defense. She was mentally unbalanced."

"Those are the hardest ones to figure out. There's no telling what she did with the plans or why she did it."

"Still, you're right. My presence in Boston at the same time as the symposium is no coincidence. Have the meetings started yet?"

"Meetings have been ongoing for two days."

"Did you connect my being in Boston with this conference?"

"Not until you told me about the anti-drone plans."

"Then why was this symposium even on your radar?"

He turned his head to look out the window. "It's my business to know."

And just like that, Beau the helpful spy morphed into Loki, man of mystery and danger.

She pulled into the loading zone of the new hotel and Beau got them a room.

He dropped onto the passenger seat and tipped his head toward the windshield. "You can park up that ramp."

Ten minutes later they were traipsing down another hotel hallway, but Deb felt less trepidation now that she had Beau by her side. Or should she be feeling more?

His concern could all be an elaborate ruse to lull her into compliance. When she least expected it, her Prospero teammates could crash the party and drag her back for questioning all at Beau's invitation. But her brothers on Team Three had to know she'd never betray them.

Then why not confide in them? The words floated through her mind, and even her answer to that question felt like a betrayal.

Beau pushed open the hotel room door. "One room but two double beds. Hope that's okay."

"That's fine." She tossed the purse onto the bed farthest from the window. "And I hope it's okay that I snag the bed away from the window."

"I was going to suggest it." He clicked the remote control for the TV and swiped a room service menu from the table. "Are you hungry? Maybe we should just eat in the room tonight."

She twitched aside the curtain at the window. "You're sure we weren't followed?"

"Positive." He waved the menu. "Food?"

"Yeah, whatever." She hadn't eaten a decent meal since Zendaris had snatched Bobby.

She plucked the special phone from her pocket and placed it on the nightstand.

Beau said, "He's sure taking his sweet time."

"He's holding all the cards." Deb shrugged out of the coat and hung it in the closet. Then she toed off the heels and stretched out on the bed, stacking a few pillows behind her back and crossing her legs at the ankles.

"I'll order for both of us if that's okay." He peered at her over the top of the menu. "You look like you could use a good meal."

"Food has been low on my list of priorities lately."

"You should know from training that you need to keep yourself in fighting condition."

"You don't get it." That's why she never confided in her Prospero brothers, either. They weren't mothers. When Zendaris had kidnapped her son, he'd carved a hole in her heart. He'd left her half a person.

Beau was Bobby's father, but he didn't know he was a father. He could talk about being in fighting condition and being aware of one's surroundings, but he was a whole person, not a shell like she'd become.

Beau shrugged and picked up the phone. He cradled the receiver against his shoulder as he read off enough dishes to feed the entire hotel.

Deb fluffed up the pillows behind her and stared at the local TV news through half-closed eyes. A shot of MIT had her leaning forward. She snapped her fingers at Beau, who was adding desserts to their order.

She simulated pressing buttons on a remote and he tossed it to her. She increased the volume on the TV.

The voice-over of the reporter droned on about a

weapons symposium. The brief report didn't mention any names until the very end.

"Dr. Scott Herndon, professor emeritus at MIT and frequent advisor to the Pentagon, is chairing the symposium, which will include a gala event on the last night to raise funds for war-torn areas across the globe."

When the report ended, Deb muted the sound. "That's it, isn't it? Sounds like a big deal."

"Anything discussed in those meetings is going to be top secret. How does Zendaris expect to get any information out of that symposium?"

"The symposium ends tomorrow." She glanced at the cell phone on the nightstand. "If Zendaris wants me to make a move, you'd think he would've contacted me by now—unless that scope to the forehead was his way of reaching out."

"I don't think Zendaris is trying to kill you. It doesn't add up." Beau perched on the edge of the other bed and rested his ankle on his knee. "Any assignment he has for you will most likely come at the last minute to give you less time to prepare. He wants to keep you off balance."

"He's doing a great job." She tossed the remote to Beau's bed and collapsed against her pillows. "He still hasn't allowed me any contact with Bobby. I don't even know for sure if he's alive or…"

"What's the matter with you?" Beau smacked his hand against his thigh. "You need that proof of life, Deb. Don't do another thing he tells you to do unless you get something on Bobby."

"I demanded it the last time we spoke, but he refused." Crossing her arms, she hunched her shoulders against the persistent chill in her bones.

"You hold some cards here, too. Before you carry out

your next assignment, you need assurance of Bobby's safety."

"What if he refuses again and threatens to hurt him? I can't play chicken with my son's life." She rubbed her tingling nose. "What makes this even worse is that Bobby wasn't in the best of health prior to the kidnapping."

"He was sick?"

"He'd been listless, which was so unlike him. I thought he may have caught a bug, but he didn't have any cold or flu symptoms."

"Did you take him to the doctor?"

She slid a glance at Beau, who'd twisted around on the foot of the bed to face her. Did he sense his connection to Bobby on some level?

"He had a doctor's appointment the day before he was snatched. The doc ran some tests on him, took his blood and urine, that type of thing. I haven't heard anything back from the tests yet, but it's only been a week."

"Then you really need to demand to see him or talk to him. What story is Zendaris feeding him?"

"I have no idea. He's only two. I'm sure he doesn't understand why I've abandoned him." She covered her face with her hands. "Once a child is abandoned, he never gets over it."

The mattress sank and Beau encircled her wrists with his fingers. "Nonsense. You recovered nicely. Hell, you're one of the most well-adjusted people I know."

"You don't know me. We spent one night together."

"That's all I need to figure someone out."

She spread her fingers and peeked at him through the spaces. "That's not saying much considering the types of people you hang out with."

He raised his brows. "When I'm not doing the spy thing, I have the most boring existence you can imagine.

My dad's a mechanic, my mom's a secretary at the local high school. Staid. Boring."

"Is that why you went all out on the career path to become one of the most feared assassins in the business?"

His jaw tightened as he shook his head. "I'm no assassin, Deb. Nobody got killed who didn't deserve it. Nobody who wasn't a threat to other lives."

Someone rapped on the door with a shout. "Room service."

Holding out his hand, Beau rose from the bed and crept to the door, lifting his weapon from its holster on the way. He stood to the side of the door and put his eye to the peephole. "Can you slide the check under the door, man? I'll sign it, send it back and you can leave the food."

"Sure."

A slip of paper sailed beneath the door and Beau plucked it from the carpet. He backed up to the credenza and signed the bill. Then he shoved it back through the door and watched from the peephole.

The waiter called out, "Thanks."

Beau waited several seconds and then opened the door and wheeled the cart into the room. "Can't be too careful, huh?"

"If he's been working in hotels a while, I'm sure he's seen everything."

Beau stationed the cart by the table and began lifting silver domes. "Looks good. You hungry?"

The steam that rose from the dishes carried some savory scents that made her mouth water. It had been several days since she'd eaten a real meal, and her stomach grumbled with the realization.

"I *am* hungry."

Beau transferred the plates from the cart to the table and pulled out a chair. "Have a seat."

Deb shook out a thick white napkin and dropped it on her lap. She started with the soup and didn't stop until she'd licked the last smudge of cream cheese frosting from her fork.

"How long has it been since you've eaten more than a few bites of food?"

She patted her mouth with the napkin. "Since the day they took Bobby."

"I thought so. You look—" his gaze dipped from her face to her body and back again "—a little thinner than when I last saw you."

Warmth crept into her cheeks and she covered the bottom half of her face with the napkin, pretending to wipe her mouth again. He should know.

They'd spent almost the entire night naked in her hotel room. They'd eaten room service that night, too, but not seated at a table with napkins in their laps. They'd lounged across the king-size bed, feeding each other morsels of food, even incorporating the chocolate cake into their lovemaking. Instead of daintily patting their mouths with napkins, they'd hauled off to the shower, together.

She coughed. "Being a mom keeps me on my toes. I don't have as much time to work out at the gym, but I get to run at the playground and throw balls and chase after a speeding tricycle."

"Sounds like you love it…and him."

Deb studied his face. Was it time to tell him Bobby was his? *Nope.* Loki wouldn't want to be saddled with a son anyway. How could he squeeze in a battle with Somali pirates between Little League games?

Beau Slater may have come from ordinary, but he didn't want to go back there.

The cell phone by the bed chirped. The fork she'd been

dragging across a plate dropped with a clatter and she half rose from her chair.

"It's him."

"Answer it. It's what you've been waiting for."

She swallowed and all the sweetness from the carrot cake dissolved like ashes on her tongue. When the phone rang for the fourth time, she dived across the bed and grabbed it.

"Yes?"

"Good job at the jewelry store. You can keep the loot."

"I don't want it. What was the point of that? Someone could've gotten hurt."

Beau jerked his thumb up, and she punched a button for the speaker.

"Someone would've gotten hurt if you hadn't followed our instructions, Deb. Just look at it that way."

"I—I'm in a different hotel. Someone was aiming a high-powered weapon into my hotel room this afternoon. I saw the beam on the wall."

Zendaris sucked in a breath. "Are you scamming me, Deb?"

"Are you scamming me? Are you trying to kill me?"

"Why would I do that? We're just getting started." He clicked his tongue. "But maybe your colleagues want you dead."

"Never." Her gaze darted toward Beau slumped in his chair, his fingers steepled beneath his chin. Why had Prospero sent the best in the business after her?

"Are you sure about that? If the mighty Jack Coburn gets wind of your betrayal, you're finished."

She ground her teeth together. "It's not a betrayal if it's coerced."

"But they don't know that, do they? Do they, Deb?"

"As far as Prospero is concerned, I'm on a leave of absence. They have no reason to suspect otherwise."

"Where are you?"

"Another hotel in Cambridge." She held her breath. Would he demand the location?

"Excellent."

"What next, Zendaris? A bank robbery? A high-speed chase?"

"A party."

She raised her shoulders at Beau. "You want me to go to a party?"

"A very special party with very special people."

"Where?" Deb licked her lips.

"In Boston. You'll be attending the gala fundraiser as part of the Symposium on Alternate Methods of Defense."

"What do you want me to do at this party besides eat, drink and be merry?"

"I want you to get close to Dr. Scott Herndon."

"Get close to him and do what?"

"Kill him."

Chapter Five

Beau bolted upright. The man couldn't be serious.

Deb choked out one word. "Why?"

"That's not your concern for now. Let's just say I'm sending a message."

"How am I supposed to kill Dr. Herndon in a roomful of people?" She shook her head at Beau, her eyes wide and glassy.

He wanted to go to her and smooth away the worry, but now wasn't the time. And what could he possibly say to comfort her? The man had her son and she'd do anything to protect him.

"I'm leaving the logistics of the crime in your capable Prospero hands, Deb. You figure it out, but at the end of the evening Dr. Herndon will no longer be drawing breath."

Beau vaulted from the chair and tapped Deb on the knee. He mouthed, *Bobby*.

She closed her eyes. "I'm not killing Dr. Herndon or anyone else until I have proof that my son is okay."

"He's fine, just a little tired. You'll see when I decide you'll see."

Beau squeezed her knee and shook his head. Zendaris needed her. She had the power right now.

"No. I need to see or talk to him before the event tomorrow night, or it's not happening."

Zendaris paused and then sighed. "All right. Not tonight. Tomorrow morning. Are you ready for your instructions?"

For the next five minutes, Zendaris explained to Deb how to pick up her ticket to the event, her identity for the evening, and the dress code. He must've given her that wad of cash in the bag to carry out her assignments without leaving a trail of credit card receipts.

When she ended the call, Beau held out his hand for the phone and she dropped it in his palm.

He examined it again, but couldn't see any way to track the number or location of the phone Zendaris used to call her. He didn't want to take the device apart in case that sent some sort of signal to Zendaris.

"I can't kill someone."

"You're not going to kill Dr. Herndon. We'll figure out a way to trick Zendaris."

"I don't see how. The death of Dr. Scott Herndon is going to be big news."

"Prospero never faked a death before?"

"Prospero may have but I haven't."

"I have, so you're in luck."

She crossed her legs beneath her and pushed the hair from her face. "You were right about demanding to see Bobby. He gave in."

"Of course he did." He dropped the phone back on the bed. "Zendaris needs you. If he harms Bobby now, you're no longer his puppet."

"You were also right about that defense symposium."

"It would've been clear to you, too, Deb, if you'd been thinking straight. That's half of Zendaris's advantage over you, and he knows it. You're rattled. But he didn't count on me."

"I never thought I could count on you, either." She grabbed his arm. "Why are you really helping me, Beau? Are you hoping to bag Zendaris on your own? I can't believe you'd put my son before that goal."

"Why do you keep asking me that question, Deb? I told you the prospect of getting close to Zendaris is tempting, but I'm not going to put a child's life at risk to do it." He traced the knuckles of her hand. "Can you put aside your trust issues for a while to believe me?"

She released his arm, leaving crescent imprints from her fingernails. "I don't know why I should trust you. I never figured you for a family man with any strong feelings for children. So it makes me wonder even more why you're torpedoing your own assignment to help me."

"Maybe I don't have strong feelings for children." He ran a hand along her thigh. "But that doesn't mean I don't have some feelings for you."

"Do you always run around jeopardizing your career for one-night stands?"

"Are you done eating?" He pushed off the bed and began loading plates and serving dishes back onto the cart.

"I'm glad I ate before that phone call because I just lost my appetite." She rolled onto her stomach and planted her elbows on the bed while balancing her chin in one palm. "What did you think of Zendaris?"

He clanged a silver cover back over a serving dish. "A scumbag of the highest order."

"I mean, do you think that was him on the phone? Have you ever heard his voice?"

"No." He dabbed at a cake crumb and sucked it into his mouth. "I know he's of Greek descent and spent time in

Italy, so the accent of the guy on the phone would match that. I thought Prospero finally got a line on him. That was the chatter."

"We did. The former nanny for Zendaris's children was able to give us a composite. We know what he looks like now—when he's not in disguise."

"But he's always in disguise."

"Just like you."

"Not always." He ran a hand through his hair, shorter than he usually wore it. "This is my real hair, my real eye color."

"You've been known to sport a beard, long hair, glasses, extra weight. Why no disguise for this assignment?"

He shoved the cart ahead of him toward the door. "I guess I wanted you to recognize me. I didn't wear a disguise that night, either."

"You didn't wear much of anything that night."

"Glad you noticed." He gripped the handles of the cart to the breaking point and wheeled it to the door.

Her low, throaty voice and half-lidded eyes had caused a jolt of lust to claim half his body—the bottom half. This was the Deb he remembered. This was the Deb he still wanted.

But she'd pushed him away after the kiss. Why the mixed messages now? Her emotions were all over the place. The fear she felt for her son caused her to seek solace, and maybe the only way she knew how to elicit comfort from him was through seduction. Maybe she just wanted some physical contact, but the only physical contact they knew was sexual.

Probably wasn't a good idea to mix business with pleasure, so much pleasure. But then it hadn't been a good idea to take this assignment in the first place. He should've come clean to Prospero about his heated fling with Deb.

He shoved the cart against the wall in the hallway and stepped back into the room. "You have a long day ahead of you tomorrow. You should get some rest. Do you have toiletries? Do you want me to pick some up downstairs? I at least need a toothbrush."

"That would be great. I flew into Logan this morning. Zendaris didn't tell me to pack a bag, so I didn't."

"I'll pick up the basics, and you can get more of what you need tomorrow when you go shopping for the party dress."

"Do you think he's watching me?"

"He seemed genuinely surprised by the sniper, and he didn't ask you the details of your hotel. I don't think so. He doesn't need to. He has his insurance.

"Keep the door locked and chained and don't open it for anyone." He strode to the window and pulled the drapes closed even though their window faced the Charles River. "And stay away from the window."

He slipped out the door and paused with his head bent until he heard the lock and chain slide into place.

Waiting for the elevator, he glanced to his left when he heard a door close. He poked his head into the corridor, but all the doors remained closed. Maybe someone had gone for ice or the vending machine.

He rolled his shoulders and stabbed at the elevator button again. He was on edge and it felt good, natural. He'd let his encounter with Deb throw him off his stride. His assignment may have changed but he was still on assignment. Still on the job.

The elevator skimmed down to the first floor without stopping. He crossed the lobby and headed for the shop he'd seen when he'd checked in.

He bought some toothpaste, toothbrushes, a comb and several other items to get them through the night and the next morning. As he grabbed the small bag with his purchases, his cell phone buzzed once in his pocket.

He exited the store and leaned against the wall outside the restaurant bar. He checked the phone's display and sucked in a breath. *Prospero.*

If he ignored the message, he wouldn't have to lie to Jack. If he ignored the message, Jack would read that as totally out of character for Loki.

If Jack wanted status, he'd give Jack status. He'd tell him he'd tracked the quarry to Boston—not a lie. Prospero wouldn't send anyone else out here to check on his progress. The stalwart men of Prospero trusted him.

That was their first mistake.

He sent a text that he might have a lead on Deb heading to Boston. The only response he got from Jack was *Roger.*

Yeah, the man still trusted him. But Beau had no intention of letting Jack down, or letting Deb down. He'd stay true to Prospero, help Deb and rescue her son as icing on the cake.

When he got back to the room, he tapped on the door and stood in full view of the peephole. The hotel staff had removed the room service cart.

The chain scraped in its slot and the door inched open. Beau pushed it wide. "Are you okay?"

Deb rubbed her eyes. "I fell asleep. What took you so long?" She yawned and held out her hand for the bag swinging from his fingertips.

She didn't need to know he'd had contact with Jack. He tossed the bag to her. "I had a lot of shopping to do."

Peering into the bag, she wrinkled her nose. "I'm going to have to do a lot better than this when I hit that party tomorrow night."

"You and me both."

Her eyes widened as she looked up. "You're going, too?"

"How else are we going to stage a murder?"

DEB ROLLED ONTO her stomach and burrowed her head into the pillow, trying to cling to the fading wisps of her dream. Its images had already slipped from her consciousness, but the dream had left her with a feeling of contentment—a feeling all too rare in the daylight hours.

She hadn't slept that peacefully since the day she'd lost Bobby, and she owed that sound sleep to the man in the next bed.

Shifting her head on the pillow, she opened one eye and drank in the sight of Beau sprawled on the bed next to hers, one bare leg hanging off the side, both arms wrapped around a pillow.

He stirred and murmured something into the pillow.

Was he having sweet dreams, too? She'd wanted nothing more than to crawl under the covers with him last night, but she recognized the urge for what it was—a need for comfort. He was already doing his part. She couldn't ask him for his shoulder to lean on in addition to everything else he was doing for her.

He didn't owe her anything. Hell, he didn't even know Bobby was his son.

She cleared her throat and the noise acted like a prod.

Beau's eyes flew open and he bolted upright in the bed. "What?"

"I'm sorry. I just coughed. I didn't mean to wake you up." In fact, she'd been enjoying studying his face in repose. Now she was enjoying the way the sheet had fallen to his waist, exposing his bare chest.

Maybe she did want more than comfort from Beau.

The fire she'd felt when she'd first met him had never died. Being with him again had ignited the kindling flame.

She averted her gaze. Her attraction for Beau caused knots of guilt to form in her belly. Zendaris had her son. How could she even be thinking about sex?

Did that make her a bad mother? The fact that she'd allowed her son to be kidnapped made her a bad mother. Cade Stark would've never allowed that to happen to his son.

She buried her face in the pillow.

"Do you want to have breakfast downstairs before we go shopping?"

"Zendaris is supposed to send me confirmation that Bobby is okay today, before the party."

Beau swung his legs over the side of the bed and planted his feet on the floor with the sheet still twisted around his torso. "He'll use that cell phone to do it. Keep it with you."

"The only clothes I have are the ones I wore yesterday." She scooted up against the headboard. "I brought some cash with me, so I'm going to pick up a pair of jeans and a few shirts."

"All I have is yesterday's clothes, too. I'm going to need a tux for tonight."

"You still haven't explained how you're going to get into that party."

"One of the guests is going to lose his ticket. Isn't that what Zendaris told you? All guests needed a ticket?"

"He said he'd leave mine for me today."

"Obviously, if he has you go to a pickup location, you go alone. He and his cohorts might be watching." Beau rose from the bed and the covers fell from his body.

His boxer briefs clung to his heavily muscled thighs,

and he stretched, the rest of his muscles shifting and bunching.

"And tonight?" Deb swallowed and tugged the sheet up to her chin. "We'll have to go separately tonight."

"Yeah, just in case he's watching the crowd. I doubt it though. He's not going to want to be anywhere near that party especially since Prospero now has an accurate description of him."

"But he's the master of disguise."

Beau shrugged. "Aren't we all? Do you want the shower first?"

"Go ahead."

When Beau disappeared into the bathroom, Deb turned up the volume on the TV. She didn't need to hear the water running and imagine how Beau looked with it sluicing across the planes of his body. She didn't have to imagine because she'd seen it—and him—in the flesh.

Amazing how that one night of unbridled passion had led to Bobby, and in a twisted way had led them back to each other. She'd figured Bobby's paternity had been her ace in the hole to sway Beau from hunting her to helping her. And she hadn't even needed it to convince him.

He'd been ready to help her as soon as she'd explained her predicament to him. He hadn't needed to hear that Bobby was his.

The shower stream stopped and several minutes later, Beau called from the bathroom. "It's all yours, and I even left you some hot water."

They hadn't had that problem when they'd showered together.

She dragged the sheet from the bed and wrapped it around her body. She shuffled toward the bathroom, clutching her wrinkled skirt and blouse under one arm.

Holding her breath, she squeezed past Beau standing at

the vanity mirror, the white hotel towel wrapped around his waist, heat emanating from his body.

"I won't be long."

"Where's the phone in case he contacts you while you're in the shower?"

She opened her hand. "I have it."

"Leave it here." He tapped the vanity.

She scooted around him to place the phone on the countertop. Then she dove into the bathroom and shut the door. Releasing a sigh, she dropped the sheet and shimmied out of her underwear.

He hadn't lied. The hot water pounded her back and she closed her eyes.

If they could somehow fool Zendaris into believing that she killed Dr. Herndon, would she get Bobby back? She believed Beau when he'd told her that he'd accomplished similar feats in his storied career. She'd known the career before she'd met the man, and he hadn't disappointed her at all. In any way.

The pounding on the bathroom door jolted her out of her reverie.

"Deb, you have a text."

She cranked off the faucet and yanked her towel from the rack. "Give me a minute."

She squeezed out her hair and tucked the towel around her body. Still dripping, she threw open the door to the vanity. "Did you open it?"

"No." He held the phone out to her and she took it with a damp hand.

It took her two tries to hit the right button to open the text message. The picture that greeted her had her sinking to the floor in a puddle.

"What is it?" Beau hovered above her. "Are you okay?"

She turned the phone out toward him, tears flooding her eyes. "It's Bobby."

Chapter Six

He crouched beside her, his bare shoulder touching hers. He poked at the display. "Can you blow that up? He's holding a newspaper."

She flicked the pads of her finger across the display and the picture of Bobby enlarged.

"More." Beau closed his hand over hers and brought the phone closer to his face. He peered at the screen. "It's a newspaper from today. Proof of life."

Pressing the phone against her heart, she breathed out, "Thank God."

"How does he look to you?"

She held the phone out again and refocused the picture. "He looks sleepy. He must've just woken up. How does he look to you?"

Beau squinted at his son's face. Would he see the resemblance? "He looks tired."

"I'm so worried he might be sick. How would they know? How would they know what he needed?"

He stood up, one hand on her head, tousling her wet locks. "One thing at a time. Let's just get him back."

Deb dressed and dried her hair before the mirror using the hotel hair dryer. Zendaris wanted her in disguise again tonight but not with the blond wig. After all, that woman had just robbed a jewelry store.

She hunched over the vanity practically touching her nose to the mirror. And this one would be an assassin.

Zendaris had given her plenty of money to effect her change of identity, and now that he'd given her proof of Bobby's safety he'd expect her to carry out his orders. Or else.

She shivered and backed away from the mirror. "I'm ready."

Beau, wearing the same jeans and blue flannel shirt from yesterday, shrugged off the wall where he'd been leaning and pocketed his phone.

Deb stumbled to a stop. "Who were you calling?"

"Just checking my messages." He patted the phone in his pocket.

"Anyone I know?" She held her breath, her gaze scanning his impassive face. Did she really expect Loki to give away anything with his expression? In his line of work, losing your poker face could get you killed.

"A new contract coming up." He raised his brows. "Do you think I'd come this far with you to double-cross you?"

"I don't know." She strode to the closet and yanked her coat from the hanger. "Just remember…"

He sliced a hand through the air. "You don't have to tell me. You won't go without a fight."

She shot him a thumbs-up. "You're catching on."

"Let's eat."

She draped her coat over her arm as he ushered her through the door. She'd misjudged him. She never dreamed he'd ride to her rescue if he didn't have a stake in the outcome. Maybe he knew subconsciously that Bobby was his but was too afraid to ask. The timing was right, although she'd fudged a little and had told him Bobby was almost two when he was really over two years old.

As they waited for the elevator, she whispered, "Do you have your weapon?"

"Of course."

She knew he had it but wanted to segue into her next question. "When am I getting mine back?"

"Just as soon as I can be sure you're not going to use it against me and go rogue."

"Why would I do that? I'm grateful for your help. I don't think I could do this without you."

He snorted. "Deb Sinclair, first female Prospero agent? That'll be the day she's helpless."

"I told you." She jabbed at the button a few more times. "I'm different from the woman you met that night."

"Not so different." His gaze raked her head to toe.

The doors opening and the people inside the car saved her from a response. They had to dissipate this sexual tension between them. It wouldn't help her cause. It wouldn't save Bobby.

Maybe they should just sleep together and get it over with. They'd probably come away from the encounter disappointed that it didn't live up to the fireworks of their one and only night as a couple.

Beau placed his fingers on her hip when the elevator reached the lobby, and Deb squirmed at his touch. She knew in her heart this man could never disappoint her.

They nabbed a table in the lobby restaurant and ordered breakfast. Beau pulled a smartphone from his pocket, not the same phone he'd been checking when she'd walked in on him. Looks as if everyone had special phones.

He tapped the display several times. "I need to rent a tux for tonight and pick up a few things for my transformation."

"Do you think we should be seen together on the

street?" Deb poured a steady stream of cream in her black coffee.

"I don't think Zendaris is following you. He doesn't even know what hotel you're staying in anymore, and doesn't seem to care. But it's not a bad idea for us to keep our distance on the street." He tilted the phone back and forth. "If you pick up a throwaway cell phone, I'll text you to let you know where I'll be, and you can do the same. Doesn't mean we can't wind up at the same shops, but let's not arrive and leave together."

Using a napkin, he jotted down the addresses of places that would be of interest to her and shoved it across the table. "Let me know when Zendaris contacts you to pick up your ticket to the ball. I want to scope out the place."

"I'm going to feel a little like Cinderella." She folded the napkin and dropped it into the bag hanging on the back of her chair.

He quirked one eyebrow. "I think I missed that part of the story where Cinderella had to take someone out."

Deb took the T into Boston and her first stop was an upscale wig store. She felt naked without Beau by her side and felt even more naked without her weapon. He should've trusted her with it.

Zendaris hadn't given her instructions about her appearance—just that she be appropriately dressed for the gala and not look anything like the jewelry store thief.

She fingered the hair of the wigs lined up on mannequin heads with blank faces. She stared into the vacant eyes of one face and felt as if she were looking into a mirror.

She'd felt empty, drained since Bobby's kidnapping.

"Can I help you?" The clerk glided forward on the thick carpet.

"I'm looking for something—" Deb cranked her head back and forth "—black. Long, straight and black."

The woman cocked her head. "That would be a very dramatic look with your pale coloring." Crooking her finger, she crossed to the other side of the store. "I think I have what you want."

Only Zendaris had what she wanted now.

The saleswoman slipped a wig off the smooth dome of one of the mannequins and held it up. "Is this what you're looking for?"

The long black locks brushed the woman's arm as it swayed in her hand.

"Perfect."

"Have a seat." The clerk patted a chair stationed before a mirror.

Deb perched in the chair while the woman gathered her hair in a ponytail, pinned it up and pulled a cap over her head. She tucked in the stray auburn strands and pulled the wig over the cap.

When Deb looked up, she saw a stranger. The silky black strands cascaded across her shoulders and down her back. Now she just needed some dark eyes.

Her next stop was a department store cosmetics counter. She couldn't bring herself to buy a bunch of expensive cosmetics, so she asked for some samples and figured she'd pick up the rest at the drugstore. Then she took a detour through the store to pick up a few items of clothing so she wouldn't be stuck wearing the same skirt and blouse for however long Zendaris planned to keep her on the hook.

She hoped to God it wasn't much longer. Bobby looked too sleepy in that picture even for morning. Did they keep him tied up? Was he imprisoned in some room? A wave of nausea hit her gut, and she doubled over the clothes rack. She had to rescue her little boy.

She scooped in a couple of breaths, inhaling the floral perfume she'd sprayed on her wrists at the makeup counter. She could do this. She could get through this. She had no choice.

She swung by the lingerie department and snapped up several pairs of panties and grabbed a pair of pajamas on the sale table. If she had to spend another night in a hotel room with Beau, she preferred to do so with a few extra layers of clothing.

The shopping bags hung from her arms and banged against her thighs as she hailed a taxi to take her to her last stop—time to find the perfect dress for a murder.

She slipped into the formal wear shop slightly out of breath. What she saw next sucked the rest of the breath from her lungs.

Beau was planted in front of a mirror, tugging on the cuffs of a black dinner jacket. His eyes met hers briefly in the glass. "You don't think the sleeves are a little short?"

The saleswoman fluttered around him like a butterfly. "Maybe a little. It's the shoulders that concern me. Yours are so broad the material is puckering across your back."

Deb pursed her lips in a smirk. Could the woman be more obvious? She cleared her throat.

The woman responded without taking her eyes from Beau. "Someone will be right with you."

That someone was another clerk who popped her head out of the dressing room area. "Have a look around. I'll be there in a minute."

Deb cut a wide swath around Beau and the fawning store clerk. She cruised the perimeter of the store, fingering fabrics and checking price tags—not that any of the dollar signs concerned her. Zendaris was picking up the tab.

A couple thousand bucks for a dress in exchange for an assassination? Her services came cheap.

The clerk from the back approached her, brushing her hands together. "With your coloring, I'm thinking a jewel-toned green. What's the occasion?"

Deb didn't have the heart to tell the girl that by the time the evening rolled around, her coloring would be completely different. "It's a formal event—gowns, tuxes."

"Ooh, the best kind. Can I show you some dark emerald-greens over here?"

Deb clung to the black dress in her hands. You couldn't wear green to a murder, could you? "I was thinking something a little more subtle. I sort of want to blend in with the crowd."

The clerk screwed up her mouth. "That's no fun, but black is definitely your color for blending in."

After several minutes of frantic activity, the girl sent Deb to the dressing room where she'd stashed three black dresses—a halter neckline, strapless and spaghetti straps.

She stepped into the halter dress first and let it drop as soon as she brought the ties around her neck—too severe. She shimmied into the strapless dress and tugged at the fitted bodice. Nice.

The clerk called from outside the dressing room door. "Do you want a second opinion?"

Hiking up the dress, Deb stepped out of the dressing room and twirled around. "What do you think?"

"It's amazing."

Deb jerked her head around at the sound of Beau's voice. Back in his jeans, he sprawled in a chair across from the dressing rooms, a bottle of sparkling water in one hand.

The clerk giggled.

"Excuse me?"

"The dress, take it. It's you."

She added a note of outrage to her voice. "I don't believe I asked your opinion."

"I just couldn't help noticing how great it looks on you."

"Mr. Shelton." The saleswoman who had been helping Beau stepped between them with a plastic bag draped over her arm. "Your tux is ready."

Beau eased to his feet. "Thanks, Adele." He strolled to the door and called over his shoulder, "Maybe we'll wind up at the same black-tie event."

He'd *better* be there.

Deb bought the strapless black dress and a pair of heels to go with it. Then she loaded her purchases in a taxi and returned to the hotel.

On the way to the elevator, she glanced at the big clock over the reception desk—past two o'clock and still no word from Zendaris on where to pick up her ticket for tonight's party. Would Beau really be able to find a way to attend?

The bigger question was how did he plan to fake an assassination at a crowded event?

By the time she reached the room, her arms were aching from the weight of her bags. She tapped at the door with the toe of her shoe.

Beau opened the door, and she transferred two bags from her hands to his.

Hoisting the bags, he asked, "What is all this stuff?"

"Since I didn't get to pack before I left home, I wanted to pick up a few things to wear when I'm not attending gala fundraisers." She collapsed on the bed, her legs hanging over the side. "Did you get everything you needed?"

He dug into one of his bags in the corner of the room and bounced what looked like a caterpillar in his hand. "Zendaris isn't the only one who can change appearances."

"What is that thing?"

He held it up between two fingers. "A fake moustache."

"You're really going all out." She kicked off her shoes and wiggled her toes. She couldn't wait to slip into that pair of flats she'd bought today.

"You didn't hear anything from Zendaris?"

"Not yet." She rolled to her stomach. "You don't think he changed his mind, do you?"

"Probably not, but that's a good thing. You want to do whatever is going to get you closer to getting your son back."

"Including murder?" She pulled a pillow against her chest and hugged it. "I don't understand how we're going to get around that."

"We will. Let's have some lunch."

"I'm not hungry." The dinner last night and the breakfast this morning had been more food than she'd eaten in a week. The meals had made her feel slow and sluggish and too relaxed. She needed to be on top of her game right now.

"Didn't your mother ever tell you that food helps you keep up your strength?" Beau cursed, realizing his mistake almost before the words left his mouth. "Sorry."

"Yeah, I never had that mother, but I know what you mean."

"I worked up an appetite with all that shopping." He peeled his key card from the glass-topped credenza. "I'm going to run to that deli down the street and pick up a sandwich. Don't go anywhere without me, and keep the door locked and chained."

He backed out of the room, shoving the key card in his back pocket. *What an idiot.* He knew Deb hadn't had a mother growing up. Her mother had been some junkie who'd abandoned her to the foster care system at the age of four.

Deb hadn't even had the advantage of being a baby ready for adoption. The older kids always had a tougher time of it, and she'd bounced around a few foster families before running away from the last one at sixteen.

The rigors and discipline of the U.S. Navy must've been a welcome change from the chaos of her childhood. And then she'd learned to fly choppers.

He jogged down the stairs and welcomed the brisk blast of air that hit his face when he bounded outside. Between all the hot and heavy lovemaking he and Deb had indulged in, it was amazing he'd learned so much about her life.

Shoving his hands in his pockets, he kept his head down as he strode to the deli. He'd feel a lot better once he donned his wig and facial hair. With that symposium in town, he risked running into people who knew him.

He'd missed the lunch rush and stood in line behind just one other customer. While he waited for his pastrami, his phone buzzed. Deb's name flashed on his display.

"What's up?"

"It's on."

"Where?"

"I have instructions to pick up the ticket at a bookstore on White Street, Flights of Fancy."

"A bookstore?"

"In a book. The ticket's going to be in a book."

"Hold on." Beau put down the phone and paid for the sandwich. "What time?"

"In an hour."

Pulling up his sleeve, he glanced at his watch. "I'm going to head over there right now, Deb. Zendaris is not going to risk leaving that ticket in a book for long. Maybe someone's slipping it into the book as we speak."

"Are you going to do anything if you catch someone?"

"No. We want that ticket, but I might be able to get a line on someone working with Zendaris. Give me the address and the name of the book."

Deb gave him the information. He could probably walk to the bookstore, but a taxi would get him there faster. He headed back to the hotel to pick one up there.

A five-minute taxi ride brought him to the bookstore, and he instructed the driver to drop him off another hundred feet down the street.

Shoving his hands in his pockets and tucking his chin to his chest, he jogged across the street and dropped his sandwich on one of the metal tables on the patio in front of a coffeehouse. Then he ducked inside to order a coffee and grab a magazine and took a seat at the table.

He shook open the magazine and unwrapped his sandwich. He alternated between taking bites of his pastrami and peering over the top of the magazine to monitor foot traffic into the bookstore.

Each time someone entered or exited the store, he snapped them with his camera. Maybe they'd get lucky. He didn't believe for a minute Zendaris would risk some stranger finding the ticket to the fundraiser by placing it too early. He'd want to know that Deb could get to the bookstore first.

A couple of likely suspects, both male, shuffled into the store and then out again in record time. Beau wouldn't dismiss any women as likely candidates, but the truth was there weren't many Deb Sinclairs in the world.

And for one hot night, she'd belonged to him.

After more surveillance pictures and several unread magazine pages, a taxi pulled up to the curb fronting the bookstore and deposited Deb on the sidewalk, sporting a long black ponytail. A pair of slim jeans and black flats had replaced the straight skirt and high heels of the past few days. Dark sunglasses hid half her face. She looked young and fresh enough to be a student in this town teeming with them.

His pulse quickened at the sight of her.

She glanced both ways and slipped into the store. The minutes ticked by on Beau's watch, each one passing slower than the previous one. He slurped the last of his cold coffee and chucked the magazine onto the table.

Several more minutes passed, and then Deb emerged from the store, her sunglasses on top of her head. She must've asked the taxi to wait because the same one barreled down the street as Deb stepped onto the curb.

Beau scraped his chair back, tossed his coffee cup and sandwich paper into the trash and dropped the magazine back in the rack just inside the coffee place.

He decided to walk back to the hotel, welcoming the cold air that needled his face. Now that Deb had her ticket to tonight's festivities, he had to beg, borrow or steal his own. He had no intention of leaving her in that lion's den by herself.

If Zendaris wanted a murder, he'd get a murder.

He used his key card to enter the room, but Deb had chained the door. Her instincts seemed to be returning to her after the shock of losing her son.

"It's me."

She shut the door and slid the chain. She greeted him holding a laminated rectangle in front of her.

Before studying the ticket, his gaze locked on her eyes, now brown instead of green. Her emerald eyes had given her face a bright, open aspect. This stranger hid secrets behind her dark eyes.

"Nice disguise."

She waved the ticket back and forth. "I thought I might be able to slip outside and give this to you once I was in, but it has a UPN code. Some attendant at the door will most likely scan the ticket so that it can't be used again."

"That UPN makes it hard to duplicate, too." He pinched the plastic between his fingers and turned the ticket over. "Looks like I'm just going to have to steal one."

"Do you think you can do that?"

He rolled his eyes and handed the ticket back to her. "You're the one fond of calling me Loki."

"I didn't realize Loki was a thief along with all his other talents."

"Some of Loki's exploits are exaggerated—" he flicked a finger at the small camera he'd taken from his pocket "—and some aren't."

"Is that a camera?"

"Yes, Madam Spy. I don't leave home without it."

"Do you think you caught Zendaris's associate?"

"Associate? That's a nice name for him." He claimed his laptop from the closet, placed it on the table by the window and booted it up. "Tell me if you recognize any of these people. Maybe the guy who dropped the phone in your pocket on that street corner."

Deb paced the room while he fiddled with the USB connection between his mini camera and the laptop. Soon the images loaded. "They're up."

Deb leaned over him, her black ponytail sliding over her shoulder and tickling his arm. Her scent, a mingling of flowers and musk and citrus, made his head swim. Or maybe it was her close proximity and the way her warm breath caressed his cheek that made him dizzy.

He tapped the keyboard to scroll through each image. "Any of these people look familiar?"

At the third picture, Deb jabbed the screen. "This guy."

Beau zeroed in on his face and blew up the image. The man in the picture also had on sunglasses that hid a portion of his face and a hat pulled low on his forehead. Was everyone in Boston sporting some kind of disguise?

"No." She wiggled her fingers at the screen. "Zoom out again. It's not his face. It's his body. The guy who bumped into me on the street in Beacon Hill had a large build, a puffy jacket like this guy and broad shoulders, a thick neck—or at least his jacket made it seem thick."

Beau hit the arrow key several times until the man's body filled the frame. "He's big, wide through the torso, neck as big as one of my thighs. Do you think it's the same guy?"

"Could be. Was he one of the first ones you caught at the bookstore?"

"Yep. He's my third suspect. Look through the rest before you settle on him." He clicked through the slideshow for her, and she halted at only one more—another big guy in a leather jacket.

"The first one had the right kind of jacket on. It could be him. His face isn't very distinctive, is it?"

"All heads and faces have distinct shapes and forms. I'm sending this one to my guy to see what comes back."

She stepped back and curled her fingers around the back of his chair. "You have a guy?"

"You have Prospero. I have a support team, too."

"Do they know what you're working on?"

"Never."

She puckered her lips and blew out a long breath. "Haven't you had to check in with Prospero yet? Aren't they demanding some kind of progress report from you?"

"I'm Loki, not a second-grader." He cropped and saved the photo and then sent it along to one of the computer banks that matched faces with a huge database of known and suspected terrorists, thugs and wannabes. "This could take a while, but then we have a party to attend."

"Three hours to go. How are you going to get that ticket?"

"I'm a skilled pickpocket." He flexed and then cracked his knuckles. "You don't think swiping one of these tickets from some distracted scientist isn't going to be child's play for Loki?"

She laughed and some of the lines that had been plaguing her face disappeared. "Not every scientist is forgetful and distracted."

"I'll find one who is." Crossing his arms behind his head, he stretched out his legs. "I had a sandwich for lunch. Do you want to eat something before the party?"

"I can't eat." Deb folded her hands across her stomach. "Too nervous. We still haven't discussed the plan for this evening. How are we going to pull off a fake murder?"

"We'll have to assess the situation first. Maybe I can get close to Dr. Herndon and make a proposal."

"He's not going to listen to some deranged stranger and agree to play possum."

"Who said Dr. Herndon and I are strangers?"

"You know Dr. Herndon?" Her newly dark eyes popped open.

"You could say that."

She huffed out a breath and her nostrils flared. "Why don't you just say it?"

"We all have our secrets, Deb."

Her cheeks flushed and she turned away.

He planned to help her rescue her son, but that didn't mean he had to reveal all his secrets. He shoved the laptop into the middle of the table. "If you don't mind, I'm going to hit the hotel gym before I start my transformation."

"That's fine." She poked her head in the closet to retrieve the small evening clutch she'd bought earlier and stuffed the ticket inside.

Did Beau suspect her of hiding something from him? Every time he mentioned keeping secrets, she felt as if he were drilling a hole into her brain to discover hers.

If he couldn't see the obvious similarity between himself and Bobby, she didn't want to bring it up. This was not the time or place to tell a man he had a son.

"I'm going to get some rest and then start my own transformation. I'm sure mine's going to take longer than yours."

He pointed to his head. "You already got started. You... It looks great, different."

"That's the idea."

He left for the gym and waited outside the door, listening for the chain. She appreciated the protectiveness but she'd feel a lot safer if she had her weapon.

He'd locked both guns in the room safe but had neglected to give her the combination. Did he really think she'd up and shoot him to escape after everything he'd done for her?

He might up and shoot her once she revealed she'd kept his son from him these past two years. He had to understand. She'd make him understand, or maybe she wouldn't have to try. Once he finished this assignment, he'd be traipsing off to his next one.

Maybe not *traipse*. Beau wasn't a man who traipsed.

Sighing, she dropped onto the edge of the bed and slipped off her new flats, and then curled onto her side.

She reached for the phone on the nightstand and clicked open the picture of Bobby holding the newspaper.

She traced his sweet face with her fingertip. "Hold on, precious. Mommy's coming. Daddy, too."

Chapter Seven

By the time Beau returned from his workout, Deb had showered, slipped into her lingerie and hugged a white terry-cloth robe around her body to let him into the room.

He tilted his head back and sniffed. "It smells sweet in here—a lot better than that gym."

"It's the perfume. I talked the girl at the cosmetics counter into giving me a few sample sizes of perfume, even though I crossed the street to buy my makeup at the drugstore."

He snorted. "Don't waste your time trying to be thrifty with Zendaris's money."

"Oh, I don't care about that." She pulled a chair up to the mirror. "I just want to be able to dump all this stuff once this mission is over. I don't think I could bring myself to throw out expensive makeup regardless of who footed the bill for it."

She spread a hand towel on the table and started lining up tubes and jars and brushes. "How was your workout?"

"I really needed it." He stripped off his sweaty T-shirt and shoved it into a plastic bag in the closet.

Deb leaned close to the mirror, but shifted her gaze to the reflection behind her. Beau must've done some shopping on his own, too. She hadn't remembered the gym shorts that now hung low on his waist.

When he raised his eyes to meet her stare in the mirror, she snatched at a bottle of foundation, knocking it over. She'd better stop acting like a love-struck teenager around him.

Her focus had to remain on Bobby and freeing him from his captors. Somehow she felt as though, if she stopped thinking about him for one minute, he'd be snatched from her.

She'd been preoccupied the day he'd disappeared. Logically, she knew her preoccupation had nothing to do with Bobby's abduction, but that didn't lessen the guilt. She didn't need any more guilt weighing her down.

"I'm going to step in the shower."

She waved a hand in the air as if she couldn't care less that he'd be in the other room—naked.

Deb applied the drugstore cosmetics with a heavy hand. The foundation changed her skin tone down to her décolletage. She stroked on black mascara, eyeliner and three different shades of eye shadow until an unfamiliar pair of deep-set smoky eyes stared back at her from the mirror. The coral blush she feathered onto her cheekbones altered the contours of her face. She'd save the lipstick until after she slipped into her dress.

The water from the shower had stopped at about the same time Deb had finished her eyes.

As she turned from the mirror, Beau burst from the bathroom with his arms spread. "Well?"

He'd purchased his own wig—dark hair brushed back from his forehead with the hint of a widow's peak. He'd changed his blue eyes with dark contacts, just like hers, and a bushy moustache and beard covered the lower half of his face.

He would look almost nerdy if it weren't for all those

muscles on display above the towel wrapped around his waist.

"Wow, you sort of look like a scientist."

His mouth formed an O amid all that hair. "And you look sort of amazing in a mistress-of-the-dark kind of way."

"Too much?" She bit her lip. She didn't want to stand out in the crowd.

"It'll work. Zendaris wouldn't even be able to pick you out."

"If he's there. I don't think he'll show his face."

"I think we can both show ours without being recognized."

"Wouldn't you want Dr. Herndon to recognize you?"

"There are other ways I can make myself known."

Which he obviously wasn't going to tell her about. She pulled the heavy dress from the hanger. "I'm going to put this thing on. Are you done in the bathroom?"

"You don't have to get dressed in the bathroom. We can just turn our backs to each other. I have to get into my monkey suit, too."

Deb staked out one corner of the room while Beau staked out the other. Did he find her modesty juvenile? Little did he know she had a hard time controlling her thoughts when confronted with his half-clothed body.

She untied the robe and let it drop to the floor. She stepped into the dress and tugged the bodice over her breasts. "Can you zip this for me?"

"My pleasure." His warm fingers skimmed her bare back as he pulled the dress together and tugged on the zipper. "There's a little hook at the top. Might take me a minute to get it with my clumsy fingers."

He could take more than a few minutes if that meant

she could continue feeling the warmth emanating from his body and inhaling his clean, masculine scent.

"There." He placed his hands on her shoulders and turned her toward him. His dark eyes kindled, a different light from his usual blue fire—but it still melted her insides.

"You look stunning."

She gave a half laugh and stepped back, almost tripping on her gown. "It's the makeup. Men always claim they like a woman with a fresh, natural face and then go all gaga over the woman with the artfully applied makeup."

"I go gaga over you, natural or made-up."

"Yeah, well, we tried that before." She brushed past him to get her heels from the closet. "Didn't work out that great."

He appeared behind her in a flash as she lifted her skirt to slip a foot into her shoe.

"It didn't? I always thought it worked out pretty great. I had no regrets. Did you?"

Balancing on one high heel, she gripped the closet door frame as she put on the other shoe. When she'd discovered her pregnancy, that night loomed as a disaster. But once she'd held Bobby in her arms, she wouldn't have changed one moment of it although her son had never had a father.

If Beau knew the outcome of their brief encounter, he wouldn't think it had worked out so great.

"I—I just mean we never saw each other after that. I didn't even know how to contact you." She had her excuse for not telling him about Bobby if it ever came to that.

He brushed her hair from her back, holding the heavy strands of the wig in one hand. "If you had known how to contact me, would you have done so?"

She whipped around and her hair slid from his grasp.

With the five-inch heels on, she could almost glare at him eye to eye. "You knew who I was. Why didn't you ever contact me?"

He parted his fingers across his moustache and around his mouth. "We didn't exactly discuss our next date, did we?"

"It wasn't the time or the place."

"Exactly. Don't forget, Deb. You were the one who slipped out at the crack of dawn, leaving me with nothing more than a scribbled note and the scent of you all over those sheets."

With his words, the memory of that night slammed against her full-force and she grabbed the closet again and closed her eyes. "I did leave you the note."

He chuckled. "Just like a woman to expect a man to figure out something from that. That note made me think you saw that as a one-nighter, and hey, if that's all I could get, I could die a happy man. But I didn't figure you wanted any follow-up, and I guess I was right since you had a boyfriend or a lover at the time—Bobby's dad."

"I'm sorry." She clasped her hands over her aching heart.

"No need to apologize." He chucked her under the chin and crossed back to his side of the room. "Now I can die a happy man."

"Don't talk about dying." She dipped her head and fussed with the skirt of her dress.

He slipped his feet into a pair of shiny black dress shoes and shrugged into his cummerbund. "Can you help me with the bow tie?"

"Of course." She flexed her fingers and he returned to her realm just when she'd gotten her breath back. His proximity made her pulse race and her skin prickle with heat.

She wanted to correct his false impression that she'd had a lover stashed away somewhere else the night she'd met him. But to do so would be to confess that he was Bobby's father. She wasn't ready for that yet—and neither was he.

They had to rescue Bobby first.

He tilted his chin up as she tied the bow tie, and his fake beard tickled her fingers. She straightened the ends of the bow tie and then smoothed her hands across the front of his starched shirt. "There you go."

"Perfect." He sidled in front of the mirror, but his gaze shifted to her. "Why *did* Bobby's father let you and Bobby go?"

"It's a long story suited for another time and another place." And that had to be the understatement of the evening.

He shrugged his broad shoulders and stepped around her to rummage in another bag. "And now the pièce de résistance."

He perched a pair of dark-framed glasses on the end of his nose, and she laughed.

Running a hand over his slicked-back hair, he said, "Overkill?"

She shook her head. "It's just that the way that tux fits you, you're going to be the hottest absentminded professor at that shindig."

His grin only served to emphasize her point. "Ladies first. You take a taxi to the Grand Marquis, I'll follow in another taxi and I'll see you at the party."

She swept up her beaded clutch from the bed and hugged it to her chest. "Shouldn't I have some kind of weapon?"

"You're not going to kill Dr. Herndon."

"Yes, but don't I need a prop or something? I have to make some kind of show of it."

His eyebrows rose above the top of his thick frames. "Show of what? Do you want to get arrested for attempted murder?"

"What if you don't make it inside?"

"I'll make it inside."

"Damn it." Deb stamped her foot and the black dress rustled around her legs. "I feel like I'm going into a boxing ring with no gloves. Zendaris is expecting me to kill Dr. Herndon, and I don't even know what the plan is."

"Technically—" Beau curled both hands around her throat and wedged his thumbs beneath her chin "—you're still my captive. I'm going out on a limb trusting you, but I don't know your real intentions. You're on the edge, and there's no telling what you might do to get your son back."

She jerked away from his warm touch, dashing a tear from the corner of her eye. "I don't like feeling helpless."

"Trust me. I'll handle this."

"You expect me to trust you and yet you just admitted you can't trust me?" She dug her heels into the carpet.

"You lied to me."

She blinked. *He knew.* "Wh-what are you talking about?"

"When I first approached you, you lied about having contact with Zendaris."

It took a few seconds for the pounding in her temples to subside. "Of course I lied. My son's life was on the line."

"It still is."

She jabbed her finger just below his perfectly tweaked bow tie. "Don't screw this up."

"I never do."

"And that's a lie." She curved her lipsticked mouth

into a smile. "You screwed up this assignment for Prospero, didn't you? They expect you to serve them my head on a platter."

He tugged on the lapels of his jacket. "Don't be so sure I won't."

THE TAXI ZIPPED through the streets of Boston on the way to the Marquis while Deb's fingers toyed with the beads on her black evening clutch. She could wipe the smirk right off Beau's face if she told him the truth.

That wasn't a sufficient reason to tell him that he was Bobby's father, but she did have to tell him. He deserved to know. What he did with that information rested with him.

Not all fathers wanted to be part of their children's lives. Not all mothers wanted to be part of their children's lives. For the second time that night, she whisked a tear away from her mascaraed lashes.

She'd dealt with her abandonment issues long ago, but she didn't want Bobby to deal with the same issues. At least he had a mother who loved him, which was more than she could claim. But she'd had Robert, and in the end that had been enough.

Her taxi joined a row of them lined up in front of the Marquis.

"Do you want me to drop you here, or wait until I roll up to the entrance?"

"This is fine." The hand that reached into her bag for some cash had a slight tremble. She wished she knew how Beau planned to pull this off.

The driver had hopped out of the taxi and opened the door for her. Must be the dress. She pressed the money into his hand and thanked him.

Closing her eyes, she rubbed her lips together. Time to

don her identity for the night. She couldn't be a nervous mom planning an assassination. That person wouldn't win her many friends.

She joined the throng of people entering the hotel, hitched up the bodice of her dress and patted the sides of her breasts to make sure they didn't spill out. Then she put on a smile and plucked her invitation from her clutch.

Lifting the skirt of her dress, she stepped onto the escalator. Tuxedoed men formed a barrier at the entrance to the ballroom, scanning invitations and checking bags. Without a metal detector in sight, it would've been easy to slip a weapon in here.

She huffed out a sigh and presented her ticket to the sentry. He waved her through, and the crowd sucked her into the room.

She claimed a glass of champagne from a passing tray and tossed back half of the bubbly liquid. Then she threaded her way through taffeta, silk and brocade all scented with expensive perfumes, and zeroed in on a clutch of people at the corner of the food table. Who didn't like talking about food?

She elbowed her way up to the trough and stabbed a shrimp with a red plastic toothpick and held it up to her neighbor. "Have you tried any of the dipping sauces yet?"

Her new friend tapped a silver dish. "Try the Thai peanut sauce."

That remark launched an exchange about allergies, the weather, the Red Sox and Anthrax. Feeling warmed up, Deb sidled up to the next group where more inane conversation bubbled from her lips.

Facing the ballroom's entrance, she tracked the new arrivals. She could pick out Dr. Herndon from a newspaper photo but not from this crowd.

Her gaze skimmed over a tall man with a full beard

and moustache and then backtracked. She released a pent-up breath. Beau had made it through the doors.

He jerked his head around as if knowing she had him in her crosshairs. His dark eyes behind the thick glasses met hers, and he cut a swath through the crowd toward the bar.

She had a sudden longing to swill something stronger than the sweet champagne making the rounds. She excused herself from her current circle and weaved through a pack of penguins to join Beau at the bar.

"Big crowd, isn't it?"

"Scotch, neat, please." Beau barely turned his head. "It is."

"I'm not sure I can even pick out the guest of honor." She rapped her knuckles on the bar. "Make that two, please."

Beau curled his long fingers around his glass and moved away from the bar. She followed, but she stood apart from him and scanned the room.

"Over by the stage."

She glanced at the end of the room where several band members were tuning their instruments. "Tall man, receding hairline, jaunty polka-dot bow tie?"

"That's receding?" He smoothed a hand over his wig. "Go get acquainted as the black-haired siren. He likes pretty women. You need to get him alone."

"How am I going to manage that? He has a million people around him."

"Use your assets." His gaze dropped to her décolletage.

She nodded. This wasn't the first time as a female agent she'd used her sex appeal on a mission—but it might be her last if she couldn't get this job done.

She lolled a tiny sip of scotch on her tongue before letting it roll down her throat, leaving a trail of fire. She straightened her shoulders, not bothering to tug at her dress's bodice this time.

Sauntering toward the stage, she rolled her hips and twirled a lock of black hair around one finger. Herndon noticed her approach from five feet away and broke off his conversation to send a smile of encouragement her way.

She tripped to a stop at the stage, and her drink sloshed up the side of her glass. She put one finger in her mouth to suck off the scotch and widened her eyes. "Is there going to be music and dancing?"

Herndon's Adam's apple bobbed once. "There is. Do you dance, Miss...?"

He held out a hand, and Deb leaned in close to clasp it. "Desiree—it's like *desire* with an extra *e* at the end— and I love to dance."

Herndon chuckled and his hand, which had grown moist, tightened its grip on hers. "I do, too. Promise you'll find me when the band strikes up the first tune."

"Absolutely, Dr. Herndon."

"You know who I am?"

"Of course." She winked. "You're the man of the hour, aren't you?"

His smile stretched from ear to ear. "I'm flattered, Desiree, and please call me Scott. I'm going to get a refill, but look me up for the first song."

She wet her mouth with the scotch and then swept her tongue over her lips. "Of course, Scott."

She turned and walked away, feeling Dr. Herndon's eyes pinned to her swaying hips. Was he going to feel stupid when he found out her true identity? Probably not when he discovered she'd spared his life.

On her way to the ladies' room, she shot a look at

Beau, chatting with two serious-looking young men. He ignored her.

She scuttled into the bathroom and hunched over the vanity. She didn't like using sex to do her job, but even a renowned scientist like Dr. Herndon wasn't immune to female flattery and charms. Was that her fault?

He wouldn't be so anxious to go off with her if she presented as a studious young woman interested in nuclear physics. She'd go for the kill after their dance and invite him outside for some fresh air.

Beau would probably make his case then.

She grabbed a silver tube of lipstick from her bag and smoothed it over her lips.

The toilet in one of the occupied stalls flushed, and a woman squeezed through the stall door, flattening the flared skirt of her gown.

She joined Deb at the vanity and caught her eye in the mirror. "Sexy dress, but you might want to watch that bodice before it becomes a sexy half dress."

Deb glanced down at the top of her dress, hugging the curves of her breasts in a desperate attempt to stay up. "Oh, thanks."

She yanked at the bodice for the hundredth time that night, but once out of the bathroom she tugged it down to its previous daring level. Her slipping bodice just might be the key to getting Dr. Herndon outside…and saving his life.

Several minutes later, melodious chords rose from the dais and Deb made a beeline for Dr. Herndon, surrounded by adoring geeks.

Dipping between the black-clad shoulders, she shook her finger at Dr. Herndon. "You promised."

Like a magnet, his gaze dropped to her cleavage. He

foisted his empty glass on one of his fans and rubbed his hands together. "I was waiting for you, Desiree."

He crooked his elbow, and she slipped her hand around his arm. He led her to the dance floor where several couples were already swirling to a waltz.

His arm dropped to her waist and he pulled her close, crushing her barely concealed breasts against his starched shirt. His heartbeat rat-tatted against her chest, his warmth heating her skin.

Ugh, he must be very excited. She bit her lip and muttered a curse at Beau Slater.

He twirled her once and stumbled as he hugged her close again.

"Are you okay, Scott?"

He wheezed. "I'm fine. Haven't danced in a while and it's a bit warm in here, don't you think?"

He couldn't have offered her a more perfect setup.

She squirmed out of his tight grip and smiled into his red face. "I *am* feeling overheated. Maybe we can get a breath of fresh air outside."

"Let's finish this waltz and it's a deal." A trickle of sweat rolled down the side of his face and dripped onto his high collar.

"Are you sure you're okay, Scott? We can sit this one out and get that air right now."

His lips moved but no sound came out. Instead, a trickle of saliva dribbled to his chin.

"Are you ill?" Great—all she needed was for Dr. Herndon to draw attention to himself.

His fingers dug into her flesh and his knees buckled. She wrested away from his hold so he wouldn't take her down with him. And down he went.

As Deb hovered over him, he clutched his throat with

both hands. Blood gushed from his mouth and he toppled over.

A woman screamed.

Deb stepped back from the blood pooling on the dance floor.

Someone grabbed her arm.

Several people crouched beside Dr. Herndon.

One solemn-faced man looked up and said to no one in particular, "Dr. Herndon is dead."

Chapter Eight

"Let's go." Beau tugged on Deb's arm again. She was the last one to have contact with Dr. Herndon, and she didn't need the police questioning her.

She stumbled against him, and he had to pull her dress up before she spilled out of it. No wonder Dr. Herndon had been so captivated. Now he was dead. Had she done it?

He led her through the crowd pressing in to see the dead man on the floor lying in a pool of blood that had spewed from his mouth. Poison.

Two security guards rushed past them. Shouts and cries swirled through the ballroom.

And still Beau fought against the tide to escape from the room. Once outside the ballroom, he hustled Deb toward the stairwell.

"It's just one floor. Can you make it?"

She hiked up her skirts and made a dainty dash for the stairs like Cinderella after the ball. Only Cinderella hadn't left any dead bodies behind.

Beau pushed through the fire door and pulled Deb out after him. The cold air blasted his face, bringing tears to his eyes. He took one step toward the line of taxis and limos at the curb and then flattened his body against the wall, taking Deb with him.

Emergency vehicles double-parked alongside the taxis, and the first responders surged into the hotel.

Holding on to Deb's hand, Beau pivoted and walked quickly in the other direction from the commotion. He grabbed the handle of a taxi door and stuffed Deb into the backseat—right after he yanked the black wig from her head and the beard from his face.

He gave the driver the name of their hotel and collapsed against the seat. His gaze slid to Deb, her chest rising and falling, wisps of auburn hair framing her face. He pressed a finger to his lips.

When they got to the hotel, they stood shivering on the sidewalk. He turned her toward the door. "You go through the lobby, and I'll go the back way."

He took the three flights of stairs two at a time. By the time he reached the room, Deb had the chain on the door.

She let him into the room and then dropped onto the bed, the black dress swirling around her.

"Did you do it? Did you kill Dr. Herndon?"

She popped up like a jack-in-the-box. "Are you crazy? Of course I didn't kill him."

All the tension he'd been carrying in his shoulders seeped out—almost all of it. "Okay, okay."

"Do you really think I'm capable of murdering someone?"

"You're a covert ops agent. You'll do what's necessary to get the job done. You're also a mom who wants her son back."

"I'm not a cold-blooded killer."

"What happened back there?"

"Poison."

"My take exactly, but how? Why? Who?"

"I don't know." Her fingers pleated the silky black material of her dress. "Everything was going as planned. I had Dr. Herndon wrapped around my finger. He would've followed me to Jupiter after that dance."

"So would've half the men in that room."

Her glance knifed him between the eyes, and he spread his hands. "That's a good thing. You were doing your job. When did you notice he wasn't right?"

"Almost as soon as we hit the dance floor—rapid heartbeat, sweating, flushed skin." She hugged herself. "He became unresponsive and then collapsed to the floor."

"It didn't look like anyone else was affected, so someone targeted him, but how?"

"His drink. He seemed to be drinking a lot. His glass was always empty or almost empty. Someone must've slipped him something in his drink."

"It couldn't have been Zendaris. He fully expected you to do the deed."

"What if he knew I wouldn't do it? He wanted Dr. Herndon dead, so he had a backup plan." She pulled the pins from her hair and they fell to the bed. "What if he knows I failed?"

"How could he know your thought processes? If he had a plant at the party, he must've noticed you moving in on Herndon."

She doubled over and her now-loose hair tumbled around her bare shoulders. "What a mess."

"Deb?"

Peering at him through a veil of hair, she said, "Yes?"

"It's not a mess."

"Dr. Herndon is dead."

"Exactly."

She sucked in her plump lower lip. "I didn't kill him. I wouldn't kill him."

"Zendaris doesn't know that. All Zendaris is going

to see on the news tomorrow is that Dr. Scott Herndon died at the party in his honor. Don't get me wrong." He peeled off his jacket and loosened the bow tie. "I'm sorry for Dr. Herndon, but his murder leaves you in the clear."

"That's...awful."

"But true."

"Do you really think Zendaris will believe I murdered Dr. Herndon?"

"Why wouldn't he? He's holding your son. He sent you to do a job. The target has been neutralized."

"But who did it?"

"Maybe someone who has the same objective as Zendaris. Maybe the same person who shot at you the other night."

She plowed her fingers through her hair and pressed her palms against her temples. "Is there some shadow operation going on paralleling mine? This *is* a mess. If someone gets to the anti-drone plans before I do, what reason will Zendaris have for returning Bobby?"

"We'll just have to beat them to it." His cummerbund gaped open and he shrugged out if it.

"How are we going to do that? I don't even know what Zendaris wants."

"You know, Deb. He wants the plans, and somehow Dr. Herndon was involved."

"Was." She shivered.

Beau knelt before her and slipped the high heels from her feet. "You did good, Cinderella."

"I used my body to entice a world-renowned scientist." She flopped back on the bed and her toes dangled just above the floor.

"You did what you had to do." He took one slender foot in his hand and massaged her instep. "You did what was required. That's what we do. It's our number one job requirement."

She hitched up on her elbows. "Do you ever get tired of it? Do you ever get tired of being Loki?"

"Sure I do." He sat back on his heels and pulled her foot onto his thigh. "But it's what I signed up for. If I had wanted to settle down in some cramped house with six kids and work nine to five every day, I would've followed in my dad's footsteps. I, too, could've worked in the family business eighty hours a week."

Her still-brown eyes glittered and he jerked back from the sparks of anger there. Why did she care if he spurned his parents' lifestyle? She'd changed since having a kid, but he supposed that was natural. Kids changed you. He saw it over and over with his friends. Not. For. Him.

"Don't get me wrong." He released her foot. "I love my folks and my older brother who stayed to help Dad with the business and will eventually take it over. I love my nieces and nephews. All nine of them—ten, my younger sister just had a baby."

"It sounds—" she swiped a hand beneath her nose "—amazing. To have all that family around."

"You know, it is." A smile tugged at his mouth. "One of my nephews cracks me up. He's always asking the most off-the-wall questions, and one of my nieces is a total tomboy. She plays just as rough as her male cousins, but her sister is a princess who won't wear anything but pink."

Hunching forward, she said, "It sounds like you know them well, like you pay attention to them as people."

"Is that surprising? They are people—each one with a unique personality." He jumped to his feet and brushed off his slacks. "You gotta see that with your own son, even though he's only…"

"Two." She rose from the bed. "Bobby is almost two."

Beau drew his brows over his nose. Hadn't they been together three years ago? She hadn't wasted any time going back to her lover. He tightened his jaw. "I'm going to get out of this monkey suit and hit the sack. Mission accomplished."

"Man dead."

"You had nothing to do with that. Let's just hope Zendaris thinks you did."

The following morning, voices from the TV intruded on Deb's hazy dreams. She burrowed under the pillow, but that failed when Beau started tugging on her feet.

"Deb, wake up. Wake up. It's on the news."

She rolled over and sat up, squinting at the images on the TV. A reporter was standing in front of the Grand Marquis, yapping into a microphone.

"What's he saying? Are they calling it a murder?"

"The Boston P.D. is going to wait for the autopsy and the toxicology report before making any kind of statement."

She grabbed the remote from the foot of the bed and increased the volume.

A blonde news anchor appeared on the split screen with the reporter. "Do the police have any reason to believe this is foul play, Dave?"

"No, Charlotte, but they are looking for this woman."

The room spun and Deb grabbed the bedspread in her fists as she stared at a grainy photo of herself entering the Marquis Hotel, her black wig hiding half of her face. "Oh, my God."

"She was the person dancing with Dr. Herndon when he collapsed. The police would like to talk to her."

"I bet they would." Beau dropped on the bed next to

her. "Don't worry. Nobody is going to link you with that picture."

"Maybe whoever poisoned Dr. Herndon was smart enough to make it look like an accident." She scooted back toward the headboard. "That's what I would've done."

He lifted an eyebrow in her direction and clicked off the TV. "Let's just hope Zendaris saw the same report."

Deb reached for the phone charging on the nightstand. "Nothing yet."

"You must be more than ready for breakfast after skipping dinner last night, unless you filled up on the appetizers at the party."

She wrinkled her nose. "I had one shrimp and after what happened to Dr. Herndon, I'm glad I didn't eat anything else."

"I'll head down to the hotel restaurant and meet you there." He turned with his hand on the doorknob. "Unless you want me to wait for you. I know you're a Prospero agent, Deb, but you're off your game. If you don't want to be left on your own…"

"I want my weapon." She leveled a finger at the closet, housing the room safe where Beau had stashed her .45.

"Fifty-one, ninety-eight."

Before the door even closed behind him, Deb scrambled off the bed and flew to the closet. She tried the combination and a red Open flashed on the display.

She swung open the door and lifted her gun from the safe. She checked the chamber and blew out a breath. Now she could handle anything.

She took the gun with her into the bathroom while she showered and dressed. Returning to the room, she scooped up the gown puddled on the floor where she'd dropped it last night. Shaking it out, she noticed a couple of shiny spots on the skirt.

Gathering the material in her hands, she brought it close to her face and gasped. Blood—dried blood. She stuffed the dress in the closet and slid the mirrored door closed.

If she had gotten Dr. Herndon outside sooner last night, could she have saved his life? She had no way of knowing. When had someone slipped him the poison? How quickly had the poison acted?

Fate had taken over last night, and it had been Dr. Herndon's time to die.

She stashed her weapon in her bag and left the room to join Beau. She could escape now if she wanted. Nothing stood in her way. She had her gun and the phone connecting her to Zendaris—and her son.

But she was fooling herself if she didn't believe Loki would find her. She hadn't even known he'd been tailing her the first time. What had he said earlier? She was off her game. Yeah, she'd given up the game completely when Zendaris had snatched Bobby.

That wasn't the real reason she didn't bolt. Beau made her feel safe, protected, like she had a chance, like Bobby had a chance.

And then there was the paternity issue.

He'd made it clear last night he didn't have kids in his five-year plan. He'd spoken of his siblings and nieces and nephews in such an offhand manner, but with such warmth. That part gave her hope.

When the elevator opened on the lobby, she sighed and flipped her ponytail over her shoulder. She'd kill to have a large chaotic family like that.

She spotted the top half of Beau's face above a newspaper, and weaved through the tables to sit across from him.

He lowered the paper when she pulled out the chair. "Still just on coffee?"

"I didn't want to get ahead of you." He snapped the paper in his hands. "And I wanted to read the coverage of last night."

"Big deal?"

"Oh, yeah."

"What's the tone of the article?"

He folded the paper and tucked it under a menu. "The reporter is being cautious, but *foul play* practically screams from every other line in the story."

"Is anyone speculating on a motive—anyone but us, that is?"

"There's a lot about the symposium and who had a vested interest in the discussions."

"No mention of Nico Zendaris?"

He swirled his coffee. "There never is, is there?"

"We—" she cleared her throat "—Prospero wants to change that—shine a spotlight on him and his organization."

"You're still part of Prospero, Deb." He put a finger on a plastic menu and slid it toward her. "The work you're doing now will benefit Prospero."

"Honestly, Beau, I just want to benefit Bobby. I want him home with me."

"I know." He covered her hand with his. "It must be tough. I can't even imagine what one of my sisters would do if her child was missing, or my brothers for that matter."

Or you? Could you imagine what you'd do if a dangerous arms dealer had your son?

Folding her hands in her lap, she looked down. She couldn't even meet his eyes anymore when talking about Bobby. She had to tell him, but she'd waited so long now it would seem as if she were just trying to light a fire under him to rescue Bobby. He might not even believe her at this point.

"Do me a favor, Deb, and eat. In fact, I should've made that a condition of returning your weapon." He flipped the menu open in front of her.

"Why did you return it? With my gun back in my possession and my first task for Zendaris completed, I could've hightailed it out of here and finished the work on my own."

He shrugged. "I didn't think there was much danger of that."

"Really?" She didn't like the sound of this. When people like Loki failed to see her as a threat, she'd definitely lost her edge.

The waitress stopped by the table, took their order and filled their coffee cups.

When she left, Beau folded his hands around his cup. "We're on the same side now. I want to help you get Bobby back. I want to help you get your life back, whether or not that's with Prospero."

Or you?

The words came out of left field and she covered her mouth with one hand as if she'd uttered them aloud. When did she ever believe she'd have a life with Beau? He was committed to life on the road, a rootless existence that didn't tie him down to the drudgery of family and hearth and home.

He'd had all of that with his big warm middle-class family. And he'd rejected it.

"Why? Why are you so willing to help me when you could've bagged me at that hotel and had me back at Prospero headquarters a few hours later? You could've collected your bonus, which I'm sure Jack was offering for a speedy delivery, and been on to your next assignment."

"Obviously, I need to give you more reassurance." He held up the index finger of one hand and reached into his back pocket with the other. He flipped open his wallet and a plastic insert cascaded down to the table.

Children of different ages, some babies, some toothless, some freckled and towheaded grinned at her from the shiny plastic. "The ten nieces and nephews?"

"Nine. I haven't put the newest one in the lineup yet."

Deb trailed her finger along the smiling faces and halted at one blond boy who made her heart skip a beat. "Who's this one?"

"That's Grant. He's my brother's boy."

Deb gulped. Grant could be Bobby's twin. Hadn't Beau seen the resemblance between her own son and his nephew? Or had he just seen a scared boy who looked tired?

God, Bobby had looked tired. Were they feeding him properly? Drugging him?

Her appetite evaporated, and she released the plastic insert. It swung over the table like a pendulum. "Cute kids."

"I'm sorry. That was probably an insensitive thing to do."

"Not at all. You want to help me and Bobby because my son reminds you of your nieces and nephews. I get it."

He cocked his head and two vertical lines formed between his eyebrows. "Reminds me? I don't know your son, but any child in danger is gonna tug at my heartstrings. Are you surprised I have heartstrings? Whatever those are. Are you surprised Loki has a heart?"

"I know Loki has a heart. I fell asleep to it beating beneath my cheek that night."

A smile played around his mouth as the waitress delivered their food. When she left, he squirted some ketchup on his plate and his smile widened. "I thought reference to that night was off-limits."

"It's going to come up, isn't it?" *And it's so much more important than you know, Beau.* "It happened. We saw each other in the buff, we made love, we shared the shower."

"Stop." He made a cross in the air with his fork and knife. "I'm going to attempt to eat my breakfast without drooling."

She grinned and attacked her own plate. On one level she wanted to feel sad and anxious over Bobby every minute of the day to keep her focus, but on another, with Beau to lighten her load, she felt human and more capable of being the kind of mother Bobby needed right now.

The kind of mother who could kick ass.

Then the white elephant on the table, the cell phone from Zendaris, buzzed twice. Deb wiped her hands on her napkin and hit the button to read the incoming text.

Beau hunched forward, his silverware clattering in his plate. "What's it say?"

She turned the phone toward him. "Good kill."

Chapter Nine

"That's a good thing, Deb." He nodded once and dug into his omelet, not wanting to acknowledge Zendaris's power to rattle Deb. "He believes you killed Dr. Herndon. That's what we want."

"But what does he want?" She dropped the phone on the table and tapped it. "Why the cryptic message? Why doesn't he just tell me what to do?"

"Because he's toying with you. Don't let him get under your skin. That's exactly what he wants."

She choked and gulped her coffee. "He has my son. That's about as far as someone can get under my skin."

"He'll tell you what to do next, don't worry. And when he does—" Beau stabbed a chunk of potato and held it up "—you're going to have another demand for him."

"I am?"

"You're in the driver's seat right now. You killed a man. You just showed you're tough enough. Now he needs to deliver on his end before you proceed."

"Bobby. I want to see Bobby again, make sure he's okay."

"This time you're going to talk to Bobby. He's going to have to put him on the phone and let you hear his voice."

Beau's words filled Deb with strength. She didn't like feeling helpless. Who did? But for her, those vulnerable feelings sucked her back to her childhood, before Robert had come into her life like a guardian angel.

She didn't want to go back to that dark place again. Now here was another guardian angel in the unlikely form of a tall, lean, dangerous spy. And he gave her hope and courage. That's what Bobby needed right now.

"Bring it on, Zendaris." She flicked the phone with her fingers. Then she finished her breakfast—every last bite.

On the way up to the room, Beau asked, "Do you want to work out at the gym with me?"

She stopped at the door. "How did you know that's exactly what I needed?"

Placing his hands on her shoulders, he dug his fingers into the base of her neck, sending shivers down her back. He knew exactly what she needed.

"I think it's time for you to get your mojo back."

"Is that why you returned my gun?"

"That and the fact that someone is running around Boston who seems to be on the same track as you. You need to be able to protect yourself."

She turned toward the door with Beau's hands still on her shoulders and slipped her card in the slot. "What if Zendaris finds out that someone else killed Dr. Herndon?"

"That's not going to happen. Why would it unless the killer himself tells Zendaris? I don't think he's going to want to broadcast that because Zendaris will see him as a rival. And we know what Zendaris does to rivals."

Once in the room, Deb changed into some makeshift workout clothes—her jeans from yesterday and a T-shirt and tennis shoes.

Beau put on the shorts and T-shirt he'd worn to the gym before and plucked the material of the shirt from his chest. "If Zendaris keeps you dangling much longer, I'm going to have to go home and pack a bag."

"Where is home?"

"An apartment in D.C."

"We don't live far from each other. I have a small house in the burbs of Virginia." To think all this time, Bobby had been close to his father. It would be convenient once Beau knew. He and Bobby could see each other. He could spend time with Bobby between assignments.

She slid a glance at Beau as he punched the elevator button. "I—I suppose a house in the suburbs sounds like torture to you."

"To me, but a kid needs that. Kids need space and greenery and—" he waved his arm "—all that stuff."

"All the stuff you had and didn't appreciate."

He leaned a shoulder against the inside of the elevator car. "Who said I didn't appreciate it?"

"What would you call it, then? By your own account, you graduated from high school, enlisted in the Marines and started training for the most dangerous missions."

"I'd call it—" he swiped his card to unlock the door to the gym "—a thirst for adventure."

"And have you slaked that thirst yet?" She grabbed a towel from the counter and hung it over her shoulder.

"Did you slake yours?"

She spread her towel on a bench and straddled it. "It wasn't a matter of slaking. I didn't have a choice. I have a son to care for, so I had to scale back."

"Exactly." He ran a hand along a row of dumbbells and grabbed one, hoisting it from its cradle. "When circumstances change, you make the necessary changes in your life."

He curled the weight up to his shoulder. "Now are you going to keep talking or pump some iron?"

She snorted. "My friend and I back home can do both."

"Men just grunt."

They continued to work out, exchanging snippets of conversation and a few grunts.

Deb stretched out on a mat, feeling a pleasant ache in her muscles. A workout couldn't relieve all her stress, but it had helped.

Then the cell phone buzzed.

She snatched it up and glanced at Beau doing flys on a machine. A few other guests had joined them in the gym, so she didn't want to yell across the floor.

She answered the phone. "Yes?"

The hated voice purred in her ear. "Good job, Deb. I knew the agents of Prospero Team Three were killers, and you didn't disappoint."

"We didn't know your wife was there."

A sharp intake of air was all the answer he gave. Then he cleared his throat. "The assassination of Dr. Herndon was just one step. Are you ready for the next?"

"Wait. I can't talk here." She scrambled from the mat and waved to Beau. She pointed to the covered patio off the gym floor, and he followed her out.

She mouthed *Zendaris*.

"Okay. I'm ready for the next step if you are."

Zendaris paused. "What are you talking about?"

"I want to talk to my son. You showed me the picture, and I killed Herndon for you. Now I want to talk to him."

"He's a toddler. He doesn't talk much."

Anger thumped against the back of her head and she took a deep breath. "He's my son. I want to hear his voice."

"I have a son, too, Deb. Prospero knows that now after capturing my children's nanny."

"You mean the nanny you left for dead? Yes, we know

you have a son and a daughter." She'd appeal to his fatherly instincts but he probably didn't have any. "So you know two-year-olds can talk, and I want to talk to mine."

Beau was nodding encouragement.

Zendaris gave an exaggerated sigh. "You're getting to be more trouble than you're worth."

"I won't do one more task until I speak to my son."

"I'll arrange it, but once I do you're mine."

"I'll do your dirty work because you have my son, but I'll never be yours."

WHILE DEB TOOK a shower, Beau clicked on the TV to see if there were any more news stories about Dr. Herndon's death, but the local news wasn't on yet and the story wasn't big enough for the national news channel to carry it.

He'd been proud of Deb today. She seemed to be getting her spine back, although he couldn't fault her for losing it in the first place. Even if one of his nieces or nephews had been snatched, he would've gone nuts.

Deb must really like kids. She'd probably like more than one. She seemed really interested in the pictures of his family. He must've come across as a real jerk the night they'd met if she believed he took his family for granted. Nothing could be further from the truth.

Had he gotten his taste for thrills and chills out of his system? He'd experienced more than a lifetime of them, enough to write three books. But the woman he settled with would have to be special—just that right mix of independence and femininity. He hadn't met her yet.

Until that night in Zurich when he'd seen Deb down the length of that bar.

For the longest time, he'd convinced himself it was all about the great sex, the hot chemistry between them.

But he'd come to realize Deb possessed all the qualities necessary to lure him in like a magnet. Spending time with her again, even under these circumstances or maybe especially under these circumstances, reinforced his belief that she had something unique, some combination of traits and beliefs that matched up with his.

Could he let her go after this assignment?

His laptop in the corner beeped, and he strolled to it and hit a key to wake it up.

The search for the identity of the man at the bookstore had concluded and a file had been deposited on his desktop.

He double-clicked on the file, and a document popped open containing pictures and corresponding text—a who's who of bad guys.

A sweet scent wafted from behind and he cranked his head over his shoulder to take in Deb massaging lotion into her hands.

"Is the search program done?"

"Yep. Returned quite a few possibilities for our bookstore patron."

"Can we look now, or did you want to get something to eat first?"

"The sandwich I grabbed on the way up to the room is enough." He spun the laptop toward her and pulled up the other chair. "Let's have a look."

They scanned through several faces, reading their criminal bios and taking a few notes on the hotel stationery.

"Anyone look familiar?"

"Prospero has had our sights on a few of these people, so I'm going to eliminate those guys right now. Nobody we looked at had ties to Zendaris. Has to be someone off our radar."

After an hour and a half, they'd narrowed their search down to five men—all the size and shape of the man at the bookstore.

Beau tapped the screen. "I'm going to do some more research on these guys. If we can locate our man, there's no telling what we'll discover."

"Like where they're holding Bobby."

"Exactly." He accessed another classified database and fed information on their five suspects into it.

Deb sat on the bed, crossing her legs beneath her. "Aren't some alarm bells going to go off somewhere when you input data into those systems?"

"Definitely."

"Will the usage be tracked back to you?"

"I have an excuse. I'm on assignment, so while someone may be tracking my search criteria in these databases, it shouldn't raise any suspicions. I use these all the time. What's the difference now?"

"The difference is you've gone to the dark side. You've joined forces with your prey."

He hit the final key and stood up to stretch. "As far as anyone knows, I'm still tracking a suspected rogue Prospero agent."

"I hope so." She plucked at the bedspread with nervous fingers. "Dinner in the hotel again or room service?"

"I'm sick of this hotel. Let's go out."

"Disguises?"

"Not the brunette from last night and not the blonde from the jewelry store. It seems that every identity you have gets into trouble. You're better off with your natural hair color."

"I was no brunette last night—that was more mistress of the dark."

"Boston P.D.'s looking for mistress of the dark now, so you'd better not bring her back."

The phone that Deb kept by her side buzzed, and her face paled just like it did every time a call or text came through. This time it was a call.

She licked her lips and answered it.

As always, she put it on speaker, and a gruff voice scratched over the line. "You ready for the kid?"

At least they knew Zendaris was probably not holding Bobby himself. Beau pressed the record button on his mini recorder.

Deb's voice, strong and sure, answered, "Yes."

More shuffling and scratching came over the line and the man's voice barked, "He's listening."

"Bobby? Bobby, is that you? It's Mommy."

A child's voice responded, "Mommy?"

"Are you okay, Bobby? Mommy misses you and will see you soon."

"Mommy, I wanna go home."

Deb squeezed her eyes shut and Beau had a strong urge to take her pain away.

"You will. Soon, Bobby. Are you getting enough to eat?"

"Ice cream."

"You're eating ice cream?" She rolled her eyes at Beau.

"'Cuz my throat hurts. I'm tired."

"Bobby, are you sick?"

"Throat hurts. Bye, Mommy."

"Bobby? Bobby?"

"He's done. Kids this age don't talk much."

Deb had slid to the floor with her back leaning against the bed. "Is he sick? He said he had a sore throat and that he was tired."

"Seems okay to me. I ain't a babysitter."

"Oh, yes, you are." Deb staggered to her feet and marched across the room. "You listen to me. You have my son. You took him, and if anything happens to him, your boss won't get one more thing out of me except a bullet to the head. Now, I'm going to ask you again. Is my son sick?"

The man coughed. "He seems okay. He's tired a lot and started whining about his throat so I gave him some ice cream. Look, you talked to him and now I gotta go. We'll be in touch."

When the man ended the call, Deb threw the phone at the bed. "Bobby didn't sound good."

"Maybe he's just tired and sleeping a lot because he's cooped up with that guy. They're probably not taking him out to play or letting him get any exercise." He walked to the bed and retrieved the phone. Deb needed this thing in working order.

"The important thing is—" he crossed the room and took her hands "—you spoke to him and he's alive."

"You're right. What do you think they've told him?"

He gathered her hands and held them against his chest. "That's another thing. They're not going to be mean to him or freak him out. They want a calm kid on their hands, or at least as calm as they can get him keeping him away from his mother. The ice cream is a good sign. They're trying to make him happy."

She chewed on her bottom lip but left her hands in his. "The sore throat worries me. He had that before…before he was kidnapped. That's why I took him to the doctor."

"Maybe it's just the flu. It's that time of year."

"The sooner I get him home, the better."

"In the meantime, I'm here to take care of his mom, and she needs more than ice cream, too. So let's go out and get dinner like we planned."

"I wish he had told me what they want from me next. I just want to get through this. I'm tired of his games."

"He'll tell you soon enough. Dinner—we have something to celebrate. You talked to Bobby for the first time since he was taken, proving that Zendaris needs you as much as you need him."

"Okay, dinner, but nothing fancy. I wore my only fancy dress last night, and that didn't go so well."

"Not for Dr. Herndon, but it couldn't have worked out better for you."

Hunching her shoulders, she pulled her hands away from his grasp. "Ugh, I don't like thinking about it that way. Some of his blood spattered on my dress, you know."

"If more than one person wanted Herndon dead, he didn't stand a chance, whether he'd danced with you or not."

"I know you're right." She scooped her hair back from her makeup-free face. "Since I had Bobby, I haven't been doing a lot of the heavy lifting for Prospero. I'm not used to these assignments anymore—the violence, the car chases, the dead bodies. I've been doing more analysis than fieldwork."

"I don't know that you ever get used to someone dropping dead in front of you."

"I'm glad it's not just a *girl* thing."

"Not." He slid his jacket from a hanger in the closet. "And we are going casual—lobster place outside of town, pick up your own food at the counter, sawdust on the floor."

"That sounds about right."

They took a taxi to the restaurant. Beau didn't think Zendaris was having Deb followed, but that didn't mean they had to drive around in the car he'd provided her.

They joined the long line of customers waiting to place

their orders and both picked out a couple of lobsters, some fried clams and coleslaw. They took their bottles of beer to a table and waited for their feasts to be delivered.

Beau had been worried that the call from Bobby would sink Deb into a depression, but she seemed revitalized—ready to take on Zendaris instead of cowering from him.

Beau had finished half his beer by the time their food was delivered to their table.

Deb's eyes widened when the server plopped the plate on the picnic table in front of her. "I may be in over my head here."

"That lobster may look big but you'll have to work to get to all his good parts."

"*Its* good parts." She wrinkled her nose. "Don't refer to it as a he."

Beau laughed and cracked open the first claw. He dug out the succulent meat and drenched it in drawn butter. When he placed it on his tongue, it almost melted. He closed his eyes. "Mmm."

"I think you have it right. Do the hard work first, and then when you're tired out eat the easy stuff."

He helped her crack her lobster, but being Deb, she insisted on taking over and doing it herself. He'd want a wife like that—someone independent, not clingy.

Not that he was thinking about a wife. His gaze shifted to Deb licking melted butter from her fingers. Not even one like this. At least not now. Or maybe ever.

"What?" She covered her face with a greasy paper napkin. "Is that gross?"

"Is what gross?"

"Licking my fingers."

"Not. At. All. You can lick anything you like." He sucked on an empty claw to discourage the wicked grin forming on his face.

She pointed at him with her little sharp fork, a piece of lobster still hanging from the end. "That's Loki right there. That look. You must've had women across the world tossing their panties in the air with that look."

He choked and a quantity of beer fizzed through his nose. "Is that why you think I got into this business?"

"I know that played a role in my Prospero teammate, Gage's, decision."

"Gage Booker, the senator's son?" He took another swig of beer, managing to swallow this one. "That's because he's a suave, smooth-talking SOB."

"And you're…"

"Not."

"Right." She popped a fried clam into her mouth and puckered her lips as she chewed.

Beau never realized eating greasy seafood could be so erotic, although he should've known better. The very first meal they'd shared together had wound up all over their naked bodies.

He tapped his empty beer bottle. "Do you want another? We're taking a taxi home, and I don't think Zendaris is going to contact you tonight."

Her face grew still and she dropped a clam that had been making its way to her mouth back into her plate. "No, I'd better not."

He could've kicked himself for bringing up Zendaris just when she'd seemed to relax a little. "Bobby's okay, Deb. Having another beer is not going to make a difference in how fast we get him back."

"It feels wrong." She crumpled up her napkin and tossed it into the silver bucket brimming with lobster shells.

"I know it does, and I'm not trying to make you forget

about Bobby's predicament, but being a nervous wreck is not going to help him."

"It's a more appropriate response than noshing on lobster and guzzling beer."

"You're not guzzling beer." He leaned forward and dabbed a spot of butter from the corner of her mouth. "Reclaiming your strength and confidence has helped him and will help him. You talked to him for the first time. That had to make him feel better."

"Him and me both, but I think I'll skip the second beer. You go ahead though."

A phone vibrated and Deb jumped. "Is that mine?"

"I think it's mine." Beau felt his pocket, his fingers brushing his buzzing phone. He pulled it out and checked the display. His heart lurched. Jack.

"I'm going to take this call outside. Can you get me another beer?"

Her green eyes glittered in her pale face. "Business?"

"Different business." He lied as smoothly as he would to any quarry he was tracking.

He scuffed through the sawdust on the floor, and pushed through the restaurant's side door to an empty porch. If Jack was calling instead of texting, it had to be important.

"Loki. What's the problem, Jack?"

"You are."

Beau's nostrils flared and his eyes narrowed as he watched Deb through the window pick up a beer at the counter. Looked like he was going to need it.

"What do you mean?"

"Cut the bull, Loki. We know all about you and Deb. You're off the case."

Chapter Ten

Maybe just one sip.

Deb tilted Beau's bottle of beer to her lips. The earthy taste of hops and grains filled her mouth and bubbled against her tongue.

Beau was right. She had to stay strong for Bobby. She couldn't turn into that spineless pile of rags she'd been when she'd first discovered his kidnapping. Her weakness had wasted valuable time and caused missed opportunities.

Who knew how much detail she'd ignored from that first phone call, from the daycare worker's information?

Swiveling her head, she picked out Beau on the side porch of the restaurant. He had his back to the window, but the set of his shoulders and the stiffness of his back screamed out *argument*.

If that was a business call, business wasn't so good.

Suspicion flared in her gut. Those old feelings and instincts that had vanished the past week were creeping back into her consciousness.

If Beau wanted her to feel empowered, so be it.

She slammed the bottle on the table and pushed to her feet. The soles of her tennis shoes kicked up sawdust on their way to the porch. She eased open the door and held her breath.

She couldn't catch any of Beau's words, but his tone was unmistakable.

She took one step onto the porch, and he spun around, gripping his phone in one hand like a weapon. His ferocity tumbled from him in waves, encompassing her and making her knees tremble. Amid all the talk of families and children and the sexual teasing, she'd almost forgotten who he was.

"Eavesdropping?"

The word hung between them, creating a veil of mistrust on both sides.

"Are you worried about what I might've discovered if I had been?"

He dipped his head and rested his forehead against one end of the phone. "The game's up, Deb."

Her heart fluttered and her knees practically wobbled. Had Zendaris discovered the truth about the murder? "What game?"

"The game I've been playing with Prospero."

Her knees crumpled, but she managed to fold onto a cold bench. She crossed her arms and tucked her hands under her armpits. "Wh-what does that mean, exactly? Do they know you've been working with me?"

"Not quite. It's not as bad as that."

She scooted further onto the bench before she slipped off and gulped in a few lungfuls of cold air. "Get to the point, Beau."

"Jack found out about us." He smacked the phone against his palm. "Somehow he discovered we'd met before, had spent the night together."

"Okay." She released her breath in small spurts where it formed gusts of fog in the air. "Did he mention how he found out?"

His brows jumped to his hairline. "Why does that matter? He's Jack Coburn, that's how he found out."

It mattered because the only people she'd told about that night were her brothers in arms—Cade, J.D. and Gage. If they'd ratted on her to Jack, it meant they no longer had her back. It meant they believed the worst of her.

"It doesn't." She shook her head and drew her hand across her mouth. "What's the upshot? Why were you arguing with Jack?"

"Did you hear any of that?"

"Just the tone of your voice, your stance, the way you turned on me when you heard my approach."

"Sorry." He ran a hand through his hair. "He's taking me off the case, Deb."

"He told you that?"

"When Dr. Herndon was murdered, he figured there had to be some connection between his death and you and Zendaris. He wondered why I hadn't made the connection, and then he found out about our connection."

"Does he know you're helping me?"

"I don't think so. If he suspects it, he didn't accuse me of it. If he believes you turned, he'd have to believe it of me, too."

"What next, Beau?" She shoved her hands beneath her bouncing legs, not wanting to hear his answer.

"He's putting someone else on the job."

She jumped up and stalked to the end of the porch and then swung around. "That's just great. I have Zendaris yanking my strings like a puppet master, some shadow spy after the same thing I'm after, and now some hired spook coming after me—one I didn't happen to share a hot night with. And Bobby's still being held captive."

If she hadn't just vowed to man-up and start acting like a Prospero agent, she'd cry.

"And me."

"Huh?" That's the only word she could manage to squeeze past her tight throat.

He hooked his thumbs in the belt loops of his jeans and drew back his shoulders. "You have me."

Those were the sweetest three words she'd heard all night. She threw herself against his chest and wrapped her arms around his waist. "You don't know how good that makes me feel."

He stroked her hair, and just like that she didn't feel like crying anymore. They'd formed a team, and with their combined experiences and resources, they'd be unbeatable.

She lifted her cheek from his chest and parked her head beneath his chin. "You don't think Jack would send one of my Team Three members after me, do you?"

"No way." Cupping her jaw, he tilted up her head. "He knows how strong that bond is. He knows their first loyalty is to you."

"But not if I broke that trust. That's what he thinks, isn't it? Maybe that's what they think, too."

"Is that what you'd believe of them?" He traced her outer ear with the pad of his thumb. "Would you naturally assume one of your team members had gone to the other side just because your boss told you he had?"

Pressing her lips together, she shook her head from side to side. "No. I'd never believe that of any of them."

"And I'm sure they feel the same way about you. I may be an independent contractor now, a lone wolf, but I experienced that same bond when I was active duty. Jack Coburn is not going to send one of your own after you."

"Then we're safe."

"Don't be too confident. There are some good people

out there, and Jack knows all of them. I found you, and it wasn't hard."

One of her shoulders rose and fell. "You're Loki."

"Yeah, well, Loki may have just ruined his reputation." He hung an arm around her shoulder and nudged her toward the door and light and people and warmth.

"I'm sorry."

"Don't be. Jack was right—any gun for hire who could be deterred by a pretty face and a one-night stand might want to look into retirement."

"Jack said that?"

"Something like it. You know Jack—a man of few words."

The warm room sucked them in, and they wandered back to their table hand in hand. "I'm going to have another beer after all."

"Why not celebrate? The charade is up and I don't have to go on lying to Prospero. I hate lying to my friends, anyway."

Deb dropped her lashes over her eyes and reached for Beau's bottle of warm beer. "Do you want a fresh one?"

"Absolutely, but let me get them this time."

He rose from the table and sauntered to the counter, way too relaxed for a man who'd just been fired.

She hated lying, too. She had to find a way to tell Beau he was Bobby's father. She'd have to wait until she had Bobby safely home and in her arms though. Beau's worry for Bobby stemmed from his concern for all children and maybe, just maybe, his feelings for her. If she told him about Bobby before they rescued him, his emotions would cloud the mission.

He'd be even more worried about Bobby if he knew he was his own…wouldn't he? At the very least Beau's anger toward her and her deception might compromise the entire plan.

She'd wait.

He returned, carrying two sweating bottles. "They replaced my warm beer for free. We've gotta come back here when this is all over."

She smiled while she took a sip of her beer. She wanted nothing more than to come back and eat lobsters with Beau and Bobby as a family. But Beau didn't want a family.

And he hated liars.

THE NEXT MORNING, Deb woke up heavy-eyed. Beau had gone to the gym early, letting her sleep in. She had to make up for the sleep she'd missed during the night. The sleep she'd missed tossing and turning and being tuned in to every little movement from the bed next to hers.

Several times, she'd imagined that Beau was leaving his bed for hers. She'd lie still and wait for his touch, wait for his masculine scent to wash over her, wait for his whispered words of want and need.

She'd waited all night long.

By the time morning rolled in, her muscles ached, she could barely move her stiff neck and a foul mood hovered over her like a miasma.

Beau had seen the writing on the wall almost immediately and taken off for the gym, telling her to get some more sleep.

The extra hours of sleep hadn't done much for her sore muscles and stiff neck, which she attributed to her workout yesterday. But sleep had softened her mood.

She had nobody to blame but herself that Beau hadn't made any moves on her. She'd made it clear the first night he'd tracked her down that her worry and desperation as a mother had shut down the spigot of sexual need and desire.

What had changed?

Every time she fantasized about Beau, black clouds of guilt would rush in on the heels of the fantasy. She'd mentally berate herself for thinking about her own desires while her little boy was being held hostage somewhere.

But it was more than sex she craved from Beau. She longed for that human connection that had been missing from her life for so long. She thirsted for the comfort and completeness of making love with a man, especially this man, the father of her beloved child.

To form that bond with Beau again would be to complete the circle of their family. She'd begun to feel as if there were some mystical power in making that connection, as if that family bond could clear a path to finding and rescuing Bobby.

Beau's laptop beeped in the corner. She eyed it but decided against mucking around with his databases and search engines.

She yawned and stretched. She could use some juice and coffee but after the lobster and fried clams and beers last night, she couldn't face another morsel of food.

Deb rolled out of bed and stumbled into the shower. The warm water and fragrant steam did nothing to wake her up, so she twisted the dial in the other direction. As the cool water hit her back, her teeth chattered and sent a wave of goose bumps across her body. That's what she needed.

She dressed in the same old jeans but swapped the T-shirt she'd worn yesterday for a fresh one.

If Zendaris kept her on the line much longer, she'd need to hit the mall again.

The door clicked and Beau poked his head into the room. "Is everyone decent?"

"If you can call these dirty jeans and T-shirt decent, then I guess I qualify."

He placed a cup of coffee on the table and held up a paper bag. "I figured you'd sleep through breakfast, so I picked up a coffee and a couple of scones for you."

"Thanks." She waved her toothbrush at his laptop. "Your computer beeped while you were gone, but I didn't want to mess up anything."

"Maybe my sources found something on our guy." He pulled a scone from the bag and bit off the corner.

"I thought those were for me." She took in his damp T-shirt clinging to his chest and the sweatshirt he'd thrown over the back of the chair. "Where have you been anyway? Since when does the hotel gym have scones and coffee?"

"I took a run along the river. I couldn't take the tread-mill in the gym—too boring."

"No suspicious activity out there? No one lurking around the hotel?"

"Do you think my replacement is going to find you that fast?" He brushed the crumbs from the table into his palm.

"I don't think your replacement is going to find me at all." She joined him at the table, where he'd pressed a few keys on the laptop, and took a sip of her coffee. "Now that you're a disgraced spy, is someone going to bust you for accessing top secret databases?"

"How fast do you think Jack works? He just fired me last night. I doubt if the entire intelligence community knows." He rubbed his hands together as lines of data scrolled down the screen. "I'm not persona non grata yet."

He pulled up a chair and nodded to the other one.

"Have a seat and start eating that other scone before I demolish that one, too."

She sat down next to him and plunged her fingers into the white bag. She broke off a piece of the crumbly scone and popped it into her mouth. "Can you make anything out of all that?"

Beau was running his finger down the monitor, stopping occasionally to jab at a piece of information as if prodding it to give him more.

"Look at this guy, Deb." He scrolled up the screen to one of the pictures they'd matched before. "He's known as Damon. He's a South American, has been involved with the drug cartels down there. He dropped off the radar a few years ago, but still has his contacts so he's not out of the game. But which game?"

"No more drugs?" She stared into the dark beady eyes of the man, hoping for some recognition.

"He hasn't been connected to the drug trade for a few years. Maybe he switched to weapons. His drug connections would be handy for Zendaris."

"Specialties?"

"Weapons. Surveillance. He's also the muscle."

"He has enough of them." She bit off another piece of scone and covered her mouth when she talked. "If he's our man, it would be great to have at least one face to pick out in a crowd."

"Exactly. I know I could recognize him again. Who knows where he'd take us if we followed him?"

"He could take us to Bobby."

"And that's the kind of break we need."

"Any of the others on our short list look good?" She swirled her coffee in the cup before taking another sip.

"Not as good as this guy."

Crumpling the pastry bag in one hand, Deb rose from

the table and tossed the bag in the trash can. She flipped through the free paper the hotel delivered, but Dr. Herndon's death didn't warrant a place on the national news scene for the second day running.

"Have you heard anything more about the investigation into Herndon's death?"

"Nothing. I guess they're waiting for the autopsy report."

"And nothing more about the mysterious black-haired seductress?"

"Nope, and since Herndon was single the media isn't crawling all over that angle."

"What angle is Jack taking? Does he think I'm responsible?"

"Involved? Yes. Responsible? Jury is still out on that one."

She carefully refolded the paper along its crease. "What did you say to Jack last night? Why were you arguing with him?"

"He'd just fired me. I was trying my best to talk him out of it." He kicked his long legs up on the chair she'd just vacated. "I admitted that we'd hooked up years ago but insisted it meant nothing and the news that I'd be tracking you barely registered as a blip on my radar."

"Ouch. Did he believe you?"

"Whether he believed me or not never came up. Fact is, I withheld information from him. You don't withhold information from Jack Coburn."

"I know." She dropped on the bed. "Look where it got me."

"Are you sure your best bet all along wasn't to tell Prospero that Zendaris had kidnapped your son?"

"No." She stuffed her feet into her tennis shoes. "When

someone has your child, your first instinct is to do exactly what they tell you to do."

"I get that, but it's not like your team members would jeopardize the safety of your son. They wouldn't have come in with guns blazing."

"I just had a feeling that Zendaris would know if I went to Prospero. I don't know how or why, but that feeling controlled every move I made after Bobby's kidnapping."

"He knew enough about your life to have someone pretend to be Robert. I can't tell you if it was a good move or a bad one to keep Prospero in the dark. You bought yourself some security but opened up some difficulties for yourself. Did you really think your boss wouldn't notice that you'd dropped out of sight?"

She sighed. "I took a leave of absence. I thought that would be good enough."

"Well, here we are."

"Yep." She tied her shoes and stomped on the carpet. "Going somewhere? Mind if I tag along?"

She crossed her arms and tilted her head. "Because you want to or because you think I need protection?"

"Does it matter?" He stripped off his T-shirt and dug through the dresser drawer where he'd dumped his purchases. He pulled out a clean T-shirt and the jeans he'd worn over the past few days. "Can you wait while I hop in the shower? I won't be long."

"I'll wait for you." Her gaze lingered on the wedges of muscle shifting across his chest and shoulders. Could she wait for him while he decided whether or not he wanted to be a father to Bobby?

She'd have to tell him first.

While Beau showered, Deb flipped through the TV channels. Had the untimely death of a scientist already slipped off the news radar? She should be thankful. She didn't need to have her picture flashed on the news again, although it added credibility to her actions for Zendaris.

And Prospero.

Had her Team Three cohorts recognized her from the grainy photo?

Beau had finished his shower faster than she thought humanly possible. He burst through the bathroom door, fully dressed and toweling his short hair.

At least he was sparing her the sight of his half-clothed body for once. She couldn't take much more temptation.

"Are you ready?" He rubbed a little gel between his palms and slicked it over his wet hair.

"Are you?" She made a circle with her index finger in his general direction. "I didn't realize Loki used so much hair product."

He held up the tube. "This? Just keeps things in order."

"Got it." She held up her hands.

"Where are we going?"

"I thought I'd take the T into Boston and follow that red line painted on the sidewalk that goes past all the historical sites. I've done it before. It takes you from Boston Common all the way to the *USS Constitution* in Boston Harbor."

"Sounds like an all-day adventure."

"What else do we have to do except wait around for Zendaris's instructions—and he seems to be taking his sweet time."

"You're right, and it'll take your mind off…things."

"My mind's never off Bobby, if that's what you mean." Deb zipped up her jacket and pressed her lips together just in case Beau thought a smile meant she'd forgotten about her son…their son.

"Hey." He pulled her toward him by the edges of her jacket and yanked her zipper up to her chin. "I know that.

You don't have to prove anything. You wouldn't be contemplating murder and mayhem at Zendaris's behest if Bobby didn't mean the world to you."

"It's just that sometimes…" Her lip trembled and she bit it.

He wrapped his arms around her and held her flush against his body. His heart beat strong and sure beneath her cheek and she closed her eyes to soak in his strength.

She allowed herself one minute of weakness, and then she pushed away from him. "Okay, let's get reacquainted with the Revolution."

They picked up a pamphlet in the Common and followed the red line painted on the sidewalk. When they hit Faneuil Hall, Deb's stomach grumbled, reminding her of the paltry breakfast she'd consumed in the hotel room—and Beau had stolen half of that.

Beau pointed to the food court. "I'm pretty sure that wasn't around in 1776, but I'm glad it is now."

"You must've been reading my mind—or listening to my stomach. I'm starving."

"I'm up for a burger and fries, you?"

"I'm going to the pizza place." She jerked her thumb toward a counter with a red-and-green-striped awning.

"Meet you back at a table in this general area. Do you have money?"

"It's on Zendaris." She waved a twenty at him.

Deb ordered a couple of slices of thin-crust pepperoni pizza, a small salad and a diet soda. Bobby had just been discovering the joys of pizza before he'd lost his appetite. A gnawing sense of worry joined the hunger pangs in her belly. She hoped Bobby's jailer was feeding him more than ice cream.

She dipped her hand into a canister, grabbed a few packets of Italian dressing and tossed them onto her plastic tray. She maneuvered through a tour group set free for lunch and claimed a table in the middle of everything.

A few minutes later Beau turned from the counter of the burger place, peering over two plates of food.

Deb waved and he weaved his way through the tables to join her, and plunked his plates onto the table.

She snatched a fry from the towering stack. "That's for eating my scone this morning."

He shoved the plate toward her. "You can have a lot more than that if you want."

"I'm good." She swallowed the fry and picked up her pizza. "How do you like the tour?"

"It's interesting. Those men who signed the Declaration risked a lot, didn't they?"

"Nothing worth having comes without some element of risk."

"I agree." He nodded and bit into his burger.

She dabbed her lips with a napkin and took a sip of her soda. She'd do well to remember that. If she wanted Bobby to know his father, she'd have to risk Beau's wrath and tell him about his son.

They ate their lunches, talking about the tour and history and their favorite players in the Revolution. They talked about everything but Zendaris and Prospero and the anti-drone plans.

They even talked about Bobby. Deb peppered her conversation with stories about him and how he'd changed her life. This had to be gradual. Once she sprung Beau's paternity on him, he had to have a feel for Bobby. She didn't want Bobby to be a complete stranger to his father.

Beau flipped open the brochure on the walking tour. "Are you up for the rest of the walk? Paul Revere's house and the *USS Constitution* and Bunker Hill?"

"Let's do it." She collected her trash and piled it on the tray. "We may not be here tomorrow."

They dumped their trash in the cans and stacked their trays on top. They went out a side door to continue their walk.

A light changed and Deb stepped off the curb. Out of the corner of her eye, she saw a car surge past the rest.

As she turned to face it, her world slowed down. The large black SUV careened through the intersection, heading straight toward her. Beau yelled out. Deb took one step and froze. Would she be continuing into the path of the car? Should she jump back?

Then she realized it wouldn't matter. Where she went, the SUV would follow.

Chapter Eleven

The SUV bore down on them, narrowly missing a car scooting through the intersection. Beau called out to Deb, but she seemed frozen, transfixed by the black vehicle.

If she didn't move within a split second, he'd have to move her.

Hell, what was he waiting for? He hooked an arm around her waist and yanked her back onto the sidewalk, smashing her into the corner of a building.

She gasped and it sounded as if she'd spent all her breath. A woman screamed—not Deb. Tires squealed, filling the air with the smell of burning rubber.

When Beau looked up, the SUV was speeding around the next corner. Someone had covered the license plate with paper.

Of course.

A woman hovered above them, panting and cursing. "Can you believe that idiot? He almost took us out."

Wouldn't be the first time.

"Are you okay, ma'am?"

"I'm all right, just shaking like a damned leaf. Is your wife okay? That moron came closer to her than me."

Deb raised her head, her eyes wide in a white face. "Oh, my God, he almost hit us. Was anyone hurt?"

The woman pressed a hand to her forehead. "No, but

it wasn't for lack of effort on that driver's part. He went right through the light and then it seemed as if he waited for pedestrians to enter the crosswalk before stepping on the gas."

Deb had sat up and was leaning against the building. A slight scrape marred her smooth cheek. "Thank God he didn't hit anyone. Did anyone get his license plate?"

"Big black behemoth—that's all I saw." She shrugged, straightened her jacket and stepped into the crosswalk again.

"Beau?"

"Big black behemoth with paper covering the plates."

Deb covered her mouth. "Then it was deliberate, and I don't think it was aimed at Miss Pink Jacket."

"I doubt it."

"What if it *is* Zendaris?"

"Deb—" he hooked an arm beneath hers "—we're not going to discuss this on the street."

She brushed off her jeans. "Let's continue this walk."

"Are you crazy?"

"What? Do you think he's going to try it again?"

"Stay close to me."

"So he can take both of us out?"

"I thought you were convinced he wasn't going to try the same stunt twice?"

"He's not, unless he has another blind car waiting in the wings."

They continued their walk, but this time, Beau kept his arm firmly around Deb's shoulders. When she squirmed under the weight of his arm, he took her hand and pulled her close, matching her step for long step.

"Why would you think Zendaris was trying to kill you when he's using you to go after the anti-drone plans?"

"Is he? Is that what he's using me for? So far he's

had me rob a jewelry store and kill a man. How is that bringing him any closer to the plans or me any closer to Bobby?"

"What do you think he's doing?"

"Playing some sadistic game. He can't get to Cade, J.D. or Gage, so he's taking all his fury out on me."

"I have a different take on it." He pulled her onto a bench looking out on a park with brown, wintry grass. "I think someone else is after the plans, knows you're after the same thing and doesn't want to lose out to you. He's trying to eliminate the competition."

"Who's he working for?"

Beau rested his ankle on his knee. "Maybe he's someone like me—a freelancer."

"Maybe he's working for Prospero."

"I was working for Prospero when the first shot was attempted in the hotel room."

Turning toward him, she placed her hands on his thigh. "Jack Coburn has excellent instincts. Maybe he knew from the get-go you weren't to be trusted."

"Thanks."

"Maybe he was testing you."

"Seems kind of convoluted to me."

"If your scenario is correct, Beau, we can't let this other guy beat us to the punch." She dug her nails into his leg. "If he gets the plans before I do, it's over for Bobby."

"Don't think like that." He lightly rapped his knuckles on her head. "We're double the trouble. Nobody is going to beat us at our own game."

She managed a weak smile. "Onto the *USS Constitution?*"

"For liberty and justice for all."

"That's the Pledge, not the Constitution."

"Conceived in liberty and dedicated to justice?"

"Gettysburg Address."

"I give up." He stood up and pulled her to her feet. "I obviously need the rest of this history lesson."

When they got back to the hotel, Beau stopped at the sundry shop and bought some cotton balls and antiseptic spray. In the room, he dabbed the scratch on her face, and she sucked in a breath.

After Beau treated her scratch, Deb hopped onto the bed and punched the pillows behind her. "If the guy in the SUV today is the same one with the high-powered rifle at the other hotel, he must be following us. That's just one of many things that scares me right now. If he's tracking us, who's to say Zendaris isn't tracking me. And if he is, he knows about you."

"Whoa, you're making a lot of leaps here."

Tilting her head back, she closed her eyes. "I just want Bobby back. I don't care about the plans, Zendaris or even Prospero. I just want to hold my son in my arms."

The mattress sank and Deb fluttered her lashes. Beau was on the edge of the bed, his blue eyes brimming with some emotion she couldn't identify.

Was it pity? She'd take that. She'd take anything from him at this point. Once she told him about Bobby, she may never get another chance to be with him.

And she wanted to be with him.

Beau inched closer. "Turn around."

Folding her legs beneath her, she presented her back to him. His strong hands closed around her neck.

"You've been on a roller coaster for over a week."

With his thumbs, he rubbed circles at the base of her neck.

"It's been more bearable since you showed up." She dropped her chin to her chest.

"This is not something you want to face on your own."

His knuckles massaged the sides of her neck. "Even if you're a tough-as-nails Prospero agent."

She huffed out a breath. "Is that what you think?"

"That's what I know. That's the woman I was attracted to in Zurich, and I've seen flashes of her in Boston—fearless, determined."

"I told you, I changed after Bobby."

"And I like this Deb even more. You're still fearless and determined—this time to protect your son—but you have some soft edges now that you were missing before."

His hands moved to her back, smoothing over the sharp angles of her shoulder blades.

"That's what having kids will do to you." She rolled her head back and hissed through her teeth when he dug his fingers into the flesh on either side of her spine.

"Does that hurt?"

"In a totally good way."

"You have so many knots in your neck, shoulders and back. You're holding all your tension in those areas."

"Are you a masseuse in your spare time?"

He chuckled in her ear, a low sound that made her mouth water.

"One of my sisters is a masseuse. She's taught me a thing or two. She claims every time I come back to the family homestead, I'm tied up in knots."

"That doesn't surprise me. You always seem coiled and ready to spring."

He lifted her hair and pressed his lips against the back of her neck. "Not always."

If she melted against him right now would he take the hint? "Beau…"

"Shh." He gathered her hair in his hands and buried his face in it. "If you don't want more, that's okay. If you do, that's okay, too. I'm not going to think you're less of a mother or less of an agent if you want to make love with me. It is what it is, Deb."

She turned toward him, and her hair slipped from his hands, falling around her shoulders. "I can't pretend anymore. I can't pretend that you're just some man who turned from a predator to a protector. You're a man who's been on my mind for the past three years."

"God, I'm glad to hear you say that." He encircled her waist with his hands. "I thought it was just me. I thought I'd built up a night of incredible sex into some epic encounter that I'd never experience again."

Stroking her hands across his shoulders, she smiled. "An epic adventure—yeah, it did feel like that."

She couldn't resist those lips a second longer. She shifted forward, and he took it from there.

When their lips met, a jolt of pure desire zapped her from head to toe. He felt it, too, because he held her tighter as if he was afraid she'd fall from the bed.

His hands tangled in her hair as he positioned her head, angling his mouth across hers. Their tongues tangled. Their breaths came heavy and hard.

Would it be like the first time they'd collided? Frantic. Eager. Breathless.

No. Tonight Beau Slater held her in his arms, not Loki. Tonight the father of her child held her in his arms.

He deepened the kiss, and stroked her back, slow and easy. Had he read her mind? This time the reckless abandon that had possessed them three years ago had morphed into a slow sensual dance.

Sitting back, he slipped his hands beneath her legs and pulled them straight, causing her to slide onto her back. He rolled up the hem of her T-shirt and trailed rough fingertips across her belly.

"This time I want to fully appreciate every inch of

you." He nudged the shirt up farther and ran his thumbs across the bottom crescents of her breasts through her lacy bra.

She gazed at him through her lashes. "Are you going to take ten minutes to get my T-shirt off?"

In one swift movement, he yanked it up and over her head. Then he placed it over her eyes. "Maybe you need to stop directing the action here, lie back and enjoy."

"I can do that."

The makeshift blindfold made every touch and every sensation a surprise, a welcome surprise. When she thought he'd continue his exploration of her breasts, he tickled the lobe of her ear with his tongue instead. When she thought he'd follow that up with a kiss to her mouth, he slid his hand beneath her bra and cupped her breast while teasing her nipple.

And on it went. Blindfolded, she became a canvas for his fingers, mouth, lips and tongue—and she still had on the majority of her clothing.

Finally, he slid her jeans over her hips and pulled them off, along with her panties. He brushed his hands along her inner thighs, parting her legs.

She held her breath, as tingles raced along her flesh, gathering in all the sensitive areas of her body. She could feel the heat emanating from his skin and knew all the rustling and clinking had come from the removal of his own clothing.

She almost snatched the blindfold from her eyes so she could feast on the sight of his naked form, but then she'd spoil his party.

He straddled her and the tight flesh of his erection brushed her belly.

Unbidden, her hips rose from the bed in anticipation.

Beau clicked his tongue. "Impatient woman."

Then he flicked her nipple with the tip of his tongue.

She gasped and began to draw her legs together, but he caught the insides of her thighs with both hands. "Keep your legs open—for me."

The growl in his voice had her quivering like a bowl of Jell-O, but she obeyed his command. Did she have a choice?

He continued toying with her nipples—tongue and fingers, pleasure and pain. His game had her squirming on the mattress beneath him.

After tweaking it, he sucked one nipple between his lips. As he pulled the aching nipple into his mouth, one finger drew a hard line from her navel to her throbbing folds.

The shock thrust her pelvis upward, and a groan escaped from her lips. "Why are you torturing me?"

He nipped her lower lip with his teeth. "Do you want me to stop?"

Raising her hands, she dug her fingernails into the first flesh they met—one hip and one arm. "Don't you dare. But can't you lift the blindfold so I can see where the next sneak attack is going to land?"

"And why would I do that?" The bed dipped on either side of her and she felt his knees at her hips.

Again, she hitched up her hips, but he cupped her breasts and squeezed them together. The hot flesh of his erection eased between the cleft of her breasts, poking her chin.

Two could play at this game.

She dropped her chin to her chest and stuck out her tongue to sweep it across his smooth skin.

He groaned but didn't stop. Neither did she. After a few more strokes, the time he spent close to her mouth increased until he stopped pumping her breasts altogether.

Hitching up on her elbows, she took him fully into her mouth. When she reached for the blindfold, he cinched her wrists.

"Not yet. I'm not done with you yet."

She gave a throaty laugh. "I thought I was just about to finish *you* off."

"You've clearly forgotten this is Loki you're dealing with—master of self-control."

He slid down her body and plunged his tongue into the warm folds between her legs. He drove her to the edge of madness with his mouth, lips and tongue.

As her belly coiled and her muscles tensed, he pulled away from her. She cried out and then amplified that cry when he drove into her.

He pulled the T-shirt from her face and scorched her with a gaze of blue fire.

She exploded around him. Wave after wave of pleasure surged through her body, and she clamped her legs around his hips to ride out the storm.

He gave a great shudder, slammed against her once, held his position for a few seconds and then continued stroke after stroke as he emptied his seed deep inside her.

When he finished he collapsed to the side of her, nuzzling her neck and caressing her breasts. "Can I just say, Madam Spy, that you're the best lay I've ever had in my life?"

"Aww, I'll bet you say that to all the lady spies." She punched him in the shoulder where her fist met solid muscle.

He grabbed her hand and kissed every knuckle. "No, I don't."

"Food, blindfolds, you're quite the inventive lover."

"I think the food was your idea."

"You started it by putting that strawberry in my... Never mind."

He had moved from her knuckles to her fingertips, kissing each one. "If I was so inventive, why'd you run back to the other guy so fast?"

Her heart skidded to a virtual stop in her chest. She did not want to have this conversation about Bobby's father. Not yet.

She smoothed her hand across the hair sprinkled across his chest. "You were Loki. You never even told me your real name."

"You never asked."

The cell phone, which was never far out of her reach, buzzed, and a breath hitched in her throat. "It's him."

Beau reached across her body and picked up the phone. He held it out to her and she grabbed it.

"Yes?"

Zendaris snarled over the phone. "Are you playing me for a fool?"

Chapter Twelve

The rosy afterglow on Deb's cheeks faded to white. Beau's heart slammed against his rib cage. Deb hadn't put the phone on speaker and being out of the loop even for a second had his blood pressure going through the roof.

"Wh-what are you talking about?"

Beau poked her thigh to get her attention. She twisted her head around and her eyes widened as if she'd forgotten his existence. She blinked a few times and pressed the speaker button.

"You told Prospero, didn't you?"

Deb choked and Beau cursed under his breath.

"I did not tell Prospero. Why would you think that? Do you really believe I'd kill an innocent man and turn around and tell Prospero about it?"

"Who said Dr. Herndon was an innocent man?"

"What are you suggesting?"

"I'm suggesting you called someone in for help."

Deb hunched her shoulders, and he tucked the sheet around her waist. Had Zendaris spotted him?

"I didn't call anyone in for help, least of all Prospero. The word on the street is I'm a traitor and Prospero doesn't suffer traitors kindly."

"Someone is shadowing you, shadowing me. I don't like it."

"Did you think a Prospero agent could turn and nobody would notice?" Her sharp tone filled Beau with admiration. This Deb Sinclair was finished with cowering and shaking at Zendaris's every command.

That's it, Deb. A good defense is a good offense.

Her attitude had thrown Zendaris off balance. He paused, and she jumped into the pause.

"If Prospero sent someone after me, it's not another Prospero agent. Coburn doesn't use his agents like that. If someone is on my tail, it's a hired gun." She formed a gun with her fingers and aimed at Beau.

"He'd better not get in the way of my plan. If he does, there will be— How do you Americans say it? A world of hurt…for everybody."

"There's not going to be any world of hurt. What are your plans? What do you want me to do next?"

"Break into Dr. Herndon's house and get the anti-drone plans."

Deb's mouth dropped open, but Beau didn't know why she was so surprised. They'd figured Zendaris had those plans in his sights.

She recovered quickly. "Where's his house and is anyone watching it?"

"His house is outside of Boston, and whether or not anyone is watching the house is your problem, not mine." He gave her the directions to Herndon's house, which Deb scribbled on the hotel notepad on the nightstand.

She held the pen poised over the paper. "Where will I find the plans?"

"Again, your problem, Agent Sinclair, not mine." Deb closed her eyes and rolled her lips inward as if to rein in her emotions.

If Zendaris had dared talk to him like that, he'd ram

the phone down his throat over the line. But then he didn't have a son to worry about.

"And when I secure the plans, we talk again to discuss the trade."

"If someone doesn't beat you to it."

Deb set her jaw. "Nobody is going to beat me to it. The trade?"

"I'm a man of my word." He coughed. "I think your son's…ah, babysitter…is getting tired of the job anyway."

"Oh?" Deb's eyes flew to Beau's face as she dropped the pen to the floor. "Why is that?"

"Your son hasn't been feeling well."

Was Zendaris telling her this news to keep her off balance? To instill urgency?

"What's wrong with him?" Grabbing a pillow, she hugged it to her chest.

She should've grabbed him instead. Beau slipped a blanket over her shoulders, his arm lingering behind her back—just in case she needed something to lean on.

"I'm sure it's nothing, but you're a mother and you'd want to know. I have a soft spot for mothers, Deb." He paused. "My daughter didn't even have the chance to know her mother."

"I'm sorry—" Beau tugged on the end of her hair "—for your daughter. Every child deserves his or her parents, both of them. What are Bobby's symptoms?"

"I'm not a doctor, and you just killed one so get to his house and get me those plans, or your son is not going to have to worry about his symptoms."

Zendaris ended the call and Deb looked like someone had just punched her in the gut. Zendaris had lured her in with his talk of mothers and his sob story about his wife, whose death was at his door, and then delivered his last words with a hammer.

Deb's hands looked frozen on the phone, so Beau pried it from her fingers and gathered her in his arms like he'd wanted to do five minutes ago. He ran a hand down her stiff back. "It's okay. You can let go now."

Her body melted against his as a sob racked her frame. "He means it, Beau. He'll kill Bobby if I don't deliver those plans. What am I going to do? We've worked so hard to keep those plans out of his hands, but I have to save my son."

"We're going to do both, Deb. We have to do both."

"Bobby's still sick." She covered her face with her hands. "He must feel so abandoned by me right now. He's not feeling well and Mommy isn't there for him. How is he ever going to recover from this?"

He grasped her wrists and pulled her hands from her face. Then he brushed his palms across her wet cheeks. "This experience is not going to scar him for life."

"It took me a long time to get over my abandonment issues. It took a father figure like Robert. A boy needs his father."

Beau swallowed. Did this mean she had plans to go back to Bobby's father when this was all over?

"You'd had a child's life of abandonment, Deb. This is two weeks out of Bobby's life. He's not going to remember. Once he feels his mother's arms around him again, he'll forget you ever left."

"I hope you're right." A shudder ran through her body. She plucked a tissue from the box on the bedside table and dabbed her nose. "I'll bet your mom never left your side when you were sick, did she?"

"My mom?" After the drama of the phone call, he began to notice the cool air on his bare skin so he burrowed back under the covers and pulled Deb along with him. "God, no. My mother was a stay-at-home mom when we were little and when we were sick, she'd hover over us with homemade chicken soup and mentholated rub and disgusting concoctions for sore throats like apple cider vinegar."

She snuggled closer to him and curled her toes against his shins. "But you loved it, didn't you?"

"*Love* isn't the word I'd settle on. Let's just say none of us stayed sick for long."

"You're just saying that." She rubbed his chest with the heel of her hand. "You felt her love right there and you've been able to carry it with you everywhere. That's the kind of love I want to give Bobby."

"And you're giving it to him. You're risking everything to keep him safe, and he feels it—" he tapped the left side of her chest "—right here."

"Do you really think so?"

"There are different types of motherly love, and different types of mothers. How cool is it going to be for Bobby to discover someday that his mom is a kick-ass spy who battled an international arms dealer to keep him safe? I'd say that beats out homemade chicken soup any day."

She turned her head and kissed his arm. "What an amazing thing to say. How did I ever think you were cool and aloof?"

"That's the image I cultivated." He tousled her long hair, which already resembled a red-hued bird's nest. "Of course, if Coburn spreads the word that I took an assignment to protect a woman, there goes my image."

Her long eyelashes drifted closed and fluttered over her eyes. "Mmm, I don't know about that. The ladies will be throwing their panties at you even more than usual."

"The ladies do not throw their panties at me."

Her lips curved into a smile against his chest, and he lightly pinched her bottom. That made her squirm against him, so he did it again, but her breathing had deepened and her lips parted in a long sigh.

He whispered into her ear, "The only panties I want are yours."

THE FOLLOWING DAY, Deb dug into a piece of French toast with a swirl of cinnamon and warm pecans on top. "I can't believe we forgot to eat dinner last night."

"Really?" Beau speared a potato on his plate and dragged it through some sticky egg yolk. "Because it seems to me that you'd skip dinner and every other meal if my stomach didn't remind us to eat."

"It's the nerves. I can't eat when I'm stressed."

He raised one eyebrow as she smothered her French toast with syrup and flagged down the waitress for another side of bacon. "You're obviously not stressed."

"I don't know what it is. I feel energized today." She *did* know the reason. Part of it included Beau's pep talk last night. He thought she was a good mom and that cut loose a heavy burden she'd been carrying on her back like a Sisyphean-sized bolder.

Maybe he'd be more willing to sign up for fatherhood once she told him about Bobby's parentage if he believed she was a good mother. And she planned to tell him just as soon as this nightmare ended.

"It probably has to do with the fact that we're in the homestretch here. You have your final orders from Zendaris, and we're close to ending this."

She held up her hands, crossing her fingers. "I hope so. Were you able to access the floor layout to Herndon's house on the laptop before we came down here?"

"I was, and we're in luck. The house is not that big."

"Maybe that's why he went to the dark side. He wants a bigger home and all the stuff that goes with it. Because if he has those anti-drone plans, he definitely crossed over to the dark side."

"It probably also has to do with his taste in fancy women."

"Tastes like that can get you killed." Deb drew a line through her syrup with the tines of her fork.

"He found that out the hard way—not that the mysterious black-haired beauty at the charity ball had anything to do with his death."

"Do you think that's how Zendaris decided to use me once he got his hands on Bobby? He knew Dr. Herndon's proclivities?"

"He would've formulated a different plan if it had been Cade Stark's son he kidnapped."

"It wasn't Cade's son. He was able to keep his son safe."

"By eventually going to Europe. Aren't his wife and child still there?"

She plucked a pecan from her French toast and sucked it into her mouth. "You are good. That information is supposed to be top secret."

"So is the layout of Dr. Herndon's house, but I managed to get a source to send it to me."

"After breakfast we go up to the room and hash out a plan for entry?"

"For entry and search. The plans could be anywhere in the house. What format do you think they're in?"

"They were in a computer file, but I doubt Herndon left them on his computer. A skilled hacker can get into any computer, which Prospero found out when we first had the plans."

He waved the waitress over for more coffee. "They could be on a thumb drive or a CD, or he could've just printed them out. Will you know what they look like?"

"Oh, yeah." She bit into her last piece of bacon with a crunch and offered the rest to Beau, who took it. "When Cade first stole the plans from Zendaris, we were all briefed on what they contained, if not the particulars. That's why I think Zendaris is using me to do his dirty work instead of one of his usual goons—that and his thirst for revenge."

Beau leaned back in his chair and crossed his arms over his impressive chest. "Don't let him pull at your heartstrings over his dead wife, Deb. Men like Zendaris aren't sentimental. They may think they love their wives and children, but they put them in harm's way every day of their lives. A dude like that would sacrifice Granny if it meant more power and money."

"You're right. All the men on my team recognized that immediately. I was the only one who felt a modicum of guilt over the fact that his wife had been killed in our raid of his factory."

"That's because you have a soft heart." He reached out and dislodged a strand of hair stuck to her cheek.

She snorted. "Nobody has ever accused me of that before, including the girls at the reform school that I busted out of."

"Tough girl." A smile hovered on his sensuous lips.

"Are you making fun of me?"

"Not at all." He held out his hands. "You might kick me where it counts."

"I'd *never* do that." The thought of doing damage to any of Beau's beautiful parts caused her to cringe.

"There's a soft side to Deb Sinclair, and obviously Robert Elder saw that."

Her nose tingled. "Robert had to sandpaper away a bunch of layers to find it, and the process wasn't always pretty. He was a marine, so he was into that tough love."

Beau hunched forward, cupping his mouth with one hand. "So am I. In addition to the blindfold, I have some furry handcuffs."

She kicked his foot under the table as all those afore-mentioned soft spots started to melt. "That was not a blindfold. That was my T-shirt."

"More coffee, sir?" The prim waitress's gaze darted back and forth between the two of them as if waiting for one of them to sprout horns—probably Beau.

"Yes, please, ma'am."

His wicked grin had spread over his face, and the wait-ress blushed to the roots of her severely restrained hair.

When she spun around, rather too quickly, Deb kicked him again. "You're a bad boy."

"I do have those fuzzy cuffs if you want to use them."

"I think we need to get our minds out of the gutter and into Dr. Herndon's bedroom—uh, house."

Pushing back from the table, he winked and dropped several bills on the table.

Deb tapped the money. "That's an awfully big tip."

"She earned it. Her ears are going to be burning for hours."

Back in the hotel room, Beau brought up the plans for Dr. Herndon's house, and they hunched over the table together reviewing the layout. They drew green lines to several possible entrances to the house and red lines for quick escape routes.

"If anyone is staking out the house, let me take care of him…or her."

Deb's red pencil went off the table. "We're not going to leave any dead bodies behind this time, are we?"

"Not unless it's self-defense. Someone shoots at me, I'm going to shoot back. It's second nature."

"Great." She rubbed out the pencil line with the tip

of her finger. "What if there's someone on the property? He's not threatening you, but he's blocking our access to Herndon's house?"

"I have a dart gun in my arsenal. Sometimes it's deadly and sometimes it's not. That will be a *not* situation."

Deb took a few steadying breaths. "If we get the plans, do I tell Zendaris? Lie? How far do we take this?"

"Far enough to get Bobby back—without compromising national security."

"You make it sound so easy, Loki."

"Anything worth having is hard, Deb. Didn't you just say something like that last night? Worth the risk? If this isn't worth the risk, I don't know what is."

She nodded. Beau always knew the right words to say. Didn't he ever stumble and fall? Didn't he ever have regrets? Didn't he ever have fears? Could she trust a man like that?

Of course, he just might regret their one-night stand when she got around to telling him about Bobby. It would break her heart if he did, but she'd have to face it. And then she'd move on.

She'd decided that giving Bobby a father had to become a priority. No more declining blind dates or brushing off the flirtations of various men at the gym, the grocery store, friends' parties.

No more daydreams about Loki—or night dreams.

She'd reveled in every second and sensation of their lovemaking last night, knowing they might not come together again. She'd have to stop comparing every man she met to Beau. It wasn't fair to the men, her or Bobby.

He needed a father, not some illusion. Not some spy on a pedestal. If Beau wanted nothing more to do with her or Bobby at the end of this game, she'd stuff her feelings down and form a relationship with someone who could be there for her and her son. Someone who could be there when the guns stopped blazing and the cars stopped screeching.

She could do it. Anything worth having was hard.

Dropping her pencil, she yawned. "I think I'm going to take a nap before lunch and finalizing these plans."

"Oh, no, you're not."

She snapped her mouth shut. "Excuse me?"

"We have a mission tonight. Your strength and agility just might save your life—and mine." He threw one of his T-shirts at her. "We're going to the gym to work out."

"You're worse than one of my Team Three members. Can we nap after the workout?"

"We can definitely go to bed after the workout."

She threw a sharp glance his way, but he'd bent over to tie his shoes.

He stood up, dragging her coat from the back of the chair and folding it over his arm. "Do you want to hang this up? Might as well straighten up a little before we leave the room to the maid."

"Sure."

He extended his arm and stopped. "Did you leave the phone in here?"

Her heart skipped a beat as she swiveled toward the desk by the computer. "I thought I left it there."

Her pulse returned to its normal rhythm when she spied her lifeline to Bobby on the other side of the laptop. "It's here. I'll take it to the gym."

Beau plunged his hand into her coat pocket and pulled out her personal cell phone. "This is your own phone, right?"

"Yeah, that's mine. Is it dead? I haven't looked at it in days. I turned it off when I got here just in case someone wanted to use it to track me down."

He pressed a button. "Completely dead. It'll work with my charger. Do you want me to plug it in? You don't have to use it if you're afraid Prospero will ping you."

She shrugged. "Might as well. I'm not sure I want to see or hear any messages on there if they're all from Prospero."

He attached her phone to his charger and then crooked his finger at her. "No stalling. Let's go."

True to his word, Beau put her through a rigorous workout—strength, agility, balance. Not that a few hours hitting the gym would prepare her for the assignment tonight, but it bolstered her confidence.

Beau was good about bolstering her confidence. And how was she repaying him?

He came up behind her and kneaded her shoulders. "How'd that feel?"

"This feels great." She rolled her head back.

"I meant the workout."

"That felt great, too." Tipping her chin at the water dispenser, she asked, "Do you want more water?"

"Sure."

She pulled two plastic cups from the dispenser and waited for the woman in front of her to fill her water bottle.

When the woman turned, she smiled at Deb. "You and your husband have a great connection."

"My...? Yeah, we do."

"It must be nice to share interests with each other." She made a face and took a swig of water. "My husband and I don't do anything together anymore. I try to get him to be more active, but he'd rather sit in the room and read scientific journals."

Deb stepped around her to fill the cups. "Even if you

liked reading scientific journals, it's not something you can do together, huh?"

"Exactly. I'm even a nurse and I don't like it. Of course, I made my husband take me to that charity ball the other night and look how that ended up."

Deb's hand jerked and the water sloshed over the edge of the cup. "Charity ball?"

The woman's eyes bugged out. "You didn't hear about that? My husband was in town for that scientific symposium on defense. That's how he got an invitation to the charity event at the end of the conference, but that bigshot scientist croaked on the dance floor."

"Oh, I did hear something about that on the news." Deb placed the cup on top of the water dispenser. "Did they ever found out the cause of death?"

"Not that I know of."

"Did your husband know Dr. Herndon?"

"Dr. Herndon?"

"The man who died."

The woman smacked her forehead with the heel of her hand. "I'd forgotten his name already. See, you know more about it than I do. No, my husband didn't know him. Of course, now my husband is using that doctor's death as an excuse to avoid parties—as if that happens every week."

"Well, I hope the rest of your visit is uneventful."

"Now, what fun would that be?" She laughed and returned to her machine.

At least the woman hadn't recognized her from the charity ball or the newspaper photo the next morning.

She handed Beau the water and he tossed it off in one gulp. "Making friends?"

Deb pitched her voice low. "Turns out she was at the little shindig the other night."

"She didn't recognize you?" He crushed the cup in his hand.

"She did not." She wiggled her fingers. "Now stop wasting cups. I'll get you a refill in that one."

"You don't have to fetch water for me, Deb."

"You gave up a lot to help me. It's the least I can do."

Later they returned to the room and scurried for the bathroom door in a mad dash. They collided and Beau wrapped his arms around her from behind, lifting her feet off the carpeted floor. He swung her around and dumped her on the bed, landing on top of her.

She panted. "Are you really going to claim the shower first after I brought you all that water?"

"Is that why you did it, so you could call dibs on the shower?"

"Actually, you go first. I want to chill out and watch TV. Maybe I'll take that nap now."

"Are you sure?" He brushed a lock of hair from her eyes. "I was just teasing about the rush to the bathroom."

She pushed at his chest. "Go, but don't be surprised if I'm sound asleep when you get out."

He kissed her nose and rolled off of her.

When the bathroom door closed behind Beau, Deb snuck a soda from the minibar and swept her newly charged phone from the table on her way back to the bed. She stretched out, hit the remote for the TV and turned on her phone. It couldn't be tracked if she just checked her messages, could it?

She scrolled through several messages from Cade, J.D. and Gage, her Prospero teammates. They'd all ganged up on her, but it didn't sound as if one of them believed she'd turned.

She kissed the display of her phone. "I love you guys."

She also had several voice mails, and the ones from Jack Coburn didn't sound all that warm and fuzzy.

When the next voice mail started, the voice of Bobby's pediatrician surprised her. "Deb, this is Dr. Nichols. Give me a call as soon as you can. We got those test results back for Bobby."

A little fizz of fear touched the back of her neck. The test results? Dr. Nichols hadn't made a big deal about them at the time of the visit—just some blood, some urine. No big deal.

In the next voice mail, Dr. Nichols's voice sounded more urgent. "Deb, this is Dr. Nichols again. I need to speak to you about Bobby's test results. I don't want to worry you too much, but it is imperative we talk."

Well, Doc, you just worried me.

Deb held her breath and pressed two to hear the next message.

"Deb, I hope everything is all right. It's not like you to ignore any issues with Bobby's health, and well, this is an issue. We need to speak."

With dread pounding against her temples, she punched the button for the next message.

"Dr. Nichols here. Typically, I wouldn't go into this on the phone, but you need to hear this information about Bobby's test results. His blood tests indicated an immune deficiency. That's why he's getting sick so much. This is definitely not as serious as it could be, but Bobby's going to need some blood, and we both know that's not going to be easy with his O negative type."

The doctor explained a few more details that would've made much more sense in person where she could've asked some questions. But she couldn't be there. She was in Boston. And Bobby was with strangers. Sick. In need of blood. Blood she couldn't give him.

The bathroom door opened. "I thought you'd be sleeping by now."

Beau padded into the room on bare feet and halted. "Deb, is everything okay?"

She had the phone clasped between her knees and she raised her eyes to meet Beau's worried gaze. "No. Everything just went from bad to worse."

His gaze darted from the phone she'd left on the bed to the one in her hands. "Not Zendaris?"

"Bobby's pediatrician has been trying to reach me."

"Why?"

"Bobby's sick."

"Oh, Deb." He crossed the room and crouched beside her. "Is it serious? Is that why he's been feeling under the weather?"

"I don't know how serious it is, but he mentioned an immune deficiency. I need to talk to the doctor."

"But not HIV or something like that?" He placed a hand on her bouncing knee.

"N-no. He mentioned that this illness is not as serious as it could be, so it sounds like it can be treated."

"That's encouraging. Now we just need to get him home and get that treatment for him."

"You don't understand." She knotted her fingers and the phone dropped to the floor and bounced once.

"I know it seems like a long shot to get him back without giving Zendaris the plans, but we can do it."

"It's not that, Beau. It's the treatment."

"What is it? Some type of blood or platelet transfusion? It's not gonna be pleasant, but I'm sure he'll pull through."

"Something like that, but Bobby has an uncommon blood type, O negative, and he needs to get blood from another O negative donor."

A deep furrow formed between Beau's eyebrows. "That's a crazy coincidence. I have the same blood type."

"I know that. I figured you did."

He sat back on his heels, his hand sliding from her knee.

"I figured you did because you're Bobby's father."

Chapter Thirteen

The room spun around him. Hell, the world tilted.

He was a father? He was Bobby's father? He didn't doubt Deb. The timing worked out, although Bobby had to be older than she'd claimed. He hadn't just turned two; he must be almost two and a half. The picture of his nephew, Zach, his older brother's kid, looked just like Bobby in Deb's picture. How had he missed that?

This also meant Deb hadn't run back to her lover or boyfriend, probably hadn't had a boyfriend at all.

It also meant she'd lied. For over two years she'd kept his son from him and then she'd kept the truth from him for over two days now.

And now his son was sick and being held captive.

"Say something."

His gaze returned to her face, strained with worry, her eyes bright with unshed tears. He swallowed the angry words that rose to his lips. "Why didn't you tell me?"

She flinched.

He'd suppressed the angry words, but his fury must've seeped into his tone.

Spreading her hands in her lap, she said, "There were a few reasons, Beau. First, I didn't even know Beau Slater was your name. You were always Loki to me. You were Loki that night."

"Cop-out."

She flinched again.

"You're an intelligence expert. There was any number of ways you could've discovered the identity of Loki. Next?"

Her fingers twisted, but she held his gaze. "Okay, you're right. Maybe I could've figured out your real name. Then what? Presented a pregnancy to a man who'd made it clear he didn't want to be tied down? A man who reveled in the spy's life—a different country every week, no home, no family obligations, freedom?"

Her words pricked him—right between the eyes. He must've really gone overboard with the James Bond stuff that night.

"Good God, Deb. That was one-night-stand pillow talk. Did you really believe I was that shallow?"

"That's my third point." She held up three fingers as if to prove it. "I was embarrassed. We had a glorious, passionate encounter for one night. And then I was supposed to present you with a son nine months later? I wasn't some giddy girl who didn't understand the ins and outs of conception. I should've used protection."

"If it comes to that, *I* should've been using protection. That's not the point. You didn't, I didn't and we produced a baby. And then you kept him from me for over two years."

She jumped up from the chair and took a turn around the room. "I didn't know how you'd take the news."

"Doesn't matter. It's not up to you to control my feelings. Stop trying to control everything." He grabbed the pillow from the chair and threw it across the room.

She ducked, even though he'd tossed the pillow in the opposite direction.

"I was scared, Beau. I was afraid that I'd present you

with our beautiful boy and you'd reject him. I couldn't bear that for my son. Not my son." She swiped the back of her hand across her cheek.

Was she bringing up her own abandonment to soften him up? The hard knot that had formed in the pit of his stomach when she'd told him about Bobby loosened.

Squeezing his eyes closed, he pinched the bridge of his nose. He'd risen from his crouch when he threw the pillow and now they stood across the room from each other, the air between them crackling with emotion.

"I understand about your fears. I do. But you brought a child into this world alone. What did you put on his birth certificate for his father? Unknown? Isn't that *your* father's name?"

Her face crumpled and a sob ripped through her body, making her slump forward. "It was hard, but I thought it would be even worse if you knew about him and rejected him. I—I thought I could find a father for him one day."

Anger pounded against his temples and he smacked his chest with his fist. "I'm his father."

"I'm sorry." She raised one arm, her fingers stretched out toward him. "I should've tracked you down. I should've told you from the beginning. I see that now. I see how you talk about your nieces and nephews, but you didn't reveal that side of yourself to me in our first meeting."

He tensed his muscles, steeling himself against her gesture. Instead of going to her, which every fiber of his being wanted to do, he snorted. "Our first meeting was a hot tangle of body parts. My nieces and nephews didn't come up."

She dropped her arm and hugged herself. "I told you about my life—the foster homes, the trouble, Robert."

"Last time I checked, you're a woman. Chicks talk."

She rolled her eyes and the hug turned into arms crossed over her chest. "Oh, you talked, Loki. You talked about the fight you had on the streets of Istanbul. The cat-and-mouse game you played with the Russian spy in the halls of the Kremlin. The Saudi princess who stripped for you in her father's palace. You talked about the high life. The spy's life. You didn't sound like father material."

His skin prickled with heat. He wanted to ram his fist into the wall. He cleared his throat. "Pillow talk."

"It left an impression."

He wouldn't let her turn this around on him. She'd made the choice, and although he could understand that choice better, it didn't change the facts.

"You should've told me, Deb."

"I know. I see that now. I saw it when you talked about your family. I made a big mistake." She swept her hands across her face. "Will you help Bobby?"

"If you have to ask that, you don't see a thing."

DEB LET THE water from the shower trickle down her face to join the tears and wash them away.

She'd screwed up. Big-time.

All the reasons she'd given herself for not tracking down Bobby's father turned to ash when confronted with Bobby's father.

She'd allowed her fantasies of Loki to sway her. The stories he'd told her in bed hadn't done anything to disavow her of those fantasies. He was everything she'd imagined him to be.

Just not father material.

She hadn't been looking for a father for her children that night. She'd been looking for a good time. She'd been looking for a hookup with a man she'd dreamed about for two years, ever since she'd read about one of his exploits in a journal.

She hadn't been mother material that night, either. Beau was right—chicks talk. And she'd talked about a dysfunctional childhood being shuttled from foster home to foster home. Antisocial behavior. Thieving and lying. And finally being taken in hand by a tough ex-marine who'd lost his own daughter to a drug overdose.

If she were a man looking for a mother for his children, she would've run the other way after meeting her.

Sighing, she cranked off the water. They still had to get through this assignment together. She knew he had her back…and Bobby's. The fact that she'd even questioned his commitment put the nail in the coffin of any kind of relationship they might have had.

But he'd be there for Bobby.

She knew that now. Beau Slater would never abandon his son, no matter what his son's mother had done or how she'd insulted him.

They'd planned to get a bite to eat before setting off for Herndon's house. She'd gladly eat crow just to sit down with Beau and try to explain herself again. Not that it would do any good at this point.

She toweled off and dressed in the bathroom. Then she poked her head out the door. She didn't know what she expected to find—Beau sitting in a corner gnashing his teeth or standing on the balcony throwing pillows into the river.

He waved her over from where he was hunched over the laptop. "Found something interesting on our bookstore guy."

The tightness in her chest eased and she strolled to the corner of the room and looked over his shoulder. The screen showed a page from the beefy man's passport.

"Quite the world traveler, isn't he?" Her voice sounded high and unnatural so she cleared her throat.

"Look at this." Beau jabbed at the display. "Didn't one of your guys track Zendaris down to a house in Colombia recently?"

"Gage Booker. He raided his compound down there, although Zendaris had already fled. That's where he found the nanny."

"This guy, Damon, was in Colombia recently. We can say with a fair amount of certainty that this man is in Zendaris's employ, and he's the one who left the invitation for you."

"It helps getting an ID and confirmation that he's Zendaris's man. Now if we could just see him again, we could follow him or get a jump on him."

"Exactly."

"Good job, Beau." She touched him awkwardly on the shoulder and then snatched her hand back. "I think I'll watch TV for a bit and then, um, did you want to get something to eat?"

Squinting, he brought his face close to the laptop where he'd brought up another document. "I think it's best if we eat in the room. We may have identified Damon here, but we still don't know the driver of the SUV yesterday."

"You're right." She backed up to the bed and sat up against the pillows against the headboard while she clicked on the TV. "Is the TV too loud?"

"No."

The hotel maid had done a good job of swapping out the sheets and making the bed, erasing all evidence of the passionate sex she and Beau had shared here less than twenty-four hours ago. Her clumsy declaration to Beau that he was Bobby's father had done a good job of erasing the rest.

She scanned through the channels, skipping over the local evening news. She didn't need to add to her depression anymore.

She stopped the channel at a cartoon with a silly sponge and a dumb-as-rocks starfish—one of Bobby's favorites. She giggled at their antics.

Several minutes later, Beau tilted his chair back to get a view of the TV. "What are you watching?"

"A cartoon—the sponge guy is trying to raise money with a singing contest, and his friend, the starfish, wants to enter but he's just so bad." She laughed again as Beau raised his brows. "I guess it's funnier when you know the characters."

"You know these characters?"

"Heck, yeah."

"Does Bobby watch this cartoon?"

"It's one of his favorites. That's their friend. He's an uptight squid."

Beau watched the cartoon through two commercial breaks, studying it as closely as he'd been perusing those documents on the laptop. Then he shook his head and resumed his research on the computer.

When the show ended, Deb flipped over to some comedy show rerun and dropped the remote on the bed. "Do you want me to order dinner?"

"Sure." He reached across the laptop and flipped open the room service menu. "Get me the steak, no potato, extra asparagus instead. Have them send up a pitcher of iced tea, too."

He tossed the menu at the bed and she dove for it before it hit the floor. She ran her finger down the columns of food.

Beau stretched and grabbed the handle of the balcony door. "You should get the...never mind."

He slid open the door and stepped outside. Leaning over, he folded his arms across the flat wooden barrier around the porch.

Deb picked up the phone and ordered a steak for herself, too. She wanted to match Beau stride for stride tonight. She didn't want him accusing her of holding them back. Of course, for that accusation, there'd have to be some passion involved and right now Beau was treating her like a casual stranger.

She studied him through the sliding door. The wind ruffled his short hair, and his strong profile stood out against the blue sky.

Was he thinking about their plan tonight or was he thinking about Bobby? Maybe he was thinking about both because if the mission didn't work out, he may never get the opportunity to meet his son.

Stop. She covered her mouth with her fist, biting into her knuckle. She couldn't think that way. It was counterproductive and flew in the face of everything Prospero had taught her. The mission had to succeed. There was no room for failure. There was no other outcome.

He stayed on the balcony until the food arrived. When the knock came on the door, he stepped into the room and retrieved his weapon from beneath the bed.

He used the same M.O. as he had a few nights ago. When he peeled his eye away from the peephole, he opened the door and rolled the cart into the room.

Instead of laying out their food on the table for the two of them, he took his own plate from the cart and brought it to the table where the computer sat.

She got it. He didn't want to eat with her. He could barely look at her.

She dragged the cart toward the bed, poured a glass of iced tea from the pitcher and placed it at his elbow.

"Thank you."

"You're welcome."

Then she plopped onto the bed and ate her steak from the cart. She didn't even like steak, but figured it would please Beau to eat what he was eating to prepare for the mission. Fat lot of good it did her.

She should've figured out two years ago that it would've pleased Beau if she'd told him they had a son together.

Beau shoved his half-eaten steak to the side of the table and leaned over to hoist the pitcher from the cart. "More tea?"

"No, thanks."

The brown liquid streamed into his glass, and the tinkling ice was the only sound breaking the silence between them. Facing the cops, a security system and a rottweiler at Herndon's house would be preferable to the strained atmosphere in this room.

Beau stirred some sugar into his tea and took a long drink, draining half the glass. "I have a black jacket you can wear and a black wool cap."

"Okay."

"We'll try the entrance we discussed first, and if there's a problem there we go around the back to our second option. Agreed?"

"Agreed."

"The most likely place for these plans in a house would be a safe. We'll search for a safe first. If there are any laptops in the house, we'll take them."

"Good idea."

"Once the police determine foul play in Herndon's death, they'll be all over his house. They may have already taken his computers."

"You're right."

"Deb." He plowed his fingers through his hair. "I don't need a yes-man. I need someone to bounce ideas off. I need someone to challenge and correct me."

She dropped her fork on her plate. "I just want to make it up to you, Beau."

"Ordering steak and saying yes to everything I throw out there is not going to make up for keeping my son a secret from me."

"I'm trying. I just want to explain…"

He sliced a finger across his throat. "Save it. I already told you I'm going to help Bobby, right now—tonight, and when he comes home by donating my blood or whatever else he needs. I'll be there for him. You don't need to worry about that."

Would he be there for her, too? Somehow, looking into his frosty blue eyes, she didn't think so. It had to be enough that he'd be a part of Bobby's life.

"Thanks. He's a wonderful little boy."

"And stop thanking me. It's what any father would do for his child."

"Not necessarily." She stabbed her fork into the steak.

His tone softened. "It's what this father would do."

She shoved the cart out of her way and brushed past Beau. Hovering over the laptop, she said, "What are we going to do if the neighbor on this side of Herndon's property has security lights? And are we going to search together or split up? Together is safer—apart is faster."

He joined her at the computer, careful not to touch her as if she had cooties.

She tried not to inhale his scent, tried not to notice his strong hands hovering over the keyboard.

Nodding, he said, "That's what I need from you."

And I need so much more from you.

A few hours later, they were ready to roll.

They'd packed their equipment in a backpack and stashed it in the trunk of Deb's car—the car Zendaris had provided for her getaway. The drive out to Herndon's house took just over thirty minutes.

Beau cruised past the house first. The leafy suburb provided some generous space between the houses.

Deb said, "At least the houses aren't right on top of each other. I don't think any neighbor casually looking out his window is going to see us breaking into Herndon's place."

"Or going to hear a breaking window."

"They will hear an alarm, though, so we'd better make sure that system is deactivated."

Beau parked the car around the corner. "Are you ready to make a run for it if we have to?"

"Didn't I tell you I used to run track in high school?"

"You told me you used to run from the cops in high school."

"That's why I was so good at track." She winked and coaxed one small quirk of the lips out of him. That was the first thing remotely related to a smile she'd seen since she'd told him the news about Bobby.

Beau pulled the pack out of the backseat and hung it over one arm as he exited the car. Deb followed, easing her door shut. A dog barked in the distance but not because he'd heard any slamming car doors.

The soles of their tennis shoes whispered on the bare pavement. If this had been fall instead of winter, multi-colored leaves would be crunching beneath their feet. Occasionally, a brown leaf skittered across the road.

Deb had tucked her hair into the cap and had zipped Beau's jacket up to her chin. If anyone did spot her, they'd see a floating white oval in the black of night.

They reached Herndon's house and crept along the side

of the front lawn. They located the low window on the side of the house that led to a back bedroom in the house.

Beau fished a glass-cutting tool and suction cup from his bag and sliced a neat square at the top of the window near the lock. He attached the suction cup to the glass and pulled, removing the glass with no muss and no fuss.

Deb whispered, "You could be a cat burglar."

He reached into the space with his long fingers and flicked the lock. "Now let's just hope he hasn't further secured the window with a bolt."

He pushed on the window sash and after a little resistance, it slid up.

As planned, Deb hoisted herself through the window, flicked on her penlight and sailed through the sparsely furnished bedroom. She turned to the left, located the mudroom and unlocked the door.

When Beau appeared out of the darkness, she jumped, banging her elbow on the washing machine.

"Careful." He steadied her by placing a hand on her back. "Let's find his office first, check for computers and safes, and then look for other likely locations for safes."

"The room I entered looked like a spare bedroom. We can skip that one."

The beam of his flashlight led the way out of the mudroom and back to the hallway. They poked their heads into the other rooms off the hallway, but Herndon had used them all as bedrooms. A smaller room off the living room contained a desk and shelves crammed with books and binders.

"Bingo." Beau swept the room with his flashlight.

A computer monitor sat on the desk, but cables dangled where it would have been attached to a CPU.

Deb pointed at the tangled cables. "Do you think the cops took that?"

"Herndon died two days ago. It's probably going to take the cops a little longer to get the approval to search his premises."

"Maybe he sent it out for repair or didn't even use it." She scanned the desk. "Is there a laptop instead?"

"Nothing. There's no computer in this office."

They rifled through the desk drawers, which Herndon hadn't bothered to lock. They checked in the small closet, but Herndon's messy office held no secrets.

Beau asked, "You okay to fan out?"

"I'll backtrack to his bedroom, and you can take the front of the house. I saw some paintings in the living room—perfect place for a wall safe."

"Whistle if you find something."

Deb sidled along the hallway, trailing one hand along the wall. She skipped the two spare bedrooms and headed straight for Herndon's private lair.

She went for the closet first and shoved aside the Oxford shirts and tweed jackets to search the floor of the closet. Shoes took up most of the space on one side and boxes of papers and awards on the other. He could've buried the plans under this meaningless stuff to throw off any potential thieves. Thick dust coated her fingers where she'd moved the boxes, so it didn't seem likely he'd hidden something here in the past several months.

She sat back on her heels, wiping the grime from her gloved fingers on the carpet. Dr. Herndon wouldn't mind now.

Her gaze skimmed the small pictures on the walls, too small to conceal a wall safe. She checked anyway.

The king-size bed dominated the room with its four posts and deep blue bedspread. It figured, since Dr. Herndon had been quite the ladies' man. He'd probably had his share of young, eager female students in this room.

A flat-screen TV faced the bed, and surround-sound speakers stared down from each corner of the room. He even had a small refrigerator tucked into a credenza with glasses lining the shelf.

Ducking down, she swung open the fridge and two bottles of wine clinked together. She stared at the books on the nightstand with headphones hooked over the drawer. He'd spent a lot of time in this room.

She dropped to her hands and knees. Robert had stored lots of stuff beneath his bed—even cash—said he trusted his bed more than a bank. Deb crawled to the bed and flipped up the bedspread. She reached for a long case and knew before she unzipped it she'd find a rifle.

A wooden box was cozied up next to the edge of the nightstand and she pulled it toward her. The small lock that secured it was child's play for her knife. She flipped up the lid and gasped.

Explicit photos of women in varying stages of bondage littered the top layer of the box. She shuffled them to the side and curled her fingers around the papers beneath.

The footfall on the carpet behind her caused prickles to run across the back of her neck. She held her breath, waiting to hear Beau's low, sexy voice.

She didn't.

Chapter Fourteen

"Get your hand away from the knife and move to the left, Agent Sinclair."

Beau drew back from the door. The man holding Deb at gunpoint obviously had no idea Deb had company in the house. Good.

The man blocked Beau's view of Deb, but he heard a rustling noise. She'd better not try anything stupid like go for her knife.

Beau took one silent, stealthy step to the right to line up behind the guy. While their unwelcome visitor was giving some other instruction to Deb, Beau was at his back in two long strides.

With one hand he gripped the back of the man's neck, squeezing with all his strength. With the other he knocked his gun hand to the ceiling.

The man didn't even get a shot off. He dropped to his knees, the gun falling from his hand.

Deb lunged for her knife and jumped to her feet. She kicked the gun away from the man's reach.

He wouldn't be needing it anyway.

Beau hoisted the backpack over his shoulder and snatched the gun from the floor. "Let's get out of here. Now."

"Is he dead? Did you break his neck?"

"With my fingers?" He snorted. "I cut off the blood flow through his carotid artery. He's out, but he'll be coming to soon, and this one usually works with a partner."

"You know him?" The whites of her wide eyes shined in the dark.

"Yes. Now move."

They crawled out through a different window in case someone was watching the mudroom door or the broken side window. When they hit the ground, they did an army crawl away from Herndon's property.

Grass, leaves and dirt clung to Beau's clothes as he crawled after Deb, silently urging her on. She'd been the complete professional all night. The atmosphere had been tense between them, but she'd never lost her focus.

He couldn't say the same for himself. Bobby weighed heavy on his mind all night—his son. What if his immune deficiency disease got the better of him before they could rescue him? What if he never got to meet him? After the failure of tonight, that possibility was too real to contemplate.

Ever since Deb broke the news to him, he'd wanted to see his son's picture again but he was too proud to ask. Or too stupid. He wanted to know everything about him. Now the only way he might know Bobby was through secondhand accounts.

No. He couldn't let that happen.

They found themselves in the backyard of the next property. This one hugged the corner lot, and if they got through the rest of this yard they'd be close to the car.

Deb had figured out the same thing. She twisted her head around and pointed to the side.

The tangle of foliage finally ended at the edge of a manicured lawn. They continued their crawl across the dew-soaked grass and skirted the brick patio. A wooden fence separated the yard from the street and they hopped it, landing on the dirt path that passed for a sidewalk in this area.

The car was waiting for them, unmolested. Beau didn't want to alert anyone along the street, so he held off on using the remote until they got to the doors. They slid inside and he tossed the pack into the backseat. Without turning on the headlights, he started the car and shot off down the road.

They didn't speak for several minutes, their panting filling the car, steam rising from their bodies.

Beau hurtled toward the freeway, careening along the on-ramp. A few cars whizzed past them, but nobody else had gotten on the freeway where they did.

Beau broke the silence. "That guy was my replacement."

"Where do you know him from?"

"Security circles. Coburn didn't waste any time. He may have already had the guy lined up before he even spoke to me. Who knows? He could've even traced my cell phone."

"How'd he figure we'd be at Herndon's house?"

"Coburn had already put two and two together. I told him you were in the Boston area and then Dr. Herndon winds up dead in the Boston area. The guy was probably just staking out Herndon's house."

"Jack's going to know you're helping me." She pulled the black cap from her head and the static electricity made her hair stand out at the sides.

"Yep." He squeezed her thigh because he just couldn't help himself despite his hands-off policy. "I'm sorry, Deb."

"Sorry? What for?"

"I'm sorry we got interrupted in our search. Sorry we

won't be able to give Zendaris what he wants—for now. But we'll get another chance. I'll make sure of it."

"Oh, yeah, that." She reached inside her jacket and pulled out a sheaf of papers. A few photos fell into her lap.

"Is that what I think it is?"

She waved the papers in the air. "I have the anti-drone plans."

BACK IN THE hotel room, they sat across from each other on the bed, passing the papers back and forth. Beau was no scientist or engineer, but he trusted Deb when she told him this is what she'd been briefed on to look for.

"I can't believe he had these plans underneath his bed. Maybe that's where we should hide them until we get them into secure hands."

She tapped the edge of one of the photos on a piece of paper. "How are we going to get these into secure hands and get Bobby back from Zendaris?"

"We'll wait and see how he wants to do the exchange before we come up with a plan."

"Bobby needs to get back home to start his treatment. The doctor indicated he'd be at risk for all kinds of viruses if we don't."

"I promise you, we will." He toyed with one of the pictures Deb had found with the plans. "I guess Dr. Herndon liked to keep all his dirty little secrets in one place."

"I told you he was kind of a perv." She peered at one of the photos. "But it looks like everyone is a consenting adult and thoroughly enjoying himself or herself."

"Especially her." He flicked a photo in Deb's direction.

She pinched it between two fingers, her eyes widening. "Oh, my God."

"What?" He rose to his knees and took another look at the picture. "This one is no more extreme than the others. It just looks like she's really getting into her dominatrix role."

"I know her." Deb tapped the photo.

"You're kidding. What are the chances of that?"

"No, I *know* her. She sold or gave the plans to Herndon."

"This woman in black leather and thigh-high boots is the one who stole the plans from Stark?"

"Abby Warren—turns out she was a psycho, not just a garden variety traitor."

"Uh-oh, you don't want a woman holding a whip to be a psycho."

Deb dropped the picture. "She led Zendaris on—promised to give the plans back to him when she'd probably already sold them to Herndon."

"Somehow I find it hard to muster up much sympathy for Zendaris. Someone cheated him at his own game—good for Mistress Abby. Someone's about to cheat him again."

"I hope he calls soon." She plugged the Zendaris phone into the charger and rolled up the plans. "We can't stash these under a hotel bed. Where should we hide them?"

"Can't we just burn them?" He snapped a rubber band around the tube.

"I have to turn them over to Prospero. It would be a feather in Jack's cap to produce these plans for the Department of Defense. Weapons experts can study them to find out how to fortify the drone missile against deactivation."

"You care that much about Prospero and Jack? He just sent a guy to capture you."

"He's just doing his job." She uncrossed her legs and dangled them off the side of the bed. "He sent you to me, too, and for that I'll forever be grateful to him."

"I think you would've figured a lot of this out on your own, Deb. In the end, you're the one who found the plans under Herndon's bed."

She folded her hands in her lap and kicked her legs. "I wasn't referring to the assignment. He sent you to me and you couldn't have been a more perfect person at a more perfect time. You offered to help me and help Bobby without even knowing he was yours."

"I could see how torn up you were about his kidnapping. A man would have to have a heart of stone to turn away from you." He traced the straight line of her spine.

"It was fate that Jack hired you before he hired that man back at Herndon's house. If he'd been the one tracking me from the jewelry store heist, Bobby would be dead. Bobby got his father when he needed his father most."

"I'd like to think that amateur would've never pinpointed your location like I did."

"He's not going to call tonight. It's almost midnight."

Deb scrambled to her feet and jumped up and down on top of the bed, scattering the kinky pictures. "I don't know about you, but I'm wound up so tightly I can't sleep."

Adrenaline pumped through Beau's system, fast and hot and unwanted. Was this Deb's invitation to a repeat performance of last night? As much as he'd enjoyed that performance, they needed to settle a few things first.

He grabbed her ankle. "You've got surplus energy? How about telling me about my son? Show me that picture again and any others you might have on your phone. Let me in on the phone call tomorrow morning with his pediatrician, so I can learn about this illness, too, and what I need to do to make it better for him."

Her cheeks flushed a pretty pink, whether from her

trampoline jumping or his request, he couldn't tell. She bounced to her knees and grabbed her purse off the floor.

"Do I have pictures."

She started at the beginning with the same picture she'd shown him in her wallet with her holding a newborn Bobby in the hospital.

She talked his ear off the rest of the night and into the morning, regaling him with stories of Bobby's first smile, first step, first word—all the things he'd missed.

He soaked it all in now, feeling as proud of all of Bobby's accomplishments as if he were...his father.

Deb's manic pace slowed. She'd shown him every picture she had of Bobby. The stories got sillier and sillier as her lashes drooped over her green eyes.

When the phone slipped from her hand and her head slumped to one side, Beau tugged the covers down and helped her crawl underneath. He joined her, fully clothed as she was.

He slipped an arm around her shoulders and pulled her close until her head bobbed to his chest. As he stared into the face of this mom who'd gone to hell and back for her son and had managed to recover the plans to the anti-drone, he realized he was looking at Superwoman.

And even Superwoman made mistakes sometimes.

The next morning, Deb had already slipped out of bed and showered by the time he opened even one eye. He watched her stuffing her dirty clothes into a hotel laundry bag.

"Are you still running on adrenaline?"

She dropped the bag. "You were sound asleep a minute ago. It was the first time I'd been awake before you, so I thought I'd take advantage of it."

"If you're sending stuff to the hotel laundry, I'd like to include the clothes I wore last night." He yanked up the bedsheets and peered underneath. "The maid is going to wonder what the heck we were doing in here with all this dirt."

She kicked something on the floor. "We'd better pick up these, too, or we'll really have her wondering."

He leaned over the bed to find Herndon's private pics littering the floor. "You'd better save the one of Abby Warren. It shows how Herndon possibly got his hands on the plans."

"What do you think he was going to do with them?" She dropped to her hands and knees and started gathering the photos.

"I don't think his intentions were good or he would've immediately turned them over to the U.S. government. Maybe he was trying to sell them back to Zendaris and that's how Zendaris knew he had them."

She straightened the stack of pictures by rapping their edges on the nightstand. "If that was his plan, he was naive. You don't double-cross a man like Nico Zendaris."

"A man who takes photos like this—" he tapped the top picture of a woman with her hands secured behind her back and a gag in her mouth "—is not naive."

She flicked her fingers in the air. "That's sex. He was dabbling in high-stakes espionage, and he was in way too deep."

"He paid the price." He lifted the receiver from the hotel phone. "Are you going to call Dr. Nichols now?"

"Don't you want to take a shower first?" She wrinkled her nose. "Besides, I don't think we're going to get to talk to Dr. Nichols on the first call, especially on a Monday morning. We'll leave a message, he'll call back. That's the way it usually works."

He threw back the covers and rolled from the bed.

"Okay, put the call in, but don't start without me. If he calls back while I'm in the shower, drag me out."

"You got it." She placed the call and as she'd predicted, the nurse told her the doctor would call her back as soon as he was finished with his current patient.

Beau rushed through his shower, and while he was running his hands through his wet hair in front of the mirror, the hotel phone rang.

He stumbled out of the bathroom, and Deb waited until he'd joined her at the table before picking up the phone on the third ring.

"Hello?"

"Deb? It's Dr. Nichols."

Since the hotel phone didn't have a speaker option, Beau had tilted his head against Deb's to hear the conversation.

"I didn't get back to you sooner because I've been out of the country."

"How's Bobby doing?"

"He has some flu-like symptoms."

"That's to be expected. His defenses are down and he's susceptible to everything right now."

"Can you explain his problem again to me now that I have you on the phone and can ask some questions?"

"Of course."

"Bobby's father is listening in."

Dr. Nichols paused. "I thought he was out of the picture."

"He's back in it now, and he's going to be Bobby's donor since he's also O negative."

"That's good news. I like seeing families come together like this."

The doctor explained about the immune system in

layman's terms, and described Bobby's condition, treatment and prognosis.

Beau held Deb's hand through it all. It sounded scary but the doctor assured them Bobby's disease was treatable and eventually curable.

"So, when can you come in for a consultation? I want to outline everything for you, there are some forms to sign and we want to test your blood, Mr., ahhh, Mr...."

"Slater."

"Mr. Slater. We want to make sure you're compatible with Bobby and get all the paperwork done. So call for an appointment within the next week, Deb."

"We will." She held up her crossed fingers.

When Dr. Nichols ended the call, Deb slumped in her chair. "We have to get him in there."

"We have the plans, thanks to you. We should have this wrapped up within a week."

"I'm just anxious to know how that's going to happen. I assume Zendaris is going to designate some meeting place, maybe even where they've been holding Bobby all this time."

Leaning forward, he gripped both of her knees. "You're not going into any kind of dangerous situation."

She rolled her eyes at him. "It's too late for that, Beau. This whole thing reeks of danger."

"I think you should insist on a public place."

"You know he'll never go for that. He's not going to shoot me...or anyone else in public if things don't work out his way. He'd be stuck if we were in a public place."

"You won't be going in alone anyway. I'll be right behind you, one way or the other."

"We won't be able to trick him with the plans. He's seen them before, and he won't release Bobby until he gets a look at them. If we give him something fake, he'll realize it right away."

Beau rubbed his jaw. "It would be nice if the plans were a couple of lines or a formula. Then we could rewrite it in disappearing ink or paper that disintegrates."

"That would be a great joke, but you're right, it would take forever to copy those plans."

"So, we hand them off and somehow get them back."

"Do you really think he's going to let them out of his sight again after all he's been through? He thought he had them once when he had one of his minions track down Abby Warren's former roommate. Turns out Abby tricked him, and us, and had already done her modeling at that point for Dr. Herndon and had turned them over to him. Zendaris is not going down without a fight this time."

"I guess we just have to wait until he contacts you before we can figure out how to handle this."

"I wish he'd hurry up. You'd think he'd be antsy to find out how the operation went last night."

Beau gestured to his phone next to the computer. "Coburn knows how it went."

"What do you mean?" Deb grabbed his phone and examined it. "Shouldn't this thing be turned off? He'll ping it and track you down."

"Not this phone—untraceable." He held out his hand and she dropped the phone in his palm. He punched a button and held out the phone for her to read Jack's text message.

She read it aloud. "'You're helping Deb? You turned?' Followed by two question marks."

"Which means he doesn't really believe it."

"Two question marks told you that?"

"Coburn's not a man given to excess emotion. Two question marks mean a lot."

"He doesn't believe you turned, but he knows you were with me at Herndon's house last night? His agent must've reported in with the bad news."

"Deb, I don't think he believes you turned."

"He sent not one, but two hired guns after me. Even if the second one was pretty useless, that's still a big commitment on Jack's part."

"He wants to bring you in. At no time did he ever give me any license to harm you."

"It doesn't make a difference. I can't allow him to bring me in."

"We have the plans."

"We don't have Bobby."

Her mouth formed into a stubborn line and he knew she wouldn't listen to his scheme right now. Maybe she'd never be ready to hear it. Maybe he had to set it into motion without her knowledge.

Hell, it's not like she hadn't been deceiving him for almost three years.

Deb rose from her chair and stretched. "I am so sick of being cooped up in this hotel room. I'd really like some fresh air."

"I don't know if that's such a great idea. For a minute there last night, I thought we'd come face-to-face with your shadow, the man who's been taking potshots at you."

"Maybe he beat us to the punch. Maybe he's the one who stole Herndon's desktop computer. He searched the house but got focused on the computer and never looked in the right places."

"How did you come to look under the bed?"

"Robert used to hide things under the bed, too. He was paranoid that way." She walked to the window and peeked through the drapes.

"Despite his paranoia, he sure did a good job with you."

"He was the only father I ever knew, and he helped me so much with Bobby. He was his father figure and role model." She held up one hand. "And I'm sorry that wasn't you, Beau. It should've been you."

The realization that he'd missed those years with his son punched him in the gut all over again. He'd have to find a way to forgive Deb and make it stick. He'd have to hold the memory of last night, when they'd talked until dawn about Bobby, close to his heart. In that moment he'd forgiven her.

He blew out a long breath. "If it wasn't me, then I'm glad it was that grizzled old marine who was there for Bobby."

"Robert told me I was wrong." She threaded her fingers together in front of her. "He told me a man deserved to know he'd fathered a child. Deserved the chance to step up. He'd gotten his wife pregnant before they married, and the day she told him she was pregnant was the day he became a man, according to him."

"You didn't listen to him?" The more he heard about Deb's surrogate father, the more he respected him.

"I didn't always take his good advice."

The hotel fire alarm blared in the room, and they both jumped at the same instant.

"What the hell?"

Deb pointed to the brightly flashing lights above the door. "This is for real."

Beau strode toward the safe in the closet. "Get the plans. I don't like this."

"It's a fire alarm."

"How many times has a fire alarm gone off in a hotel where you're staying?" He punched in the combination of the safe. "Once, twice in all the times you've stayed in a hotel?"

"You think this is a setup?"

At least she wasn't arguing with him. She grabbed the dark jacket she'd worn last night and slipped the rolled-up plans with the photo of Abby Warren inside the breast pocket.

Some shouts resounded in the hallway, and Beau peered out the peephole. "Everyone's leaving."

"We have to leave. What if it's a real fire? And even if it isn't, I'm sure security or the fire department is going to do a check of the rooms."

Who else was going to do a check of the rooms, or more specifically, this room? "It sure is an easy way to clear out all the rooms, isn't it?"

She patted her chest. "I have the plans with me. All anyone's going to find in here is a bunch of disguises and some stolen jewels in the safe. He's welcome to them. Of course, if the cops find those we'll be in a world of trouble."

"It's not the cops I'm worried about."

They joined several people in the hallway, chattering as they made their way to the stairwells.

Before one of the men swung open the stairwell door, Beau stepped in front of him. "Hold on. You should always check to see if the door's hot first."

He pressed his hand against the fire door and stepped back. "It's fine."

The man mumbled as he brushed past Beau on his way into the stairwell, "Who's he, Fireman Bill?"

Beau met Deb's dancing eyes above the hand covering her grin. "I'm sorry, but you are kind of bossy."

"Someone's gotta take charge around here."

People thronged the stairwells, the guests on the top

floors pushing and shoving to get to the bottom. Beau positioned himself behind Deb to protect her from the human onslaught.

He bent forward and whispered in her ear, "I'm glad this isn't a real emergency."

Hotel personnel ushered them out a side door into the chilly morning. Guests in coats hastily thrown over bathrobes or pajamas blinked in the bright light. Others warmed their hands on coffee cups from late-morning breakfasts. Businesspeople in their suits and smart coats checked in with hotel staff and then slipped into taxis to do their morning work. A group of school kids shoved and giggled while their chaperones gave them the evil eye.

Beau tensed his muscles and scanned the crowd. Had someone pulled the fire alarm to lure him and Deb out of the hotel? The man Coburn had hired as his replacement didn't know their location if he had to stake out Herndon's house to surprise Deb.

What about Zendaris? Maybe he figured Deb had the plans and would get a jump on her before working out a trade for Bobby. His gut rolled. He did not have a lot of confidence that Zendaris would return Bobby once he got his hands on the plans.

Zendaris didn't want just the anti-drone plans. He wanted revenge on Prospero Team Three, and now he had the perfect opportunity to get it.

Someone shrieked and Beau reached for his weapon. He cranked his head around to see one of the schoolgirls in the shrubbery.

Deb patted his arm. "Easy, cowboy."

"I don't like it."

"Neither do I. It's freezing out here." She hunched her shoulders, turning up the collar of the jacket she'd borrowed from him.

Beau curled his arm around her waist and felt for the plans secured in her inside pocket. "Just don't drop these."

"And I thought you were just trying to warm me up."

"I can do that, too." He wrapped both arms around her and pulled her close, the plans crinkling between them. She remained stiff in his embrace, probably not sure what it meant.

Hell, *he* didn't know what it meant. His feelings for her ping-ponged between anger, understanding, admiration and pure unadulterated lust.

And something else—something much more.

With the fire trucks still parked out front, hotel security waved their arms and shouted an all-clear. The hotel guests began shuffling back into the building, heading for the elevators.

Beau steered Deb back the way they'd come. "Let's take the stairs. It beats waiting in line for the elevator."

They jogged up the three flights of steps and pushed through the fire door on their floor. They'd beaten most of the other guests back inside.

Beau slid the key card into the lock and pushed open the door. He stepped back to allow Deb in first.

When the door slammed, a gust of cold air greeted them. A rash of goose pimples raced up Beau's back, but it didn't have anything to do with the temperature.

"Deb, get down." He reached for his weapon for the second time this morning, but this time it was no school-girl he confronted. And it was too late.

A man dressed like a firefighter emerged from the curtained balcony, holding a gun in front of him with two hands. "We finally meet face-to-face. Now hand over those plans."

Chapter Fifteen

Deb felt the papers warm against her chest and held her breath. She could sense the tension vibrating from Beau's body.

The man pointing the weapon looked familiar, even in his firefighter disguise. *Damon.*

Zendaris was double-crossing her. He'd had no intention of returning Bobby to her. Her rage crashed through her body in hot waves, and she clenched her fists, her nails biting into her flesh.

"Slide your weapon across the floor, Loki." Damon aimed his gun at Deb's head. "Or the broad gets it right now."

Deb's pulse jumped. Zendaris had known all along that Beau had been helping her? Was that the reason for the betrayal? Had the man she'd believed was Bobby's savior turned into his destroyer?

Beau slid his weapon from his shoulder holster, placed it on the carpet and slid it across the floor. "Did Zendaris ever plan to return the boy?"

"Zendaris?" The man practically spat the word. "You still don't get it, do you?"

"What don't we get, Damon?"

The man smiled—his white teeth standing out in his

brown face. "You're good, Loki. I'd heard you were the best. But I'm better."

Deb licked her lips. "Zendaris is not getting the plans until I get my son."

Damon cursed and this time he did spit. "I'm not working for Zendaris. I'm on my own now. I'm starting my own business, and it's going to start with those anti-drone plans."

Deb didn't know whether to laugh or cry. If this man got the plans from her, she'd never see Bobby again. But this was not a Zendaris double cross.

She shot a glance at Beau's stony face.

He spoke, barely moving his lips. "You work for Zendaris."

"I *did* work for Zendaris. I told you, I'm striking out on my own, and I want those plans." He wiped his mouth with the back of his hand, but his aim stayed steady. "Zendaris is supposed to be so brilliant, but I'm the one who watched this Prospero agent. I'm the one who discovered she'd hooked up with Loki. I'm the one who attached a GPS to the car Zendaris left for her."

"Does Zendaris know that?" Beau was flexing his fingers.

"Why should I tell him? *El jefe.* He wants all his peons to call him *el jefe. El pendejo* is more like it."

Beau asked, "If we have them, what do we get in exchange for the plans? Zendaris has the boy."

Damon hoisted the gun higher. "You get her life."

"Why don't you just kill me now?" Deb spread her arms wide. She'd die without Bobby anyway. "That was you who tried to shoot me at the other hotel and run me down with the car, wasn't it?"

He nodded. "I wanted you dead. I told Zendaris I could recover the plans from Dr. Herndon, but I guess he didn't trust me. I figured with you out of the way, he'd go with plan B—me. But now that you have the plans, I'll just take them from you."

He'd obviously already searched the room and hadn't found them. Deb opened her mouth to deny she had them, but Beau held up his hand.

"You killed Dr. Herndon?"

"I had to get him out of the way. I knew you two would pull some trick to make it look like Herndon died. I had to make sure it happened."

Deb threw her arms out to the side. "You were at that party, too?"

"Don't feel bad. I didn't recognize you two, either. I posed as security and then slipped some poison into those 7 and 7s he was downing faster than a sailor on leave."

"Why didn't you tell Zendaris about your accomplishment?" Beau asked.

"Why would I? He'd only wonder why I stepped in. The man doesn't trust anyone."

"If we give you the anti-drone plans now, you'll leave? You won't hurt Deb?"

"I don't care about her. Prospero's never going to get their hands on them again anyway. I already have a buyer. Give me the plans and I'll let you both go. You'll have to deal with Zendaris anyway."

"The plans aren't here."

Deb stared at the floor.

"Where are they?" Damon narrowed his eyes.

"We left them in the car."

As soon as the words were out of Beau's mouth, Deb grabbed his arm. "No. We can't give him the plans. We'll never get Bobby back."

"You're more important to me than your son. I can't

lose you. I'll handle Zendaris. I'll figure out a way to get your son back."

Deb's fingertips tingled. Damn, they made a good team.

She choked out a sob.

Damon snorted. "Yeah, yeah, you'll work it out with Zendaris. Where's the car?"

"In the hotel parking lot."

"If you're lying to me, your girlfriend dies. Or maybe I'll bag Loki and start my business with some street cred."

"I'm not lying." Beau pointed to the gaping door of the safe. "You've already searched the room. You know the plans aren't here."

"Then let's get moving." Damon waved his gun. "And don't try anything on the way to the parking lot, or you're both dead and I'll find the plans myself."

They shuffled toward the stairwell with Damon behind them. Nobody saw them, but after the fire alarm nobody would look twice at a fireman walking through the hotel with two guests.

Deb hoped Beau had a good plan up his sleeve because Damon would have to pry these papers out of her cold, dead fingers.

They crossed a corner of the lobby to reach the walkway to the parking structure, receiving only cursory glances from the few people they encountered.

Damon's fireman getup clanked and squeaked as he lumbered behind them. Beau, in his dark jeans and dark jacket zipped up to his chin, looked like a long, lean panther beside Damon.

A long, lean, swift panther unencumbered and coiled to spring.

Yeah, Loki had a plan.

They climbed up one level and then two. Beau had

left the car on the second level when they'd come back from Herndon's house last night, but they continued to the third level. And beyond.

By the fourth level, Damon wiped sweat from his brow and growled. "Where is this damn car?"

"It's on the roof."

When they ascended to the top level, the wind whipped through the sparse parking lot where only a few lonely cars waited.

"Is this a joke? Your car's not up here." Damon grabbed Deb's arm and pulled her toward him, so close she could smell the coffee on his breath.

"Sure it is. It's the one on the end. Keys are in my pocket."

Damon tightened his grip on Deb. "Pull 'em out real slow or she dies right here and now."

Beau pulled a set of car keys from his pocket, dangling from his finger. They dropped to the ground.

"Oops." Before asking for Damon's approval he ducked to sweep them up.

He rose with a knife in his hand.

Deb didn't even see him swipe at Damon, but Damon grunted and his arm loosened. She plowed into his shin with her heel and ducked from his grasp.

He roared like an injured animal, and Beau slammed his arm upward with a sickening crack. The gun dropped to the pavement, and Deb scooped it up.

By the time she rose, Damon was on his knees, his right arm hanging loosely at his side, Beau's knife against his throat.

"I guess you're not going to bag Loki." He tipped his head at Deb. "Put the gun on him, Deb."

"Done. Now where's my son, you SOB?"

"I'm not—"

Beau smacked the side of his head with his fist. "Yes, you are. Where is Zendaris keeping the boy?"

"Why should I tell you that?"

"Because if you don't, this *broad* is going to shoot you. Don't forget, she's a Prospero agent trained to kill." Beau shrugged. "And if she won't, I will."

"I'm a dead man anyway if Zendaris ever finds out about my betrayal, and he will find out if I tell you where he's stashing the kid."

"Not—" Beau ran the tip of his blade beneath one of his fingernails "—necessarily."

The big man licked his lips. "Whaddya mean?"

"If you tell us where the boy is, I can make arrangements for you, arrangements that will keep you out of Zendaris's clutches."

"How?"

"You don't need to know how. I'm Loki. Just know I can do it."

Deb's mouth watered. Damn, the man was sexy when he talked like that.

Damon's eyes shifted from the knife in Beau's hand to the gun in hers. He swallowed and nodded once. "He's holding the kid in a warehouse in Crosstown, out by the south end."

Deb clenched her teeth to hold in her scream. Zendaris had promised to keep Bobby safe. Crosstown wasn't safe. Since this whole nightmare started she'd believed only half of the stuff coming out of Zendaris's mouth— including his claim that he'd trade Bobby for the plans.

Now she had him right where she wanted him.

"Address and layout."

Damon gave Beau the information, and he must've committed it to memory since he hadn't written down one word. When Damon was done, Beau turned to Deb.

"Hand me the gun and take the keys to the car. Drive it up here and get my black bag out of the backseat."

She left him holding Damon at gunpoint and hoped to God nobody stumbled onto the scene. They'd have a lot of explaining to do.

She wheeled the car up to the rooftop and parked, blocking the view from the stairwell in case one of the three owners of those cars came up here.

The men were still in the same position. In fact, they looked carved from stone.

She dragged Beau's bag out of the back and unzipped it. "What do you need?"

"Rope, syringe."

Damon's legs bounced on the ground. "That doesn't sound good."

"If I wanted you dead, you'd be dead." He handed the gun to Deb again while he secured Damon's hands behind his back. "Now stand up and walk toward the car.

"Pop the trunk, Deb."

"Wait." His feet skidded to a stop. "You're not cramming me in there."

"Relax, Damon." Beau pricked the needle in the back of Damon's neck. "You won't feel a thing."

As Damon slumped forward and stumbled, Beau folded him into the trunk and covered him with blankets.

"What are we going to do with him?"

"Leave him for somebody to find."

"Not the cops. He'll be back on the streets in minutes."

"Not the cops." He slammed the trunk down on their captive.

"Not the FBI or CIA? He'll talk. Zendaris can't know about this. We have him where we want him now. We have Bobby's location, and we can get the jump on him."

He cupped her face in his hands. "It's all right, Deb.

Our friend will be out for hours. By the time he comes to and I place my anonymous call, our business with Zendaris will be finished."

"How can you be so sure?"

"Look—" he smoothed his thumbs across her cheeks "—Damon's betrayal of Zendaris and his stalking of you were the best things that could've happened. To know where Zendaris has Bobby in advance of your meeting with him is priceless. We've got this."

He landed a kiss on her mouth—the first since she'd dropped the bombshell about Bobby. It felt good. It felt like a promise.

When he released her, the cold air hit her face, snapping her back to reality. They couldn't promise each other anything—not until they rescued Bobby.

She jerked her thumb at the car. "Where are we taking him?"

"I think it's safe to leave him here for now." He swept his arm across the parking lot. "Doesn't look like a lot of people park up here."

"Will he be warm enough in the trunk?"

His brows show up. "You're worried about him?"

"He gave us Bobby's location. I don't want him to die."

"He's not going to die, and if he does? He may have given us Bobby's location at gunpoint, but he didn't seem to care what Zendaris had in store for him once you couldn't deliver the plans. I'm not going to shed any tears if the guy dies of hypothermia."

Beau moved the car to a location away from the stairwell and blasted the heat in the car just to make Deb happy. "If you want to come out here and start the engine every few hours to make sure he's warm, knock yourself out."

She clutched the phone in her pocket and dragged it

out to stare at the display for the hundredth time that day. "Why hasn't he called?"

"He'll call when he's ready, which is fine because we have some work to do before he calls." He patted his chest as they descended the parking structure stairs. "You still have those plans safe and sound?"

"You were right about keeping them with us. If I'd tried to hide them in the room, Damon and the plans would be on their way to Istanbul or wherever."

He draped his arm around her shoulders. "Did I ever tell you about a fight I had in Istanbul?"

"You don't have to tell me stories." She smacked her hand against his hard stomach. "I've seen you in action, Loki. I'm a believer."

"Good. Then you're going to trust me now on how this is going to go down." He kissed the side of her head and pulled open the door of the lobby.

She stiffened and blocked his entrance to the hotel. "I don't like the sound of that. Why are you already warning me to trust you?"

Reaching over her head, he pushed open the door. "Let's get back to the room first."

When they got to their room, Deb rounded on him. "What are you planning to do?"

"Now that we have the plans and know where Zendaris is keeping Bobby?" He aimed his fingers into a gun and shot at her. "Bring in the reinforcements."

"Reinforcements?"

He yanked his cell phone from its charger and turned it on.

"Th-they might ping you and discover our location."

"Ping away. I've already given them our location."

"What? You're bringing in Prospero?"

"Specifically, Team Three—Cade Stark, J.D. and Gage Booker."

"You already contacted them?"

"Before our fake fire alarm and they're all on their way."

She sank to the edge of the bed. "What if Zendaris finds out?"

"How's he going to find out? This is Team Three we're talking about here. I don't know why you didn't trust them to begin with, Deb. Those guys have your back. They knew you hadn't turned." He typed a message on his phone. "I'm giving them the warehouse location now."

Fear and uncertainty swirled through her body, pumping up her adrenaline. "Unless they're lying. What if they just said that and instead they're on their way to bring me down?"

The bed dipped as he sat beside her and took her fidgeting hands in his. "Not everyone is out to bring you down. Look at Robert. You probably wondered what some old ex-marine wanted with a teenage girl he'd caught stealing from him. And all he wanted was to help you. I didn't even know Bobby was my son when I'd decided to help you. Team Three, those guys are your brothers. Let them help you, too."

"It's just—" she gripped his hands and fought the tears "—I've been doing it on my own for so long."

"You don't have to. Your brothers in arms are on the way, ready and willing to do anything to get Bobby back. And I'm here, ready and willing to be a father to Bobby— and more if you want it."

Her heart jumped, but she dared not look at his face. Did he mean he'd stick around? Want to be a family? Or had he said that to shore up her courage for the battle ahead?

She'd take it for now.

She dragged in a breath. "Where are they going to be?"

"We're not going to meet anywhere. We're doing this by secure text. I'll wait for their responses, but they'll probably move in and do surveillance on the warehouse before any meeting Zendaris sets up. We need to make sure Bobby's physically located at the property first. If they go in there with guns blazing and Bobby's not there, we'll tip Zendaris's hand."

"This is really happening." She jumped up from the bed and paced the room. "Where are they now?"

"J.D. was coming in from Colorado, Gage from Texas and Cade from Europe. Given the time zones and the fact they're all coming in on private jets, they should be here soon."

"And Jack? Does Jack Coburn know?"

"He knows."

"Why didn't you tell me?" She folded her arms and wedged a shoulder against the wall.

"I didn't want to worry you and I wasn't sure what role they could play, but as long as we had the plans I figured they had a right to know."

"I don't know whether to feel betrayed or happy."

"That's kind of how I felt when you told me about Bobby."

The pulse in her throat throbbed. "I never meant to betray you, Beau. I did it to protect myself, and yeah, because I didn't trust that you'd be there for Bobby."

He crossed the room to her slowly, his gaze never leaving her face, their electric connection as strong as it was the night their eyes first met at that bar in Zurich.

When he reached her, he curled one arm around her waist and cupped the back of her head with the other. "Woman, I know why you did it and it still pisses me off. But, God help me, it's not enough to make me give you up."

His kiss weakened her knees, and she had to cling to his neck so she wouldn't melt at his feet. His lips slid from her mouth and touched her cheeks, nose and eyes. As they hovered near her mouth again, she whispered, "I'm so sorry."

He ended her apology by sealing his lips over hers.

For the next hour, they communicated back and forth with Prospero Team Three. The three of them were on their way to Crosstown with enough ammunition and supplies to start a second revolution.

Beau assured them he'd let them know as soon as Zendaris set up the meeting. They agreed that if they got confirmation of Bobby's presence in the warehouse, they'd move in.

"I'm hoping that's the case. I really have no desire to meet Zendaris face-to-face." She toyed with the edge of the room service menu. "D-do you think even if they saw Bobby, they'd wait for the meeting so they could nail Zendaris, too?"

"I think—" he smoothed his thumb across the back of her hand "—they will do whatever it takes to secure Bobby and deal with Zendaris later. At least we have the anti-drone plans."

She shook her head to clear it of doubts. "You're right. You know, I joined the team later. One of the original members died on assignment. Jack replaced him with me. As the only woman, I always felt a little on the outside."

"Their actions today will forever prove that false." He picked up the menu. "Is it just me, or did we totally forget to eat?"

"Between fake fire drills and stuffing a fake fireman into our trunk and inviting the cavalry out to the rescue, yeah, I think we've been a little too busy to think about food."

"I'm usually never too busy to think about food." He leaned over and kissed her mouth. "Or other things."

She snatched the menu out of his hands. "When you talk like that, it makes me believe all the stories about Loki, including the ones I'd rather not think about."

"Totally exaggerated. Now let's order some room service."

"Ugh, can we go down to the restaurant to eat?"

"It's the same food. Are you getting tired of looking at my face?"

She trailed her fingers across his stubbled jaw. "Never, but now that Damon is safely in my trunk, it would be nice to get out of this room and sit at a table."

They sat across from each other in the hotel restaurant, and Beau picked up his sandwich. "Same sandwich I would've gotten upstairs."

"But we get the added bonus of listening to the couple arguing at that table and the toddler throwing his food at that one."

Beau scratched his jaw. "Does Bobby do that?"

"Occasionally."

The phone buzzed and Deb dropped her fork. *This is it.* "It's a phone call."

"Answer it and tell him to call you back in five minutes." Beau waved for the check and stuffed two French fries in his mouth.

"Yes?"

"Do you have the plans?"

"Yes. Can you call me back in five minutes so I can have some privacy?"

He clicked his tongue. "You mean you're not holed up in your hotel room crying your eyes out?"

No, I'm working on double-crossing you.

"Five minutes."

Beau tossed some bills on the table. "Did he ask you about the plans?"

"I told him I had them."

They rushed back upstairs and just as Deb stepped inside the room, the phone rang. She answered and put it on speaker.

"What do you want me to do?"

"Meet me at the Central T stop on the Red Line. You'll be picked up and taken to your son where we'll make the exchange."

Deb laughed but it came out more like a snort through her dry mouth. "Do you think I'm stupid? You'll have me picked up and killed while you steal the plans. No, thanks. Next."

Zendaris sighed. "You really need to work on your trust issues, Agent Sinclair. If I tell you where Bobby is first, who's to say you won't enlist some help? You see, I have trust issues, too."

She rolled her eyes at Beau. "I can drive to the T stop, and you can have me followed to make sure I'm on my own. I'm not playing games. I have the plans and I want my son back."

"I think I can work with that. But we'll leave a car for you, so we can make sure there's no tracking device on it. And you'll be following another car to the location, so you're not getting the address in advance. If we pick up any tail on you, it's over."

"I'm bringing my weapon. So there'd better not be any funny business when I pick up the car or follow the other car."

"I think two distrustful people just worked out a deal. Be at the T station at nine o'clock tonight."

Zendaris ended the call, and all of Deb's strength evaporated. She sat on the floor, the phone cradled limply in her palm.

"You did it." Beau pulled her to her feet and swung her around. "The terms are great."

She finally got her mouth working. "Where will you be?"

"I'll be waiting at the warehouse. We'll all be there, waiting for you, Deb."

Covering her face with her hands, she murmured, "I'm scared. I'm scared for Bobby."

"I am, too, but this is our best chance."

She parted her fingers. "You're scared, too?"

"Damn right. I'm scared I'm never going to get the chance to meet my boy. I'm scared I'm going to lose you. I'm scared that the great Loki can't live up to his reputation."

She threw her arms around his broad shoulders. This wasn't just about her anymore. This man deserved a chance with his son, the son she'd denied him for two years.

"Don't be scared, Loki. We can do this."

Chapter Sixteen

Deb was the luckiest woman alive.

Beau surveyed the cache of weapons and explosives and equipment that Team Three had arrayed before him on the floor of the abandoned warehouse. These guys meant business.

They'd secured the abandoned warehouse on the same property as Zendaris's, coming in under the guise of a food truck making a delivery. Even if anyone at Zendaris's warehouse had seen the truck coming in, they'd put it down to commercial activity involving the food bank in the area. Plenty of food service warehouses crouched in the shadow of the Suffolk County Jail.

Not the safest place to keep a kid—unless the kid wasn't yours and you didn't give a damn about his health or safety.

He'd hated leaving Deb at the hotel to make her way to the Central T station alone, but she was no wilting flower. She had a weapon and she knew how to use it.

His place was here with her support team, and what a team it was. How could she ever have doubted these guys for a minute?

"You ever work much with explosives, Loki?" J.D. shook his head. "I mean, Slater?"

"Some. My style is more stealth."

J.D. patted the cheek of Gage Booker, the senator's son, and said, "We don't let Gage here get too close. He doesn't want to damage his pretty face."

Gage laughed. "You're the one who needs to watch out, J.D. It's your wedding coming up."

"Yeah, maybe I'd better go wait in the truck."

Cade Stark kicked up his feet on a crate while he loaded ammunition into his gun. "We haven't caught a glimpse of Deb's son yet. Make sure she realizes that when this is all over. It's not about nailing Zendaris. It's about rescuing her son."

"He's my son, too."

Silence settled over the small office space.

J.D. broke it with a whistle, and Booker coughed. "Zurich?"

"She told you?"

Booker held up his hands. "She told me she'd met you while on assignment out there, but the hotel during that time was like a spy convention. I never put two and two together when Deb announced her pregnancy."

Stark said, "Deb's on the private side. Zendaris tried this same scheme with my son. That's why he and my wife are in Europe right now. I want nothing more than to bring this SOB down, but your boy comes first."

"I appreciate that."

Booker caressed the scope on a high-powered rifle. "You told her to get them outside, right?"

"Yeah. Zendaris knows she's skittish and even agreed to let her bring her weapon, but he'll make her give that up. She can trade her weapon for the concession of meeting outside."

J.D. checked his watch. "Gentlemen, I believe it's time we took up our positions."

Booker had the sniper's position on an opposing warehouse's rooftop. J.D. would also be on top of a warehouse with several mobile explosive devices. Stark had the peripheral area covered for any incoming personnel and to stop Zendaris's escape, if it came to that.

And Beau planned to be as close to Deb and Bobby as he could possibly be in case anything went wrong and to follow the action. He'd never admitted fear to anyone like he had to Deb this afternoon in the hotel. She had such an exalted image of the great Loki, he'd almost convinced himself that she'd turn away from him in disgust once he'd revealed how scared he was.

She hadn't.

Beau slipped out of the warehouse into the cloudy night. A storm was brewing for tomorrow, but for tonight at least they didn't have to battle the elements. One battle was enough.

He crept along the side of the abandoned warehouse. Zendaris's people wouldn't be expecting anyone to be in the area. The deliveries had died down by five o'clock. A couple of workers from the food bank had wandered over to check on some supplies, but there had been no activity since.

Zendaris's warehouse was a hulking shape backed up to a chain-link fence. Beau dropped to his belly and crawled toward a foul-smelling Dumpster several yards from the warehouse door.

And waited.

DEB'S CLAMMY HANDS had almost slipped off the steering wheel several times during the drive, especially when she thought her guide was veering in a different direction from Crosstown. Now as she followed him through the gates of the warehouse area, she let out a pent-up breath.

Her gaze darted among the dark shapes that littered

the property. Could her Team Three coworkers already be here? *Brothers,* Beau had called them—brothers in arms. If they were truly here, she'd never doubt them again.

Of course, she was leading them right to Zendaris and the anti-drone plans—something all of them thirsted for.

The car ahead of her parked in front of a windowless warehouse and she gulped. Was that where they'd been holding Bobby? She pulled in behind her escort. She left the plans on the seat of the car and scrambled from the front seat, clutching her weapon.

A pair of lights on the outside of the warehouse came on, bathing the pavement with a yellow glow. Good. They couldn't claim it was too dark to stay outside.

Stay outside. That's what Beau had told her to do.

The driver of the car didn't say a word. He stood beside the warehouse with his arms crossed. Had he taken Damon's job? Had Zendaris wondered what had happened to Damon?

He was probably being interviewed by a CIA agent about now. Beau had abandoned the car with Damon in the trunk somewhere out near Roxbury and gave the tip to Jack. In a gesture of good faith, Jack would let the CIA have a crack at Damon first.

Another car roared through the gates, cutting its lights. Deb jerked back as the car swerved next to hers.

A bald man jumped from the driver's seat and opened the back door of the black sedan. A slim man of medium height emerged, straightening the cuffs of his jacket. Deb could smell Armani.

He adjusted his dark sunglasses, tipped the brim of his fedora and smiled. "Agent Sinclair. May I call you Deb? I feel like we have such a connection."

"I feel like I have a bad taste in my mouth that I can't spit out." She raised her weapon.

He chuckled. "I have to admit, I like my women… softer, but you'd be a handful in bed. Guess you weren't that good if the father of your child abandoned you. You know a lot about abandonment, don't you, Deb? Just think, if circumstances had turned out differently and that old marine hadn't turned your life around, you could've had a job with me."

He'd picked the wrong tactics to use with her. Insults only made her stronger, fiercer. If he liked his women soft—he was gonna hate her.

"Where's my son, you slimy piece of excrement?"

"Where are my plans, you bitch?"

"I have the plans, but you're not getting them or my gun until I see my son, bitch."

He swept his arm forward. "He's inside. I'll take you to him, and you can bring the plans with you. Once I verify their veracity, I'll give you your bratty sick kid."

"No. I'm not walking into a trap." She waved her gun. "Bring him out here, to me. I'll secure him in the car and give you the plans."

He caressed his chin as if he had a pointed beard on the end of it—like the devil. He'd sent imposters in his place before, but she was confronting the real Zendaris. She could smell it.

He snapped his fingers at the man by the warehouse door.

To Deb's relief, the flunky turned and unlocked the door. The warehouse swallowed him up and then spit him back out several minutes later. In his wake, an older black man was carrying Bobby in his arms. He must've been the one who'd impersonated Robert.

Deb willed her feet to stay planted on the ground. She still had her weapon pointed at Zendaris and she couldn't lose that advantage. "What's wrong with him?"

The man holding him answered. "Just sleeping. He's okay."

"Wake him up."

The man shook Bobby a little and said a few words. Bobby popped his head up and shifted his arms and legs.

She blew out a breath. "Put him down and let him come to me."

"Wait." Zendaris held up his hand. "I'm the one giving the orders. You're still holding a gun on me and I don't have the plans. You could grab your son and shoot me."

"Your men have guns on me." She shrugged. "If I shot you, they'd shoot me or Bobby. I'm not going to risk that."

"Sort of a Mexican standoff here, eh?" He snapped his fingers at the man. "Put him down. I want my plans."

The man put Bobby on the ground, and Bobby blinked and rubbed his eyes. With her gun still on Zendaris, she called to her son. "Bobby, it's Mommy. Come to me."

"Mommy!" His little feet slapped the ground as he ran toward her. He threw himself at her legs, wrapping his arms around them. She wanted nothing more than to pick him up in her arms, but this farce wasn't over yet.

Zendaris held out his hand. "The plans. Or I really will have my men shoot both you and your son before you can even get a shot off."

Something whizzed through the air and Zendaris's mouth hung open.

This is it. Deb took a step back.

A form hurtled from behind the Dumpster. Beau yelled, "Get down, Deb."

In one motion, he swept Bobby from the ground and wrapped his arms around both of them as he tackled them. Deb heard more whizzing noises above them. A car started, and then stalled.

Beau dragged her and Bobby a few more feet away from the chaos, his body still covering theirs.

He looked over his shoulder from the ground. "How many? How many men does he have with him?"

"Zendaris."

"Down."

"Driver."

"Down." He spoke into the mic clipped to his jacket, and she realized he wasn't talking just to her.

"Man who had Bobby."

Deb overheard a voice coming through Beau's earpiece. "He ran back into the warehouse. J.D., launch the smoke bombs."

Deb screamed over the new noise and tried to cover Bobby's ears. "My escort."

"Down."

Cade—it must've been Cade—replied, "I got someone exiting the gate."

Someone else shouted, "All clear, all clear."

Beau spoke into his mic. "Verify. Verify the all-clear."

Nobody answered. The connections had been lost.

Black smoke poured from the warehouse and Deb squeezed her eyes shut. It was over. The nightmare was finally over.

"Zendaris not down, not out."

Gasping, Deb lifted her head and Beau sat up to face Zendaris's weapon pointed at them.

Zendaris was propped up against the car, the open door serving as a shield from any incoming bullets. But there wouldn't be any incoming bullets because the other three had thought the drama was over and had left their posts.

He pointed at Beau. "Who the hell are you?"

"Just a curious bystander."

"Another Prospero robot, most likely. Do you really have those plans, Deb?"

"Yes." The gun Deb had been holding on Zendaris before all hell broke loose was gouging her hip. She shifted toward Beau to push it in his direction. "The plans are in the car, but you'll never get away with them. My Prospero brothers will be here in seconds."

"Maybe they will, but I'm going to take a few of you down before I go, starting with you."

Her gun flashed before her as Beau swung it free while throwing himself in front of her and Bobby. Two shots echoed in the night and Bobby whimpered in her arms.

Beau rolled from her body and crouched beside her. "Are you okay?"

She struggled to a sitting position, pulling Bobby into her lap. Touching Beau's face, she whispered, "Are you?"

"I am now." He pointed the gun at Zendaris's body, coiled on the ground.

"What the hell happened?" Gage ran toward Zendaris and kicked the gun from his hand. "How did he survive that shot to the heart?"

Beau rose to his feet and extended his hand to Deb. "Bulletproof vest. Your shot knocked him down, maybe even knocked the wind out of him, but his vest saved him."

"Damn fedora. Couldn't get a clean shot at his head."

J.D. and Cade had arrived, too, picking through the weapons and trying to ID the men. "That's gotta be everybody."

Deb stroked Bobby's face. "Are you okay, my love?"

He nodded. "Where were you, Mommy?"

"I was trying to get you home."

Beau touched a finger to Bobby's nose. "Didn't you know, Bobby? Your mom is Superwoman."

Epilogue

The light breeze caused a ripple through the meadow of Colorado wildflowers, and the bride resembled another flower as she floated along the edge of the meadow, her white skirt billowing behind her.

Deb sipped champagne, and the bubbles tickled her throat. "Let's go congratulate the bride and groom."

She grabbed Bobby's hand and rested her fingers on Beau's arm. The crowed parted for him as he led her to J.D. and J.D.'s new wife, Noelle. Crowds would always part for Loki.

Deb kissed Noelle on the cheek and hugged J.D. "This is it, cowboy. You're a married man. Are you going to put down roots in Colorado?"

"We'll probably go back to D.C. at first. This is Noelle's brother's place. We've just been helping him out." He kissed his wife's hand.

"It's beautiful."

Like a magnet, their little group drew the others. Gage, looking like a *GQ* model, approached with a dark-haired beauty—Zendaris's former nanny.

Cade, with his beachy-blonde wife by his side and their little boy skipping in front of them, joined them as well.

Deb studied each of their faces. Even though Robert was gone, she still had a family. These men were her brothers, and she knew now she could trust them with her life and her son's life. She should've realized that before.

They stood silent for a moment, consciously aware for a split second that they shared a special bond—not just the Prospero Team Three agents, but the people they loved. The people Zendaris had targeted. They stood frozen, as if drinking in the beauty and inhaling the freedom of the moment.

Then they all began to talk at once.

Cade clinked his glass with Deb's. "I guess we owe Zendaris for leading Deb straight to the anti-drone plans. Dr. Herndon was probably ready to put them back on the market."

"Now the Defense Department has them." J.D. draped his arm around his bride's shoulder.

Gage snorted. "Better the DOD than the CIA. You should've seen that compound the Agency had down in Panama."

"This is a wedding. Enough shop talk." Cade's wife, Jenna, ruffled Bobby's hair and smiled at Deb. "He's so cute. Is he better now?"

"He's getting stronger every day, thanks to his dad." Deb brushed her hand across Beau's back.

He caught her hand and kissed her fingers before going back to his conversation with Gage's girlfriend, Randi, about Colombia.

Jenna's son, Gavin, pulled on his mom's arm. "I wanna run over there, Mommy. We can see horses."

Jenna put her finger to her lips. "Just a minute, Gavin. Deb, is it okay if I take Bobby with us? I don't know about your little guy, but mine's just itching to get his fancy clothes dirty."

Deb crouched next to Bobby. "Do you want to go with Gavin and his mommy to see the horses?"

"Can Daddy come?"

"He'll come in a minute. Go play with Gavin."

Jenna took both boys by the hand and called after Cade to join them.

J.D. and Noelle peeled away from the group to dance with their new in-laws, and Gage pulled Randi into the wildflowers where they disappeared from view.

Beau jerked his chin toward Bobby with the Starks. "He looks good, huh?"

"Looks good, feels good. The transfusions worked like a charm." She hitched her arms around Beau's neck and kissed his chin. "He's so happy to have his daddy in his life—we both are."

"And his daddy is happy to be there. He fit right in with the cousins, didn't he?"

"Your family is completely turning his head. He's already clamoring for ten brothers and sisters."

He dragged her close and whispered in her ear in a way that still gave her shivers, "Should we get started on that request?"

"We can work on it, but let's wait a few years before actually creating another perfect child. You're seriously considering Jack's offer to join Prospero, aren't you?"

"I am if he'll have me."

She kissed him. "I'm giving you a very good recommendation."

"Thanks, babe. That'll go far because you know about all of Loki's exploits, don't you?"

"I don't want to know about *all* of them." She put a finger on his yummy lips that she couldn't stop kissing.

"Really? Because I have one I don't think I told you about before."

"Watch yourself."

"Did I ever tell you about the one where I was in this bar in Zurich?"

She tilted her head to one side. "Hmm, I don't think so."

"So, I was in this bar in Zurich, relaxing after a particularly perilous assignment."

"Fascinating."

"I looked across the room and my eyes locked onto the most intriguing woman I'd ever seen in my life."

"She sounds dangerous."

"You have no idea."

"What happened? Did she turn out to be a double agent? Lead you on a high-speed chase through the mountains?"

"Something much scarier than that." He traced her lips with his fingertip. "She made me fall in love with her."

* * * * *

INTRIGUE…

BREATHTAKING ROMANTIC SUSPENSE

My wish list for next month's titles…

In stores from 15th November 2013:

❏ Cold Case at Camden Crossing — Rita Herron

& The Cradle Conspiracy — Robin Perini

❏ Justice is Coming — Delores Fossen

& Yuletide Protector — Julie Miller

❏ Undercover Twin — Lena Diaz

& Dirty Little Secrets — Mallory Kane

Romantic Suspense

❏ Colton Christmas Rescue — Beth Cornelison

Available at WHSmith, Tesco, Asda, Eason, Amazon and Apple

Just can't wait?

Special Offers

Every month we put together collections and longer reads written by your favourite authors.

Here are some of next month's highlights— and don't miss our fabulous discount online!

On sale 6th December   On sale 1st November   On sale 6th December

Save 20%
on all Special Releases